Praise for *New York Times* bestselling author

JAYNE
ANN
KRENTZ

"One of the hottest writers of romance today."
—*USA TODAY*

"Krentz's flair for creating intriguing, inventive plots; crafting clever dialogue between two perfectly matched protagonists; and subtly infusing her writing with a deliciously tart sense of humor are, as always, simply irresistible."
—*Booklist*

"A master of the genre…nobody does it better!"
—*RT Book Reviews*

"Ms. Krentz has deservedly won the hearts of readers everywhere with her unique blend of fiery passion and romantic adventure.… It is this gratifying intricacy that makes each and every Krentz book something to be savored over and over again."
—*Rave Reviews*

"Jayne Ann Krentz entertains to the hilt."
—Catherine Coulter

D1308188

**Also available from
Jayne Ann Krentz
and Harlequin HQN**

Wildest Dreams
"The Cowboy" (*Tough Enough* anthology)
Dangerous Games
The Man in the Mask
Twist of Fate
Gambler's Woman

And coming in April 2014

Ruthless Love

JAYNE
ANN
KRENTZ

WRITING AS STEPHANIE JAMES

RECKLESS NIGHTS

HARLEQUIN® HQN™

Recycling programs
for this product may
not exist in your area.

ISBN-13: 978-0-373-77827-0

RECKLESS NIGHTS

Copyright © 2013 by Harlequin Books S.A.

The publisher acknowledges the copyright holder of the individual works as follows:

STORMY CHALLENGE
Copyright © 1982 by Stephanie James

RECKLESS PASSION
Copyright © 1982 by Stephanie James

Printed in U.S.A.

CONTENTS

Dear Reader,

Those of you who read my books know that these days I write contemporary romantic thrillers as Jayne Ann Krentz, historical romantic suspense as Amanda Quick and futuristics as Jayne Castle. At the start of my career, however, I wrote classic battle-of-the-sexes-style romance using both my Krentz name and the pen name Stephanie James. This volume contains two stories from that time.

I want to take this opportunity to thank all of you—new readers as well as those who have been with me from the start. I appreciate your interest in my books.

Sincerely,

Jayne Ann Krentz

STORMY CHALLENGE

Chapter 1

Later, she would ask herself how she could possibly have missed all the danger signals emanating from the man. With the inevitable wisdom of hindsight, she would feel the lazy menace in him as clearly as she now felt her own deeply intrigued response, and Leya Brandon would wonder bitterly why her normally astute mind and intuition had betrayed her.

It was to be only the second time in all her twenty-seven years that she had allowed herself to be misled by a man, but Leya would take little comfort from that fact. She rarely needed a second lesson in anything.

But for the moment, on the dance floor of the secluded inn on the wild Oregon coast, Leya wasn't thinking of the future. The man held her in such an intimate dancing embrace that she was obliged to rest both hands on his broad shoulders. The way he shaped the curve of her waist made it impossible to concentrate on anything but the present. Leya tipped back her neat head, the long, sable-dark braid falling dramatically over one shoulder and across her breast, and smiled up into Court Gannon's sensuously narrowed tortoiseshell eyes. The look she met in the gold-flecked gaze caused her fingertips to flex ever so slightly against the subtly rough texture of his jacket.

The inviting, waiting look in Court's eyes deepened as he felt the small movement on his shoulders.

"You feel like a kitten trying to decide whether or not to settle in for the night," he murmured in soft amusement, turning his head slightly to touch her wrist with his lips. It was the lightest, most teasing of caresses, yet Leya was aware of the small shiver which coursed through her.

"Not for the night," she made herself answer, with a smiling ease that took a surprising amount of effort. The realization that it was going to be difficult to refuse Court's imminent invitation to share his bed hit her with some force. My God, she thought wonderingly, I've only known him two days! "But a few more dances would be welcomed," she concluded softly.

"It will be my pleasure to provide the dances," he growled in his dark, heavily shaded voice. "But I warn you I intend to use the time to my own advantage." The large, strong hands at Leya's waist tightened meaningfully and the golden brown eyes gleamed.

Leya's full, generous mouth curved a fraction more as she regarded her partner from beneath thick eyelashes. "Coming from someone who doesn't believe in exerting himself unnecessarily, that sounds rather energetic," she observed teasingly.

"The operative word is unnecessarily," he drawled. "And

I'm coming to the conclusion that having you for an entire night is going to be very necessary, indeed!"

Leya felt the warmth flood her face even as she tried to retain her normally abundant common sense. "There's a certain lack of subtlety in your approach tonight," she accused chidingly as she sought for a light way of handling the increasing sensual tension between them.

"I've had the impression from the beginning that the usual games weren't going to be necessary between us, Leya," Court retorted almost gently, his eyes searching her features for the truth of her feelings toward him.

"It's not a question of playing games, Court," she replied, the smallest of frowns drawing her dark brows slightly toward each other. "It's a matter of being sure. Why does a man imply a woman is teasing or playing games when she is only trying to test the depths of her own reactions and those of the male involved?"

"Because he's horribly afraid that if he allows the woman to probe her feelings too deeply, she'll talk herself out of going to bed with him!" Court said and grinned candidly.

"So he deliberately tries to make her feel guilty by accusing her of being a tease?" Leya shot back, silver-green eyes deepening with a nonverbal rebuke.

"Exactly. Can you blame us? All's fair in love and war!"

"Situation ethics, Court? I'm surprised at you. I would have thought you were the type of man who lives by a definite set of principles," she mocked.

"And doesn't alter them to fit the situation? Well, in a

sense, you're right." He smiled unabashedly. "It's just that the principles I choose to live by are my own."

"Developed by you and for you?"

"Umm," he agreed, his fingers kneading the contour of her lower waist with blatant pleasure.

Leya felt the pleasure in his hands as it communicated itself to her and knew she was going to have difficulty when it came time to say good-night. She refused to think of how difficult it would be when the moment for goodbye came, as it would in only a few short days.

But vacation romances, however pleasant, were doomed to appallingly short lives, she told herself firmly. They were meant to be enjoyed on a superficial level and then forgotten—light flirtations that could be ended without serious regret. For Leya, that meant not having to live with the knowledge that she had given herself casually to a man who wouldn't remember her name by the time his next vacation arrived.

But regardless of what happened between them, Leya knew she wouldn't forget Court Gannon's name for a long, long time. Nor would she forget anything else about the man with the tortoiseshell eyes and matching hair. Large and solidly built without being an ounce overweight, he topped six feet by about one inch, she estimated, and she found pleasure in the way his wide shoulders narrowed into a lean waist and strong thighs.

There was power in this man, and Leya was honest enough to admit it attracted her. Only later would she tell herself she should have been wary of that primitive attraction. But the mastery and strength were cloaked in what was, for Leya, an enormously appealing laziness and self-control.

The variegated deep gold and dark brown of his thick hair was cut short in an apparent effort to tame the broad wave that threatened to fall across his wide forehead. More than once, Leya had been forced to exercise a degree of control in order to restrain herself from reaching up to thrust curious, sensitive fingers through the curve of that hair. She knew her own weakness for tactile sensations and deliberately avoided the temptation.

Heavy brows and long lashes shielded the well-spaced and deep-set brown-and-gold eyes. A bold, no-nonsense hand had chiseled Court's face, leaving an aggressive nose and an unconsciously arrogant tilt to the strong chin. Broad, jagged planes that left no room for soft handsomeness marked the high cheekbones and tightly fleshed skin beneath. The column of his neck was strong and browned in the same sun-colored shade as his face and hands. The tan was an excellent foil for the crisp whiteness of his shirt collar and cuffs. Leya flexed her fingers once again, enjoying the texture of his richly woven wool jacket. He wore the close-fitting slacks and coat with an ease that suggested expensive if conservative tailoring.

Leya had no notion why she had looked up from the book in her lap yesterday morning to find Court Gannon watching her from across the heavily beamed and elegantly rustic lobby of the inn. She had responded automatically to the mildly prickling sensation of being observed and lifted her head to meet the unexpected impact of the gold-marked eyes. The moment she had acknowledged his presence, he had started forward with a deliberate, lazy stride that brought him inevitably to where she curled in the corner of the old Victorian couch in front of the roaring fire. There had been a few other people seated nearby and she had told herself he was heading for one of them until it became apparent she was the focus of his attention.

A little uneasily she had listened to his brief, polite introduction as he seated himself beside her, stretching out long legs toward the huge stone fireplace which dominated that end of the room. The initial unease had been natural enough, given the fact that Leya had no illusions about being an eye-catching beauty.

The truth of the matter was that she thought of herself as rather average. An average five-and-a-half feet in height, an average, perhaps overly rounded figure that required an average amount of dieting and an average, attractive set of features. She knew full well she had above-average intelligence and sense of humor but she didn't really expect most men to notice or appreciate those two virtues. Especially not clear across the lobby!

In spite of her own dismissing assessment of her looks, more than one man in the past had been attracted by the very un-average and unusual combination of long, sable-brown hair with the strange silvery green of her eyes. The effect was a subtle one and not usually noticed consciously at first, but it was there. It allowed Leya to wear the strong, bold colors she favored. Her features were feminine but not soft. They betrayed the intelligence and self-awareness lying underneath, as well as the strength those two factors ensured. Her firm chin, straight nose and perceptive eyes were gentled a bit by long lashes and the ready curve of her mouth.

No, not a great beauty, Leya had told herself wryly, and dressed as she was yesterday in well-washed jeans and a brilliant burnt orange velour top, it was natural enough to wonder why a stranger had picked her out of the crowd. Of course, she had added in silent amusement, the crowd was very small. It was winter, the summer tourists were long gone, and not everyone favored the fiercely rugged southern Oregon coastline at this time of year. Only those with a penchant for the intriguing wildness of a storm over the sea or the mystery of a fog-shrouded stretch of beach came at this time of the year. They felt themselves amply rewarded.

"What are you thinking about?" Court broke into her thoughts to demand suddenly, the rather hard line of his mouth quirking at the corner as he studied the flicker of thought in her eyes.

"Yesterday," she admitted simply.

"What about yesterday?" he persisted softly, using his hands to press her more intimately against his hard leanness. He was using the dance as an excuse to make love to her,

Leya realized with a small sense of shock. She felt her pulse quicken in response to the barely disguised arousal in him.

"The way you came toward me through the lobby as if you knew me." She smiled. "I was afraid you were some-one I should know, whose name I couldn't remember!"

"You were right," he told her meaningfully. "I was some-one you should know. The only reason you couldn't re-member my name was because I hadn't given it to you yet."

"That opening conversational gambit of telling me the ending of the novel I was reading was clever, too." Leya grinned cheerfully. "It ruined my plans for the entire day, since I had intended to spend the whole of it reading that book!"

"I wanted you free to spend the time with me."

"So I gathered," she said dryly. "But it wouldn't have worked if you hadn't turned out to be every bit as lazy and uninterested in tennis as I am!"

"Oh, I knew we were two of a kind from the moment I spotted you across the lobby," he assured her humorously, the laughter reaching his eyes and warming them nicely. "Let's face it, only a certain type of person is going to come here at this time of the year."

"Someone who has no aspirations to be the next tennis star or golf hero?" she quipped, aware that the music was drawing to a close.

"Someone," he told her deeply as he took her arm and guided her back to the small table, "who understands that walking along a beach at dawn is life's only important sport!"

"I'm afraid my dedication to the ideal falls somewhat short," she murmured ruefully as she took the seat he held for her. "I have to admit to finding dancing a very interesting alternative. And for someone who claims to be too lazy to do anything except walk for exercise, you do a pretty good job on the dance floor!"

"But dancing with you isn't a form of exercise," he pointed out, lifting the glass snifter in front of him and taking a man-sized swallow of the potent cognac.

"No?" Leya inquired, arching one brow with a hint of warning.

"No," he confirmed, heedless of her faintly quelling expression. "It's a prelude to making love to you, and I would never," he added in a soft rasp, leaning forward to watch the color in her face, "make the mistake of classifying sex with you as a sport or a game!"

"Court!" Leya snapped, determined to let him know that he had stepped too far out of bounds. "That's enough on the subject. You wouldn't want me to think you have a one-track mind, would you?" She made an effort to inject a caustic note into the small setdown she had attempted to deliver. But it was difficult to maintain that faint air of outrage beneath the glittering light in his eyes. Her real reaction to his blatantly sexual talk was an unfamiliar weakness that left her feeling pursued. Leya Brandon was not accustomed to the role of hunted female. And, she promised herself silently, she did not intent to allow this man to treat her as prey. She was glad he found her attractive because the feeling was mutual, but she had very definite ideas on equality in a relationship. She also had very definite ideas on the depressing nature of relationships based purely on sex. The last thought firmed her mouth and Court was far too observant not to have seen the faint hardening in her silvery green eyes as well.

"A one-track mind is exactly what I seem to be developing around you, Leya," he confided with a sensual twist of his lips. "Do you know what my first thought was this morning?"

"What?" she asked warily, reaching for her own snifter and sipping delicately. In the candlelight the deep emerald color of her long-sleeved gown glowed. The light reflected warmly from the unusual green pendant set in gold that hung in the deep opening of the dress.

"I thought that it was all wrong I should be waking up alone. You should have been there with me," he whispered, with such intensity that Leya blinked uncertainly.

"I've told you the conversation has gone far enough," she breathed, forcing her willpower to the fore. It was not a characteristic in which she normally found herself deficient. "I suggest we either switch to another topic or say good-night."

"You don't like knowing that I want you?" he queried whimsically. "Or are you afraid of admitting that you want me, too?"

"If you think you're going to trap me into answering a double-edged sword of a question like that, you're considerably less intelligent than I originally believed you to be!" she informed him loftily, forcing back the rush of laughter she was experiencing.

"It was worth a try." He shrugged with massive resignation, an answering grin in his eyes. "Well, what would you like to discuss? I'm at your service, I assure you. At least until I can think of a way to steer the conversation back to my main interests!"

"Limited though those interests appear to be?" she mocked.

"There's nothing limited about them," he informed her kindly. "You're just jealous because I know how to establish priorities and stick to them!"

Leya flung up a hand in laughing self-defense. "Enough! I'm going to choose a topic and you're going to do me the courtesy of following my lead!"

Court lounged back in his leather-padded chair and smiled benignly. "You leave me little choice. I am, after all, wearing the clothes of a gentleman tonight."

"And you always suit your actions to your clothes?"

"Not always, but as a special favor to you tonight, I'll make the effort. That is until the clock strikes twelve," he concluded with a theatrical salute of his snifter.

"You have a pumpkin waiting to take you back to your room at midnight?" Leya asked interestedly, leaning forward to prop her elbow on the table and rest her chin on her palm. The green stone at her throat gleamed softly in the light; a gleam that was reflected in her eyes. She smiled.

"Don't worry," he told her. "There's room for two inside."

"About my conversational topic," she began determinedly.

"Yes."

"Have you had a chance to read that contract my brother wants me to sign, so that he can go ahead and hire this high-powered consultant he's found?" Leya plunged into the question that had been on her mind ever since she'd given the papers to Court for his opinion.

"I've read it. I went through it before I picked you up for dinner," he admitted quietly, a new note of seriousness entering the heavy-timbred voice. Across the table, the tortoiseshell eyes met hers.

"Well?" she pressed a bit grimly. "Do you agree with me?"

"That it's dangerous? It could be in the wrong circumstance," Court said slowly, evenly. The cognac swirled gently in his glass.

"I knew it!" Leya stated with unhappy satisfaction. "As soon as Keith gave it to me I knew there was something crazy about the whole setup!"

"I said it could be dangerous in the wrong situation," Court repeated calmly, watching her face closely. "You were wise to be cautious, Leya, but there are some mitigating circumstances involved here."

"Such as?" she challenged.

"Such as the fact that you know your brother, and I know the other party named in the contract. The man he wants to hire."

"You know him!" Leya stared, totally astonished by this information. "You know this C. Tremayne? But how could you? Where would you have run into him?"

"In Silicon Valley," he told her, using the slang expression for the area around San Jose, California, where so much of the new high-technology electronics industry was based. It had been so named for the semiconducting material that had helped revolutionize solid-state electronics.

"You worked down there for a while?" Leya demanded, confused. "I didn't know you were in engineering. I thought you said something about finance...."

"I've worked with several electronics firms, helping them secure venture capital. It takes money to do first-class research and I help them find it," he said, as if it were the simplest thing in the world.

Leya knew there was a lot more to it than he implied, but she had other things to pursue at the moment. "So you've met Tremayne? What do you think of him?"

Court smiled. "He's not the ogre you've convinced yourself he is, for a start."

"He must be!" Leya scoffed. "What sort of creature besides an ogre would try to tie my brother to a contract like the one I gave you to read?"

"A man who has as much to lose as your brother and

wants to protect himself as well as his client," Court explained tersely.

"All the protection is on Tremayne's side!" Leya exploded in disgust. "The way that contract is written, he's tied his salary into the profits. If my brother's company does well, Tremayne stands to make a tidy sum, far more than a normal salary for consulting!"

"And if Brandon Security Systems goes under, Tremayne loses said fortune."

"What about that business of insisting on full decision-making authority?" Leya persisted irritably. "He's virtually setting himself up as president of the firm!"

"From what I know of him, Tremayne doesn't make decisions by consensus," Court admitted dryly. "He wouldn't go into a situation like this unless he had the power to do what needed to be done, without having to refer everything to a committee."

"But the main reason Keith insists on having the man in as a sort of chief consultant is because he's hoping to learn from Tremayne! If Tremayne won't be bothered with discussing his decisions, what good will that do Keith?"

"If Tremayne has agreed to guide your brother over the next couple of years, until Keith has enough experience under his belt to take on the full responsibility of running the firm, you can rest assured he'll do as he says. In my experience, Tremayne is a man of his word. He just wants it clear from the outset that for the duration of the contract, he's in charge. If you ask me, your brother is showing a lot of sense. After all, it must be damned intimidating to suddenly inherit a large business at the age of twenty-five. You did say he was a couple of years younger than you?"

Leya nodded morosely. "I realize he's had no experience in running the firm. After all, everyone assumed Dad would be in charge for years...." Grimly, she turned her thoughts away from the sudden death of her parents the previous year in a plane crash in Europe. She and Keith had both put the grieving behind them. Coming to grips with the present was the important thing now.

"From what you've told me, your brother never really had any intention of taking over the reins," Court noted quietly, his eyes probing.

"No. It came as a complete surprise when he decided to assume the responsibility instead of just selling out," Leya admitted. "He seems a new man lately, as if he's found himself." She shook her head, thinking of the way her brother had been drifting since graduation from college. "That's why I hate to put the squelch on this idea he has of apprenticing himself to Tremayne, but..."

"But you're afraid he's agreeing to a contract that will ruin him?" Court concluded understandingly.

"You read it. It's rather binding, wouldn't you agree?" Leya retorted brusquely, running her finger idly around the rim of her snifter and watching the play of candlelight on the liqueur inside.

"Yes, but your brother's interests are well protected, Leya. Don't forget, you still hold half the firm's shares in your power. If Tremayne proves dangerous, it wouldn't be impossible to fire him. All you'd have to do is to get Keith to agree he'd made a mistake. The contract is only truly binding as long as all parties are satisfied. Keith is just asking for a chance to do things his way. Are you sure you're not playing the part of the overprotective big sister?"

Leya lifted her eyes, the metallic green gaze narrowing in response to the small accusation. "No," she snapped. "I'm exercising my obligations as co-owner of the firm. The agreement Tremayne wants signed needs both my signature and my brother's. My father left Brandon Security to both of us."

"With the understanding that for the most part you would be a silent partner, you said," Court reminded her gently but firmly.

Leya winced. "I may have told you a little too much of the background of this deal before I asked your advice," she grumbled, annoyed with herself.

But it had been so easy to talk to Court last night. She was still amazed at the relaxed and communicative atmosphere that had sprung up between them from the start. One thing had led to another and before she knew it she had been discussing the main reason she had secluded herself at the inn for a week. She had promised Keith a decision on whether or not to hire Tremayne by the time she returned to Santa Rosa, the town in northern California where she made her home and ran her book business.

Court smiled. "I think your basic decision isn't whether

or not to sign the contract, it's whether or not you're going to let your brother really assume control of the firm."

Leya gritted her teeth, forcing herself to consider the justification of his comments. "I have never been a bossy older sister!"

"You strike me as the type of woman who could get quite bossy," he chuckled.

"Except that I'm too smart to make that mistake with my own brother. I don't want him to hate me!"

"How about with a lover? Would you make the mistake of trying to dominate a man in a relationship?" Court pounced provocatively, sitting forward with a deliberate air. The gold-flecked eyes glittered with teasing challenge.

Leya smiled with serene superiority, aware of the heat in her veins. "That's different," she demurred. "Everyone knows a man is happiest in a relationship when he's properly managed."

"Funny, I always heard it was women who were content when they'd been mastered!" Court purred.

"A myth," she responded breezily. "Fostered by all those old Rudolph Valentino movies featuring sheiks who carried their women off into the desert!"

"Not to mention all those other films featuring masterful types such as Gable and Bogart and..."

"So Hollywood got off on the wrong track," Leya retorted, lifting one nearly bare shoulder dismissively. "Most of the films were made by men, so it stands to reason they emphasized male fantasies."

"That theory doesn't explain all the women in the audiences." Court grinned.

"Who can ever account for an audience reaction?"

"Who can ever account for a woman's reaction?" he countered.

"I stand by my theory," Leya declared, removing her chin from her palm and settling back into her chair. "And I have *not* been a domineering older sister!"

"Then why break a precedent and start behaving like one now?"

Leya took a deep breath. "You really think I ought to go ahead and let Keith hire Tremayne?" For the life of her she couldn't explain why she should value this man's advice. But some instinct said he knew what he was talking about. There was a sense of sureness and authority about Court Gannon that made itself felt. You had the feeling that he knew what he was doing and his advice would be solid.

"Yes. You asked for my advice and I'm giving it. I think you ought to sign and let your brother get on with the business of learning how to run the company he's inherited, which you don't particularly want. He sounds like a young man who's found what he wants to do in life. Let him do it. Not all of us are that lucky at twenty-five!" he added with a wry smile.

"Sad but true," Leya sighed, shaking her head with an answering smile. Her own most depressing memories of thinking she knew what she wanted were from her twenty-sixth year. Well, she learned her lesson. There was no point in rehashing the subject. Her smile widened deliberately as she considered the man across from her. "Did you know where you were going and what you wanted when you were twenty-five?" Privately, she put his present age at around thirty-five or thirty-six.

Surprisingly, he paused to consider the question. "In some aspects of my life I was quite certain of what I wanted," he finally said slowly.

"You sound as if you're trying to hedge the question," she accused softly.

"A man's privilege," he shot back easily, eyes laughing. Then he went on in a careful tone. "I guess the truth is I knew what I wanted as far as my career was concerned, but there were until quite recently some very open-ended questions about what I wanted in my personal life."

Across the table, Leya caught the sudden blaze of intensity in him, and a part of her wanted to turn and run. The flash of cowardice was so unexpected she found herself swallowing in nervousness. It took an astonishing amount of self-control merely to stay seated and force a deliberately unconcerned expression.

"I don't see you as the unsure type," she confessed lightly.

He looked as if he were about to pursue the statement and then appeared to change his mind. "Tell me something," he said instead, eyeing her. "If you had so many qualms about signing this contract, why didn't you make it a point to meet with this C. Tremayne and judge him for yourself?"

Leya blinked at the change of topic and then lifted

a negligent hand. "If you must know, I chose this particular week for a vacation because Keith informed me Tremayne was trying to set up just such a meeting. I felt—" she broke off, searching for the right word "—as if I were being pushed. The man didn't handle it very politely, you see. He simply told my brother to bring me to the office on a certain day and time this week, and he would handle me." She grimaced in mild displeasure.

"So you immediately disappeared on vacation?" One heavy brow lifted.

"I told Keith I'd take the contract with me and make up my mind while I was away," she explained, aware that she was tapping one foot gently under the table. She had the impression Court was about to condemn her for failing to go through with the meeting, and Leya didn't appreciate the prospect of criticism from him.

"I can see you think you know what I'm going to say next," he teased. "But you're wrong."

"Am I?"

"Yes. I'm not going to tell you that you should have stayed and had the meeting with Tremayne."

"Why not?" she demanded dryly, positive that was what he was thinking.

"Because I'm too happy to have you sitting across from me tonight," he retorted smoothly. "I'm very glad you're here and not back in Santa Rosa!"

Instantly, Leya relaxed, her lips curving warmly and the silvery green glance softening. "So am I," she agreed gently.

"And I wouldn't have wanted to forgo this encounter for all the semiconductors in California," he finished, voice thickening with male anticipation, an ancient, primitive anticipation that had the power to send answering shivers of alarm and excitement through her.

"Thank you," she whispered, trying to sound only as if she were responding to a polite compliment.

"You're welcome," he growled in soft laughter. "Are you ready to come up to my room now?"

Some of the silver in Leya's eyes coalesced into a harder substance, even while her heart picked up a beat. "Your subtlety is slipping again."

He smiled with only a touch of the predator. In fact, an onlooker would need to be quite alert to notice the implication of the flashing teeth because the heat in the golden eyes was so overpowering. "You have to come up to my room," he said patiently.

"Why?" she demanded starkly.

"Because the contract is there. I left it on the table by the window."

"I'll get it in the morning," she evaded, acutely aware of the fencing match in which she was engaged. The contract was nothing more than a polite excuse for the war of wills.

"I don't want to be responsible for it overnight," Court insisted. "It represents your brother's whole future."

"You could bring it downstairs now," Leya suggested huskily, her eyes never leaving his.

"I'll compromise and bring it to your room," he announced with a totally false magnanimity that amused Leya in spite of the intriguing danger of the situation.

"Do you ever give up?" she whispered curiously.

"No." It was a simple statement of fact and she believed him. Unconsciously, Leya ran the tip of her tongue over her lower lip, tension heightening all her senses. He waited.

"You can't come to my room. Not tonight," she finally told him quietly, her eyes meeting his in a direct, honest look.

"And you won't come to mine," he confirmed.

"I...can't..."

"You mean you're afraid," he corrected softly.

She drew a long, steadying breath. "Perhaps." She didn't try to deny the accusation and saw him nod in satisfaction.

"I'll settle for that tonight."

"What?" she almost yelped, suddenly outraged. "You *want* me to be afraid of you?"

The sexual tension seeped out of her body to be replaced by affronted feminine anger. The green glance hardened and she watched him through suddenly narrowed lids.

"With a woman like you, I think it might be a necessary first step." Court returned her annoyed expression with one of glittering male certainty. "It ensures that I have your full attention!"

Leya stared at him, trying to decide whether to laugh or to kick him. The humorous side of her nature, nearly always in the ascendency anyway, won. She grinned recklessly.

"Are you sure you'd know what to do with my full attention once you had it? Remember, you don't approve of bossy women!"

"I am nothing if not resourceful," he assured her, rising to his feet in a smooth, coordinated movement that appealed to her notions of masculine grace. He smiled deliberately, invitingly, reaching down to take her hand and tug her gently up beside him. "And I'm perfectly willing to let you try managing me."

"Because you don't think I can do it?"

"Why don't you try it and find out for yourself how much you can get away with?" he retorted easily, leading her out of the lounge and into the main lobby of the inn.

"What would happen to your poor masculine ego if I were successful?" Leya taunted, pleasantly aware of his fingers entwined with hers as he led her through the lobby and on towards the darkened, glass-walled room which overlooked the pounding surf. The emerald dress swirled around her ankles as she moved.

"It would probably be shredded," he sighed in mock despair, guiding her through the empty, shadowy room to stand before one of its huge floor-to-ceiling windows. Below them, the wind-tossed waves crashed hugely on the rocky beach, driven by the first gales of an incoming storm. What little moonlight there was illuminated the scene in a mysterious, enchanting way. As always, Leya felt herself respond to the power of the landscape.

She felt Court's hand tighten abruptly on her fingers and knew instinctively that he was equally affected by the sensual impact of the scene. She was overwhelmingly aware that the teasing, baiting, inviting approach he had been exercising all evening had given way to something much more elemental and far more dangerous.

She also knew with intuitive self-honesty that the real danger lay in her own reactions to this man who had moved from stranger to confidant in only a couple of days. Now he was pressing his status to that of lover, and Leya told herself she must be cautious.

"We seem to have the place to ourselves. And if we sit down over there in that alcove, no one coming in will even see us. Come here, Leya," Court commanded in a low, deepening tone that pulled at her.

A moment later, Leya found herself sinking quite naturally across his knees, her head against his wide shoulder. The silver in her eyes turned to rich platinum just before his mouth covered her own.

Chapter 2

Leya's first reaction to the touch of Court's lips was that his kiss wasn't exactly what she had subconsciously expected. There was nothing tentative or uncertain about the caress and his arms held her securely enough, but there was some quality in the way his mouth played on hers that didn't fit her preconceptions. A provoking delicacy she hadn't anticipated.

Intrigued and curious with a deeply feminine curiosity, Leya wound her arms lightly around his neck, her fingertips toying with the oddly attractive gold and brown of his hair. She knew a genuine pleasure in the feel of the crisp stuff and gave a small, soundless sigh. The overall effect of the tiny escaping breath was to part her lips slightly, invitingly.

But Court made no move to take advantage of the little surrender. Instead, he continued lightly, almost teasingly to sample first the corners of her mouth and then the fullness of her lower lip. As Leya began wondering at the restraint and lack of explosion in his passion, he lifted his mouth from hers and began a fragile trail of exploration along her cheek to the edge of her lowered lashes.

Just as his lips dropped the smallest of kisses on her sensitive eyelid, his hand, which had been lying along her waist, moved. It slid upward to rest a fraction of an inch below the curve of her breast. There was a sense of impending intimacy in the touch that made Leya's pulse race.

"Oh, Court," she breathed, every nerve in her body tightening itself into a high-strung tension that was as exciting as it was uncomfortable. She felt she ought to be pushing his hand away, refusing him too many liberties, but she couldn't do that because he hadn't yet taken those liberties. So far, the depth of the intimacy was only implied.

"You look very lovely in emerald green," he offered in the softest of whispers, and the hand that had been waiting under her breast shifted once again. Leya waited for it to close possessively over the small, full curve of the green bodice, knowing she should resist when it did so. For a brief instant, she would know the feel of his hand and something in her wanted that.

But his fingers did not move to explore her breast as she had expected. Instead, he picked up the long, thick braid of sable-brown hair and toyed with it. Slowly, he lifted the length of it and drew it around her exposed, vulnerable throat, raising his head to drink in the picture she made.

"I think I know why cavemen were fond of dragging their women home by the hair. Something rather primitively sensual about the notion." The gold in Court's eyes flowed into the shadowy brown, melting it, turning it to molten amber.

Leya watched him from beneath her lashes, fiercely aware of the rope of hair around her throat. "No," she managed in faint amusement. "The ones who got dragged home by their hair were the ones who couldn't think for themselves."

"And you're much too smart to wind up in that category?" he murmured, tightening the braid ever so slightly.

"Yes." It was the simple truth.

"It isn't merely a question of intelligence, Leya," he grated, lowering his head once again to graze upon her parted lips.

"No?" she countered with amused scorn. She felt his mouth nibbling gently on hers and wanted to grab him and hold him still so that she could learn the full impact of his kiss. Her fingers tightened in the hair at the back of his head as if she would follow through with the impulse. This teasing, tantalizing string of caresses she was receiving was not enough.

"No." Court smiled. She could feel the smile against her mouth and wanted to use her teeth very carefully, warningly on his lower lip. But she didn't quite dare. "No," he muttered again on her mouth. "It's not just a matter of intelligence. There are some women, perhaps only one in a lifetime, that a man wants to be very sure of. One he would like to chain with golden bonds…!"

Leya shivered and knew he felt it. "Do you want to put golden chains on me, Court?" Her words were barely audible as she sensed the quickening of her breath and knew his fingers had released the braid to stray to her throat.

"Yes!"

There was unexpected passion in the single word, but it was not echoed in his caress, and Leya stirred restlessly against him, beginning to seek a closer touch, more of his warmth.

"I think," she murmured daringly, uncertain of her motives but knowing she wanted to provoke him a bit further, "that you have the makings of a rather possessive man."

His fingers stroked the base of her throat, drifting downward in lazy threat, and Leya shifted without conscious volition, turning into the caress, like a small cat.

"I am a very possessive man," he stated quietly. "And I will be a very possessive lover."

"When you find a woman who will let you put a chain on her?" Leya smiled in mocking challenge, watching him through slitted lashes.

"I don't plan to ask her permission," he drawled. "The chain will be in place soon enough, whether she likes it or not."

"Because you're so much smarter than she is?"

"Because I'm so much stronger and more ruthless than she is," he corrected at once. "And I've learned how to set priorities."

"You must feed that ego of yours several pounds of raw meat a day. It certainly isn't undernourished!" Leya's eyes gleamed as she met his opening examining gaze. With her hands, she traced a path through his hair to his temples, where only the faintest hint of gray could be seen in full light. It wasn't detectable at all in the shadows tonight.

"Neither is yours," he retorted with a small grin. "You're very sure of yourself, aren't you, Leya Brandon?"

"Does that bother you?"

"Do I look bothered?" he growled, swooping gently to touch his tongue to the tip of her ear.

"No," she admitted ruefully, her eyes closing in response to his tiny caress.

"That's because I know what I'm doing, little Leya."

"And what exactly are you doing, Court?"

"Baiting my trap," he explained at once. The fingers he was using to trace patterns on her throat hovered at the green gem now.

"Are you going to explain that?" she demanded, wondering if he would touch her more intimately in a few seconds. He was so close and his hand was warm and inviting...

"No," he murmured cheerfully. "I'm not. There will be time enough later."

"A man of instant decision," she taunted, turning her cheek toward his questing, sampling mouth. It was all becoming too much, she thought in gathering frustration. She wanted him to touch her, try to take her by storm. She would have to halt him eventually, of course, but in that moment she longed to know the range and depth of his passion and desire. The urge to find out if he really wanted her and wasn't simply playing with her was overwhelming. What was it about this man that affected her so fiercely? She couldn't remember knowing such a physical impatience in herself before in her life. Not even when she had thought herself so much in love with Alex.

"A man who knows what he wants," Court rasped in soft agreement with her teasing assessment.

But if he truly wanted her, why wasn't he pushing and

taking and demanding with his hands and his lips? Leya wondered distractedly. There had been nothing timid about his approach earlier in the evening! But, then, there was nothing particularly timid about him now, she acknowledged uncomfortably. It was this waiting, teasing, tantalizing quality in him that was frustrating. Frustrating and intriguing, she realized vaguely, her fingers sliding to the muscles of his shoulders and beginning a gentle, kneading massage.

Frustrating, intriguing, and… Suddenly, Leya smiled inwardly. And safe. That was the missing explanation. For all his dangerous words, he was letting her know with his body that she was safe with him. Or at least as safe as she wanted to be.

With a sigh of satisfaction at having solved the puzzle, Leya relaxed against Court's chest, deepening her own kisses as she framed his rugged face between her palms. Her self-confidence flowed serenely through her blood even as she deliberately assumed the aggressive role. The excitement was like a fire in the pit of her stomach as she kissed Court full on the mouth, probing into his warmth with the tip of her tongue. She wanted his response, needed it…

She felt his almost stoic resistance to the torment of her tongue and sought to overcome it. Her body twisted against him, and her nails gently raked the side of his tanned cheek. She imagined herself in roles she'd never played: a femme fatale, a seductress, a siren.

The urgency in her grew, unchained now by any nagging, feminine fears. She was safe with this man. She could manage him. He was willing to let her set the pace...

"Give a woman a little taste of power..." Court groaned hoarsely under her soft assault, and Leya felt the reckless laughter bubble up inside herself.

"I didn't notice you giving it to me," she husked. "I thought I was taking it!" She left off the intimate duel she had initiated with his tongue and went in search of new territory to conquer. She found it in the vulnerable tip of his earlobe. Delicately, she closed her teeth on it and was rewarded by the shudder she felt in his hard, massive frame.

"Umm," he growled softly, his hands moving on her back as he tightened his hold slightly. "For someone who's been busy refusing my invitations to bed, you're certainly turning into a little temptress all of a sudden!"

"That's because I've finally figured you out," Leya whispered exultantly, her breath coming quickly between her parted lips as she ran her hands over the front of his shirt and played with a button or two.

"And what's the big secret?" he challenged, eyes gleaming in the darkness.

"You're not nearly so wicked as you'd have me believe," she informed him, leaning her head back and smiling at him with lazy invitation. "You said it, yourself. You're wearing the clothes of a gentleman tonight, and deep down you're going to behave like one."

"Ah," Court exclaimed as if seeing the light. "You're feeling quite safe with me now, is that it? None of the fears you almost admitted to earlier?"

"None."

"Not even a little nagging fear that you might just possibly be off in your judgment of me?" he persisted easily.

"Nope." Leya laughed very softly, her eyes glowing.

"Who am I to argue with a woman's reasoning and logic?" he murmured, lowering his head to nuzzle the cord of her throat.

"Who, indeed?" Leya quipped, wrapping her arms around his neck again and holding him close.

She plunged in where she had left off, glorying in each new response she was able to elicit from him. But with each shudder and groan and husky exclamation she drew forth from Court, there was an equally intense reaction in her own body.

The moment came when his large, powerful hand floated possessively upward to cup her breast, and instead of pushing it away as she had once thought to do, Leya made no protest. She was far too caught up in her own needs now. The wish to draw forth his male desires had unwittingly fed her own. She was aware of the touch of his fingers as they sought the nipple beneath the silky material of her dress, but her reaction was to arch against his hand, not push it aside.

"Oh!" she mouthed, feeling the tip of her breast harden. A shudder tore through her, and she shut her eyes against the dizzying weakness that assailed her frame. The thin lace of her bra offered no protection and through the two layers of fabric, Court's fingers stirred the other nipple to life with a coaxing, seductive pattern that sent ripples of pleasure along Leya's nerves.

Her soft moans were muffled against the side of his neck as Court kissed and then nipped the exposed portion of her shoulder. She felt the touch of his teeth and dug her nails into the fabric of his jacket.

And she never quite knew when the moment came that Court actually reversed the seductive assault, making her the one under attack. One moment, Leya felt herself marvelously, supremely in command of the situation, reveling in her power; the next, she was helplessly responding to the increasing urgency in his kiss and in his hands.

She was only dimly aware that Court had suddenly captured her shaking, questing fingers as they searched for a way beneath his shirt, holding her palm to his mouth and turning his lips into it for a second before smiling beguilingly, sensuously down into her passion-filled eyes.

"I think it's time we went upstairs, darling," he whispered huskily. "This is much too public a place for what comes next!"

"Next?" she repeated, feeling idiotic, but unable to think clearly.

"I'm going to make love to you, my sweet Leya, and I want the privacy of my own bed in which to do it!"

Somehow, he got her to her feet, absorbing the weight of her as she leaned heavily against him. With his arm supporting her around her waist, Court walked her wordlessly toward the stairs. When she turned her head to look up at him helplessly, he merely smiled with promise and undisguised desire.

Leya felt the stairs disappearing one by one beneath her

feet, and a small voice in the most distant corner of her mind began yelling faintly that time was running out. Soon she would be on the landing and then in the hall outside his room...

How had it come to this? Leya shook her head slightly, partly in an attempt to clear it and partly in an attempt to understand what had gone wrong. She hadn't intended to go to his room tonight, she remembered that much very distinctly. No, she had kissed him because it had seemed eminently safe to kiss him. He had been restrained, gentlemanly. He had let her control the embrace, contenting himself with teasing, tantalizing caresses, which were unthreatening.

Court brought them to a halt outside his room, inserting his key into the lock, one arm still firmly around Leya. *Unthreatening,* she reminded herself grimly, as she raised her lashes to meet his eyes. The realization of what had happened hit her fully just as Court swung open the door and started to propel her gently into the room.

"No!" she breathed wryly, refusing to budge. "It's not going to be that easy, Court Gannon!"

"You mean," he soothed, swiveling to face her as she stood planted on the threshold, "it isn't going to be that easy for you to back out of it after having come this far."

"I didn't get this far on my own!" she flung back, her self-control returning in a fierce rush as the full precariousness of her situation hit her.

"No," he agreed, his mouth quirking upward. "You dragged me right along with you."

"Don't blame me for any wrong ideas you've gotten!" she declared regally, crossing her arms in front of herself and glaring at him. "All I started were a few kisses in the sitting room downstairs…"

"Don't you think it's time you finished what you started?" he interrupted, stepping close and curling his hand around the nape of her neck.

"There seems to be some question here of just who was seducing whom!" she stormed, feeling abused.

"Yes, but I was hoping you wouldn't realize it until tomorrow morning," he complained sadly.

"You admit you planned everything that happened? Letting me think you were going to behave like a gentleman and then allowing me to…to…" Words failed her.

"To seduce yourself and me, too? Well, yes. It seemed a simple enough plan." He shrugged.

Leya stared at him, thoroughly amused and thoroughly annoyed by the rueful expression on Court's hard features. She bit her lip and then shook her head in exasperation and sudden affection.

"Oh, Court, you idiot," she murmured softly. "I can't possibly go to bed with a man I've only known two days! After this vacation is over, we'll both be going our separate ways. I couldn't bear a casual little affair like that, don't you see? If that's really all you want or need, it would be best if we part friends tonight…" Her voice trailed off beneath his glittering gaze. His mouth twisted in self-mockery.

"Do you really believe that?" he whispered, the fingers behind her neck tightening. "Do you really believe all I'm after with you is a vacation fling?" He gave her the slightest of shakes.

"But, Court, what else can there be?" she exclaimed unhappily.

"As much as we want there to be, Leya," he said simply. "And speaking for myself, I want a great deal!"

"Oh, Court!"

"When you look at me like that," he muttered, "I have to believe you want there to be a great deal between us, too!"

Leya sucked in her breath, her eyes shining brighter than the gem at her throat. In the face of the emotions flaring between them, she could find nothing intelligible to say. It was too soon to hope and too late not to do exactly that. In desperation, she resorted to a bit of poor humor.

"Court, this is all so sudden," she whispered on a gurgle of laughter.

A slow smile crossed his hard face, reaching his eyes, and he tugged her close against him, letting her bury her heated face in his jacket. For a long moment, he held her that way, saying nothing at all, and she was content.

Eventually he released her, setting her a foot away and retaining a firm clasp on her shoulders while he gazed perceptively down into her questioning face.

"But no more games, Leya. We're both too old for that sort of thing!" he said tersely, and she winced at the forcefulness in him. He meant it.

"Men seem to think anything that doesn't end in bed is a game!" she accused, making the same point, she realized, for the second time that evening.

"It is," he avowed at once.

"That's not true, Court!"

"It is for us," he said gently.

"I won't be rushed," she stated proudly, lifting her chin in automatic defiance.

"But that's exactly what I want to do," he retorted, his fingers digging almost painfully into her shoulders. "Rush you off your feet and into bed where I can make very, very sure of you."

She stepped back, out from underneath his hands, and eyed him with a mixture of speculation and longing. "You," she declared on a muffled groan, "need a good lesson in the evils of possessiveness!"

"I can't help the way I am." He refused to look apologetic. Instead, his tortoiseshell eyes seemed to be eating her.

She hesitated, feeling the undeniable pull on her senses and the equally undeniable instinct to flee while she still could. She knew she was in danger of falling in love with this man she had known so short a time, and she wanted desperately to believe he might be falling in love with her. But she must control the situation until they both were sure. With Court Gannon, she must play it safe, very, very safe...

Summoning a smile, she faced him with an astonishing amount of composure, under the circumstances. "Good night, Court. I had a very—" she paused and the smile broadened "—informative evening. Shall I see you in the morning?"

For a moment, the line of his mouth hardened, and she

wondered if she was going to be allowed to escape after all. Then, he inclined his head almost formally.

"I'll pick you up for breakfast."

"Thank you. Now, as I'm here, anyway, I may as well take my brother's contract," she continued with a determined lightness. It was difficult trying to dispel the physical tension he was purposely building between them, but Leya was not without a strong will of her own.

"It's over there on the table." He watched her walk across the room and pick up the papers, a thoughtful look creasing her brow as she scanned them once more.

"Oh, hell," Leya muttered in surrender. "Have you got a pen? I might as well sign these and put my brother out of his misery!"

Wordlessly, he handed her the pen and watched intently as she flipped the pages over to the one requiring signatures. Without giving herself time to think, Leya slashed her name onto the page with a casual dash that, in a feminine way, was not unlike the equally bold scrawl on the opposite side of the paper. She glanced at the man's name once more as she tossed down the pen.

"C. Tremayne," she repeated, straightening the document and folding it into thirds. "I warn you, Court Gannon," she said with half a smile, "if that man ruins my brother's future, I'll come after you with a skinning knife!"

"You won't have far to look," he promised, a curious brightness in his eyes. "I intend to be somewhere in your vicinity!"

"You're very certain of him?" she asked quietly, the wry humor fading from her voice as she met his gaze.

"He'll deal honorably with your brother," Court stated grimly.

"Do you know anything else about him? I mean, besides his business ability?" Leya asked curiously.

"What do you want to know?" Court returned non-committally.

Leya tapped the folded contract against her palm and considered that, eyes twinkling. "Well, is he married?"

"No. Would it matter?"

"I guess not. Merely curious."

"You know what curiosity did to the cat."

"Are you implying I shouldn't probe too deeply into C. Tremayne's personal life?" Leya grinned impishly.

"He's a man," Court tossed back with deceptive casualness, retrieving the pen.

"Ah-ha! Meaning he's a womanizer?" Leya charged brightly, enjoying the new game, especially since Court seemed rather reluctant to play. "A heavy drinker? Lots of silly macho?"

"You have got it in for the poor guy, haven't you?" Court grumbled, slanting her a disgusted look.

She sighed regretfully. "I can see I'm not going to get a lot of juicy gossip out of you! Why do men always stick together?"

"Because we have so few defenses against the female of the species. Don't worry, Leya. Tremayne will take care of Brandon Security Systems and teach your brother what he needs to know." There was a mild pause as if something had only recently occurred to Court. "You don't seem overly concerned about what Tremayne's failure to honor the spirit of the contract would do to your share of the inheritance."

"I'm not," she said carelessly, truthfully. "I have no interest in Brandon Security. I don't even know why Dad left me a portion of the shares. He knew I had all I wanted in my bookshop."

"Totally self-sufficient?" There was an amused mockery in the question.

"Completely," she confirmed, lifting one brow in a faintly quelling glance. It was the truth. She had built the shop into a successful enterprise, and she had done it on her own.

"Your father probably left you an interest in the firm so that you could act as a guardian angel for your brother in precisely such a situation as this one. He must have known Keith was not yet fully capable of handling the business," Court suggested placatingly, as if making a faint attempt to atone for his remark about self-sufficiency.

"I suppose," Leya allowed, losing interest in the matter. "Well, I'll drop this in the mail tonight so that it will go out first thing in the morning. It will get back to Santa Rosa before I do." She waved the contract briefly and started forward just as if Court weren't standing between her and the door.

But in spite of her air of determined self-confidence, Court didn't step aside. She was forced to halt in front of him, as he stood with his back to the door, his hands behind him on the knob. There was an almost grim, brooding aspect in the tightened lines at his mouth and eyes. For a moment, he said nothing, watching her as she stopped warily a few steps away.

"Court?" she tried tentatively, uncertain of his mood. Carefully, she smiled, striving for a cool, calm look, when what she secretly wanted to do was give in to a very primitive urge to run. "Is breakfast still on?"

"How long will you be staying here at the inn?" he asked, ignoring the trivial question of breakfast. He watched her as if she were a small, nervous animal he wanted to catch. Prey, Leya thought uncomfortably. He really did see her as prey. Her only defense was not to act as if she saw herself the same way!

"Five more days," she told him coolly, agreeably, as if the conversation were quite normal and hadn't taken on overtones of the sort of raw menace that can only exist between a man and a woman. The menace might be present, she thought bracingly, but so were the intervening layers of civilization. She wasn't in genuine danger. Not unless she wanted to be! She returned his watchfulness with a polite, questioning glance, her head high. "And you?"

"About the same," he returned laconically. The gold-flecked eyes went to the contract in her hand and back to her unruffled expression. His voice deepened several shades to a throaty male command that was part plea. "Stay with me tonight, Leya. Please."

"Court," she said gently, "we've already discussed this. I can't. It's just…too soon." Her hand moved in a helpless, ineffectual gesture.

"You're afraid of me?" he rasped.

"Of course not!" she denied, trying to smile. She refused to think about the different aspects of fear. Not now. Now, she had to keep all her wits and self-control about her. She could do it. She knew herself to be both intelligent and strong, and she called on both qualities in full measure.

"You don't have to be afraid, Leya," he coaxed, as if she hadn't just disavowed any fear. "My trap is baited very pleasantly, I promise. You won't even hear it when the door shuts behind you."

"And in the morning?" she persisted in a distant voice, thinking that walking out of this room tonight was going to be one of the most difficult things she had ever done.

"By morning, there won't be any more talk of going back to your own bed at night!" he growled thickly, his eyes moving over her in a near-physical touch.

Leya swallowed at the sheer audacity of his words, her hand clutching the contract in a desperate, white-knuckled grip. "No," she whispered. "I need time, Court. A little more time…" Her words were a plea and she hated that. It wasn't like her at all!

"Time for more games?" he rapped.

"No! Time to be sure!" she flung back, growing angry. Couldn't he understand? For a long, heart-stopping moment, she wasn't at all certain he would even try to see her side of the matter, and then his lids dropped in a speculative, slitted glance. She was keenly aware of the fact that he was literally putting a tight grip on his instincts and desires. Civilization was asserting itself.

"I'll see you back to your room," he finally announced, turning to open the door. He caught her arm as she walked forward, tucking it under his in a proprietary hold.

"And then?"

"And then I'll come back here and take a cold shower!" he exploded in a muffled tone that served to lighten the atmosphere between them as nothing else could have done.

"Poor Court." She giggled as they walked down to the lobby so that she could request an envelope and stamp from the front desk. "You really did have your plans made for this evening, didn't you?"

He glanced down at her laughing, upturned face. "With my propensity for laziness, I have had to develop a talent for being organized. It's the only thing that gets someone like me through life!" His mouth twisted laconically, and the golden eyes were rueful.

"I know what you mean!" she retorted with instant honesty. "I function in the same way. I imagine there are bound to be a few problems when two people like us meet!" They stopped at the desk.

"Nothing insurmountable, I'm sure," he drawled, watching as she addressed the envelope and dropped it into the slot. She ignored his words.

"Well, that's that. Keith's day will be made when he gets the letter," Leya sighed, dusting her hands symbolically as she allowed herself to be led back up the stairs to her room.

"And now we can concentrate on the two of us," Court insisted smoothly.

At her door, he turned her briefly into his arms, his

rough, strong hands cupping her head while he examined her face. His thumbs idly worked the delicate area of her temples. "One last time, Leya, will you..."

"No," she cut in, smiling up at him. "The thought of you in a cold shower is too engaging to ruin!" She felt her confidence return in a warm tide, as she dug out her key. One simply had to maintain a sense of humor about life, she thought.

He shook her admonishingly, a reluctant amusement in his eyes. "For that remark, I promise you that one day you'll be joining me in a shower!" He bent down and dropped a swift, hard kiss on her mouth. "Good night, Leya. I'll see you first thing in the morning!" With that he was gone.

But meeting Court for breakfast wasn't quite the first thing Leya did the next morning. On the spur of the moment, she picked up the telephone after she had dressed in her jeans and a bright yellow sweater.

"Hello, Keith." She smiled into the phone. "I thought you'd like to know I signed the contract last night. It's in the mail."

"Leya!" Her brother's delighted voice came down the wire. "For that news, I'll even forgive you for having awakened me at such an ungodly hour! You won't regret it, you'll see. By the time Tremayne and I are finished, Brandon Security Systems will be number one on the West Coast!" There was a satisfied pause. "I knew once you'd met the man, you'd realize I was aware of what I was doing!"

Leya frowned uncomprehendingly. "But I haven't met

the man," she began, about to tell him she'd met someone who knew Tremayne instead.

"Didn't he find you? I gave him the address of that inn. He said he would be up there in a couple of days." Keith sounded puzzled.

But puzzlement wasn't Leya's chief reaction to this piece of information. She was far too bright, too good at putting clues together to remain confused for long. It was, she thought with cold bleakness as she sat on the edge of the unmade bed, phone in hand, unfortunate that she wasn't quite bright enough to have realized what was going on before her brother dropped the clue.

"Leya?" Keith's voice prompted.

"A tall man?" she questioned dismally, already knowing the answer. "With brown-and-gold hair and eyes the color of tortoiseshell?"

Her brother laughed. "That sounds a bit dramatic, but an accurate description, I guess. I take it the two of you hit if off fairly well if he convinced you to sign that contract so quickly?"

"Oh, I have nothing but the highest admiration for your Mr. Tremayne," Leya said in soft bitterness. "An extremely clever man."

"Leya? There's nothing wrong, is there? You don't sound your usual self…"

The knock on the door brought Leya's head up with a sharp jerk. Her fingers tightened on the receiver. "You'll have to excuse me, Keith. Your idol has just arrived to take me to breakfast," she whispered slowly.

"Fine," Keith sang out in cheerful satisfaction. "Give Court my best, will you? Tell him I'm looking forward to working with him!"

"I'll do that," Leya promised and set the receiver back in its cradle very gently, then got up to answer the door.

Chapter 3

He must have known she was aware of the deception the moment she opened the door, Leya thought in cool fury. She saw the darkening of Court's eyes as he took in the set, distant expression on her face. He was every bit as smart as she was. No, that was unfair, she thought sardonically, he had just proven himself smarter. Yes, this man would know at once that he had been found out. But she wouldn't take even the smallest risk that he hadn't yet guessed.

"Good morning, Mr. Tremayne," she managed in a tight, hard voice she almost didn't recognize as her own. Her hand on the door trembled with the full force of her anger, and it took all her inner control to keep from raking the side of his face with her nails.

"Good morning, Leya," he returned quietly with such coolness that she found herself digging her nails into her palm. "I take it you couldn't resist calling your brother to tell him the good news?" he added dryly. He watched her with a hard, grim look that suggested he knew exactly what she was thinking.

She tilted her chin in chilling disdain, taking in the dark

slacks that hugged his narrow hips and the maroon sweater with an open-collared cream shirt underneath. So cool, so calm, so very much the winner in their unfair skirmish. A skirmish she hadn't even guessed she was fighting.

"Congratulations," she murmured flatly. "I can only apologize that the victory was so easy for you. It must be depressing to not even get a run for your money out of your opponent. Or perhaps you prefer the easy wins?"

He reached out with one large hand and jerked the door a couple of inches, just enough to pull it free of her death grip. Automatically, she stepped back a pace as he advanced into the small room, filling it with his massiveness. He closed the door behind him with disciplined care.

"The contract," he told her bleakly, "was not the important thing between us. I wanted it out of the way."

The corner of Leya's mouth turned down in self-disgust as she faced him, the long sable braid falling across the front of her yellow sweater. She had put on boldly yellow, brightly casual earrings to go with the sweater, and their strong color was a warm note against the darkness of her sleek hair.

"I see," she flung back tersely. "For you, a victory over a woman has to be asserted in bed, is that it?" Her scorn ricocheted around the room, returning to strike again and again, but it seemed to do little damage to his tough, male hide. "For the record, when would you have told me the truth?"

"When I had you safely in bed," he admitted with such readiness that it was all she could do to keep from throwing something at him.

"You're despicable!"

"I'm practical. Done my way, things would have been a whole lot easier than they're going to be now."

"You mean you would have been more satisfied with yourself if you'd managed to seduce me as well as get my name on that contract!" she blazed. "God! What kind of man are you? To think that last night I actually thought you had something of the gentleman in you! I can't believe I've been so incredibly stupid!" She turned away, crossing her arms tightly below her breasts and walked stiffly to stand in front of the mirror over the dressing table. How could she have been such a fool? This was worse, far worse than last time...

He moved to stand behind her, not touching her fiercely hunched shoulders. The gold-and-brown eyes met the flaring brilliance of her silver-green gaze in the mirror.

"That's the hard part, isn't it, Leya?" he prodded knowingly. "The knowledge that you were tricked."

"Being played for a fool rarely appeals to even the most good-natured people," she shot back scathingly.

"But it's much worse for those of us who have a fairly high opinion of our own intelligence, isn't it?" he pointed out. "I told you last night I'm not the only one cursed with a healthy ego!"

Leya trembled at his words, not because of what they implied but because of what they were making her realize. It wasn't merely her ego that had been affronted by his scheming. Deep inside, she felt betrayed. And it was that feeling which was so hard to bear. It didn't help telling herself she had no reason to carry the pain that deep. The critical thing was that she must not allow him to know the full extent of the blow he had delivered.

"Rest assured," she bit out furiously, "my ego has definitely taken a beating. Perhaps that information will take the place of the seduction you seemed to need to sweeten your victory?"

In the mirror, his face tautened. "We've got a lot to talk about, Leya. Come down to the beach for a walk. I want to explain everything, honey..."

"You're crazy if you think I'd so much as walk down the hall with you after what you've done!" she stormed, whirling and planting her hands on her hips. "You've had all the victory you're going to get. Leave me alone!"

"I'm afraid that's not possible," he sighed.

"Would you like a little assistance from the inn manager? I'm sure he would be glad to stop you from harassing one of his guests! I'll call him!"

"Leya, calm down. I'm going to talk to you so there's no sense in ranting at me in an effort to make me leave. I'm not going anywhere without you!" There was a quiet steel in Court's voice that underlined the statement very distinctly.

"What can you possibly have to say to me? I have no wish to listen to your gloating!"

"I have no intention of taunting you about the contract, you little fool...!" he started heatedly.

Leya flinched at the word. "Must you call me that to my face? I'm only too well aware of my foolishness!"

"Damn it! I didn't mean it like that! It's only that I'm getting impatient with you and the phrase slipped out..."

"Because it's what you think I am! A fool! Well, even fools learn eventually, Court Tremayne—" She broke off with a scalding look. "What the hell is your full name, anyway? Not that it matters!"

"Courtland Gannon Tremayne," he said evenly, his mouth tight.

"As I said, it doesn't really matter!"

"Sure it does," he retorted promptly. "It's much easier to swear at someone when you know his full name!" There was the smallest hint of amusement in his face.

"You'll have to forgive my sense of humor this morning," she grated. "It's at a low ebb."

"Come down to the beach, Leya, or at least down to breakfast," he murmured coaxingly. "We have to talk."

"I'm not setting foot outside this room in your company. Can't you get it through your thick head that I don't want to see you again? You certainly seem bright enough on other matters!"

"You're determined to be stubborn about this?" he demanded in soft warning.

"Why not? It goes along with being foolish and having an oversized ego!"

"When it comes to being foolish, I'm the one who should be accepting the honors!" he snapped, putting out a hand to grasp her thick braid. With a quick tug, he forced her closer, ignoring the sharp gasp of anger and pain from his victim. "I should have kept you in my room and in my bed last night. We wouldn't be going through this little scene now if I had!"

"I can only be grateful that some remnant of my own common sense was at work last night!" she hurled back vengefully. "I can't bear to think of how much more foolish and stupid I would be feeling this morning if I had let you seduce me!"

"That's not the way it would have been. You would have understood…"

"If you think I would have been so awestruck by your incredible lovemaking that I would have forgiven you the deception, you're out of your mind!"

He drew a sharp breath, and she knew he was waging an inner struggle with his temper. The knowledge that she had succeeded in upsetting him to some small degree was satisfying.

"Listen to me, Leya Brandon," he charged, his grip on her hair bordering on the painful. "You're going to get the full story of how I wound up involved in this situation whether you like it or not. I would prefer to do my talking down on the beach where the breeze can evaporate some of your heat, but if you insist, I'll do it here. Take your choice. Either way, you're going to hear me out!"

"You can't force me to listen to you!" Leya wrenched

her head, trying to free the braid, but she only succeeded in hurting herself.

"Want to bet? I'm a hell of a lot bigger than you are!"

"Don't you dare threaten me!" she hissed, slightly appalled at his vehemence. Why couldn't he take his victory and leave?

"I'd rather reason than threaten, but you seem beyond the reasoning point! I'm not leaving you alone until you've heard me out, Leya."

She stared at him, knowing he meant everything he said and unsure how to handle his iron will. Short of screaming, there wasn't any obvious way of getting him out of her room, and a walk on the beach didn't sound all that bad. She needed to get some of the churning anger out of her system. Perhaps she could go for the walk and let him ramble his excuses. When he'd had his say, she could simply turn her back on him. There might be some satisfaction in showing him he couldn't talk his way out of the situation. The only thing that bothered her was why he should even want to try. Unless having her signature on the contract wasn't reassuring enough for him...

That last thought decided her. It also jolted her. She had to remember that this wasn't just between herself and Court Tremayne. Keith was involved. And Leya still held fifty percent of the shares of Brandon Security. If she chose to try and get Keith to listen to her... Yes, Tremayne might have reason to be concerned.

"All right," she agreed ungraciously. "I'll go for the walk."

He relaxed visibly, releasing the chain of her braid. "Thank you, Leya."

"Don't thank me," she grumbled, turning away to collect her down jacket. "I'm going under duress. I can't understand what you're hoping to accomplish!"

"I only want to explain, that's all," he protested, watching as she zipped the front of the dark blue jacket. His eyes traveled over her with a curious possessiveness that annoyed Leya.

She said nothing as they went to his room, waiting in the hall while he picked up a sheepskin coat. He didn't try to persuade her inside, appearing to realize she'd been pushed far enough for the moment. In silence, refusing his proffered arm, she stalked beside him down the path leading to the rocky, untamed beach. The aftermath of the previous evening's storm had left the usual calling cards of carelessly tossed driftwood and broken shells. The tide was out and the sea moved sleepily under a gray sky.

Leya felt herself being absorbed into the scene, her senses responding as they always did to the feel of the ocean environment. It appealed to her love of the tactile quality in life, and when she accidentally caught Court's shrewd glance, she knew he was aware of the effect. Grimly, she closed her face so that he wouldn't start congratulating himself on that bit of perception, too!

"Well?" she prompted coldly. "Let's have it. I'd like to get the postmortem over."

He shoved his hands into the fleece-lined pockets of his jacket and shot her a narrowed glance as they walked.

"I met your brother a few months ago when he first began looking for a consultant."

Leya said nothing, her eyes fixed on the far end of the beach.

"We met initially, though, not because of my financial background but because of some work I've done with security electronics. He was interested in some of my—" Court hesitated "—some of the results of my basement tinkering."

Leya did glance up at that and as quickly away. What was it to her if he liked to work with his hands occasionally? She certainly didn't want him thinking they might have something in common!

"He was interested in exploring some of the possibilities of a gadget he found out I had put together. One thing led to another and we started talking business."

"Keith needed a consultant for the business and you needed a way of marketing your latest gadget, is that it?" Leya murmured, leaping to the obvious conclusion.

"Not quite," he shot back dryly. "There were other markets for my little security device."

"But none that offered you control of the company at the same time, I'll bet!"

"Shut up, Leya," he told her peaceably enough. "I'm trying to explain."

Leya lapsed back into silence. Didn't he realize nothing he said could possibly alter this feeling of betrayal inside her?

"Keith and I eventually reached an agreement acceptable to both of us, and then he explained about your position in the firm."

"The silent partner who wasn't being too silent!"

"But who seemed to have no interest in Brandon Security except to babysit her brother!"

Leya winced at that. Was that how Keith had taken her resistance to the idea of the contract? She had never interfered in his life before, and it was only her basic good sense that had prompted her to do so this time!

"He told me a great deal about you, honey. He's very fond of you, and he's got a lot of admiration for his independent, successful older sister. But he's found what he wants to do in life, Leya, and he's determined to do it his way. He wants you to remain the silent partner and let him run Brandon Security."

"You mean let *you* run it, don't you?" She gritted her teeth.

"I've got the experience in both electronics and finance the firm needs right now. Brandon Security is in trouble, Leya. Your brother won't be able to salvage it on his own. He's got the intelligence to see that, and he's got the guts to take the necessary steps to save it. Two years from now, he'll be a very smart, very street-wise young businessman. I'll see to that."

"We'll certainly find out if you're telling the truth, won't we?" Leya smiled with brittle, dazzling brilliance. "The contract is on its way back to Keith, and you're in charge of

Brandon Security for the next two years. Bring me your report card at the end of that time and we'll see how you did!"

He came to a halt, swinging around to face her with his feet braced slightly apart. Without a word, Leya stopped, raising her cold green eyes to meet his piercing gaze.

"I don't intend to wait two years for you to forgive me, Leya."

"Why do you need my forgiveness at all?" she countered recklessly, the sea breeze loosening tendrils of dark hair and whipping them around her throat.

"Because I want you," he said with flat honesty.

Leya gaped at him in open surprise, and then her teeth closed with a snap. "Oh, come off it, Court. Who's playing games now? You don't want me nor do you need me. Not any longer. You've gotten what you wanted!"

"No, I haven't. Not yet. But I will!"

"What you lack in romance and subtlety you certainly make up for in directness, don't you?" she mocked, outraged.

"I think," Court said slowly, examining every inch of her furious face, "that I began wanting you after your brother had told me something about you. From the way he talked, I knew I was going to find you interesting, to say the least. And I had to admire the way you'd picked up on the possible dangers in that contract we wanted you to sign. I was quite annoyed when you didn't bother to keep the appointment I'd set up for us to meet, and when I discovered you'd taken the contract and disappeared, I decided to find out for myself just what you were really like."

"So you came sneaking up here, pretending to be someone else..." Leya began in a voice that shook.

"I came up here to find out if the real-life woman had the same laughter and challenge in her eyes that I'd seen in the portrait in Keith's office," he drawled softly, deeply.

Leya bit her lip, remembering the portrait her father had commissioned shortly before his death and had hung in the office that was now Keith's. Then she opened her silver-green eyes very wide and spoke in liquid tones.

"Look closely, Courtland Gannon Tremayne. I'm not laughing."

He reached for her, and she stepped hurriedly back out of range, a derisive sound on her lips. Why did he continue to lie to her? It made no obvious sense! "I don't know what new game you're playing now, Court, unless you're afraid I'll turn my brother against you and make it difficult for you to do what you want with Brandon Security. But whatever it is, don't expect me to be fool enough to fall for your lies again! I know it's asking a lot in view of the current evidence, but try and credit me with some intelligence!"

"Leya, when you spontaneously asked me what I thought of that contract yesterday, the opportunity of getting it out of the way was too good to miss. But I didn't force you to sign it! You signed it because my arguments in favor of it were sound. They still are. Forget it now. That business is behind us where it should be. It had nothing to do with you and me in the first place."

Her eyes slitted at the note of urgency in his voice. "Do you really believe I'm going to simply forget what you've done to me?"

"I haven't done anything to you, damn it! Not yet, at any rate!" he growled feelingly, almost as if he were the persecuted one, Leya thought incredulously. "The contract isn't important. It was between me and your brother and should never have involved you in the first place. Naturally, I used the easiest method available of getting it out of the way..."

"So you could concentrate on me?" she scoffed, knowing he was lying and almost wishing he wasn't. But that was ridiculous. She wanted to be free of this man, not to discover he might actually be attracted to her after all!

"Yes!" he snapped back, frowning.

"What a waste of time," Leya said with a patently false regret. "I'm no longer in a mood to be the focus of your undivided attention, flattering though the offer may be!"

"You didn't seem to mind last night," Court pointed out righteously. She saw his hands shift slightly at his sides and knew with a sense of triumph that he wanted to grab her and shake her. If nothing else, Court Tremayne was learning he wasn't going to have everything his own way!

"Last night I thought you were someone else, though, didn't I?" Leya tossed back very sweetly. "It was a simple case of mistaken identity. Probably could have happened to anyone." Her voice hardened. "Thank heavens I found

out the truth in time!" She whipped around, the braid flying over her shoulder to hang down the center of her back.
With grim briskness, she resumed her walk in tight-lipped
fury. This time, however, the fury was at her own runaway
tongue. She shouldn't have tacked on that last line. It had
been far too revealing and she could only hope he wouldn't
pick up on it.

Court caught hold of her braid, yanking her to a violent
halt before Leya had gone more than a few steps.

"Ouch!" she yelped, incensed at the small pain. "Let go
of me, you sadist!"

But his response was a further, somewhat gentler tug that
nevertheless managed to pull her slightly off balance and
into his arms. At once, he steadied her by clamping her resisting body tightly against his broad chest.

"In time for what, Leya?" he demanded as she wedged
her hands against his shoulders. "Why are you so glad you
discovered who I was by this morning?"

"No special reason," she taunted, pushing with a disgust-
ing lack of effect against his unyielding body. The silver in
her eyes glinted as she lifted a resentful gaze to meet his
probing one. "It's not at all uncommon for a woman to like
to know the real name of the man who took her to dinner!"

"That's not what you meant, you little shrew. Tell me
the truth! Or shall I do it for you?" he offered menacingly.

"You wouldn't know how!" Leya was acutely aware
of the manner in which Court's small store of patience
seemed to be depleting itself. But what did she care if he lost

his temper altogether? There was nothing he could do to her now!

"You're telling yourself you're glad you found out the truth because you came very close to winding up in my bed last night, and there is every possibility you would have come even closer to doing so tonight. By the end of our week here together, you would have belonged to me completely and that frightens you, doesn't it? You've realized you might have fallen for a man who made you feel like a fool."

"That's not true! You don't scare me in the least, Court Tremayne, but you do annoy the hell out of me! Kindly let me go!" Leya blazed, horrified at his perception. Her palms on his shoulders curled into fists as she struggled to escape his grasp.

"Do you think I don't know how far gone you were last night?" he snarled, disregarding her futile efforts to free herself. "I didn't have to let you go back to your own room, Leya! With very little effort, I could have kept you with me until morning and we both know it. I was the fool last night because I was trying to play the gentleman. It seemed to be what you wanted, and I, like an idiot, wanted to please you. I took a risk and let you go, and look where it's landed us!" His very male indignation would have been humorous if Leya hadn't felt equally indignant.

"How dare you act the injured party!" she nearly shrieked.

"Because I'm feeling injured!"

Before Leya fully comprehended his intent, Court had pinned her head in the crook of his arm, dragging her back against his shoulder and holding her immobile for his kiss. Even as her mouth opened in angry denial, he was crushing the resistance there with his own lips.

Leya, whose recent memories of his kisses comprised images of tantalizing, haunting, teasing caresses that urged and beckoned, was stunned by the devastating domination Court now exerted so effortlessly. Instinctively, she tried to wrench her face away from the marauding punishment, but she couldn't move so much as an inch in his grasp.

"No!" she shouted into his throat, her single word muffled in the warm heat there. Instantly, she was disciplined for her verbal rejection, Court's teeth closing painfully on her lip until she opened her teeth and allowed the invasion of his tongue. It found hers hiding in the dark cavern and forced it into a hot, savage duel that brought a moan from deep in her throat. Only when he seemed satisfied that he had subdued the defiance did he withdraw, his voice grating on her mouth.

"There's no point in fighting me, little Leya. I'm staking my claim, putting my seal of ownership on you, and you're going to learn the limits of my chain!" His hand went possessively to her breast.

The silvery green eyes flew open to glare into the molten brown ones so close to her own, Leya's flaming anger sparkling clearly. Too clearly, if she had but known it. There was far more than anger in the gems of green. There was a feverish brilliance reflecting the depth of her passionate outrage.

"You egotistical, overbearing, arrogant creature! Take your hands off me this instant! And don't have the gall to talk to me as if I were some sort of pet or slave you can own!"

He grinned with feral savagery, his fingers on her jacket splaying to cup the whole breast underneath. "But I am going to own you, honey. It's the only way with a woman like you. You have to be quite certain which one of us is in charge or you'll run me ragged. I'm much too lazy to let you do that to me!"

With a quick movement he obviously hadn't expected, Leya jerked one arm free and swung it. Not in the typical, useless feminine slap, but in a short-arced, forceful punch to his ribs. The thickness of his sheepskin coat blunted the impact somewhat, but there was nevertheless a satisfying thud and she heard the sharp breath between his lips.

"You little vixen!" He snagged the offending hand and crushed it in his own. "I'm going to wind up doing something we both might regret before this is over, and you'll have no one but yourself to blame!"

His head came down again, bruising her mouth. When she went taut in protest, he deliberately moved to bury his face in the curve of her throat, forcing her to accept the burning string of kisses that he trailed from the pulse to the nape of her neck. He held her tightly against his shoulder, trapping one of her arms between their bodies and holding her flailing wrist in the manacle of his grip. With his free hand, he began unzipping her down jacket.

"Court! Don't!" Leya's voice was muffled in the sheepskin. He paid her words no attention, sliding his hand smoothly under the yellow sweater and up to her breast. At the touch, her breath was suddenly blocked. When his fingers undid the front clasp of her bra and slid across to begin a rough teasing pattern on the nipple, she could only suck in air on a gasp.

"Listen to your body, not your head, sweetheart," Court ordered thickly as he held the prize of the hardened top of her rounded breast. "God knows mine is screaming loudly enough at me! I can't believe yours isn't clamoring just as madly. We want each other, little Leya. Why shouldn't we satisfy that want?"

"There are a few things missing from this relationship, damn you!" she rasped, knowing herself helpless to continue fighting the effect he had on her for long. It enveloped her, absorbed her, seduced her sense of touch in the same way that the isolated beach did. The heat of his body was a delicious counterpoint to the crisp, chilled breeze. The earthy, tantalizing scent of him filled her nostrils like the smell of the sea, and the feel of his hands was as alluring as the sight of a storm on the waves. He could not have chosen a more overwhelming setting than the beach to make overwhelming, mastering love to her, she acknowledged miserably.

"What's missing from our relationship, Leya?" he whispered beguilingly, his hand slipping down from her curving fullness to flatten appreciatively on the skin of her stomach. He must have sensed her reaction because in another moment he was letting his fingertips trespass inside the waist-band of her jeans. Leya shivered violently. Desperately, she tried to pull her wandering senses together, too conscious of the new seduction in his lips as they explored the exposed nape of her neck.

"Try love for starters!" she cried into his shoulder.

"It will come in time," he assured her in soft persuasion. "Give yourself a chance. You can fall in love with me…"

"I'm not particularly interested in a one-sided situation!" she hissed.

"You want me to fall in love with you?" Court gave a soft, knowing chuckle. "Even if I were to fall in love with you, I'd be a fool to admit it, wouldn't I? Especially at this point! You'd use the information like a loaded gun!"

Leya ground her teeth, hating the humor she felt in his chest. He was determined to make a joke of it!

"We'll worry about falling in love later," he went on easily, sliding his hand along the edge of the jeans until he reached the small of her back. She could feel him playing with the tiny, fine golden hairs he found there, and her body throbbed in response. "There are other matters to settle between us first," he concluded, sounding decisive.

"Love isn't the only thing I'd want out of a relationship," she swore forcefully. "There are a lot of other things you're equally incapable of giving!"

"Such as?" He put out his tongue and touched the small bones of her shoulder with its tip.

"Such as respect and equality, to name a couple!"

"Now that's an unfair accusation," he muttered. "I have every intention of teaching you to respect me. It's one of my highest priorities, in fact."

"That's not what I meant, damn you!" she wailed, wishing she could move just enough to sink her teeth into him or pummel his ribs again. But he still held her caged.

"Ah, you're afraid I don't respect you!"

"It's quite obvious you don't!"

"You're wrong, Leya. I have a very healthy respect for your strength and your intelligence and your independence. The same sort of respect I have for a female lion. But a man has to tame wild things somewhat if he intends to enjoy them in some measure of safety. I wanted to try a gentling approach first. That's why you got off so easily last night. But if that doesn't work..."

"I'm surprised you are willing to devote the energy it would take to control me," Leya ground out bitterly. "I got the impression you enjoyed a leisurely approach to life!"

"I do. It's one of the things we have in common," he grinned and she felt his teeth on her skin. "Don't worry. This little flare-up between us is a temporary thing. Once the dust has settled, we'll both be able to lapse happily back into our normal, serene lifestyles." He sounded pleased at the prospect.

Leya froze in sudden anguish. My God! she thought helplessly, he sees me as some sort of temporary toy to relieve a small stretch of boredom he's passing through! It was either that or he was convinced she would undermine his influence with Keith. Those were the only two reasons Leya's agile mind could come up with for Court's apparent interest in her as a lover. She had been an idiot during the past two days to think he was genuinely attracted to her!

And how typical of a man to think that the best way of controlling a woman, whether for one's own pleasure or for business reasons, was to take her to bed!

Chapter 4

"If you've quite finished with the explanation you brought me down here for, do you mind letting me go back to the inn?" Leya managed to mumble into Court's shoulder.

She felt his alert silence and then he said carefully, "That depends. Are you going to accept the explanation?"

"You actually want me to forgive you for your deceit?" she muttered disbelievingly.

"I want you to understand why I did it and let us both start over again. Hell, Leya," he went on wryly, "I know we've gotten off on the wrong foot because of that contract...."

"Your perception is blinding!" she interrupted scathingly.

"But I'm asking you to forget it and let us start fresh," he persisted doggedly. "I want you so much, little Leya, and I know the feeling is mutual. You can't hide it from me. In the past couple of days, we've gotten too close."

"And if I don't agree to forgive and forget?"

He sighed deep in his chest. "Then we'll do things the hard way."

"Meaning?" she gritted, as his hand slid out from under the sweater. The loss of its warmth was unexpectedly de-

pressing, and she could have kicked herself for the irrational reaction.

"Honey, don't push me," he replied steadily. "Just give
me a chance. Please?" Slowly, he loosened his grip, not setting her completely free, but allowing some distance between them.

Leya watched him through resentful eyes, disgusted to
find a tiny spark of humor flicker to life at the effort he was
making to appear encouragingly repentant.

"You don't grovel very well," she noted grimly.

"Is that what you want me to do?" he rapped interestedly,
tortoiseshell eyes flickering with an unreadable expression.

"It would be a start, but don't fret," she added quickly,
flinging up a hand. "I don't expect it of you!"

"Leya, from now on I guarantee that everything between
us will be honest and straightforward," he replied earnestly.
His large hands moved to zip up the down jacket.

"Or else they'll be sneaky and underhanded. One of the
two, right?" she retorted cheekily, rapidly regaining her
nerve as she recognized that his impassioned anger of a few
moments earlier was fading.

"I'm trying to be patient..." he began forcefully.

"Why? Because you're hoping I'll give in to your blan-
dishments and therefore be much less taxing to handle?"

The hint of a smile touched his mouth. "I'll have to admit
life would be simpler if you decided to be reasonable."

"Oh! You're impossible!" Disgustedly, Leya thrust her
hands into her pockets and stalked back up the beach to-

ward the distant inn. She didn't look up as he fell into step beside her, but she heard the questioning note in his voice.

"Leya?" He was waiting for her ultimate answer, she realized, asking if she was going to make things difficult for him.

And it struck her that Court was still wary of her. True, he had her signature on the contract, but she retained half-ownership of the firm. As long as she held fifty percent of the shares, she could still represent a threat to his control. He himself had pointed out that all she would need to do was convince Keith they'd made a mistake...

Something inside her despaired. She didn't want to think Court was really so unscrupulous. She didn't want to acknowledge the possibility that he was still scheming. With a small inner sigh, she realized why. She was attracted to the man. Attracted to him in a way she had never been attracted to anyone else. She simply didn't want to believe the worst of him. In spite of the evidence!

But she had to be realistic, she told herself fiercely. The only thing she could be sure of was that Court wasn't completely confident of her. He was prepared to exert himself if she proved rebellious. He was equally prepared to accept her surrender immediately. But what would he do, she wondered acidly, if she didn't give him the clearcut answer he wanted? It was a poor punishment for the humiliation he had put her through, but it was all she had.

"I'll have to think about it," she told him coolly.

"Think about it!" he exploded. "What do you mean,

think about it? Either you're going to accept the situation or you aren't!"

"Whatever you say, Court," she replied demurely, trying to take some satisfaction from his obvious frustration. It was hard. She didn't want the satisfaction of punishing him. She wanted the satisfaction of knowing he really wanted her!

"What do you think you're playing at, Leya Brandon?" he growled. "You were ready to commit murder when you opened the door this morning. A few minutes ago you were shivering in my arms. Make up your mind, damn it!"

"I'll try," she promised mockingly. "But first I think I'll have breakfast. There's nothing like a brisk morning walk on the beach to stir up an appetite, don't you agree?"

She watched him out of the corner of her slanting green eyes and saw the look of wariness and confusion tautening his features.

"Then what?" he prodded belligerently.

"After breakfast? Why, then I think I'll make arrangements to head back to Santa Rosa, of course. I'm sure you'll understand when I say my vacation has been spoiled!"

"There's no need to turn tail and run." He had apparently reached the conclusion that she was afraid of him.

"I'm not running," she assured him with forced serenity. "I'm flying. There's a plane out of that little town up the coast that connects with a major airline. I'll be home by noon."

There was a heavy silence.

"I drove up," Court said finally. "I'll drive you back."

Leya was startled. "No thanks," she managed. "It's a full

day's trip by car and I don't think I want to be cooped up with you for that long."

"Leya!"

"Yes, Court?" she said with vast, insincere politeness.

"I said I'll drive you if you're determined to go back to Santa Rosa today!"

She sensed his uncertainty and impatience and wondered at it. A part of her longed to believe it stemmed from the fact that he was finding his victory hollow. But she knew better than that. The only reason Court was making an effort to maintain some relationship with her was because he was nervous about the power she still held over him. True, Keith practically idolized the older man now, but if his determined sister went to work on him, who was to say she might not be able to convince her brother they'd made a mistake? She still held a fifty-percent ownership in Brandon Security.

But the thought of spending several more hours with Court was suddenly too tempting. Leya was honest enough to admit to herself that she was looking for excuses to put off a final break in their relationship. She didn't want to say goodbye. Regardless of his reasoning, Court was offering her an excuse to stay close to him for a few more hours. And Leya, fearing she was a fool, found herself grasping at the straw.

"All right, Court."

In the end, the trip back to Northern California proved to be the battleground of a very delicate, very careful war.

Leya realized within the first hour that Court was determined to use the time to his advantage.

He knows he hasn't handled this well, she found herself thinking in surprise. He's realized he needs more than my signature. He needs my cooperation. She realized a little grimly that he was going to try and ensure that cooperation by trading on the attraction between them. What frightened her was the possibility he might succeed in doing exactly that! She remembered their lovemaking the previous evening and on the beach that morning and shivered. She had never known such depths of passion with any other man. It was unique. Court Tremayne was unique. And telling herself she was a unique idiot didn't seem to do much good.

There were no outright confrontations. Court was obviously going out of his way to try and mend the fences he'd ripped apart. Leya caught his deceptively casual glances from time to time as he drove with an assurance that seemed second nature.

Leya was careful to steer the conversation in relatively harmless directions, but Court was equally bent on making his case. The subtle battle raged back and forth.

"Honey," he began determinedly at one point, "when you've had a chance to think about it, you're going to remember how much we were enjoying each other during the two days we just spent together. We learned a lot during that time and…"

"Just look at those fantastic redwoods!" Leya interrupted in an awestruck tone. "Do you realize how old these trees are? The whole forest seems so…so primeval, doesn't it? A piece of the earth lost in time." As the magnificent coastal redwoods drifted past the car window, Leya focused her attention entirely upon them.

"I've lined up an apartment in Santa Rosa," Court tried again later. "I want you to see it..."

"Oh, darn," Leya muttered, her fingers going to one ear. "I've lost an earring. It must have fallen on the beach this morning and I just now noticed it."

She heard Court stifle a groan of dissatisfaction at her refusal to get involved in an intimate discussion. "Was it expensive?" he muttered.

"Well, yes, considering the time I put into it," Leya grumbled. That was no less than the truth, she thought. She really ought to go ahead and get her ears pierced.

That succeeded in surprising him. "Time?" he asked with sudden interest, casting her an appraising glance. "Do you make jewelry?"

She nodded.

"Including that green thing you were wearing last night? I liked that. It was very unusual." He sounded genuinely admiring.

"I make all my own jewelry." She shrugged, a little sorry she had brought up the topic by noticing her missing earring.

"No kidding? You have a little workshop?"

"Well, yes," she returned distantly.

"Do you sell your stuff?"

"Oh, no. I only make things for myself or for friends. Just a hobby."

"I'm surprised you don't have your ears pierced," he re-marked knowledgeably. "I've heard women say it's a safer way to wear good earrings."

"I'm a born coward," Leya confessed, smiling slightly in spite of herself.

"Is that the reason you haven't done it?" He grinned. "You amaze me. I wouldn't have thought you would be afraid of a little thing like that!" He seemed, she thought in annoyance, delighted at the news of this fault in her character!

"I don't see many men rushing out to do themselves a physical injury for the sake of fashion!"

He laughed. "I'm sure everyone, male and female, makes some sort of painful effort in the never-ending chore of trying to attract the opposite sex! I've got friends who jog miles and then lift weights. Painful in the extreme, I should think!"

"And what sort of painful effort do you put forth, Court?" Leya demanded, eager to put him at least vaguely on the defensive.

"My effort is that of acting with a semblance of civilized behavior when what I really want to do is reach out and drag you straight into bed," he retorted immediately, eyes darkening with a sudden intensity that was unnerving.

Leya felt the blood rush into her face. She had walked right into that one.

They stopped for dinner early in the evening, and it was dark before Court, following Leya's terse directions, finally drew his very sleek foreign car to a halt in the quiet neighborhood.

For a moment, he sat in silence surveying the old two-story structure with its encircling porch, graceful windows and gingerbread trim. The new wooden siding was painted a rich butterscotch and the trim was in white. Her home dated from a warmer, more inviting era of house design, and Leya had taken loving care of it in the two years she had owned it.

"You live here?" Court's voice held something besides admiration, and Leya's head swung around sharply. What could he possibly find to criticize about her beautiful home?

"Yes," she told him tartly.

"Alone? In a big place like this?" His considering, dangerous glance told its own tale.

"It's a bit late to be worrying about who I might be living with, isn't it?" she taunted.

"It's a bit late for you to be telling me about it," he corrected in a hard, raw voice that alarmed her. "But better late than never, I suppose. Let's get it over." He shoved open the car door with a savage push.

Leya saw the thin, brutal line of his mouth, the uncompromising set of his shoulders, and realized she was looking at a man who had psyched himself into a battle-ready frame of mind in about five seconds flat.

"Court!" she yelped belatedly, realizing what she'd done. Hastily, she scrambled out of her side of the car and raced forward to catch his arm.

"Court, there's no one in there," she said breathlessly,

tugging at his sleeve. "Stop acting the demented lover! The neighbors might see you!"

"If he's not there, where is he?" Court ripped out, shooting her a look of smoldering rage. "When does he get home at night? Or have you two got some sort of *modern* relationship? One that lets you go off on vacation while he does the town? I warn you, it's not going to be like that between us!"

Leya swallowed, realizing with inner disgust that it was going to be harder calming Court back into a rational state that it had been getting him out of it in the first place. Was he really this upset at the thought of her living with a man? Was his interest in her more than merely business? She didn't have time to dwell on the possibility now.

"Don't be ridiculous," she ordered disdainfully. "I'm not sharing that house with anyone. It's all mine! But it certainly wouldn't be your concern if I did have a male roommate," she went on spirited, her eyes glittering. "What in the world did you think you were going to accomplish by barging into my home like that, even if there had been someone there?"

"That's obvious! I'd have thrown him out!" The adrenaline in him was fading, but the expression in the molten eyes remained hard.

"You'd have had absolutely no right! I've given you no excuse to think…"

"Are we going to stand on your front porch and discuss what has turned out to be a purely hypothetical point?" he asked with sudden rough humor, his hand grasping the long dark braid on her shoulder and tugging affectionately.

"Yes, we most certainly are! We're going to get something very clear between us, Court Tremayne! I will not have you embarrassing me in front of friends and neighbors..."

"Never," he promised solemnly. "Wouldn't think of it!" The outrageously pious expression on his face made her want to hit him.

"Nor will I have you making scenes with any of my *male* friends," she emphasized.

"How many of them are there?" he demanded interestedly.

"Will you be serious?"

"Anything you say. I am hereby seriously asking you out to dinner tomorrow night," he said at once. "Seven o'clock okay?"

"I haven't even said I'll go out with you!" she blazed, thoroughly irritated now.

"You didn't give me all this trouble during our two days at the beach," he complained on a note of smothered laughter. "Can't you close your eyes and imagine yourself back there, B.C.?"

"B.C.?" she questioned warily.

"Before Contract."

"You're an idiot," she sighed.

"But a lovable one," he argued, bending his head to drop a feathery kiss on her nose. "Besides, it takes one to know one. Come on and I'll get your bags out of the car."

Twenty minutes later, Leya watched from her screen door as the sleek black car pulled away from the curb and thought herself extremely lucky to have rid herself of Courtland

Gannon Tremayne so easily. It could have gotten nasty, she reflected uncomfortably as she turned away and locked the door behind her. Fortunately, he had convinced himself that she would be dutifully waiting at seven o'clock tomorrow night to go out to dinner with him and that seemed to satisfy him. His goodbye kiss had been short and fierce.

And what would happen, she wondered with grim interest, when he arrived and found her gone? Because she certainly didn't intend to go out with him the following evening. She needed time to think.

Automatically, she dialed her brother's number to let him know she was back in town.

"I thought you were going to stay for a few more days," Keith responded a moment later, sounding vastly surprised. "What happened? Weather turn too bad? A volcano erupt?"

That last guess wasn't far from the truth, Leya reflected wryly. It occurred to her she wasn't sure yet how much she wanted to tell Keith. Her pride was at stake here. Did she really want to admit to him what a fool she had been? And then there was the fact that Keith sounded so happy to know she'd signed the contract. Did she really want to ruin his working relationship with Court before the partnership had had a fair chance? What if Court turned out to be the salvation of Brandon Security after all?

"After I'd made up my mind about the contract, I saw no reason to hang around," she told him evasively, not wanting to acknowledge the fact that she was making excuses to herself. Why was it so difficult to take a hard stand against

Court Tremayne? Why was she trying to find a reason to give him a chance?

"Court was a little upset when you failed to show up for the meeting he'd planned," Keith went on with a chuckle. "I was a bit worried that he might rile you when he finally found you but I gather everything went okay. He's a great guy when you get to know him," he assured her enthusiastically. "I'm going to learn a lot from him."

Leya couldn't think of an intelligent response to that comment, so she mumbled something noncommittal and largely inaudible.

"Say, as long as you're back early," her brother continued, "you might want to drop by Sue's tomorrow evening. She's giving a cocktail party and said to be sure and extend the invitation to you if you got back into town in time." Susan Adams was a mutual friend of long standing.

Leya didn't hesitate. It was the perfect answer. Now she had an excuse not to be at home for Court tomorrow night! "I'd love to. Thanks for telling me. What time?"

"Six-thirty or so. It's a buffet, so we won't starve," he told her cheerfully. "I'll see you there. And Leya?"

"Yes, Keith?"

"Thanks for signing the contract." The phone clattered into the cradle.

For a long time, Leya sat silently beside the phone, gazing with unseeing eyes out over the cheery clutter of her living room. The inside of her home, as friendly as the outside, reflected its owner's lack of concern for unnecessary order. Leya's financial accounts for her bookshop were accurate to the penny, but the interior of her home was warm and delightfully chaotic. The difference represented an essential aspect of her character, and she was far too intelligent not to be aware of it. She had long since accepted her leisurely approach to life, seeing no point in overexerting herself in nonessential areas. The house was clean, but on its best days it remained—at least to an impartial observer—mildly disorganized. That didn't bother Leya in the slightest. She knew herself to be smart enough to set her own priorities in life, and perfect housekeeping simply wasn't one of them.

But where, she asked herself thoughtfully as she viewed her highly eclectic décor, did Courtland Gannon Tremayne fit into her list of priorities? She shook her head, her eyes roving idly over the excellent nineteenth-century end tables and the twentieth-century batik wall hangings. Why was she tacitly admitting to herself that, even though she had every reason to mistrust him, her instinctive reaction to Court was to believe he would honorably uphold his end of the contract? Her teeth clenched for an instant. When she thought of how close she had come to letting him seduce her!

There was no doubt about it, she acknowledged sadly, her pride had been the chief casualty in their small war. It had been a long time since a man had so completely played her for a fool. She closed her lashes against the memory of Court's kisses and her own mindless response.

But it wasn't only the passion she remembered, it was the humor they had shared and the conversation and the walks on the beach. It all added up to a very dangerous package, and if she had half the brains she credited herself with, she would tell Keith everything and demand they unite to fire the man!

Well, she decided as she slowly got to her feet and made her way into the cozy bedroom with its huge brass bed, she would have a small breather in which to think about what she wanted to do.

Leya was still running through her reactions to Court the next afternoon as she turned off the shower and reached for one of the huge, brilliant red towels that decorated the cheerful red-and-white bathroom. Most of the day, she had been unable to think of much else besides the man, and the fact annoyed her. Perhaps the party this evening would take her mind off the puzzle he presented.

The towel wrapped around her torso and tucked in just above her breast, she pulled a brush through the unbound deep brown hair until it fell in a rich mass down her back. She would rebraid it when she had dressed. Maybe she would twine through her hair the beaded metal ribbon she had completed last week, she thought, opening the door of the warm, steamy bath and stepping into her bedroom.

A scream rose in her throat even as she recognized the large male figure standing by the window. She barely stifled it, her hand going to her mouth in classic shock. Immediate fear was replaced at once by unadulterated outrage.

"Court! What the hell do you think you're doing in my bedroom! How dare you?" She clutched automatically at the fastening of the towel but her mind was churning with too much anger to be overly cautious at that point.

He turned, gold-misted eyes sweeping the length of her figure encased only in the towel and coming to rest on the flaming silver-green gaze. Something stirred in his expression. Something primitive and masculine and dangerous. But he smiled. And that smile made Leya more wary than anything else he might have done.

"I came to take you to the party," he said simply, not moving.

"The party," she repeated stupidly. "But…"

"I know we had a date for dinner, but I'm agreeable to a change of plans. Fortunately, your brother filled me in on the change, though. Otherwise there might have been a most unfortunate misunderstanding between us." Still he didn't move, watching her with his hands clasped casually behind his back. Leya had the impression he did that to keep from reaching for her throat.

"I never said I would go out with you this evening," she started aggressively. Going on the offense was the only thing she could think to do under the circumstances. Perhaps she could bluff him.

"You allowed me to believe you were accepting my invitation and you know it," he returned coolly.

"You assume far too much!"

"Because I want you so much," he countered. "Although at the moment I might find it more satisfying to beat you than make love to you!"

"How did you get in here?" she shot back suspiciously,

her mouth hardening with hostility. "The front door was locked. I know it was locked!"

"Ah, but not with a Brandon Security Systems lock," he murmured. "You really should use the family brand, Leya. It's very good, and living alone in a big house like this you should take every precaution!"

"This is the first time in two years I've had any reason to worry!"

"Are you worried, little Leya? If so, then I commend your intelligence."

"Are you resorting to threats, Court?" she demanded boldly.

"I told you once I prefer the easiest, least taxing methods."

"Get out of here!" she hissed violently.

He moved abruptly, starting toward her with long, lean strides that ate up the distance between them before she could get back into the bathroom and lock the door. Her hand was on the knob behind her when his fingers closed on her bare shoulder.

He jerked her toward him, bringing her close against his long-sleeved yellow shirt and dark brown slacks. He wasn't wearing a necktie, and the open collar revealed the tanned line of his throat and the beginnings of crisp, curling chest hair.

"Stop it!" Leya clutched frantically at the towel's insecure fastening, which was threatening to come undone under the violent treatment it was receiving.

He grasped both of her wrists and pulled them around

behind his back, forcing her head to tip up and her eyes to meet his.

"The only way you're going to keep that towel in place," he pointed out with drawling amusement, "is to stand very close to me. The fact that it's still between us is your best hope right now."

"Take your hands off me," she snarled, knowing herself physically helpless and hating the sensation. "You're behaving like a...a..." Words failed her.

"Like something besides a gentleman?" he suggested almost mildly, eyes gleaming as he forced her close. "But you have only yourself to blame for that, don't you? A *lady* who makes plans to break a date shouldn't expect too chivalrous a response from the man involved!"

"I've told you, I never agreed to go out with you tonight! You ordered me to do so, but for your information, that is not considered the same as an invitation!"

"Details," he growled softly, lowering his head to touch her forehead and then her cheekbones with his lips. "But I'm willing to let bygones be bygones. Unlike some people I know! Show me you're sorry and I'll show you how lenient I can be. Come on, Leya, a pretty little apology," he coaxed with mocking charm as he feathered her face with more and more warm, tiny kisses. Kisses that beguiled and cajoled just as they had that night she had almost wound up in his bed, Leya reminded herself fiercely, as she tried to retain her basic good sense.

"Court, you've had your big scene," she muttered, aware of the heat in her body and terribly afraid he must know of it also. She had so little on that she was literally unable to clothe her reactions. "Please get out of here and let me get dressed!"

"But I like you wearing only a towel," he whispered deeply, his teeth nibbling at her ear and the sensitive area behind it. "You seem much less formidable this way, do you know that? And the softness of your hair is an invitation to any man, especially one who happens to be in your bedroom."

"Please!" she almost begged, acutely aware of her body's rising tide of response. How could she let this—this *liar* take advantage of her? What was wrong with her? But she had been thinking of him all day, and it was as if his sudden and totally unexpected presence in her room was the result of her overactive imagination. As if she had somehow conjured him up out of thin air from the sheer force of her thoughts!

She heard his muffled groan and knew his own body was leaping into hard, demanding alertness. It called to her on a nonverbal level, seeking her, wanting to bury itself in her warmth. The gentle, teasing quality of the kisses changed gradually, deepening into the heavy, drugging, seductive caresses that had left her so helpless on the beach the previous morning.

"You can't hide from me, honey," he grated, his mouth sliding moistly, burningly along her cheek to cover her lips in a plundering, arousing kiss that shook off the last of the gentle cajolery and bared the uncompromising male desire beneath.

"I know you want me. It's only your silly female pride

standing in the way," he murmured against her bruised lips. "But I've apologized for that business with the contract. Forgive me for that and I'll forgive you for trying to sneak out tonight!"

"It's not that simple, damn you," she wailed, her lashes moving restlessly against her cheeks as she felt the throbbing in her stomach.

"Yes, it is," he countered throatily. "It's as simple as getting rid of the towel between us!" With that he moved against her, his chest crushing her breasts for an instant before he stepped back a couple of inches.

The red towel gave up the battle and slipped soundlessly to the floor at their feet.

"No!" Leya whimpered, and then her words were swallowed up as he forced his tongue deeply into her mouth and his arms released hers to encircle her still-damp, nude body.

It was getting worse, she thought frantically while she could still think at all. Every time he held her she was less able to resist, less able to deny him. She felt the firm thrust of his strong thighs as he lowered his hands the length of her back and arched her hips into him. His fingers snarled themselves in the long ends of her hair and used the leverage to force her head back further so that his mouth could explore her throat.

"God, Leya!" he swore, his lips branding her. "I love the feel of you. I could get lost in your body. So much passion waiting for me, so much pleasure. I've wanted you since I first saw you across the lobby at that inn! You're going to drive me crazy if you don't admit you want me, too!"

"But that's not enough!" she gasped as his fingers dug into the soft flesh of her buttocks. A violent shiver rocked her.

"It's a damn good start!" he retorted, using his grip to force her into full awareness of his growing desire.

The unmistakable desire in him was a commanding, aggressive pull on the very core of her femininity. It stirred her loins and weakened her knees until she was clinging to him for support.

"Yes," he whispered in thick triumph as he felt her clasping hands move over his back. It was as if he were accepting a surrender she hadn't voiced aloud, and it shook her back to awareness as nothing else could have done in that moment.

"Let go of me, Court!" she ordered in a rough, shaking voice. "We're going to a party, not to bed!" She struggled wildly, as much against the masculine triumph she perceived in him as against the force of her own desire. He was not going to make a complete fool out of her!

"Sweetheart, don't fight us both. You can't possibly win," he purred huskily in her ear, his hands gentling her spine. "It's going to be all right. Let me show you how good it's going to be between us. You can trust me…"

"About as far as I can throw you!" With a last, desperate push, Leya wrenched herself free and grabbed madly for the towel. She clutched it tight around her trembling body and backed slowly away from him. He followed her with his eyes but made no move to recapture his victim.

"You've got a lot of nerve telling me to trust you after what you did to me!" she blazed, sweeping one hand harshly through her disarrayed hair. "And now you've come sneaking into my house like a common thief!"

"You'd better hurry if we're to get there on time," he interrupted absently, glancing at the thin gold watch on his brown wrist.

"What?" she managed, taken aback. She eyed him in confusion. "If you think I'm really going to that party with you…"

"You just said you were," he reminded her with deceptive casualness. A casualness that didn't hide the underlying steel. "You said we were going to a party and not to bed. You wouldn't think of backing out of a second date with me, now would you?"

"Court—!" Leya began wrathfully, a growing conviction that she was being manipulated eating into her bones.

"Get dressed, Leya, or I'll help you," he ordered calmly.

"The only thing you'll do is get out of my bedroom! Now!"

"Darling," he murmured in a tone of weary patience, "I'm trying very hard to tame my shrew with kindness and a degree of gentleness but if she doesn't learn the limits of how far she can push me that way, I'll be forced to try another technique. The choice is up to her. Which is it to be?"

"You're insufferable!"

"You're intoxicating. Even when you're scowling at me," he retorted smoothly. "Fifteen minutes? I'll wait for you downstairs."

Leya stared at his broad back as he sauntered out of the

room. Never in her entire life had a man ever told her she was intoxicating.

She deliberately stretched the fifteen minutes to twenty but didn't quite have the nerve to push it any farther. It wasn't that she was the least bit afraid of Court Tremayne, Leya reassured herself, it was just that he was a great deal larger than she was and he was currently blocking the only exits out of the house. And she had been intending to go to the party anyway.

With any luck, she told herself in renewed spirit as she descended the stairs a few minutes past the deadline, she would find some opportunity at the party to repay Court for his ill-treatment. At the very least, she would make certain she had another ride home. Keith would be there and he could be relied upon to provide transportation. Court Tremayne might be escorting her to the event but she didn't intend to allow him to bring her home!

The subject of her thoughts lifted his streaked brown head as she came toward him, tossing aside a magazine on gemstones as he got to his feet. He was smiling with that curious, proprietary smile of a man who thinks he has only to put out his hand and the prize will be his.

"More of your own handcrafted jewelry?" he asked, his eyes going to the unusual chains at her neck, which nestled in the hollow of a high-standing oriental collar. The dress was a boldly marked sheath of red and gold.

She nodded curtly, stepping lightly aside to collect her shawl as his fingers reached out to touch the necklace. The small evasion served its purpose, but when she glanced at him again she could have sworn she surprised a strange degree of hurt in the tortoiseshell eyes. It was gone in an instant as his hand dropped to his side.

"You can't avoid it forever, you know," he cautioned softly as he took her arm and started toward the door. He slanted a glance down at her profile, his eyes lingering on the dark braid. "Sooner or later you'll have to forgive me. Why not make it now? Tonight?"

"Think how much easier that would be for you," she scoffed sweetly. "No need to exert yourself at all!"

He grinned wryly. "I knew you'd understand."

"Sorry, Court, you're not getting off that easily," she muttered waspishly.

"What are your terms?" he demanded cheerfully, opening the car door for her.

"I'm still drafting them."

"Let's hope I don't entirely run out of patience before you decide how I'm supposed to make up for my misdeeds," he observed politely.

It was only as she walked into the party on his arm that Leya finally found something to take her mind temporarily off the matter of her entanglement with Court Tremayne.

She would have preferred almost any other diversion. Across the room, she met the sophisticated and cynical blue eyes of the one other man in her life who had succeeded in making a fool of Leya Brandon.

Alex Harlow lifted his glass in the faintest of salutes.

Chapter 5

"Who is he?"

Ten minutes into the flurry of welcome and introductions, Court managed to growl the question into Leya's ear. Any hope that he hadn't sensed her almost imperceptible stiffening as they had come through the door died.

"Who?" she tried, stalling uncertainly for time, although she wasn't quite sure why. The drink in her hand was cold, and Court was standing so close she could feel the heat of him. The two sensations seemed to feed her fever-pitched light-headedness. Once again, she wished desperately she wasn't so susceptible to the tactile quality of life.

He scolded her with his glance. "That guy with the light brown hair on the other side of the room, wearing a black turtleneck. You can't miss him, Leya," he added derisively. "He's the one trying to eat you alive with his eyes. The one person you haven't smiled at yet. Who the hell is he?"

"Why do you care?" she countered, sipping at her drink and smiling over the rim of the glass at their hostess. Sleek, charming and blonde, Susan Adams had made no secret her fascination with Court from the moment she had greeted him. She was flicking speculative glances his way as she circulated among her guests.

"It's always nice to know the name of the guy you might have to pound to a pulp later!"

Leya flinched in astonishment, covering the reaction quickly with a less than humorous smile. "I can certainly understand your interest in getting a person's correct name. I've got some strong feelings on the matter myself!"

"Leya!" he snapped out, and she knew he had just run dry of patience. He took a sip of the Scotch in his glass and waited, golden eyes pinning her. The tension in him was a lazy, coiled cat waiting to leap.

Leya quickly decided the best approach was to brazen out the situation.

"You wouldn't want to pound him, Court. You'll probably like the man. The two of you have a great deal in common!" The flashing silver in her green eyes hardened, and cool mockery edged her curving lips.

"What's that supposed to mean?" There was unmistakable anger in him now.

"A year ago I was on the point of considering marriage to him," Leya said carelessly, taking another sip from her drink. What did she care if Court knew the truth? He knew so much about her already, she thought grimly. "I thought we were in love, you see," she added confidingly, her tones laced with heavy self-mockery.

"And?" he prompted harshly through set teeth.

"And—?" Leya snapped her fingers with assumed nonchalance. "Presto! He made a fool of me." The silver in her eyes gave them a dangerous gleam.

"How?" Court grated. "Don't make me drag it out of you sentence by sentence, damn it!"

Her eyes widened. "I don't see why I should let you drag it out of me at all."

"Because whatever happened is still affecting you. You look as tense and brittle as glass. I can't figure out if you want to go over to him and throw yourself into his arms or strangle him!"

"Does it matter?" she purred, not quite looking at him but aware of his braced tension as if it were a palpable thing. It made her feel even more keyed up.

"It matters! And stop drinking that stuff as if it were soda pop," he ordered in a short-tempered rasp.

"My, you are in a domineering mood this evening," she noted with biting amusement. Deliberately, she took another sip.

"I'm in a mood to whale the daylights out of you, Leya, so you might want to exercise a bit of caution."

"I was wrong back in Oregon when I accused you of having a one-track mind," she murmured smoothly, beginning to enjoy herself for some unknown reason. "I'll have to admit you've got at least two tracks when it comes to dealing with women: sex and brutality. Have you had a lot of luck with the combined approach in the past?"

"I've never had to try combining them," he drawled in a deadly cool tone. "But for you I'll make an exception. Tell me who he is, Leya, or I'll start with the brutality first."

"My brother will break your neck!"

"Your brother hasn't even arrived yet. Besides, he's got enough sense to stay out of a situation like this!"

Leya considered him, her neat head tipped to one side, her eyes bright and daring. "His name is Alex Harlow. Want to meet him?"

"Not particularly." Court faced her coolly. "Finish the story."

"There's not much to tell." She shrugged. "He used me as a cover for his relationship with a friend of mine. A married friend. I discovered what was going on the day she announced her divorce to marry Alex. End of story."

"Not quite," he disagreed dryly, "Did he wind up marrying your presumably ex-friend?"

"Oh, yes. As soon as her divorce was final. I'm sure you'll understand when I tell you I haven't seen much of either of them socially since!"

"Is his wife here tonight?"

"I haven't seen her," Leya muttered, downing another swallow of her drink.

"Then—" Court put out a hand and forcibly removed her glass "—putting the facts together we are forced to the conclusion that he's on the make this evening. You're not to get near him, is that clear?" The brown-and-gold eyes confronted her with absolute command.

Leya lifted one eyebrow in response. "Jealous, Court?" she teased. "Or just worried that you don't have as much control as you would like over the 'silent partner' in Brandon Security?" The challenge hung in the air between them, goading and provoking.

He set her half-empty glass down on the table behind him and straightened slowly, his eyes never leaving hers. "Would you like me to admit to the jealousy, little Leya?" he drawled.

"Yes," she retorted unhesitatingly, lips curved in near-laughter. "Yes, I think that might be fun!"

"I have to assume from that statement that you've never felt the full weight of a man's jealousy," he stated very softly.

Leya pretended to consider that and then shook her head decisively. "No, I can think of a few occasions when I've been privileged to witness what's been labeled jealousy. Frankly it appeared to be a rather crude form of pouting. Like little boys who don't get their own way and go off in a corner to sulk. Would you sulk if I went over and spoke to Alex?" she asked with a strange brightness.

"No, Leya, I won't sulk," he said in a hard voice.

"Ah, well." She pretended to sigh. "It was only an outside chance. Still, it might have been fun."

"You're wrong on that point." Court looked as if he were going to pursue the subject and then broke off, glancing over her shoulder. "There's your brother. He just walked in the door."

Leya didn't look around. "A gorgeous blonde on his arm?"

"Well, she's definitely blonde. I guess you could say she's gorgeous, that is if one didn't mind a certain lack of intelligence around the eyes. Why?" Court glanced down at her wry expression.

"Since when has a man minded a certain lack of intelligence in his dates? Could I have my drink back, please?" she added with undue politeness, green eyes on the glass behind him.

"No. You've had enough."

"I haven't even finished my first drink, for heaven's sake!" she muttered furiously.

"Maybe in a little while you can have another. Provided you don't down it like water."

"You certainly are out to ruin my evening, aren't you?" she groaned.

"Chalk it up to my naturally perverse nature. You never answered my question about the blonde your brother came in with. Don't you like her?"

Leya did bother to glance around briefly at the question, her green eyes moving swiftly over the lovely young woman standing beside her good-looking, dark-headed brother.

"Never saw her before in my life," she admitted freely. "So I really can't say if I'll like her or not."

"How did you know she was blonde?" Court demanded curiously.

"That's all my brother's been dating for the past year. Blondes. Beautiful and, for the most part, empty-headed blondes." Leya frowned, slanting Court an upward glance. "Are you going to encourage or discourage that tendency in him during the next two years?"

"Your brother's contracting with me to teach him about

business, not about women," Court murmured politely. "There's not much I could do about it, anyway. It's a taste a man either outgrows or he doesn't."

"Really? And have you outgrown your taste for gorgeous blondes?" Leya tossed back with an ease she didn't feel. Susan Adams was still sending interested glances in Court's direction.

"Yes, in point of fact I have," he growled, meeting her eyes very directly.

"How long did the taste persist before you saw the light?" she taunted.

"Until quite recently," he confessed airily.

"You mean my brother could go on another ten years dating those creatures?"

"Unless he gets lucky before that." Court grinned suddenly. "And finds himself a wasp-tongued shrew with hair the color of a jungle cat. Don't begrudge him the blondes in the meantime, though. They're the ones who will make him appreciate the shrew when he finds her! Come on," he went on firmly, taking her arm, "we'd better go over and say hello. Keith's seen us."

Effortlessly, Court pushed a way through the crowd toward the other couple, dragging Leya along in his wake like a toy. She did manage to snag a glass from a passing tray, however, and had it secured in the hand farthest away from her escort by the time they reached Keith and his blonde. Her brother's green eyes met hers as she approached on Court's arm. His eyes lacked the silver tinge of her own, but the dark brown of his hair was similar. And the basic underlying intelligence, she had always thought, was pure Brandon. That opinion remained in place in spite of his recent decision to sign the contract with Court Tremayne.

"Hi, Leya," Keith greeted her affectionately. "Glad you could make it tonight. Sorry you cut your vacation short, though. Good evening, Court—taking good care of my sister?" The vivid green of his eyes absorbed the protective way Leya's arm was tucked under Court's and the abnormal brightness in his sister's eyes.

"You can trust me to look after her," Court said easily, smiling at the blonde. "Who are you in charge of tonight?"

"This is Angie." Keith grinned cheerfully. Angie didn't appear to be blessed with a last name but she didn't seem to mind as the introductions were made. Her beautifully made-up blue eyes were full of a sultry invitation and the sexy red pout of her mouth was glistening with too much lip gloss.

"I'm glad to see you and Court hitting it off so well, Leya," Keith remarked with a poorly concealed smile.

"Did you have a few doubts?" Leya charged sweetly, lifting her glass for a swallow.

"Where the hell did you get that?" Court interrupted before her brother could respond. He reached for the glass, but Leya managed to neatly sidestep.

"If you'll excuse me, I think I'll find the ladies' room. Don't go away, Court, I'll be right back!" With a quick turn on her heel that swirled the red-and-gold skirt around her ankles, Leya swept off into the crowd, glass clutched tightly in her hand. She could feel Court's eyes on her for a moment but knew he wasn't following. When the prickling sensation at the back of her neck ceased, she veered from the direction in which she had been going and headed for the terrace instead.

There was no one else outside to share the cold night air and the view of Santa Rosa's lights, so Leya sipped her drink in peace, her arms folded against the chill. And she thought about the same thing she had been thinking about all day: Court Tremayne. The only break came when her mind went briefly, angrily to the presence of Alex Harlow. But upset as she was at seeing Alex's cynical, handsome face again, there was no denying that Court somehow loomed the larger of the two in her mind tonight.

"Hello, Leya." Alex's voice came from the shadows behind her. Well, hadn't she been half expecting it? Wasn't that the real reason she'd come out here alone for a few minutes? To see if he'd follow? She knew what that look in his eyes had meant when she'd first seen it from across the room. Court was right. Alex Harlow was on the make tonight.

"Good evening, Alex." Her voice was amazingly calm as she turned and leaned against the rail. He walked toward her, the black turtleneck and dark slacks helping him blend into the darkness around him. The heavy-lidded blue eyes found hers and held them as he advanced. There was a time, she reflected, when that look could have made her heart beat faster.

"You're looking lovely tonight," he said quietly, halting a couple of steps away. He said it the way he'd always said it, in a soft, seductive drawl that made it clear he knew when a woman had dressed for him. But she hadn't dressed for him tonight, Leya thought in silent amusement. She'd dressed for Court. The admission went almost unnoticed in the increasing excitement of the moment.

"Thank you," she replied demurely. "And where is your wife?"

"Haven't you heard?" Alex asked quietly. "We've split up."

"I'm sorry to hear that, since the two of you went to such an effort to get together." If he caught the thread of sarcasm in her words, Alex didn't acknowledge it.

"Everyone makes mistakes, Leya." There was a slight pause. "I tried calling you earlier this week. There was no answer."

"I've been away for a few days," she replied, her arms stretched out on either side of her, resting on the cold metal railing as she lounged backward. The drink was clasped in the fingers of her right hand, half-empty.

"With him?"

"Him?" she questioned, eyes gleaming up at Alex's sardonically curved mouth.

"That man you came with tonight. From what I could see he appears to think he owns you."

"Does he?" she smiled.

"Don't be sarcastic, honey," Alex advised almost gently. "It isn't like you."

Leya's smile broadened. "Oh, I don't know about that. There are some who say I'm a natural shrew."

"Then they don't know you, do they?" he countered,

stretching out his hand to stroke the side of her jaw with caressing fingers.

"Perhaps it's you who doesn't know me," she suggested, resisting the urge to pull her head away from his touch. God! Was it only a year ago she would have been thrilled?

"I know you," he stated with confidence, letting his fingers slip down further to tilt her chin. "I know you very well."

"Why did you try to call me this week, Alex?"

"Can't you guess?"

"Maybe. But I'd rather be sure," Leya whispered with a hint of invitation she knew he'd pick up immediately.

"When I first met you, Monica was the only thing on my mind."

"And I was a means to get to her?"

"Yes, I'm afraid so," he admitted in a tone that said he clearly expected her to forgive the deception. "It was only later that I realized what I'd thrown away in my efforts to win the wrong woman."

"Really?" Leya whispered skeptically. "When did you make that discovery?"

"You have gotten hard, Leya. Was it because of me? Because of what I did to you?"

She wanted to laugh and barely restrained the outburst. If he honestly thought she was acting uncharacteristically now, then it could only mean he'd never learned much about her true nature a year ago. But whose fault was that, she asked herself honestly. Hadn't she always been on her best behavior around Alex? She'd never fought with him, never given him the sharp edge of her tongue. Never, she suddenly realized, pushed the relationship to the point where they would have had to discover which of them was the stronger.

"Please don't feel guilty about my current attitude," she replied serenely. "I assure you I come by it naturally. You needn't take the blame for having turned me into a bitter woman. You might be interested to know that I'm really not bitter at all," she added, reflectively.

"Not even a little?" he pressed, bringing his face close to hers so that his mouth hovered an inch above her own. "I hurt you, Leya, didn't I? But I can make up for all that."

"How?" she asked simply, making no effort to pull away but feeling no great interest in the impending kiss. She viewed his mouth almost clinically.

"By starting over..." He kissed her slowly, lingeringly, with all the old expertise.

And Leya felt nothing at all except distaste. She stood very still, her arms still resting on the railing and waited for him to finish. How could she ever have been even mildly excited by his embrace, she wondered. But she knew the answer to that. It came as soon as Alex's arms went around her waist. Alex's kiss meant nothing now because she'd been exposed to Court Tremayne's lovemaking. It was Court her body craved, not Alex or any other man.

The realization was stunning and the problem it presented seemed overwhelming. But she would have to deal with it later. At the moment, it was Alex Harlow who held her and invited her with his caresses to restart an old romance. And it didn't seem quite fair that he should escape scot-free for the way he had treated her a year ago. He had made a fool of her and it seemed only appropriate that he should suffer the same experience. The possibility of revenge made Leya's eyes glitter with a hard platinum light.

"Do you want me back, Alex?" she asked dreamily, mouth curving softly as he lifted his head. "Is that the truth?"

He looked down into her uptilted face and she knew he saw only what he wanted to see there. He was convinced he had only to lift his finger and she would fall back into his arms.

"I think we would do very well together, Leya, my sweet," he whispered, his hands pressing her waist. She felt the beginnings of male arousal in him and was pleased. "This time we would start from scratch with no other woman involved. Yes, I want you back. Tonight. Come with me, Leya. I'll take you out to dinner and we can sort everything out between us."

"That sounds very pleasant, except for one thing," she murmured, her laughter threatening to well up and overflow.

"What's that?" he prodded persuasively, eyes gleaming.

"My fiancé." Leya dropped the small bombshell with no compunction whatsoever, glorying in the shock it had caused. "The man I'm with tonight. I'm in love, Alex, with a man who makes your kisses seem like cold dishwater. Looking at you now I can't even imagine what I ever thought I saw in you!"

"What the hell are you talking about?" he blazed, his

hands falling away from her waist as if they had been burned. The blue eyes narrowed angrily.

"You heard the lady," said a hard, cold voice behind them.

Leya swung a momentarily startled glance over Alex's shoulder, her eyes colliding with Court's as he walked toward them. How long had he been standing in the shadows? she wondered frantically. What would he do? She prayed he would hold up his end of the deception, take the role he'd been assigned, and not ruin her small revenge.

"You two are engaged?" Alex demanded, stepping away from Leya and turning to face Court, who kept coming until he was close enough to slide an arm around Leya's waist.

"It was supposed to be something of a secret until we were ready to announce it, but I gather she couldn't resist telling you." Court turned his head to glance down at Leya as she stood tensely in the circle of his arm. He smiled with all the possessive warmth of a real fiancé, and she realized abruptly he was going to help her. Relief flowed through her veins, and confidence reheated her nervously cold body.

"Why didn't you say something earlier, Leya?" Alex snapped, his anger flaming as he caught sight of the laughter in her sparkling green eyes.

"I'm sorry, Alex," she apologized without any sign of contrition. "But you have to admit the opportunity was simply too good to pass up. If you could have seen the look on your face!"

"It was all a joke? Letting me kiss you like that?" he blazed, incensed.

"I'm afraid so. Why should I be interested in you after all this time, when I'm quite happily engaged to marry another man? Let's face it, Alex, we didn't exactly share an undying love!" Leya grinned, delighting in his reaction.

"You don't seem to mind having a fiancé who goes around kissing other men in the moonlight," Alex muttered to Court, clearly looking for a way of salvaging his pride. The two men faced each other across the short distance. Both were tall, but Court had a couple of inches on Alex. He also had a suggestion of strength that was lacking in the younger man. Strength and experience.

"From what I saw," Court replied in a leisurely tone, which was nonetheless menacing, "you were the one kissing her. Now that I *do* mind. In fact, you could say I take definite exception to that," he added lazily.

Leya felt the spring-tight tension in Court through the sinewy arm that crushed her against him. He was angry but he was in complete control.

"How do you know it wasn't her fault?" Alex mocked bitterly, sliding an accusing look at Leya's cheerfully smiling face. His eyes hardened at the humor in her. There was no worse way to hurt a man than to laugh at him, she thought.

"Oh, I know Leya well enough to know what she's like when she's enjoying a kiss," Court informed him with a cool certainty that left no doubt in his listeners' minds that he had Leya's physical reactions well catalogued. Leya would have blushed but for the fact that she was having too much fun.

"Is that so?" Alex began aggressively. "Well, let me tell you I knew her a long time before you came along and I…"

"One more word and I'll throw you over the railing," Court interrupted with distinct intent. "Now why don't you take your humiliation like a man and slink off somewhere? I promise to keep Leya away from you in the future. You needn't be afraid she'll exercise her claws on you again."

"Good night, Alex," Leya chimed in at once. "So nice to see you again. I enjoyed it immensely."

"Why, you little—"

"I know it's a temptation, but don't say it," Court advised. "You know how it is—if you actually say it, I'll have to do something about it."

Without a word, Alex swung furiously off into the night, heading toward the doors opening onto the terrace. In a few seconds, he had disappeared.

For a moment, silence reigned under the cold night sky, and then Leya tried to take a sip from the glass she was still clutching in her right hand. But it was no use—the laughter bubbled over and spilled out, making it impossible to swallow.

"Oh, Court." She grinned, twisting to look up into his face. "How can I ever thank you? That was fabulous! Did you see the look on his face? He was positively livid!"

"Enjoy yourself, Leya?" he asked laconically, his arm still wrapping her close. Once again, he removed the glass from her fingers, setting it down on the railing this time.

"Enormously," she assured him, deciding not to make an issue out of his insistence on taking the drink away from her. She was feeling much too charitable at the moment.

"And it wouldn't have had nearly the effect without you showing up when you did. Perfect timing!"

"Thank you. I'd been standing there for some time, you see, trying to decide when to make my appearance," he murmured, his rugged features cast in an unreadable expression as he gazed down at her gleaming silver-green eyes.

"Well, you chose an excellent moment. I'm very appreciative. That man deserved everything he got and more. Would you have really thrown him over the railing if he'd insulted me?"

"Yes, I think so," he said calmly.

"Terribly energetic," she pointed out.

"There are occasions in life when one must bestir oneself and put forth the effort," he observed. "Are you really feeling quite grateful for my assistance, Leya Brandon?" he added, taking a sip from his own glass.

"Oh, yes," she assured him cheerfully enough. She could feel the effects of the alcohol in her bloodstream, but she didn't feel drunk, merely pleasantly high.

"Grateful enough to let my help with your revenge this evening cancel out the grudge you're holding against me?" He waited for her response, a quirking smile on his hard mouth.

"What are you talking about?" she whispered, sobering quickly and twisting enough to put some space between the two of them. He didn't try to stop her.

"I'm talking about forgiving me for that business with the contract and letting our relationship go back to where it was before you found out who I was."

"You think you've made up for what you did by helping me out tonight?" Her voice was husky and there was a new pounding in her veins that wasn't induced by alcohol. She was remembering the lesson she'd learned in Alex's arms a few minutes earlier. The lesson had taught her that it was Court's embraces she wanted. Court's...love?

Dear Lord! Was she going to be an even greater fool and fall in love with the man? Leya screamed silently. She saw the way he was watching her, waiting for her to say that the score between them was settled. How did he truly feel about her? How could any woman know whether a man like this had genuinely fallen for her or whether he was still interested only in controlling a potentially difficult unknown quantity?

And how could she ever learn the answer to that question unless she took the risk of giving him another chance?

"I think you owe me a great deal for what I let you do tonight," he said quietly, deliberately pressing his case.

"You mean for using you?"

"Wasn't that what it amounted to?" he retorted with an edge on his words.

"I suppose so," she acknowledged.

"Come on, Leya. You can be more honest than that!"

"All right, so I used you a bit. What harm did it do?"

"None, but I want some payment for the privilege, and I think forgiving me for the way you feel I treated you in Oregon is little enough recompense."

She glared at him, trying to sort through her chaotic

emotions. Could they start over? Had he really begun to feel something important for her?

"And if I said we were even?" she hedged carefully.

"Then we could take up where we left off. Get to know each other better..."

She eyed him speculatively. "Is that what you want?"

"Yes, it's what I want."

Was he telling the truth or was he still worried about the threat she represented to his control of Brandon Security? But she sensed that his desire for her, at least, was honest. Could they build something lasting out of such a fleeting emotion? All her instincts urged her to take the risk of finding out. She could never be satisfied with herself or with life if she didn't seek to know the true limits of this relationship.

The sudden knowledge answered all her questions. She would take the challenge and the risk of discovering the truth about his feelings for her.

Warily, as if she were reentering the lists for another round of combat, Leya inclined her head once and whispered, "Yes, Court. I'm willing to start over again. That is," she added in a small voice, "if it's true that you deceived me because you really wanted to pursue our relationship and not just to get my signature on the contract."

"It's the truth, Leya," he told her huskily.

He stepped forward, sweeping her into his arms. "Leya, my maddening little shrew. I know how you must have felt when you discovered I'd deceived you. I would have felt the same. But I was so sure that once I had you in my bed nothing else would matter! I'm glad you've had your re-

venge by using me. We can put it all behind us. I handled
you all wrong, I know that now. You're a lot like me, and
I should have—"

"There you two are!" Keith's voice called cheerfully
into the darkness. "We were wondering where you'd disappeared. I take it everything is settled? I'll have to hand it
to you, Court! You sure know how to tie up loose ends!"

There was a distinctly admiring note in his voice. One
that finally made Leya lift her head from Court's shoulder
in sudden alertness.

Still clasped in Court's arms, which had tightened at the
sound of Keith's words, she looked past the massive shoulder and directly into her brother's smiling gaze.

"What are you talking about?" she demanded, in a tone
of voice she hadn't used on him since eighth grade, when
she'd finally learned little brothers were more easily handled with cajolery than threats, especially when they started
getting bigger than their sisters.

"Your, er, relationship with Court, here," Keith returned,
picking up some of the vibrations but not yet paying them
sufficient heed. "The last thing Court said to me before
slamming out of the office to find you at that inn up in
Oregon was that he had an awful premonition he'd been
fated to tame the green-eyed witch who was laughing at
him from the picture on my office wall. He said the one
sure way to control a troublesome female was in bed. I'll
admit I didn't expect an engagement so quickly. But Alex
Harlow is telling everyone…"

Keith broke off, grinning at his sister's stunned expression. "Haven't you learned yet, sister dear, that the only thing that prompts Court out of his easy chair or his workshop is a challenge? He'll do whatever he has to do in order to win. Why do you think I wanted him on the side of Brandon Security?"

"A challenge," Leya repeated, the metal in her eyes glowing with white heat as she stepped back out of Court's slackening embrace to face him.

"That's what this has been about all along, hasn't it? You *did* come up to that inn in Oregon intending to seduce me because that seemed like the easiest way to overcome the challenge I represented. You didn't take one look at me and suddenly decide our relationship was more important than the contract. You established a relationship in order to get that damned document signed! To control me!"

"Leya, listen to me," he began determinedly. "You've got it all wrong! Your brother doesn't know what the hell he's talking about. You and I—"

"No, he doesn't. He automatically assumed you were planning to marry me," she exploded violently. "Me, I know better. I know you'd never get *that* carried away with a mere challenge. An amusing little affair, during which you made certain I kept my interfering hands off Brandon Security, would be more to your taste, wouldn't it? Well, just in case you're not getting enough excitement out of the diversion, let me spice things up a bit!"

With that, Leya grabbed the half-full glass standing on

the railing and hurled the contents at his yellow shirt. As the alcohol and ice soaked him, she whirled and walked off the terrace.

Chapter 6

Her exit scene lacked only a small touch of practicality to keep it from being perfect, Leya reflected a moment later as she swept into the party and realized she didn't have a convenient ride home.

It was the little things that could so easily trip one up in life! In disgust, Leya grabbed a drink off a passing tray, reminding herself she hadn't been allowed to finish one yet, thanks to Court. She was making her way over to a far corner of the room, where it might have been possible to stay out of sight until her brother reappeared from the terrace, when Susan Adams glided up to her. Why were half the women in California blonde?

"I was wondering where you'd hidden yourself, Leya." Susan's eyes were lit with an interest that didn't fool Leya for a second.

"I've hidden Court outside on the terrace," Leya told her sweetly. "But as you can see, I'm not the least bit hard to find. Don't worry, Susan, I'm sure he'll be back in a moment." The thought bred an unpleasant anticipation in Leya's own mind, however. What was she going to do when he returned from the terrace and came gunning for her?

There wasn't much he could do to her in a room full of people, she told herself bravely and wondered exactly how much her own brother would be on her side. Keith's admiration for his newfound mentor seemed very high. So high that he was happy to consider Court as a brother-in-law! Of course, that event was unlikely in the extreme, Leya thought glumly, taking a swallow of her drink. Court might bestir himself for a challenge, but something told her he had enough sense of self-preservation to keep from being so caught up in the battle that he'd go to those lengths!

"He's a very fascinating man, your fiancé," Susan was saying chattily, her bright eyes on Leya's brooding expression. "I must say the news came as a surprise, though. I had no idea…"

"My what?" Leya knew she sounded almost as startled at the statement as Alex had earlier. She frowned at Susan.

"Isn't it public knowledge yet?" Susan murmured with totally false anxiety. "I'm sorry if I wasn't supposed to know, but frankly the whole room will know fairly soon. Rumors like this get around a party quickly, and several people here know you or your brother…"

"Who told you that I was engaged to Court?"

"Alex Harlow. You remember him?" Susan's prompting on the name was quite unnecessary, Leya thought. She was well aware of what had happened a year ago. "He seemed very upset about something and left a few minutes ago. You wouldn't know why he was angry, would you?" she added hopefully. Susan loved to know details.

"Haven't the foggiest," Leya retorted dryly. "As for this

engagement business," she began, intending to squelch the stupid rumor as quickly as possible. She was interrupted before the blow could be dealt.

"Leya! Just heard the news! Congratulations. That tall man with the bedroom eyes is the one, I take it?" Alice Compton came forward, a sandy-haired escort in tow. Alice's cheerful expression was full of genuine goodwill.

"Bedroom eyes!" Leya exclaimed vengefully. "Court doesn't have bedroom eyes. That sort of narrowed, sultry look is a sign of chronic laziness, not passion!" For the life of her, she didn't know what made her say that, but the impulse was irresistible.

"I resent that," murmured a familiar gravelly voice behind her, as Court's hand snaked around her waist and removed the glass from her hand. "Let's go home, little Leya, and we'll find out exactly which emotion you're seeing in my eyes!"

The laughter of those who heard the remark covered Leya's gritted exclamation. She turned to lift mocking liquid eyes up to his. "I wouldn't want to put you to the effort, darling," she purred.

"Don't fret, sweetheart," he returned with a patently insincere assurance, "I've been fortifying myself at Susan's buffet table. I think I can work up the energy!"

Under cover of more laughter from those around them, Leya bared her teeth in the parody of a charming smile. She confronted the deep, warning gleam in the tortoise-shell eyes and felt the overall intent in him as if it were a tangible electrical charge. He made no move to touch her but the threat in him was blatant.

"Oh dear," she observed nastily. "Did you have an accident with your drink?" Her eyes ran mockingly over the dampened shirt front. A mixture of excitement and anger raced along her nerve endings as their confrontation began to escalate.

"Would you believe it? I seem to have gotten in the path of a young lady who'd imbibed a little too much this evening. But that's all right. I've got a dry shirt at home. Are you ready to leave?"

"No, I'm not," Leya murmured in satisfaction. "Unlike the poor young woman whose path you crossed, I haven't had a chance to imbibe too much. I haven't had a chance to finish even one drink tonight!"

"Pity," he drawled heartlessly. "But if I'm going to make the effort to overcome my chronic laziness tonight, then the least you can do is try and keep from passing out on me!" His meaning was abundantly clear.

Keith's voice interrupted over the ensuing roar of laughter from a gathering crowd. He pushed his way toward where his sister and Court were faced off, his green eyes laughing. Blonde little Angie was beginning to sulk at the lack of attention she was receiving, Leya had time to note.

"Are you two going to stand there and make a scene instead of officially announcing the engagement?"

"Yes!" Leya gritted willingly. She could think of nothing more satisfying in that moment than a knock-down, drag-out scene in which she was the undisputed victor! Her eyes never left her opponent's face as he growled his answer almost simultaneously.

"No," Court said quite clearly. "We are going to make the announcement and then go home and conduct our scene!"

"I certainly hope you enjoy giving a performance on your own, because I intend to stay right here at the party!"

"Leya, my charming wife-to-be," Court said with vast politeness, "I will give you a choice. You may leave this party on my arm or over my shoulder. Take your pick!"

She felt the threat in him, but Leya's own emotions were vibrating at too high a pitch to care. The platinum sheen in her eyes clashed with the molten gold in his and she smiled dangerously.

"Is that a multiple-choice question?" she asked interestedly.

"It is."

"Then I choose 'none of the above'!" Leya whirled away, intent only on getting out of range as quickly as possible. But the amused crowd hemmed her in, trapping her very conveniently for Court, who didn't hesitate.

"I'll bet," he offered as his hand struck, encircling the small bones of her wrist like a manacle, "that you never did very well on multiple-choice tests in school!"

Leya gave a squeak of very real alarm as she felt herself yanked off balance. Before she could clutch at something, anything, she felt the impact of Court's shoulder in her stomach and then she was staring down his back at the floor, her heavy braid falling past her head.

For an instant, the wind was knocked out of her and, unable to protest, she heard her captor speak quite matter-of-factly to the roomful of people.

"You'll excuse us, I'm sure, while I take Leya home, so that one of us can beat the other into submission in private!"

Leya gulped air as Court began striding for the door.

"Keith!" she cried furiously. "Do something!" Desperately, she tried to twist her head high enough to see her brother, who spread his hands helplessly.

"What can I do, Leya? The man has an iron-clad contract to do just about anything he likes with Brandon Security!" The laughter in him was pure Brandon. "And you signed it yourself!"

"I'm not part of Brandon Security!" she charged ominously, knowing she had been carried almost as far as the door.

"Yes, you are," Court corrected as he put his free hand on the knob. "You're the silent partner, remember?"

"Damn you!" Then, knowing she needed the last word before the door closed, she said to the ring of delighted faces, "For the record, there is no engagement!" The last memory of the party was that of Keith's laughing eyes.

But her own silver-green gaze contained no humor at all as Court dumped her unceremoniously into the front seat of his car a moment later, slamming the door as she righted herself. He was sliding in beside her on the opposite side of the car before Leya had straightened up and found the door handle. He turned in the seat, filling the whole front cockpit with his strength and will, or so it seemed to Leya. His arm stretched out along the back of the seat, his hand resting threateningly behind her head as she twisted to face him.

"How dare you?" she choked, her fury and humiliation rising up like a tide. "How could you do a thing like that to me? You had absolutely no right to drag me off like that and...and make a fool of me! Again!"

"You asked for everything you got, Leya Brandon," he bit out and she abruptly realized there was no laughter in him, either. Their scene at the party might have amused the bystanders, but the two participants were in deadly earnest, locked in a battle that had escalated to major proportions.

"Only from your point of view," she spat. "Personally, I see myself as an innocent victim!"

"Shrews are never innocent victims! I'm still damp from that drink you threw all over me in a fit of temper, remember! And after all I'd just done for you, too!" he added, plainly outraged. In the darkness of the cold car, his eyes gleamed down at her.

"All *you* had just done! You've got your nerve! You simply walked into a private scene between me and another man..."

"Walked in just in time to hear you making use of me to revenge yourself on said other individual! Talk about nerve, Leya, you don't seem to be lacking in it! I heard you tell Harlow you were in love with me, that my kisses made his seem like cold dishwater. That's called playing one man off against another, little witch, and I don't like being part of your games! I was willing to tolerate it so you could have your revenge on me, too, but..."

"Tolerate it! You did a hell of a lot more than tolerate

it! What did you hope to accomplish by letting everyone think we're lovers? Was it all part of the challenge, Court? The challenge I seem to represent to you? I can see how it all started, naturally. First, you were annoyed when I didn't meekly show up at the meeting you'd arranged so that you could browbeat me into signing that contract. Then, after you'd tricked me into signing it, you couldn't satisfy your damn male ego, which only knows one kind of victory over a woman. I realized what was happening before you got me into bed and that really annoyed you, didn't it? Made the challenge all the greater, didn't it? Then, tonight you deliberately came to my rescue and backed up my story to Alex. That gave you the opening you needed to renew your campaign to polish off your big win at Brandon Security! And I, like the complete fool I've shown myself to be lately, fell for it. I actually let you talk me into giving our relationship another chance!"

"You've got it all figured out in your own brilliantly twisted fashion, don't you?" he grated. Out of the corner of her eye, Leya saw the hand resting beside her head close into a fist.

"Go ahead and deny it if you can! The only thing I don't understand is why the hints of marriage to Keith? Why let him think you're serious? But I suppose those were just tactics, weren't they? Little flanking maneuvers to push me in the right direction?"

"Which happens to be my bed! And that's where you're going to wind up, sooner or later, Leya my shrew," he flung back, "because you know what I think? I think you were telling Alex Harlow the truth tonight, even if you were using it for your own purposes!"

"What the hell are you saying?" she blazed, infuriated anew.

"I think you are in love with me! I think you fell in love with me back in Oregon!"

"In only two days?" she scoffed, secretly appalled at his analysis. "Not likely!"

"What does time have to do with it? I could have taken you that night you signed the contract and you know it! I could have done it the next day, even though you were furious at me. When I held you and touched you on the beach, you were responding in spite of yourself!"

"You'd like to think that's the truth, wouldn't you? That I'd actually be so overcome by your mastery of seduction I'd fall in love with you regardless of what you did to me! Much more satisfying than just getting me into bed and more efficient, too! A woman in love is probably a lot easier to control than one who will merely consent to go to bed with you. That would give you a hell of a victory, wouldn't it?"

"Leya, you're becoming totally unreasonable. I'm taking you home!" Court threw himself around in the seat, shoving the key into the ignition and slamming the expensive car into gear.

Leya could read the fury in him and the control he was exerting over it. It radiated out to every corner of the vehicle.

"Thank you," she bit out icily. "Home is precisely where I want to go!"

In the dimly lit interior, she saw him lift one heavy eyebrow but he said nothing. She sat in frozen silence as he drove with an economy of movement and wished her own self-control wasn't so weak.

Oh, the anger was a bracing enough emotion, but the slight trembling in her lower lip was caused by another feeling entirely, one she didn't want to acknowledge but which forced itself on her awareness. Leya was far too honest to pretend she didn't understand what her mind and body were crying out. For a while, there on the terrace this evening she had wanted very badly to say the score between herself and Court was even, to declare a truce and start over. And Court was smart, too smart not to guess that for a few moments he had been close to getting what he wanted.

But why? she wondered bitterly. What kind of man would get so intrigued by the kind of challenge she represented? What kind of man needed to assert his victory over a woman by dragging her off to bed? The answer had to be only a man who knew his victory wasn't secure.

"Where are we going?" she suddenly demanded suspiciously.

"I told you, I'm taking you home. My apartment. You wouldn't want me to catch cold in this damp shirt, would you?" he added mockingly.

"It won't take that much extra time to drop me off at my home, first!"

"Heartless creature," he murmured, not changing direction.

"Court!"

"Leya." He sighed. "We're going to talk this out tonight and my apartment is the logical place to do that."

"Afraid of giving me the home-court advantage?" she snapped.

"I suppose," he nodded wryly. "Maybe I'll feel safer on my own turf. I've had it with your crazy reasoning processes. To think I once thought you an intelligent woman!"

"Your insults don't bother me, Court," she managed tightly. "Perhaps if you think I'm not too bright you'll lose interest in the game!"

"I'm not the one who wants to play games, Leya, but if you force me into them I can guarantee I'll play to win."

"Your threats don't bother me any more than your insults!"

"In that case, you've got a lot to learn." But he sounded calmer now, as if he were determined to be reasonable in the face of a totally unreasonable woman's tirade.

He also sounded implacable, and although she made a few more attempts to talk him out of it, Leya knew with great certainty that he wasn't going to take her back to her own house until he'd had his say on his own territory.

The ride was concluded in chilly silence. When at last Court drew the car into the parking lot of an exclusive condominium complex, Leya finally roused herself sufficiently to note caustically, "I thought you said you had an apartment."

"I'm renting one of the condos from the owner." He shrugged. "It feels like an apartment."

The thick, verdant landscaping lent privacy to the individual units of the complex. The condominiums were modern, typically Californian in style with cedar siding, interesting angles, and a great many windows. Not at all as cozy and welcoming as her own home, Leya decided smugly.

"Come on, let's get inside. I'm cold." Court switched off the engine, heading around to Leya's side of the car but failing to arrive in time to assist her.

He said nothing about her obvious desire to ignore the intended courtesy, merely taking her arm firmly in his and leading her up the flagstone path.

"I can't imagine what else you have to say this evening," she grumbled as he silently opened the front door and ushered her into a pleasant but, to her eyes, uninspiring living room.

"Why don't we simply call the whole thing quits?" she added, taking in the politely neutral cream-colored carpeting, the bland but expensive beige-and-tan modern furniture and the touches of teakwood in the end tables. "You've won the basic prize by getting me to sign that contract. Have the grace to be content with the major victory!"

"What?" he demanded with the first hint of humor since they had left the party. "And imply you aren't as important a victory as the contract was? I wouldn't think of insulting you so!"

"Why not? You've already insulted me by telling me I'm not particularly bright." Leya chose one of the rounded tan chairs near the fireplace and flung herself into it with unconscious grace. Arms stretched out along the curving back, she crossed her legs with deliberate elegance and disdain and eyed him coolly.

"But you know that really isn't true, don't you? And therefore it was very ineffective as a slander. I only said it out of annoyance," he told her dismissingly, his eyes following her movements.

Leya gritted her teeth. "Why should you be annoyed at a challenge, Court? My brother says it's the only thing that gets you excited in life!"

"Where does everyone get this notion that I'm attracted to difficult problems?" he demanded, lifting golden brown eyes toward heaven in a beseeching gesture.

"Aren't you?" Leya ground out, gazing at him morosely from under her lashes.

"Not in my private life," he retorted feelingly, coming across the room with a slow, stalking stride.

"Nonsense," she shot back caustically. "A challenge is a challenge. Tell me about this flaw in your character, Court Tremayne. What is it with the idea of a challenge? Were you the kind of little kid who couldn't resist a dare?"

"If we're going to get involved in a discussion of my childhood, you'll have to excuse me while I change my shirt, first." His hands went to the buttons of the yellow fabric and Leya glanced pointedly away. "Why don't you make us some tea while I, er, slip into something more comfortable. I think you'll find everything you need in the kitchen." He paused. "And stop looking at the furniture that way. It's not mine. It came with the condo."

He turned and walked out of the living room, leaving

her to do as she liked about the tea. Fingers drumming on the arms of the chair, Leya considered the options and decided to make the beverage. She'd *known* the furniture hadn't been his, she told herself wryly. She had the feeling his normal décor would be a lot more like her own: bright, positive and warm.

The condo kitchen was as sleek and modern as the rest of the place. A copper teakettle sat invitingly on the almond-colored stove, and with very little rummaging, she found the teacups. They were conveniently near the stove, exactly where she kept her own at home. She and Court even organized alike!

"There," he informed her, walking back into the living room a few minutes later buttoning a dry shirt, "that's better. Now I can discuss my character flaw without danger of catching cold!"

Leya set the tea things down on one of the teak tables and watched as he knelt in front of the fireplace and began to stack kindling.

"Perhaps talking about it will help you work it out," she agreed sweetly, too sweetly.

"You're very kind. I don't think you're asking out of anything more than clinical interest, but I'll try and explain, anyway," he sighed, striking a match and bending his head momentarily over the flame.

There was a pause while he lit the fire, and then he sat back on his heels, studying the blaze intently until he was sure it had caught. He rose with a lithe grace that appealed to Leya's senses in spite of her mood, and sank into the chair across from her. He stretched his legs out in front of himself, slumping into the cushions and regarding her with a brooding air.

"About your lifelong problem," she prompted acidly.

"Oh, yes, my passion for challenge," he groaned, reaching for his tea. "You were wrong about me being the kind of little kid who's always accepting a dare, you know."

"Really?" Leya's voice held only cool, polite interest.

"I was an only child, you see, and I never did enjoy playing with other kids. Much preferred the pleasure of my own company. I wasn't antisocial, you understand," he put in with mock reassurance. "Just not interested in a lot of things that amused my contemporaries. I like to spend my time in the basement with my tools and my electronics."

Leya half smiled in spite of herself. The image was all too familiar. "Did your parents worry about your preference for solitude?"

"No," he chuckled. "Did yours?" He smiled at her with keen perception.

"No, I was lucky," she admitted. "Mom and Dad seemed to understand. They were kind enough to let me curl up alone with my books and my rock polisher!"

"Rock polisher?" He grinned.

"I had a little lapidary shop in my corner of the basement. It's how I became interested in jewelry making. But we were discussing your problems, I believe," she added determinedly. She was not about to let him charm her tonight!

"Well, where was I?" he said, leaning his head back in the chair.

"Your basement."

"Yes. I had a ham radio set up down there and all sorts of electrical test equipment. I used to send off for those build-it-yourself kits, and then one day…"

"You built it yourself without a kit?"

"How did you guess?"

"It was inevitable."

"Perhaps," he nodded quietly. "At any rate, I began having more fun tinkering and putting odd things together on my own than building from a set of plans. But when it came time to go off to college, it wasn't engineering that intrigued me, it was finance. Creative finance, as they say. I was attracted to the things that could be done when money was cleverly applied. The two interests, electronics and finance, sort of flowed together."

"Where did you go to college?"

"Berkeley."

"You were born in California?" Leya prodded, interested even though she knew she ought to be just the opposite.

"Umm. I was raised in a little town on the San Francisco peninsula. How about you?"

"Here in Santa Rosa," she confided. "But I chose the University of California campus in Santa Barbara when it came time to go off to school. Berkeley always seemed much too big, too urban for my tastes."

"Your choice doesn't surprise me," he told her softly, eyes warming. "The Santa Barbara campus would be a good setting for you, being right on the ocean. You seem to have an affinity for windswept beaches…"

For a charged moment, the memories of Oregon hung between them, and then Leya deliberately pushed them aside.

"The beaches there were nice, but the degree in English was quite useless!" She smiled. "Until, that is, I took some business courses. I had never been particularly interested in business, but I found I did rather well. By the time I graduated, I had decided I was the entrepreneurial sort."

"The bookstore?"

"Dad lent me the money to get started." Leya smiled suddenly. "Said he had complete faith in the Brandon talent for making money. I paid him back, too. Within a year the store was making money and now it brings in a very nice income. I'm thinking of opening up a branch out at the new shopping center."

"You weren't interested in taking over your father's business?"

"No, I'm much too independent. I'd never work well in a large managerial setting, even if I were the boss. Too many other people to consider. I think Keith will do it well, though. He likes directing others and pulling a team together."

"I agree, and when I've shown him a few of the ropes regarding finance and marketing..."

"We seem to have lost the train of thought here," she interrupted smoothly. "How *did* you come to be such an authority, anyhow?"

He shrugged. "When I graduated, it soon became apparent that I was never going to be happy working nine-to-five for someone else."

"Not enough *challenge* in the daily grind of engineering and accounting?"

"I wish you would stop using that word," he complained good-naturedly, his eyes laughing at her. Leya felt herself slipping dangerously back under the spell of the easy camaraderie they had discovered in Oregon. She must keep her distance tonight, she warned herself severely.

"Think of a better word," she invited pointedly.

"In any event," he began firmly, "it became obvious that my attention span was relatively short when it came to the mundane things of life, such as holding a regular job. So I started working on a contract basis."

"Choosing only the most interesting little puzzles to work on?" Leya drawled knowingly.

"Well, there's not much point in picking and choosing contracts unless one selects only the most interesting and profitable, is there?" he countered quellingly. "Besides, contract work gave me time for my basement tinkering."

"What's the longest contract you've ever accepted?" Leya demanded, eyes narrowing.

"This one," he answered honestly. "The idea of trying to help save Brandon Security and get a piece of the action if I was successful represented an interesting—" He broke off, wincing.

"An interesting challenge?" she supplied helpfully, watching him demurely over the rim of her cup.

"Vicious little thing, aren't you?"

"What do you do when you're not busy confronting the current challenge?"

"Lapse back into happy isolation in a basement or spare room somewhere," he admitted promptly. "Or head for the solitude of a beach. Just like you."

Leya ignored the bid to draw a parallel with herself. "What about the blondes you mentioned at the party? Do you drag them down into your basement or to the beach?"

"I wondered when we'd get around to them," he chuckled.

"I'm asking when do *you* get around to them?" she retorted.

"Whenever the mood comes over me!"

"Do you see each new one as a challenge?" Leya asked kindly, incredibly irritated at his admission.

"Hardly," he quipped blandly. "My women tend to be in the same category as your Alex Harlow. Pretty but rather self-centered and not too bright."

"Have you ever married one of them?" Leya couldn't resist the question. At his age, it would be quite natural if he'd been married.

There was a distinct pause while Court considered his answer. "I came damn close once," he finally admitted softly. "We were engaged before I realized my mistake."

"What was the mistake, Court?" Leya pressed tightly. "Almost succumbing to a challenge?"

"My mistake," he told her flatly, eyes narrowed, "was in thinking she was different from the others. I was lucky. I found out in time she wasn't. She wanted what the others wanted, but she was better at disguising her goals than most."

"What happened?" Leya hated herself for asking, but she couldn't stifle her curiosity.

"She thought I was going to be offered the chief executive position at the firm for which I was working at the time."

"And?"

"And I was," he said simply. "But I declined. When she found out, she declined me."

"Were you very hurt?" Leya asked tentatively, astonished at the wave of compassion for him which suddenly moved her.

"My pride more than anything. When I realized that, I also realized I'd had a very narrow escape!"

"And you've been cautious since then, right?" she hazarded, smiling gently. "Stuck to the nonchallenging blondes who are easy to handle?"

The flash of mutual understanding that passed between them was impossible to ignore. Leya knew exactly what Court had felt when he discovered he had been used. She'd been through it with Alex. Court proved he was on the same wavelength when his eyes met hers directly and he said softly, "Is that so different from what you've been doing since Harlow?"

"What do you know about what I've been doing since I dated Alex?"

"Your brother told me. He said you've been seeing a string of easily managed types who do exactly as they're bid or find themselves out of the running."

"I'll have to speak to my brother. He clearly has no feeling for family loyalty," Leya sighed irritably.

"Is it true?" Court probed.

"What if it is?" she returned aloofly, chin lifting. "Can you blame me for not wanting to get burned again?"

"No, I've been just as cautious," he murmured soothingly. "I always make it a point to find out the price first now. I didn't like being used, either. Maybe we've both been waiting for the right, uh, challenge."

"Court!" The tension in the room suddenly elevated again.

"I'm only teasing you, honey," he said quickly. "Couldn't you please take pity on a basically peaceful, leisurely male who wants a peaceful, leisurely relationship with you?"

He looked so persuasively pleading that Leya almost forgot herself. Then her lower lip firmed.

"Everything you've told me so far only points up the fact that whatever attraction I hold for you is on the level of a…a novelty," she whispered dejectedly. "I think my brother was right. When you get involved in a suitable challenge you like to win. Somehow, in your mind I've become part of the challenge of Brandon Security, and you want to make sure I'm under your control. Are you afraid I'll try and turn my brother against you? Or use my shares to block your decisions?"

"That's got nothing to do with it!" he glowered. "How many times do I have to tell you this is strictly between you and me?"

"I might have believed you if my brother hadn't come out

on the terrace when he did tonight. But hearing him describe you storming out of his office when you found out I wasn't showing up for the meeting and that—that awful remark about controlling women by taking them to bed! How do you expect me to believe you after hearing all that? It's clear you saw me as a thorn in your side. A woman you're determined to bring to heel the only way you know how. It's no use, Court, you're not going to talk me into bed!"

He set the teacup down on the end table with a warning clatter.

"You are a stubborn, illogical little shrew, and I've had it with trying to reason with you tonight!"

He was on his feet with an electric movement that was much too fast for a man who didn't believe in athletic endeavors.

Before she could safely set down her teacup and leap to her feet, he was reaching for her wrist and pulling her up in front of him.

"Let me go, Court. If you can't conduct a civilized conversation, then you may as well take me home!" With a regal tilt of her dark head, she indicated the door. "I'm sure you'll understand my stubborn, illogical reasons for wanting you to do so!"

The tortoiseshell eyes were alive with male purpose, and his hold tightened on her wrist.

"I'm not taking you anywhere except into my bedroom," he drawled. "If we can't communicate verbally, we'll rely on more primitive techniques!"

Chapter 7

"Court, this has gone far enough," Leya declared forcefully, calling on her total reserve of willpower. "You've done nothing but manhandle me this evening and I've had it!"

"You're telling me!" he agreed with heavy mockery, ignoring her attempt to free her wrists. "You're determined to run me to a frazzle, aren't you?" he went on accusingly, his face very close to hers, his eyes sweeping over her parted lips. "I've told you time and again I'm not a terribly energetic man. Why do you do this to me?"

"You're the one who started it!" she gasped, infuriated and desperately trying to retain some semblance of self-control. "You insist on playing the heavy-handed male and then wonder why I object!"

"You force me into that role because you keep playing the part of the recalcitrant, willful female."

"You forget," she charged defiantly, "that's my main attraction for you! If I turned meek and willing, you'd probably lose interest immediately!"

"Is that why you behave this way?" he asked, as if understanding had just dawned. "You're trying to hold my attention?" He looked very pleased.

"No!" she stormed, incensed that he had deliberately misunderstood her.

"Then why don't you try being meek and willing and see if that succeeds in getting rid of me?" he suggested helpfully.

"Because by the time I found out whether or not that would work it would be a trifle too late!"

"I've got news for you, honey," he retorted, stooping to swing her high into his arms. "It's already too late. Much too late."

"Court!" Leya was clamped tightly to his broad chest, and the heat of him threatened to burn her fingertips through the material of his shirt. "Put me down this instant! I will not be...be carried off for your amusement!"

"When you discover something amusing in all this," he told her encouragingly, striding toward the hall, "let me know. Personally, I'm not laughing."

"I'll never forgive you!" She tried valiantly as he rounded the corner with due caution for her head.

But already she could feel the excitement churning in her veins, almost swamping her with its intensity. She didn't want it to be like this, not with so much unresolved between them. But she couldn't deny to herself that she wanted him. She had wanted him since their meeting in Oregon. And she was very much afraid it was amounting to something much deeper and more dangerous. With feelings this chaotic, was love very far away?

"You already forgave me earlier this evening out on that terrace," he pointed out, kicking open the bedroom door with a careless foot. "You said we could take up where we left off in Oregon. This, in case you've forgotten, is where we left off!"

"Not quite!" she hissed as he tossed her down lightly onto a wide, low bed and flipped on the small lamp standing on the bedstand. "We were still getting to know each other. We weren't sleeping together!"

The room was as sleek and modern and neutrally colored as the rest of the condominium. Low-profile teak furniture and cream-colored carpeting and drapes were relieved by a suitably modern abstract painting hanging over the bed. The quilt on which she lay was a fat, fluffy goosedown affair that had probably cost a fortune. Too bad it had been done in beige. A part of Leya insisted it would have looked much better in a vibrant red.

"We weren't sleeping together only because you hadn't gotten around to admitting you really wanted me," he drawled, baiting her with a caressing, knowing glance as he straightened. "But now that you've crossed that hurdle—"

"I never admitted that!" she almost screeched, nails digging into the quilt. At least not out loud, she added in silent justification.

"Yes, you did. I distinctly heard you tell Alex Harlow that you were in love with me and that you planned to marry me," he reminded her with deep satisfaction. "That's the main reason I refrained from throwing him over the rail, you know. I decided you'd done a good enough job of punishing him for daring to kiss you."

"You beast! You know I only said that to get some revenge! I didn't mean it!" But how much of it had she meant?

The words she had used so easily to revenge herself on Alex had come quite readily to her tongue. It was easy to say she was in love with Court. Too easy.

"You can say it again tonight, then," he told her agreeably. "And this time you can mean it!"

She watched, wide-eyed, as he began unbuttoning his shirt. The sight had a certain mesmerizing quality that caught at her senses. When he started on the cuffs, the shirt front now hanging open and revealing the dark mat of hair on his chest, Leya finally summoned the will to move.

She flung herself without any warning to the far side of the bed. But fast as she was, Court was even faster, diving across the low, wide bed and snagging her around the waist before she could get to her feet.

"My God!" he breathed, aggrieved. "Why didn't someone tell me taming shrews was such hard work? If this keeps up much longer, I'll need a rest cure!"

"Damn you!" Leya wiled as he hauled her down, pinning her beneath him and using his weight to crush her gently into the quilt. "Isn't there any way of making you see reason?"

"Stop fighting me," he whispered, his voice deepening as his gaze burned over her. "I can be a very reasonable man. All I ask from you tonight is the truth, or at least a portion of it."

"What portion?" she hissed scathingly, already violently aware of the warmth and weight of him as it overwhelmed her senses.

"At least admit that you want me!"

His hands gently caught her wrists and pinned them on either side of her head; his mouth hovered an inch above her lips. Leya's breath was beginning to come more quickly as her nerves registered the impact of him.

"You mean give you the victory you want," she corrected dismally.

"Think of it any way you like," he rasped. "Just stop fighting me long enough to let me show you how good it will be between us!"

Leya watched him in the soft light, her eyes heated emeralds as the sensual tension deepened and vibrated all around them. A strange lethargy seemed to grip her limbs, strange because even though it made her feel weak, it also made her pulses pound in mounting excitement.

She did want him so, she acknowledged to herself, swallowing thickly. How could she deny it if he tried to force the confession from her with these tactics?

"You look very good lying across my bed, your dark hair on my quilt," he said quietly. "I want you so badly, my little Leya, and I know you want me. I saw it in your eyes that first night in Oregon."

He shifted slightly, raising himself far enough to finish peeling off the shirt and hurling it to the floor. Then he reached down and slipped off his shoes, still anchoring her carefully.

One of Leya's evening sandals had already fallen silently to the floor beside the bed. Court pushed the other one off her foot and then stretched out along her length again.

"Court, please don't do this," Leya began, uttering each

word with great care. She knew she was trembling now, and she also knew the reaction wasn't one of fear or anger.

He held her wrists in one hand above her head, letting his fingertips trail sensuously down the length of her throat.

"And tonight," he muttered, "you will play your games with no one else. I told you once in Oregon that I will be a very possessive lover, my sweet Leya. I meant it. I'm going to make sure that you know the limits of the golden chains…"

"Chains work both ways," she whispered, her nails curving into her palms. Instinctively, she lowered her lashes, watching his face through them. "The one who attaches a chain must continue to hold on to the other end. He is as much a prisoner as the one he would control."

"Do you think I don't know that?" Court growled, eyes blazing with a lambent flame. And then he was burying his lips in the scented place behind her ear.

Leya shivered again uncontrollably, and he abruptly released her hands, sensing her body's incipient capitulation with masculine certainty. Leya knew she was succumbing to the sensual power of the moment, knew she wanted him, perhaps even loved him. How did a woman resist the man she wanted when he let her know the full extent of his need as Court did now? How did a woman resist the man she was coming to love?

"Leya, Leya! Please don't deny me tonight," he begged. "Can't you see how I need you!"

She felt the passion in him as it mingled with her own, drawing them together in an elemental way that was nearly irresistible. It had been building throughout the evening, she knew, from the moment she had walked out of her bath to find him waiting for her.

He shifted, pulling her tightly against him so that he could find the zipper of her dress. She turned her face into his warm skin, inhaling the intoxicating maleness of him as he slipped the gown down over her shoulders. He lowered it slowly, tantalizingly, his lips following the receding barrier as sand birds follow the ebbing wave.

Tonight he did not tease her and tempt her with the seductive method he had used that last night in Oregon. Tonight Court set the pace, as if he wanted there to be no doubt this time about how it would end and no doubt about which of them was in final control.

"Oh, Court!" she breathed as his hand found her unprotected breast. She had worn no bra beneath the red-and-gold dress and he groaned softly as he claimed the treasure he sought. Her skin tingled as his fingers prompted forth the nipple, bringing it to a peak of hard desire that seemed to feed his own need.

"You could so easily drive a man over the edge, little Leya," he muttered as his lips burned a string of kisses up the curve of her throat. "All this passion combined with that damned independence! Harlow was a cretin to let you slip away from him. But I can't complain about his stupidity," he grated roughly. "It made things so much easier for me!"

"Easier!" she exclaimed huskily. "What do you mean? What would you have done if I had belonged to Alex by now?"

"Taken you away from him!" he declared savagely, and

then his mouth closed hotly over hers, forcing apart her lips. His tongue swept inside just as his fingers tightened ever so slightly on the sensitive nipple. The combined attack sent a shiver roaring along Leya's spine, and she arched instinctively.

"But you would never have belonged to Alex," he rasped against her mouth a moment later as he broke the contact reluctantly. "You're much too smart for him. It would have been funny watching you handle him tonight if it hadn't been so infuriating watching you let him kiss you! I should punish you for that piece of impudence," he concluded on a thick groan as he lowered his mouth again.

Leya knew a surge of feminine triumph as she realized Court was far past the point of being able to punish her tonight. He was thoroughly caught up in the emotional turmoil seething around them, and the knowledge thrilled her. Deliberately, she allowed her fingers to wander down the line of his ribs to the hard waist.

He drew in his breath sharply when she unclasped his belt buckle and toyed with the opening of his slacks.

"Little wanton," he whispered on a husky note of laughter. "I knew you were a born tease the first day I met you! There's only one way to handle a tease." He pulled the dress lower, sliding it down over her hips and off completely.

"How do you handle a tease?" she challenged deep in her throat, loving the feel of his hands as he stripped off her pantyhose and left her in only the red lace bikini briefs.

"Make sure she plays the game out to the very end, of course. She'll learn her lesson!" He nipped her shoulder, letting her feel the edge of his teeth in a sharp caress that made her gasp.

Instantly, her trembling fingers clutched the skin of his hips, pushing aside the unbuckled slacks. Then she slid her palms up the sleek back, pausing to probe and explore as she headed for the fine hair at the back of his neck.

He moved, settling himself on his side and using his strong hands to tug her against him, letting her feel the rising need and the pounding of his heart.

"You're mine, Leya," he almost snarled as his fingers curved around her hips, dragging her against him. His lips haunted the region of her breast in deeper, more demanding kisses. "Admit it!" he commanded, and then his mouth fastened on her nipple. A second later she felt his tongue begin a delicate pattern and finally his teeth.

"Oh!" she moaned, her body enjoying the deliciously ravaging caresses beyond anything it had known in the past. "Oh, my God! Court! I want you so much!" The words were torn from her on a breathless cry as she wrapped her arms around his neck and clung.

"Enough to admit you belong to me?" he charged, his heavy thigh trapping her twisting, writhing legs. "Enough to admit that from now on no other man has a claim on you?"

She heard the passionate demand in his words and wondered at it.

"Answer me, Leya!" he gritted, pushing her onto her back and lowering himself roughly between her legs. She felt the harshness of his slacks against the smoothness of her inner thighs and opened her eyes to find the melting gold and brown flaming over her face.

"I want you, Court," she whispered, her fingers gliding through the curling hair of his chest. "You are right about that," she confessed softly. "I've wanted you from the beginning."

It felt good to admit that much, she realized. It freed her somehow, made it possible to sink more deeply into the quicksand that was dragging at her, inviting her, overwhelming her...

"That's a start," he grated with a measure of satisfaction and relief in his voice as he slid passionately down her body, raining kisses over her breasts and on the soft skin of her gently curving stomach. "It's a beginning, at least."

Her hands locked in the thickness of his hair as he sank his teeth ever so carefully into the vulnerable flesh of her thigh.

Leya moaned and his hands held her still when she would have writhed against him.

"A start, Court?" she gasped. "What else would you have of me?"

"Everything!"

He began working his way back up her body. She could feel the rough texture of his slacks between her naked legs, knew the strength of his need as he arched himself intimately against her.

"Everything, my darling Leya," he continued more gently, curling his tongue around a taut nipple and cupping the breast with soft possession. "And I'll have it before this night is done. I must have it!"

She shuddered at the force of his demand and wondered if she would be able to resist. Already she was unbelievably caught up in the maelstrom of his lovemaking. How much would she surrender before morning?

The power in him flowed over her, summoning forth a response Leya had never dreamed she was capable of generating. Her nails raking across his shoulders in small violent attacks seemed to excite him further.

His fingers feathered the inside of her thigh, the softness of her stomach, and the sensitive skin of her breast and throat. He touched her everywhere, as if he couldn't get enough of the feel of her.

At last, with impatient, wrenching movements, he stripped off the remainder of his clothes, lowering himself quickly back down beside her and pulling her into his arms.

"My God, Leya, I dreamed about this last night after I'd taken you home, do you know that?" he gritted, running exploring hands down to the ultra-sensitive area at the base of her spine. "I could see you here beside me, telling me that you wanted me, that you weren't going to punish me any longer for what had happened in Oregon..."

His fingers dug gently, intoxicatingly into the resilient flesh of her buttocks, and Leya gasped, her own hands gliding up his smoothly muscled chest. She bent her head, kissing the male nipples with a sensuous abandon.

"Oh, Court," she breathed again and again, wonder and

chaotic emotion in her words as she contemplated what was happening.

"It's all right," he soothed passionately, stroking her back and pulling her ever closer. His mouth was hovering in her hair and he kissed the top of her ear. "Tonight we start over, just as we agreed at the party. You won't regret it, Leya, I swear. This was meant to be. You've already admitted you want me. The rest will be easy…"

"Will it, Court?" she whispered, the words almost blocked in her throat.

"The only thing standing in our way was your need to avenge yourself, to get even for the way I had deceived you in Oregon. You did that tonight. I can't blame you, I've told you that. Hell, I would have done the same. We're a lot alike, you and I."

"You think you understand me so well," she murmured into the skin of his shoulder.

"Yes," he agreed unhesitatingly, twisting his legs around her restless limbs and preparing to push her gently onto her back. "And very soon I will understand you even better. I will know exactly what drives you wild in my arms and what it takes to make you curl against me like a kitten. I will hear you tell me exactly how much you want me…"

"I want you."

"And need me…"

"I need you."

"And trust me…"

Leya went very still in his arms. He felt it instantly and

she lifted her lashes to find him staring down at her flushed features.

"Leya?" he growled almost harshly.

"What, Court?"

"Tell me you trust me. Admit that, just as you admitted that you wanted me and needed me!"

She felt the compelling urgency in him and blinked, confused. "Is it so important?"

"Yes, damn it! Tell me!"

She licked suddenly dry lips, aware of the violent tension in him and uncertain how to deal with it. "I want you, Court. Let that be enough for tonight."

"No, it's not enough!" he rasped, lifting his hands to tighten them fiercely around her shoulders. "I want to know everything!"

"Court!" His name was a helpless cry torn from her lips.

"Leya, please! This isn't a game!"

She was shaken by the intensity in every taut line of his face, unnerved by the tightness in him.

"I know it's not a game," she breathed. "That's why I can't give you what you ask. Let it be, Court. I want you—I've given you that much of a victory. Take it and have done!"

"You haven't forgiven me for what happened in Oregon, have you?" he snarled. "You aren't satisfied with your revenge."

"I'm not plotting revenge, Court," she gasped. "Not anymore. If I were, I wouldn't be here beside you, telling you that I want you and need you…"

"Leya, don't do this to me! To both of us!"

She was shocked at the words, and the knowledge that he was genuinely serious about his demand was almost thera-peutic in its effect on her will. It was a therapy she could have done without, she thought sadly.

"Is that all you can think of, even now? Winning com-pletely? Can't you take the compromise I'm offering? What's so important about having my trust? Or do you need that to assure yourself you've conquered the challenge completely?"

"Leya, you don't understand! I have to know you trust me. If you can't say the words, then I'll know you haven't yet satisfied your need for revenge. It's not a question of con-quering a challenge, damn it. Can't you get that through your head? I know you needed to punish me, but you've done that. You can't keep doing it!"

"I'm not punishing you!" she hissed, beginning to push against his hard body. "You're asking more than I can give. Stop insisting on total victory, damn it. I thought that, if nothing else, we could at least go to bed together as equals, both of us admitting that we wanted each other. But you can't even compromise that much, can you? You can think only in terms of...of defeating me completely!"

With a final exclamation of male outrage, he gathered her flailing hands tightly in his fist and pushed her flat onto the bed. His eyes raked her softly gleaming body, lingering hungrily over the wantonly vulnerable curves.

"Look at me," he growled violently as she lay stretched out helplessly beneath him. "Look at me and try to guess just what a man could do to a soft little thing like you if he wanted to defeat you completely!"

He saw the hint of uncertain, bright-eyed fear coloring the silver green of her gaze and smiled savagely. "That's right, little shrew. A man who was intent on 'total victory,' as you call it, would have a very clearcut option open to him at this point, wouldn't he? Do you even realize just how helpless you are right now?"

He grasped the sable braid and pulled it significantly across her exposed throat. Leya trembled.

"Court! You wouldn't. You wouldn't rape me," she managed painfully, lying very still as her active imagination filled in the details. To be taken in rage and violence! The thought sickened her, repelled her, frightened her on the most primitive of levels.

"No," he agreed furiously, "I wouldn't. And something tells me that of the two of us, I'm the bigger fool!"

He wrenched himself away from her, his feet hitting the carpeted floor beside the bed with a thud. With swift, forceful motions, he threw on his clothes and tossed hers across her sprawled body.

"Get dressed," he grated. "I'm taking you home."

She watched him walk out of the room, trembling so badly she could hardly pick up her garments.

She found him pacing the floor in front of the fireplace when she finally emerged a few minutes later, some of her dignity and spirit mercifully restored along with her clothes. He looked up at once and halted, eyes shimmering with an enigmatic expression.

"I'll have to give you credit, Leya," he drawled as his

gaze swept her from head to foot. "You have an instinct for good weapons."

"What are you talking about?" she muttered, coming forward slowly, warily.

"I expected to be punished for what happened in Oregon. It was inevitable you'd want revenge. I accepted that, thought I could deal with it and then put it all behind us. I talked myself into thinking I had convinced you that tonight's scene with Harlow constituted sufficient vengeance. But—"

"Will you stop talking like that?" she broke in angrily, her hand moving in a gesture of denial. "I'm not plotting revenge!"

"No, I suppose you aren't. It came instinctively, didn't it? You seized the one weapon against which I don't have a defense. You've denied me your trust. How the hell am I supposed to fight that, Leya? How do I convince you you've punished me enough? How do I win back your trust, for God's sake?"

She stared at him in silence, aware of the ragged frustration in his words. He was absolutely right. Unwittingly, she had found a way to deny him his final victory.

"I don't know, Court," she whispered. "I don't know."

Chapter 8

Revenge, Leya thought grimly the next morning as she dragged herself out of bed after an almost sleepless night. Was that what she was seeking by denying Court her trust? Was she doing it deliberately?

No, she told herself as she showered and dressed in a white skirt and multistriped blouse. It was nothing as simple and straightforward as that, regardless of what he thought. She had none of the satisfaction she'd had when she'd gotten even with Alex. There was none of the bubbling, cheerful amusement at seeing a foe vanquished. All she felt was depressed and unhappy. There was a strong wish that things could have been different between herself and Court; that things could have gone on the way they had started in Oregon.

But Oregon was behind her and reality was back. Leya clipped on turquoise earrings that matched one of the stripes in the blouse and headed downstairs to breakfast. There had been something very final about the way Court had driven her home in silence last night and left her at the door. Had he finally accepted the impossibility of continuing any relationship?

★ ★ ★

The renovated downtown mall area of Santa Rosa slumbered peacefully, waiting for the shopping day to begin as Leya parked her small, sassy little car in front of Brandon Books. As early as she was, it looked as if Cynthia was ahead of her. She glimpsed a figure moving about in the back of the shop as she slipped her key into the door.

"Hi, Cynthia," she called, shutting the door behind her. "It's only me, Leya."

"Leya! What are you doing here? You're supposed to be on vacation!"

Cynthia Dalton, the young black woman Leya had hired to help out part time, straightened from the box of new books she had been unpacking and smiled in welcoming surprise. She was an attractive person with an even more attractive personality and a liking for the book business.

Her close-cropped hair was cut with a touch of sophistication that emphasized the intelligent brown eyes and high cheekbones. This morning she wore the gold-hoop pierced earrings Leya had made for her as a birthday present earlier in the year and a stylishly casual pantsuit.

"I got back early from Oregon," Leya explained, not wanting to go into details. "But don't worry, I still want you to finish working full time this week. It will give us a chance to do some planning for that expansion into the shopping mall."

This job was important to Cynthia, who was working part time and taking college classes in business administration at night. Leya knew she had been happy to get in the extra hours at the bookstore when her boss had announced her sudden vacation plans.

"Couldn't stay away, hmm?" Cynthia teased. "Well, don't worry. No major disasters around here. I thought I'd change the science fiction display today and finish unpacking this new shipment of romances. You know how many of our regulars will be pouring into the shop today looking for them."

Leya nodded, idly circling around behind the counter and picking up the latest copy of *Publisher's Weekly*. She flipped through it absently, glancing at the announcements of new books.

"Been busy?"

"The usual daily crush. Nothing out of the ordinary. A lot of kids in the afternoons after school but they seem pretty well behaved. They're going wild over that new war game we put in the front window display."

Leya looked up and grinned in spite of herself. "We should declare a business holiday in honor of our brilliant decision to include war games and space-movie paraphernalia in our regular inventory. Do you realize that we've attracted a whole new crowd of customers? The people into that stuff are as much a breed of addict as the folks into mysteries, westerns, and romances! Bless their little hearts!"

Cynthia nodded in satisfaction, switching on the automatic drip coffeemaker on the little stand behind the counter. "There are worse habits in this world than books and games. We're doing humankind a favor the way I look at it!"

"And we're not doing too badly ourselves, either," Leya

murmured, glancing thoughtfully around the well-organized shop. Unlike her home, the place was neatly arranged with easily identifiable categories. Mystery buffs knew exactly where to head the moment they arrived, as did the World War II history types and the science fiction fans.

The shop concentrated on paperbacks and, thanks in part to a good location, had been an immediate success almost from the start. The addition of the exciting and sophisticated space and war-games section had given it another boost.

The morning wore on, with Leya deliberately refusing to think about the previous evening. She buried herself in plans for the new branch of Brandon Books, going over sketches, estimating order quantities and discussing hours of operation with Cynthia.

She was involved with a shelving plan, working at the back of the shop while Cynthia handled the customer traffic, when a shadow fell on the paper in front of her. She looked up to find Court standing beside the small table on which she was sketching. She started, not having heard him enter the shop.

"Hello, Leya," he said softly, but there was a cool wariness in the tortoiseshell eyes, instead of the masculine assurance that had always been there in the past.

"Hello, Court," she said carefully, wishing he wouldn't tower over her in such a fashion. He was dressed in a lightweight business suit, a single slash of color in his tie relieving the overall darkness of the outfit. Leya got to her feet in an automatic attempt to counteract the overwhelming sensation his presence provided.

"The woman at the counter said you were sitting back here," he told her by way of explanation. "I came to see if you will have lunch with me."

"Why?" The question came out stark and cold.

"Why do you think?" he retorted, a trace of impatience in his words now. "We have to talk."

"There's nothing to talk about, Court," Leya said wearily.

"The hell there isn't! Leya, you can't act as if nothing happened between us!"

"Will you please keep your voice down? I don't want the customers to hear you!"

"Then have lunch with me!"

"Or else you'll make a scene?" she mocked, her hands doubling into fists at her sides, her eyes defiant.

He ran a hand through his hair in clear exasperation. "I didn't come here to start a fight. I came to ask you to lunch. Please?"

She sensed the effort that had gone into the tacked-on plea and tilted her head slightly to one side, considering him. "Haven't you had enough from me, Court? I'm sorry if I couldn't satisfy your male ego completely, but..."

"Stop talking like that. Look, I want to get things back on a normal footing, Leya, for all our sakes."

"All? You're worried about my brother's reaction to our little, er, misunderstanding?" she asked tightly. "You're afraid I'll turn him against you and make your plans for Brandon Security more difficult to execute?"

"No!" he exploded and then obviously took a grip on himself. "Will you come with me, Leya?"

She met his eyes, saw the willpower he was using to keep from losing his patience, and realized there was something satisfying in that. He was making an effort, perhaps his first real effort to treat her as someone besides a woman he was arrogantly confident he could have.

"Sure, Court, I'll have lunch with you," she told him with sudden breeziness and smiled as he looked taken aback. "Just let me tell Cynthia where I'm going." Suddenly, she felt like the confident one.

He followed her down the aisles of books, his eyes roving over the shop's interior with undisguised curiosity.

"Cynthia, this is Court Tremayne. He works with my brother at Brandon Security."

Cynthia smiled warmly, and Court nodded politely, his eyes softening as he shook hands.

"You two are running quite a large operation here," he observed, glancing around again. "When Keith explained about the book business, I assumed it would be a much smaller affair."

"Bookstores have to be fairly large to be profitable," Cynthia explained, when Leya showed no signs of responding to the implied question. "The new one we're opening out in the mall is even bigger."

"Who will manage that branch?"

"I will." Cynthia smiled, slanting a curious glance at a silent Leya. "I'll have finished school by then and can work full time."

"Court is taking me to lunch, Cynthia. I'll be back in an hour, okay?"

"No problem. I brought a sandwich, as usual. Have a good time." Her dark eyes followed Court and Leya out of the shop, a speculative smile on her lips.

"There's a sandwich shop on the corner," Leya began briskly as they stepped out onto the sidewalk. She started off without waiting for his nod of agreement, only to find her wrist lightly caught and held.

"I have a better idea," he said softly as she came to a stop and looked up at him inquiringly. "There's a nicer, more private place at the other end of the mall. I tried it once with your brother. We'll go there."

Leya hesitated knowing that for "private" she could read "intimate."

"All right—you're buying," she finally agreed flippantly.

Retaining his grip on her hand, Court started off in the other direction, his long strides forcing Leya to hurry.

"What is it you wanted to talk to me about, Court?"

"I'm impressed with the bookstore, Leya. You should be proud of having beaten the odds."

"What odds?" she frowned, disconcerted at the note of honest admiration in his voice.

"The odds against small-business success," he smiled, glancing down at her as they reached the restaurant. "You must have a real flair for the free-enterprise system."

"Is that why you came by today? To see if I really do know anything about business? To find out how much of a threat I might be to Brandon Security with my shares of stock?" she asked sweetly as they were shown to their table.

He shut his eyes, drew a long breath. "No. I meant what

I said with no hidden meanings. I *am* impressed. A simple compliment from one businessperson to another. Take it or leave it."

She eyed him as she picked up the tasseled menu. He was serious. Abruptly, Leya knew she was willing to help him with the truce.

"Okay, Court, I'll take it the way you say you mean it," she said calmly.

"Thanks," he muttered dryly, watching her smile as if he didn't quite trust it. "A glass of wine?"

"Fine."

They gave their orders and then the intimacy of the small booth closed in around them. Leya felt again the tension that never seemed absent when they were together, regardless of the circumstances.

"Now what did you really want to talk about, Court?" she finally asked softly, swirling the chilled chablis in her glass.

"You know very well what the subject is," he stated quietly, holding her eyes steadily. "We have to figure out where we're going from here."

"That's simple enough. Back to work. We both still have half a day left."

"Leya!"

"Okay, okay," she apologized, her fingers moving restlessly on the stem of the glass. "Suppose you tell me what you want from me. I was willing, too willing, to give much too much last night. If you've come to demand even more of me—"

"But I am, Leya," he interrupted tersely. "I want a lot more. Can't you understand that?"

"You don't let up, do you, Court?"

"Honey, listen to me! I'm not going to give up on what we had together in Oregon!"

"It's gone, Court."

"That's a lie! When I take you in my arms—"

"Please! Don't talk like that! You're embarrassing me!" she gritted, flushing furiously. "This is a public restaurant!"

"I'm sorry, but you're making this so damn difficult," he muttered, swallowing a gulp of wine. The gold and brown of his eyes flowed over her intently, aggressively. "Can't you see what you're doing with this stupid plan of revenge? You're stringing me out on a rope that has no apparent end. If you picked a finite sport of punishment, something we could get over and done with, I could deal with it. But this business of telling me you no longer trust me..."

"What am I supposed to do? Tell you I'm willing to let bygones be bygones? Forget what happened and pretend I have no reason not to trust you?" she hissed wretchedly.

"Yes!"

"How?" she blazed.

"You could if you loved me," he whispered in a deep, dark growl, his eyes heating.

Leya froze, appalled. No! she wanted to scream at him. No! I don't love you. How could I possibly love you? But the words wouldn't come. They were blocked in her throat as she realized she didn't have the strength to say them.

"You ask too much, Court," she whispered stonily.

"Do I? More than you could have given if you had never learned about my deception? More than we would have had together if we were still in Oregon?"

"We'll never know, will we?" she countered tightly.

"Yes, damn it! We will know! I'll find a way if it kills me!"

"Why are you so upset about this?" she asked belligerently. "I'll give you my word not to interfere with Brandon Security. What's the matter? Don't you trust me, either?"

"How many times do I have to tell you this has nothing to do with Keith's business? This is strictly between us. Leya, give me a chance, damn it. Don't insist on throwing away everything we could have together just because you're angry at me. That's juvenile!"

"So now I'm being childish?" she retorted, arching one eyebrow quellingly. "You're not pleading your case very eloquently, Court. No woman likes to be told she's behaving in a juvenile fashion!"

"Even if it's the truth?" he shot back.

"Especially not then! But it's not the truth, is it? If I were really behaving like a foolish child, I would let you talk me into forgetting everything that happened. I'd let you give me a pair of rose-colored glasses. It's the adult in me that learns from mistakes, Court. It's the adult side of my nature that warns me to be so cautious about trusting strangers!"

"But you're implicitly demanding that I somehow prove myself before you'll agree to give me another chance! How does a man do that? There aren't any dragons out there waiting to be defeated in your name! There's nothing I can give you that would convince you you've misjudged me. Tell me what the hell I'm supposed to do!"

Leya blinked at the grimness of his tone, uncertain how to deal with him in this mood. He was angry, impatient, frustrated and intent on changing her mind about him. She felt as if she were holding a powder keg.

"Trust is a fragile thing, Court," she began carefully. "It would take time—"

"How much time?" he interrupted at once, pouncing on the words.

"More time than you would probably be willing to spend on the project!"

"Tell me!"

"I don't know," she groaned, wondering how they had ever gotten into a bargaining situation like this. "I suppose we would have to get to know each other all over again…"

"No," he declared flatly. "But you could give me another chance," he countered at once, spearing a radish in his salad as if it were threatening to attack him.

"What's that supposed to mean?" she demanded warily.

"Exactly what it sounds like!"

"Court!"

"Have dinner with me tomorrow night at my place," he commanded intently, his eyes half pleading, half demanding. "Spend some time with me. Let me show you I'm still the man you were falling in love with in Oregon."

"Who said I was falling in love with you?" she demanded fiercely.

"The man you might have fallen in love with if I hadn't

turned out to be such an unreliable bastard," he corrected wryly, holding up his fork placatingly. "Please, Leya?"

She hesitated. "Do you promise not to try and seduce me?" she muttered broodingly.

"No," he admitted at once, looking contrite.

"Then forget it!"

He sucked in his breath. "Leya, have dinner with me and I'll promise not to force you into bed or anything else you don't want. That's as much a promise as I can give. Not that you need it," he went on in obvious irritation. "You can always use your ultimate weapon if things start getting too involved!"

"My lack of trust would be enough to stop you in another situation like last night?" Leya narrowed her eyes skeptically. He might have halted his lovemaking last night out of sheer annoyance at her unwillingness to grant him a complete victory, but that was certainly no guarantee he would do it again!

"You've known from the beginning I would never force myself on you," he told her with cold pride. "I didn't in Oregon when I probably should have and I won't do it here. At least give me that much of your trust!"

Leya stared at him, uneasily remembering that he was right. He could have pushed her into bed that night at the inn when she'd signed the contract. The electricity had been flowing heavily between them, and it wouldn't have taken much for him to overcome her defenses. That was nothing less than the truth, she acknowledged with painful honesty.

"All right, Court. I'll come to dinner at your apartment."

The corners of his mouth lifted in unexpected wry humor, and the familiar charm warmed his eyes. "The first step is always the hardest, sweetheart," he consoled her gently. "But I'll see you won't regret it."

Cynthia glanced up an hour later when Leya walked back into the shop, her dark eyes full of questions.

"Don't ask, Cynthia," Leya advised dryly. "I'm not sure I understand myself."

"He, uh, wouldn't by any chance be the reason you cut the Oregon vacation short, would he?" her friend asked perceptively.

"He is," she admitted grimly.

"I like him, Leya."

"I did, too. For a while."

Cynthia was a good friend to know when not to press an issue like this one. Both women went back to their work without further discussion of the matter.

She hadn't really committed herself to anything, Leya assured herself the next day as she slipped a bottle of wine into a carrying bag and slid into the front seat of her car.

She was wearing a pair of straight-legged jeans with the cuffs rolled up to adjust the length. The dark sable braid lay across the breast of her cheerful yellow blouse, and a bright gold medallion glittered at the hollow of her throat.

No, there was no commitment involved in simply accepting Court's dinner invitation. And she wanted so much to be with him, she thought self-deprecatingly. She was willing to accept his patently false assurances because it gave her an excuse to agree to the date.

But she would make certain he abided by his own promises, Leya told herself staunchly as she parked the car in front of Court's rented condominium. She would not let him lure her here and then seduce her! If he truly wanted a genuine relationship, he could darn well work at it!

"Don't look at me as if I were Dracula inviting you into his castle!" were Court's first words when he opened the door to her that evening.

"Sorry," she murmured wryly, stepping inside and thrusting the wine toward him. "Do I look a tad cautious?"

"You look as if you're expecting me to close the door behind you and lock it," he grumbled, taking the wine and running a quick, appreciative eye over the label. "This looks terrific. Come on and I'll pour you a glass. Maybe it will relax you."

She followed him toward the kitchen, her eyes roving curiously over the dinner preparations. Two very thick steaks waited on a grill and a variety of lettuces had been torn into a glass bowl. A pile of scrubbed mushrooms waited in a frying pan.

"You really have nothing to fear tonight," he told her, deftly removing the cork and reaching for two long-stemmed glasses.

"No?"

"No. But I think you know that or you wouldn't have come. Admit you had to trust me a little in order to risk accepting the invitation this evening!" he challenged.

"Oh, I think you're busy regrouping your forces, trying to plan your strategy. I figure I'm safe enough until you decide how you're going to make your next move!" she told him with a deliberately teasing smile as she accepted the wine.

He caught the smile and his eyes returned it. "You're such a stubborn little thing," he sighed. "What am I going to have to do to make you stop fighting me?"

"Stop seeing me as a challenge," she retorted instantly. "Who knows what might happen if you simply saw me as a woman without any connection to Keith Brandon and Brandon Security."

Court quietly helped himself to a hot pepper from the snack plate. He learned back in the tan chair, relaxing visibly as if having gotten her this far he could afford to do so. He was wearing a khaki cotton shirt and close-fitting slacks. The masculine essence of him struck at her senses as it always did, making her fingers tingle to touch him.

"How can I ever make you believe I want you for purely personal reasons?" he asked a little grimly.

"I've never doubted your reasons were personal," she got out with a blitheness she was far from feeling.

He groaned and set down his wineglass with a small clatter. "I think we'd better find a more neutral topic." He got to his feet and reached for her hand. "Come here, Leya."

"Where are we going?"

"The bedroom," he told her with relish.

"The hell we are!"

"The *other* bedroom," he clarified, relenting. "You

showed me something of yourself today and I mean to return the favor."

Curious, she allowed herself to be guided toward the second bedroom of the condominium. He threw open the door with an expectant glance down at her face.

"You asked me once what I did when I wasn't working. Well, this is part of what I do."

"A ham radio?" Leya walked forward and surveyed the sleek transceiver and related equipment arranged on a long table.

"I got into it when I was a kid and I've never managed to kick the habit," he confessed, watching her closely.

"I've always wondered what people talk about on these things," she said, turning to him with a quick smile. "I mean when they're not using them in emergency situations."

"I'm afraid the conversations tend to be fairly similar. The weather, radio equipment and things like that. After all, the important thing is making the contact. I've talked to people in Japan and Eastern Europe. There's something fascinating about communicating with other hams so far away."

"Fascinating? Or challenging?"

"Leya, my sweet, if you're not awfully careful I'm going to withhold your steak tonight and feed you hamburger, instead!"

"I'll behave!" she promised instantly, laughing up at him as she lifted the stack of QSL cards and started flipping through them. "What are these?"

"Cards from people I've talked to documenting the contact. When I get the card, I enter each communication in that logbook over there."

"Well, I must admit, I prefer the idea of you industriously bent over your radio in the evenings to the picture of you industriously bent over a blonde!" she teased lightly, setting down the stack of cards.

"Meaning you wouldn't be jealous of the ham radio?" he inquired interestedly.

"If you're trying to make me admit I'd be jealous over the blondes…"

"No," he said quickly, brushing aside the statement. "I'm serious about the radio."

She frowned, not understanding. "Why on earth would anyone be jealous over a radio?"

"You'd be surprised," he said dryly.

"You spend a lot of time talking to *blondes* over the radio?" she taunted.

"Of course not. But I have been known to spend a lot of time on the equipment itself. Sometimes when I get started I can't walk away from it for hours. I've found that women aren't always so understanding about that kind of, er, involvement."

Leya laughed with sudden comprehension. "Sounds like me in my jewelry shop. Once I get going, I often can't quit until the current project is finished."

"Somehow," he said softly, "I had a feeling you'd understand."

Their eyes met in a curiously charged moment of mutual perception and strange recognition. Leya felt the ten-

sion around them and had to force herself to break it before
it grew to dangerous proportions.

"I'm getting hungry," she said lightly, moving toward
the door.

He stepped back to let her pass. "What a coincidence. So
am I." He turned on his heel. "Let's get those steaks ready."

As if those few moments in the "ham shack" had initiated
a truce both wanted to maintain, the conversation during
dinner slipped back into the easy camaraderie that had ex-
isted in Oregon. In its own way, Leya realized belatedly, it
was every bit as seductive as Court's outright lovemaking.

"How are you finding things at Brandon Security?" she
asked politely, helping to clear the table and stack dishes in
the sink. Neither suggested being so rash as to actually wash
the plates and utensils.

"Challenging," Court retorted dryly, grinning at her as
he carried in the last of the dishes from the dining-room
table.

"I think I'm going to learn to hate that word," Leya complained, wiping her hands on a towel.

"Join the crowd," he invited succinctly.

"Seriously, Court, are things very bad?"

"You mean with the company or with me?"

"Court!"

"Okay," he said placatingly, his eyes laughing at her. "No,
things aren't that disastrous, but there's going to be a hell
of a lot of work involved during the next two years. Your
father hadn't kept the manufacturing line updated."

"I thought he had started pouring a lot of money into

that. There certainly wasn't much left when he died except the business."

"He'd made a start but a lot more needs to be done. And the research and development end of things has also gone downhill. It's a competitive market, security devices. A viable company has to consider research as important as manufacturing and marketing. The sales staff looks fairly decent, and your brother's commitment is total. Given that, things will work out, but it will take some basic reorganization and some rough priority setting."

"And the hope that the crime situation stays sufficiently unpleasant in the United States to produce a strong consumer demand for Brandon's products," Leya remarked wryly.

"Unfortunately, there doesn't appear to be any danger of a lessening in demand. One of the first things I'm going to do when I move into your house is harden it."

"Who says you're going to be moving in!" Leya exclaimed, whirling to confront him. "And what do you mean by hardening it?"

"Sorry, slip of the tongue," he apologized meekly while Leya glared at him suspiciously. "As for hardening it, I meant make it more secure. The locks on your doors and windows would be child's play to someone seriously interested in entering illegally."

"You mean as you did that day you were waiting for me when I came out of the bathroom?" she reminded him irritably as they ambled into the living room and settled with equal lethargy back into their chairs.

"I didn't consider that a case of illegal entry," he murmured coolly, the gold in his eyes shimmering with memory. "I was coming to pick you up for a date, as I recall."

"This conversation is turning unsubtle. I can always tell when your patience is wearing thin, Court. You start losing your subtle approach," Leya declared, frowning into the fire, her arms resting along the curving back of the chair.

"That's a pity," he drawled, watching her profile. "I meant tonight to be very subtle, indeed. Why don't you come over here and let me show you?"

She turned her head at the wistful tone in his words and met his eyes.

"Show me what, Court?" she breathed, feeling the sensual tug of unseen golden chains.

"How subtle I can be," he replied softly, eyes warming with a heat that communicated itself to her. He didn't move, but it was as if he were reaching out to her, drawing on the ends of the chains. "Remember how it was in Oregon, honey? No force, no demands except the ones you, yourself, create. You have my word. I won't even come and get you. I'll let you do everything on your own."

Chapter 9

Unable to deny the restlessness his words and eyes elicited, Leya got to her feet, resolutely crossing to the fire. She didn't hear him get to his feet behind her, but she knew he was there, only inches away. He could have put his hands around her waist and drawn her back against him, but he didn't.

"Do you know how badly I want to make love to you, Leya?" he asked in a voice that had turned faintly raspy with desire.

She felt the flutter along her spine and stood very still, her eyes focused on the flames in front of her. "I thought you wanted the words first, Court. I thought you wanted to know how much I *trust* you," she said quite distinctly, knowing that if he put out his hand she would tremble beneath the touch. He probably knew it, too. Every time he touched her, she seemed to have less and less resistance, Leya thought dazedly.

"Can't you give me the words, Leya?" he begged a little thickly, lowering his head to drop the tiniest of shivering kisses on the back of her neck.

Leya flinched, as she had known she would, but she couldn't bring herself to step away from the implicit danger.

"And hand you your victory on a silver platter?" she asked, sensing his arousal and the control he was exerting over himself. It touched a chord of excitement deep in her body, emboldened her in some strange fashion.

"It's not a question of victory or challenge," he whispered, once again touching his lips to her nape. She knew he must have sensed her inner tremor. "When you realize that, you'll realize you're only hurting both of us by being so stubborn."

His hands went to her waist, settling there lightly, with no compulsion. Slowly, she turned within the circle of the embrace and met his eyes with a searching gaze.

"Am I hurting you, Court?"

"You're driving me crazy!" he gritted before taking her lips in the most feather-light of kisses. "And, yes, it hurts!"

Of their own accord, Leya's arms wrapped themselves around his neck, her body urging a closer contact with this man who could inflame her senses so easily. It would be safe tonight, she told herself silently. He wouldn't dare risk forcing her beyond the limits she wanted to set. He wouldn't want to jeopardize the future victory. Would he?

But he was leading her on again, his mouth persuasive, coaxing, cajoling, but not demanding. As she had the night at the inn, Leya felt herself responding to the safe lovemaking he seemed to promise.

Her body inclined toward his and she felt his hands slide down the length of her spine, seeking the intimate feel of her. He stood braced, his feet slightly apart and gently urged her hips against his lower body, inviting her into his warmth.

She groaned against his mouth and parted her lips, luring him into the sensual investigation he sought.

"Leya!"

Her name was a husky whisper as she moved against him and his hands tightened perceptibly. She moved her head, seeking the tanned column of his throat and felt him tremble as she scorched kisses down to the opening of his khaki shirt.

She loved this, she realized dimly. She loved the feel of him, she loved his response...

"You really are intending to drive me crazy, aren't you?" he growled, his fingers digging erotically into the curve of her derriere.

"And if I am?" she taunted, alive with the scent and feel of him.

"I'll just have to endure the punishment, won't I?" he mocked gently.

He moved, taking a step backward and sinking into the sofa, pulling her into a gentle sprawl on top of him.

She met his eyes, saw the deep male need there and responded to it. Slowly, she bent her head and kissed him, drawing out the teasing, provocative caress until she felt him shudder beneath her.

His hands held her more tightly against him, his legs stretched out so that she lay between them. Her own inner urgency grew as she began to explore the warm skin that disappeared beneath the collar of his shirt, and she was so engrossed with undoing the first button she encountered that she was hardly aware of it when his hands slid under the material of her yellow blouse.

Then, quite suddenly, his fingers were circling her breasts, seeking the sensitized nipples, and she knew he had undone the clasp of her bra. The electric shock of his touch brought her temporarily back to reality.

"Court, I don't—"

"Hush, Leya," he breathed, his fingers sliding under the small, full weight of her breasts while his thumbs probed the tips. "This is the way it was meant to be between us. We've both known that from the beginning."

"Court, I won't let you push me into bed!" she cried softly, almost beseechingly.

"Are you sure about that?" he half smiled, some of his natural arrogance seeping through to alarm her.

"Some victory that would be!" she taunted desperately, knowing the precariousness of her situation now.

"What makes you think you'd be unwilling?" he charged roughly, eyes glittering as he raked her features. His fingers moved again on her breasts, and when she trembled in response, satisfaction flared in his gaze.

"You might succeed in forcing a response," she conceded, knowing it was useless to protest that fact. "But that wouldn't give you the victory you'd have if I were to admit I trusted you again, would it? I think you like your challenges completely conquered, Court Tremayne, not just partially!"

Something dangerous flickered through him, communicating itself to her body, and she suddenly sensed the deep masculine instinct that wanted to have done with the taunts and defiance.

"For a woman who's intent on not offering me a challenge, you seem very good at throwing down the gauntlet," he finally rasped warningly. "What would you do if I chose to pick it up?"

His hands closed like steel bands around her waist, holding her immobile.

"What are you talking about?" she demanded, feeling the prickle of fear.

"What if I decided not to wait for the words and simply took what was offered? And it was offered, Leya," he reminded her with a touch of savagery. "Two nights ago you were more than willing! Perhaps I should have carried matters a little further. Another few minutes and you might have been willing to say anything I wanted you to say!"

"Well, I certainly didn't have to worry about that happening, did I?" she flung back, incensed. "You made it very clear that the only way you want me is the way most flattering to your ego! You were in a rage last night when you drove me home. I think you would have cheerfully thrown me out the door if you hadn't felt somehow obliged to take me back home!"

"Did that bother you, sweetheart?" he breathed, some of the impatience in him fading. "Did it hurt *your* ego to know I could call a halt, get dressed and take you home?"

"I don't know what dazzling conclusion you think you've reached about my behavior," she began furiously, not liking the direction the conversation was taking.

"Did you think last night was easy on me?" he soothed, reaching up to toy with her dark braid as he smiled with affectionate amusement. "Don't you know how hard it was to take you home last night? Don't you know how I spent the remainder of the night staring at the ceiling of my room and thinking about how good you had felt in my arms? About the softness of your breasts and the way your nipples flower under my fingers like buds bursting into bloom? Don't you think I was in misery remembering the invitation in your eyes, the feel of your legs alongside mine?"

"Court!" she squeaked, turning several deepening shades of red at his totally unexpected verbal lovemaking. His eyes poured gold over her.

"Oh, I suffered last night, if that's what's worrying you," he assured her softly. "I wanted very badly to slip golden chains around you and listen to you make the sweet sounds of love."

"But you didn't want me badly enough to take me on my terms. You wanted a full surrender first!" she retorted accusingly.

"Maybe," he husked, cupping her face between rough palms and pulling her head down to his. "Maybe I do want to feel more certain of you. Is that so very strange?"

"Feeling certain of someone is not the same thing as… as demanding a complete surrender!"

"In our case," he said quite steadily as he dragged her mouth down onto his, "I think it might be!"

He swamped her now with the force of his passion, unleashing all the uncompromising desire he had been holding in check. She felt the rising need in him and wanted to cry out. But her lips were captive to his.

He shifted his weight with a strong movement that reversed their positions on the sofa. In an instant he was covering her, letting her know the full weight of him as he began undoing the buttons of the yellow blouse.

"Court, no!"

"What's the matter, Leya?" he murmured into her throat as his hands once more claimed her breasts. "You have no need to fight me this time. I won't demand a confession of undying love and trust from you tonight!"

Pushing aside the fabric of the blouse, he bent his head to curl his tongue around the peak of her breast. Leya shuddered, her hands clenching in the thickness of his hair.

"Please! I don't want us to…"

"Last night you wanted it. You'll want it again tonight," he vowed.

She tried to move her legs, only to have him take advantage of the action and thrust his own between hers. Her senses spun.

"Oh!"

He ignored the small cry, his fingers sliding down the material of her jeans to find her hips in an urgent caress. She felt his tongue dip enticingly into her navel and her body arched upward instinctively.

"At least you can't hide your physical response!" he groaned, letting her feel his teeth on the softness of her stomach in an exquisite touch.

His fingers trailed down to play with the back of her

knee, massaging it through the jeans in an amazingly erotic movement that brought small moans from Leya's throat. Her hands glided down onto the muscles of his shoulders, and she dug in her nails with catlike intensity.

"Oh, my God, Court! Please!"

"Please, what, Leya?" he challenged, edging slowly back along the length of her body. "Please make love to you? I will. And I won't make the mistake I made last night."

"What mistake?" she demanded hoarsely, delighting in the feel of him as she pushed her hands under his shirt and clung to his strong back.

"I won't make any demands you're not prepared to satisfy," he swore. "We'll try it your way!"

"My way? I don't understand! What are you saying?"

She didn't want to think, but some restless part of her mind kept forcing her to do so. Something was wrong. She had to get a grip on the situation and herself. She *had* to! Already his fingers were undoing the snap of her jeans.

"Stop it, Court! What do you mean you won't make any demands? That's exactly what you're doing!"

"No, I'm not. I haven't asked anything of you, yet," he said tersely, his fingers gripping the waistband of her jeans as he prepared to drag them down over her hips. "I haven't made you swear your trust or your faith in me or your undying love…"

Leya began to panic, realizing he was intent on pursuing the sexual goal without any of the words that would make it right. She twisted, struggling to loosen his grip, but he leaned the full weight of his body against her.

"What's the matter, Leya?" he rasped, raising his head to meet her now frantic gaze. "This was the way you wanted it last night, remember?"

"No! Not this way! You don't understand!"

"What don't I understand? You didn't want the words. All right, I agree to accept your terms!"

She heard the thread of harshness in his voice, felt it in the way he was handling her, and wanted to cry. Desperately, she pushed against his shoulders.

"Please," she begged, her lips trembling as she watched him, wide-eyed and terribly uncertain. "I don't want you to do this to me. Please, Court!"

"What do you want, Leya?" he demanded tightly, his hands stilling on her hips. "I'm trying to do this your way. Tell me what you want!"

"Damn you! Stop pushing me like this!" she wailed, doubling her hands into fists against the muscles of his shoulders. "I know what you're trying to do! You're trying to force me into a corner where I'll admit anything you want!"

"How can a man force a woman to say she trusts him?" he taunted bitterly.

"By pushing her to the point where she will say the words he wants rather than go through with the lovemaking without them!" Leya stormed furiously.

For a stark second, a curious silence hovered in the air. Then Court spoke very softly.

"Why should the words matter? Why can't you go through with the physical side of things without them? You were willing last night…"

"Last night—last night I was wrong," Leya returned in a heavy, unhappy whisper. "Last night I hoped…"

"What did you hope, Leya?" he prodded.

"Nothing," she said dismally. How could she explain that last night she had somehow hoped making love together might put things right between them? It was the kind of illusion women had tempted themselves with forever. And it was just as false now as it had been thousands of years ago. It took the words to make it right. The words of genuine commitment.

"You hoped that we would say all the right things to each other in the throes of passion?" he hazarded roughly.

"Yes!" she admitted with a hint of arrogant defiance. She would not let this man crush her spirit tonight!

His eyes blazed into hers for a long, unwavering moment, and then, so quickly that it startled her, he sat up, swinging his legs to the floor. His hand continued to rest on her vulnerable, naked stomach.

He turned his head to meet her questioning gaze. "Does it strike you," he began dryly, "that we think along the same lines? Now, all we have to do is get the timing coordinated!"

She edged carefully out from under his absently possessive hand, pulling her blouse around her and beginning to button it with unsteady fingers.

"You mean last night you wanted the words before the sex and tonight I wanted them," she agreed flatly, not looking at him.

"Tonight, I was the one who talked himself into thinking

they could be put off until later," Court said gently, putting out a hand to touch her dark braid. "With any luck, maybe we've both learned something."

She glanced up sharply and found the gold of his eyes warming her intently.

"Court…"

"Come on, Leya," he ordered gently, getting to his feet. "It's time you went home."

She lay awake in bed a long time that night, thinking. Trust. It lay at the bottom of the issue. There was no denying the physical attraction between herself and Court. Instinctively, she knew that scenes such as the one she had just been through and the one the previous evening could repeat themselves indefinitely until one or the other of them succumbed to the lure of satisfaction without commitment and understanding.

But was the commitment Court wanted from her the same as the one she wanted from him? She had trusted Alex Harlow once and suffered the humiliation of being used. Court Tremayne was the only other man to have gained her trust to such an extent. And once again she had played the fool for a man.

Or had she? Court could have taken her tonight. Why hadn't he? Was it really so important to him that she commit herself fully? Did he need her trust because he needed *her?*

Deliberately, coldly, Leya applied the calculating, analytical portion of her mind to the enormous problem with which she was confronted. The pattern of moonlight on the ceiling shifted several times before she began to see a solution in it.

She needed to dissociate herself from Brandon Security in Court Tremayne's mind, she finally realized. She needed to find out how long his interest in her would last if she were no longer connected with the business. Perhaps then they could truly start from scratch.

But what would she do if she took the step of severing all ties with Brandon and then found out Court lost interest in her?

Leya closed her eyes briefly against the potential misery and then firmed her resolve. There was no other way to clear the cluttered path between herself and Court. If they were to have another chance, she must take the one step to create the opportunity.

"I'm going to have to run over to Brandon Security and see my brother this morning, Cynthia," Leya announced the next day when she walked into the shop. "Will you mind holding the fort alone for a while?"

"Nope. I was prepared to do it all this week, anyhow, remember?" Cynthia chuckled, handing her boss a cup of coffee.

"He should be at work in another half-hour," Leya noted, accepting the coffee gratefully and perching herself on one of the tall stools behind the counter. She smoothed the denim skirt she was wearing with a red-and-white checked blouse and smiled wryly. "I've stopped dropping by his apartment unexpectedly in the early mornings!"

"You mean after the door was opened a few times by various females?" Cynthia laughed knowingly.

"Why are they always blonde, Cynthia?" Leya complained, thinking of her conversation on the subject with Court the night of the party. "And they all seem to look alike, too. I'm not sure how my brother tells them apart. Something about the eyes always looks the same!"

"Your brother is a smart man," Cynthia assured her sympathetically. "When it comes time to get serious, he'll pick one he can talk to out of bed as well as in it!"

"I hope so!"

They chatted a few minutes longer over coffee, and then Leya glanced at her watch. "I'd better be on my way if I'm going to catch Keith before he gets involved in a meeting or something. You've got the number if you need me."

"Right. Don't worry about this place. I'll call if anything goes wrong."

"It won't. I just have to have the illusion that I'm useful once in a while," Leya grinned, heading out the door.

But the grin disappeared as she slid into the front seat of her car. The stop at Brandon Books had been a delaying action and she knew it. The real business of the day lay ahead of her, and there was no sense putting if off any longer.

With a feeling that she was deliberately concocting her own doom, Leya pulled out into the early morning traffic and headed for the offices of Brandon Security Systems.

Several minutes later, she walked past a secretary's desk with a smiling nod and entered her brother's sanctum. She still experienced a pang on occasion when she did it, remembering how her father had once occupied the office. But the sadness didn't last long anymore. Keith had made the place his own in the months since he had moved in, and once inside, Leya was no longer disturbed by memories.

"'Morning, Leya, what's up?" Keith asked cheerfully, closing a folder he had been scanning. "Enjoying yourself with my new consultant?"

"Funny you should mention that," Leya began dryly.

"Uh-oh. I have a feeling Court should be here to handle this."

Keith eyed his sister warily. Smart younger brothers usually learned to assess a sister's moods early in life, Leya reflected wryly. And Keith was, as Cynthia had noted, smart.

"Not at all," she told him far too smoothly, dropping into a nearby chair. "This is between you and me, brother dear."

"The last time you called me 'brother dear' you wanted to borrow my motorcycle," Keith said reminiscently. "It was returned with a crumpled wheel."

"Dangerous things, motorcycles," Leya murmured sympathetically. "I'm glad you've had the sense not to buy another one."

"I've, uh, developed other interests."

"So I've noticed. But I'm not here to borrow anything today," Leya went on briskly, crossing one knee gracefully over the other and swinging her toe idly.

"You're here to chew me out for not having come to your rescue the other night when Court carried you off over his shoulder?" he hazarded, lifting one eyebrow.

"No, although an impartial observer might think I had

cause to do so," she retorted, silver-green eyes glinting dangerously.

"Most impartial observers would have the sense to realize it doesn't pay to interfere in an argument of a domestic nature," Keith shot back easily, lounging into his chair. "Are you sure I shouldn't call Court in here? He's on a tour of the manufacturing facilities at the moment, but I can have him paged." Keith waited hopefully.

"I've told you this is between us, Keith."

"Okay, let's have it," he sighed in obvious resignation. "What do you want from me?"

"Nothing at all. I'm here to give you something." Leya fixed him with a cool, calculating glance.

"What?" He didn't look anxious to receive any gifts, she decided, smiling inwardly. A smart younger brother.

"My shares in Brandon Security Systems."

"Your what?" he demanded in stunned amazement. "Why the devil would you want to do that?" Keith leaned forward, resting his elbows on the wide mahogany desk, his green eyes staring at her.

"You know I've never had any real interest in the firm."

"Yes, but…"

"And now that you've hired yourself a man of great expertise to assist you in getting the company back on its feet, you don't need my 'silent' input any longer!" The hint of sarcasm was barely concealed.

"But this is part of your inheritance from Dad, Leya!"

"I don't want it or need it. You're the one who's taken

to the business like a natural, Keith. There's no reason you shouldn't have it all."

"But Dad wanted you to have something!" he protested, waving a hand helplessly.

"He gave me my start in the book business, remember?"

"That was a loan, which you paid back!"

"Interest free," she reminded him with a smile. "And he gave it to me at a time when none of the banks would have touched me with a ten-foot pole. Besides, there was the money from the sale of the house, which you and I split. Believe me, Keith, I'm more than content with my inheritance."

Her brother eyed her thoughtfully, absently tapping the tip of a pencil on his desk. "This has something to do with your relationship with Court, doesn't it?"

"How did you guess?" she mocked grimly. "It may very well put an end to that relationship."

"But you're hoping it won't?"

"That's my business, Keith. Do I ask you pointed questions about all those blondes?"

"Yes!"

"Liar. I haven't asked any for ages!" she argued.

"Leya, I don't know what you're up to, but..."

"Don't worry, Keith, I know what I'm doing. And I truly don't want the shares in Brandon Security. I should have turned them over to you months ago," she added sincerely. She reached into the thin leather case at her side. "I've brought the papers with me. We should be able to take care of everything today."

"Are you certain this is what you want, Leya?" Keith asked slowly, scanning her face a few minutes later as they concluded the business.

"Yes, but there is one other small item," she drawled.

"I knew it!" he gritted with morbid satisfaction.

"I want you to make it very clear to Courtland Gannon Tremayne that there is no longer any gain to be had in remaining 'interested' in me," Leya said decisively, even as the raw pain of what she was doing cut deep.

"So that's it," Keith breathed, nodding his head finally in understanding. "You're an idiot, Leya. The man wants to marry you."

She flinched. "He's certainly never said anything about marriage to me!"

"Knowing you, you haven't given him a chance! You're probably still mad at him for deceiving you up there in Oregon!"

"He told you about that?" she asked disbelievingly.

"Yes, he did, and I think you're a fool to hold it against him!"

"Would you trust someone after he'd done something like that?" she hissed angrily.

"Depends on the someone. I'd trust Court," Keith declared forcefully.

"You've got a bad case of hero worship!" she accused, getting to her feet and starting for the door. Her glance halted at the bare spot on the opposite wall. "What did you do with my picture?" she turned back to ask curiously.

"Court asked me for it," Keith said briefly, watching her

expression with great interest. "He's got it hanging in his own office now."

"He does?" Leya swallowed her surprise.

"Umm. I suppose he enjoys having an image of his *victim* handy to gloat over!" Keith retorted nastily.

Leya slammed out of the office.

Chapter 10

The ringing of the doorbell shortly after Leya had returned home from work was not entirely unexpected. Court was not a coward. With a distinct feeling of impending disaster, Leya uncoiled herself from the couch and made her way toward the door.

Court stood on the threshold, still dressed in a business suit and dark tie, his gold-and-brown hair damp from a faint sprinkling of rain. The tortoiseshell eyes gleamed.

"Good evening, Leya," he said politely, propping himself against the edge of the door with one large hand. "I understand you've had a busy day."

"I merely took care of some business matters," she retorted loftily, her heart pounding with a strange hope. Was he here to mock her or woo her?

"So I gather. Get your jacket, I'm taking you out to dinner."

At the note of command in his voice, she stiffened. "I'm not very hungry."

"Then I'll force-feed you. I'm taking you out to eat, Leya, and to discuss our future. Don't bother fighting it, I'm not in a mood for your stubbornness this evening."

"What's the matter? Can't you say what you want to say right here? It shouldn't take long!" She faced him bravely.

"I'll give you the same choice I gave you the night of the party," he said politely. "You can come out on my arm or over my shoulder."

Leya drew herself up to her full height and fixed him with an angry glare. Why couldn't he get it over with right now? What was the point in dragging everything out? Either he was still interested or he wasn't. It should be so damned simple!

"Very well," she announced disdainfully, "if you're going to be that way about it!"

"I am," he assured her, but there was a slight smile in his eyes.

Leya didn't volunteer a word during the short drive to a nearby steak house, and Court didn't bother to open the conversation until after he'd ushered her into the darkened lounge and ordered both of them a drink.

"I needed that," he muttered thankfully a few minutes later as he took a swallow of the scotch and settled into the chair. His jacket had been removed and slung over the back, and he'd loosened his tie. He looked like any other businessman relaxing after a hard day at the office, Leya thought fleetingly, stifling an urge to touch his sleeve soothingly.

"Sleep well last night?" he inquired pleasantly.

"Don't be ridiculous," she responded tightly.

"Neither did I. I gather you spent the hours lying awake staring at your ceiling in useful contemplation, however," he went on blandly.

"You've talked to Keith?" she said as coolly as possible, her fingers curling around the cold glass in her hand.

"This afternoon. So you finally decided to turn your shares in Brandon Security over to your brother, hmm? Should have done it long ago."

"It would have made everything so much *simpler,* wouldn't it?"

"Much!" He lifted his glass for another swallow.

"And you're a great one for taking the easiest path to a goal!" she went on sarcastically, sipping moodily at her drink.

"I try," he agreed modestly, watching her from beneath lowered lids. "But even I have to stand back in admiration of your talents along that line."

She eyed him sharply. "Meaning?"

"Meaning you very neatly removed the one obstacle I was powerless to remove. If I'd asked you to give up your shares in Brandon Security, you would have been certain I was determined to get you out of the picture."

"And now I've done it for you," she concluded morosely.

"Why?" he asked quietly.

She moved a hand in a small gesture that conveyed her inability to fully explain. "I…I wanted you to stop seeing me as an obstacle you had to overcome in order to have control at Brandon Security."

"I wonder how long it will take you to realize the full implications of what you did when you abdicated your rights at Brandon," he mused thoughtfully.

She frowned, bewildered.

"Don't you realize how much trust you demonstrated, sweetheart?" he said with a hint of a smile.

"I did no such thing! I merely decided to opt out of the stupid game we were playing!" she protested righteously.

"And leave your little brother to my mercy?" he murmured.

"What's wrong with that? You're going to... Oh!"

"Precisely. When did you stop worrying about my having designs on Brandon Security? When did you decide I would honor the spirit of the contract and not take advantage of Keith?"

She glanced away, her teeth sinking into her bottom lip briefly.

"Now it really is just between you and me," he went on softly. "You very graciously removed the one factor which was unduly complicating things, leaving us free to get on with this nutty relationship!"

"Is it still the 'challenge' thing, Court? Do you still have to take me to bed to prove something to yourself? There's nothing left to win! I removed the prize when I gave the shares to my brother. The game is over."

"The game isn't over until you admit you belong to me!" he gritted, his hand tightening vengefully around his glass as his temper clearly frayed. "And you *do* belong to me, Leya Brandon. I've seen it in those silver-green eyes since the first night I took you in my arms on the dance floor! The problem all along has been to get you to admit it!"

"You're so damn sure of yourself!" she snapped in sudden fury.

"I'm staking my hope of future peace of mind on the fact that you're going to belong to me, yes!"

"You'd like that, wouldn't you? It would satisfy that monstrous ego of yours to have me admit that!"

"It would certainly go a long way toward soothing it," he agreed bleakly, obviously making an effort to rein in his impatience. There were grimly etched lines around his mouth, and the determination in him was palpable.

You could tell just by looking at the man that he never gave up once he'd accepted a challenge, Leya thought miserably. She should have known giving away the stock wouldn't solve everything. No, she decided, something had changed.

He'd decided he wanted her and he was going to have her. But at least he wanted her now for herself, not as a way to buy himself into Brandon Security!

"If you thought I was proud to throw myself into your bed the moment you showed any interest in me after I'd given away the stock, you were on the wrong track," she told him bitterly. But at least she was no longer a challenge directly connected with Brandon Security!

"For a couple of basically intelligent people, we're having a lot of trouble lately with words, aren't we?" he shot back.

"What do you suggest?"

"I suggest," he told her with sudden gentleness, his eyes gleaming, "that you let me make everything much easier for you."

"How?" she began suspiciously. "I'm not going to go to bed with you in an attempt to 'communicate'!"

"I've known all along that part of the problem is your

pride," he said soothingly. "I've known it because you're a lot like me. Given the same set of circumstances, I'd have had a few problems along that line myself."

Leya felt like a pet rabbit being stroked by a wolf. "Very generous of you," she told him dryly.

"But I think you were trying to accomplish something important today by giving your stock to Keith. I think you were asking me to show you that my interest in you extends beyond the business. And I'm quite prepared to do that."

"You're going to be understanding about my pride problem?" she mocked warily.

"Definitely." He smiled, eyes crinkling beguilingly. "I've got a way to get around all the words."

"Ah! You're going to try and get me into bed without them after all!" she nodded wisely.

"It may come to that, but I'm going to try something else first."

Leya licked her lower lip with a short, quick stab of her tongue as she considered him cautiously. "Now what are you up to, Court Tremayne?"

"Intrigued, are you?" he chuckled, half turning in his chair to dig into a coat pocket. "That gives me a decided advantage, you realize."

He removed a small jeweler's box from his coat and swiveled back around to face her. The green velvet box rested on the palm of his hand as he held it out to her.

"A ring?" she asked disbelievingly, her untrusting eye going from the proffered gift to his glittering gaze.

"No, not a ring. A ring is easy to slip on and off. In

our case this will represent a more binding commitment, I think." He made no move to force the gift into her hand, merely holding it out to her with a waiting quality in his expression.

The atmosphere grew very still and dangerous. Leya couldn't take her eyes off the small green box, in spite of the sensation of menace. He was right. She was intrigued now. Not a ring? Of course not. That would have been too much to hope for. Court wasn't asking her to marry him.

"Come on, Leya," he coaxed on a note of amusement. "Take a risk."

She frowned and reached out to pluck the box from his hand. Her imagination was working overtime, she chided herself. There was no danger here.

"Open it," he prodded gently.

Surprised at the degree of boldness it took, Leya snapped open the green velvet lid and gave a small exclamation at the beautifully worked emerald earrings inside. Her knowledgeable eye admired the delicate craftsmanship and the quality of the stones before she had a chance to really think about it.

"They're…they're lovely, Court," she finally managed, a trifle breathlessly. "But I can't accept a gift like this. We're not…that is, we aren't…" She stumbled to a halt, staring at the earrings as if mesmerized.

"Leya, I once asked you how I would know when you'd forgiven me for what happened in Oregon. If you wear those earrings, I'll have my answer."

Leya glanced uncertainly up from the contents of the box.

"But, Court, they're for pierced ears. I can't wear them," she hedged, feeling quite flustered.

"You can if you want to badly enough," he pointed out, the corner of his mouth lifting faintly.

"I...I suppose I could reset them onto a clip," she began, thoroughly unnerved. "I mean, assuming I do want us to start over...which I do, Court, you must know that!" she ended in a sudden burst of honesty.

"I'm not talking about starting over, honey," he said, voice deepening. "I'm talking about making a commitment. If you want me as the man in your life, the man you trust and want, you'll wear those earrings as they were meant to be worn."

She met his eyes in sudden understanding. "That's supposed to be the easy 'nonverbal' way out of my, er, situation?" she gasped, shocked.

He sucked in his breath, eyes gleaming as he reached out to cover one of her hands with his own. "Leya, I've known from the start that I had nothing with which to attract and hold you except myself. You don't need financial security, you're not consumed by loneliness, you're not a naturally clinging vine. You don't need or want any of the things the women I've known usually want. Like a fool I tried to forge a physical bond between us, hoping that would chain you to me. The night you told me you could give me everything but your trust I realized that chain would never be sufficient, either."

"Court, I..." she floundered, not knowing what to say. Was he trying to tell her he loved her or only desired her?

Whichever it was, there was not doubt but that he still wanted her surrender!

"I know you feel cornered," he went on deliberately, his fingertips stroking the back of her wrist in lazy circles. "But so do I. My instincts tell me to grab you and take you to bed. My intellect tells me that would probably ruin everything. I don't know how to break the impasse unless you'll tell me for certain that you can trust me and that someday you might be able to love me. I want a commitment from you, Leya, so that I can know for sure you're willing to put the past behind us."

"What sort of commitment are you going to offer in return, Court?" she whispered, knowing she was trembling.

"Anything you want, Leya," he told her evenly. "Name it."

His eyes drilled into her, waiting for her response. She tensed, her hand trembled under his. He felt it and closed his own fingers more tightly around hers.

"Honey, I'm not asking for an immediate answer. Think about it," he urged. Then his mouth relaxed slightly. "And think about how much easier it will be to show me how you feel rather than having to say the words!"

"Should I be reading 'surrender' for the word 'commitment'?" she asked pointedly.

He hesitated and Leya nodded grimly.

"I thought so. You're still thinking in those terms, aren't you, Court?"

He shut his eyes and then opened them to gaze fully into her accusing stare. "I need to know you're mine, Leya. I need to know your commitment to me is total. Perhaps that is asking for a surrender."

"Perhaps!"

"All right, then, it *is* asking for a surrender. But I've already said you can ask anything of me in return!"

"You want me that badly?" she whispered.

"I want you that badly."

And then he was calmly getting to his feet, shaking off the mood that had settled around the little cocktail table. "Ready for dinner?"

"Court, listen to me. About these earrings..."

"They're yours, Leya. Do with them what you want, but if you decide to wear them I'm going to take it as an act of... surrender. The end of hostilities." He smiled gently, taking her arm and leading her toward the dining room. "That's enough on that subject. Come have dinner with me and let me tell you about my hard day!"

"Court, this is ridiculous! I will not let you do this to me!"

"Feed you? But your brother assures me the steaks here are fantastic and I have a hunger for some blood-red meat!"

"I'm surprised you don't ruin your own appetite with comments like that!"

But she wound up having dinner with him, as she had known she would from the beginning of the evening. Actually, she reflected at one point as she chewed rare steak, it wasn't an unpleasant meal. Court talked only of casual things, making no mention of what lay between them like live ammunition. And, as she had been before, Leya was

gradually absorbed back under the spell of the companionship that sprang up between them on occasions when they
were not discussing their own relationship.

"About next Saturday," he said at one point, helping himself to the rest of her baked potato, which she showed signs
of leaving. "I was thinking that a drive into the wine country might be nice."

"Over to Napa Valley? Well, I suppose…"

"I know you've probably done it a thousand times, living
so close and all, but I haven't ever done the winery tour,"
he said persuasively.

"All right," she said, discovering she didn't want to argue.
"We'll go."

He left her on the doorstep after dinner, his good-night
kiss a restrained, gentlemanly caress that astonished Leya.
She stood at the window and watched him drive off into
the night, conscious of the green velvet box burning a hole
in her jacket pocket. When the taillights had disappeared,
she dropped the curtain into place and headed morosely
toward the kitchen.

Why was it, she thought sadly as she checked the back
door and turned off lights, that of all the men she had met,
it was Court Tremayne who had the power to make her feel
this way? Jangled, uncertain, filled with longing.

Snagging an unfinished novel from the coffee table, she
climbed the stairs to her bedroom. She set the deceptively
innocent green box on the nightstand and crawled under
the covers a few minutes later.

But it was impossible to concentrate on the novel. Her

gaze kept straying to the green box, and twice she picked it up to gaze at the emerald earrings inside. They truly were lovely things, she thought with a sigh. If she were to accept, what would she ask of Court in return? What did a man mean when he said "anything"?

When she finally struggled awake the next morning after a fitful night, the green box was the first thing she saw as she opened her eyes. It stood on the nightstand where she had left it, taunting and teasing and daring her. It was certainly a reflection of the man who had given it to her, she thought with a groan, pushing back the quilt.

And the fact that she was even considering getting her ears pierced told her a great deal about her present state of mind, Leya decided grimly.

Because it was a perfectly ridiculous thing to do! What could it possibly prove? She *had* to be in love to even consider such a thing!

But perhaps, just as she'd needed some proof that Court's interest in her extended beyond Brandon Security, he needed a symbolic commitment from her.

The thought made her catch her breath. Was Court really so unsure of her? He always seemed so confident, so much in control. Yet here he was asking her to do something as ridiculous as getting her ears pierced just to seal their relationship.

The little box continued to haunt her. Court's request was crazy, yet hadn't she behaved just as crazily when she'd grandly turned over her shares in Brandon to her brother?

Only a woman in love would take such a situation seriously, Leya told herself wryly several times a day. Only a woman in love…

She *was* in love. Why go on denying it to herself? She was not a coward, either. She could admit the truth, she decided staunchly. And the next move, silly as it was, was definitely up to her! She would have to take the risk of making a commitment or face the much graver risk of losing Court.

By Saturday morning, she had resigned herself to that fact, knew it with a sureness that defied argument. She had been in love since the weekend in Oregon. And she knew that, compared to her feelings for Alex Harlow, this sensation was unique.

As she stepped out of a warm shower and rubbed herself briskly with the red towel, Leya acknowledged that there was no comparison between her feelings for Court and what she had experienced for a boy like Alex. Court was a man and he touched her elemental femininity in a way Alex never could have done. It was easy to take revenge on Alex. It had become impossible to exact it from Court.

Yet he was sure that she had done exactly that by denying him her trust, Leya reflected as she slowly dressed in jeans and a bright red top. But who had she been punishing with her refusal to say she trusted him?

Could it be that the punishment had been self-inflicted? She had been more angry at herself than him that morning when she had discovered the deception. Angry at her failure to see through the scheme; angry at her apparent stupidity.

She had told Court the truth when she said she hadn't plotted revenge. Instead she had kept telling herself she didn't trust him because she had wanted to keep the re-minder of her lack of intelligence firmly fixed in front of her. She hadn't wanted to admit another man had made a fool of her.

He had created a weakness in her that she didn't relish acknowledging, even to herself. That night on the terrace when he'd backed up her revenge against Alex, she'd found herself wanting to abandon her defenses against Court. She'd been on the verge of accepting his offer of a truce when her brother had appeared on the scene and reminded her of the weakness in herself.

But the thought of admitting her love for a man who had made it clear he only felt desire was another assault on her pride. Court was right. That pride was a factor in the situation, a very big factor. Was she going to be too arro-gant to confess her love for a man who had shown her the weakness he could create in her?

But Court had found a way around the necessary words, she remembered as she walked back into the bedroom brushing her long dark hair. She stood silently for a mo-ment, staring at the dangerous green box.

The drive through the rich Napa Valley was exactly what she needed, Leya decided a couple of hours later as she set off on the winery tour with Court. It was pleasant to sit back in the depths of the expensive car and let the beguil-ing companionship overtake her. Court made no mention of the earrings or anything else that might add a note of tension. He had been the soul of restraint all week.

It was fun tasting the various products of the vintner's efforts and selecting bottles to purchase and take home. They argued good-naturedly over the merits of Chardonnays and Cabernets, bought cheese and sourdough bread, and picnicked at a scenic point overlooking acres of neatly trimmed vineyards. True, it was a little chilly to eat in the open, but there was something cozy and intimate about dropping crumbs on Court's leather upholstery.

They talked about wine, electronics, jewelry making and business, everything, in short, except the state of their strange relationship. It was a very pleasant day, one of those days when Court felt "safe" to Leya.

They took the organized tour offered by one of the larger establishments, exploring the huge cellars and delighting in the tangy scent of fermenting wine. Once, as the main party of tourists passed momentarily out of sight behind a huge redwood vat, Court reached out and dragged Leya close for a quick, hard kiss that took her breath away for an instant.

"Couldn't resist," he explained matter-of-factly when she blinked her surprise.

But later that night after an evening spent dining and dancing at an elegant restaurant secluded in the vineyards, Leya felt compelled to take Court's hand as he was about to leave her with grave politeness on her doorstep.

"Wait," she said impulsively. "There's something I want to show you."

He arched an eyebrow in inquiry, but said nothing as he followed her into the house. Without a word, she led him

firmly toward the stairs and knew by the sudden tightening of his hand what he was thinking.

"No," she said, slanting a mischievous smile up at his
suddenly urgent eyes. "We're making a right at the top of
the stairs, not a left."

Left was the direction of her bedroom. She felt the humor
in him as she determinedly guided him right and threw
open a door at the end of the hall.

He shot her a quick look and then whistled soundlessly as
he walked past her into the functionally designed interior.

"Quite a setup." He nodded approvingly as he scanned
the workbench.

Leya relaxed slightly at his obvious appreciation of her
jewelry workshop. She watched in anticipation as Court
bent over the assortment of fine tools and delicate appara-
tus. Little glass boxes filled with thin wire, earring clips,
and other odds and ends lined one end of the table. A collection of polished rocks was housed near it. Sheets of ham-
mered metal were stacked nearby.

He smiled at her across the short distance separating them.
"I can see you getting lost in here for hours at a time." He
picked up one of the small tools lying on the end of the
counter.

"It's a hobby," she said offhandedly, not wanting to fully
admit just how much she was enjoying his interest.

"Why did you show me your secret hideout tonight?" he
murmured deeply, setting down the tiny tool and walking
slowly forward to stand in front of her.

"I don't know," she whispered honestly. "Perhaps because it was such a lovely day…"

"And perhaps because you instinctively wanted to show me how much we really do have in common?" he mused, cupping her face gently between his hands.

"I…I'm not sure why I did it. It was an impulse," she shrugged.

"Do you realize why today felt so good?"

"Why?"

"Because it felt like Oregon again," he told her softly.

Leya hesitated, knowing he was right.

"And I'm going to do my damnedest to create a lot more days just like this one," Court swore, bending to kiss her in a sweet, drugging way that made her want to bury herself in his arms.

But he didn't give her the chance. His leave-taking was warm, filled with sensual tension, but very restrained.

Exactly like the leavetaking of the next several nights, Leya thought in wry amusement as the week progressed. Court had established a truce, she had allowed him to do so, and he intended to maintain it.

The planning for the new branch of Brandon Books went beautifully during those days, with everything seeming to fall satisfyingly into place. And the nights were filled with a fairy-tale prince who was all grace and charm and re-strained desire.

Leya knew she was being wooed, and she also knew Court was intending for the romance to have a thoroughly definite goal. But he carefully said nothing about that goal.

It was only when she slipped dreamily into bed at night, and glanced at her nightstand to see if the green box was still there, that Leya allowed herself to remember the ending Court wanted.

It was over a dinner of curried lamb and green salad, which Leya had fixed on Sunday night, that Court made his announcement.

"I'm going to have to go back to the Valley tomorrow for a few days to wind up matters on a project I was finishing before I moved here," he said calmly.

"San Jose? Silicon Valley?"

"Right. I should be back in time for that party your brother is giving Friday night. You'll be there?"

"I hadn't heard about it," Leya shrugged, accustomed to her brother's offhand invitations. He would probably have called her the day of the party to invite her.

'But you'll be going?" Court persisted, helping himself to more chutney.

"Probably. Why?"

"Because I'll know where to come looking for you when I get back into town, won't I?" He grinned. "I'd pick you up but I don't know what time I'll be back so I'll volunteer to drive you home, instead. That's always the more interesting part of the evening, anyway!"

Leya bared her teeth good-naturedly at him from across the table and he laughed.

There was no denying that the dreamlike quality of the days and evenings faded considerably when Court left town.

Leya found herself eagerly awaiting the phone calls that came regularly after dinner.

"Are you sure you're not calling just to check up on my whereabouts?" she accused cheerfully on Tuesday night.

"Am I displaying a lack of subtlety again?" he sighed.

"A bit, but that's all right. Your phone calls are much better than television."

"Thanks!"

He told her how his work was going, asked about hers, and somehow it was nearly an hour before he hung up.

The green box was waiting in its usual place on the night-stand when Leya went to bed that night. She lay very still in the darkness for a long time, staring at it and remembering the warmth in Court's voice on the telephone.

She crawled back out of bed and reached for the extension phone. Deliberately, she dialed Cynthia's number.

"Cynthia, I have a personal question to ask you," Leya began carefully.

"At this hour of the night?"

"Does it hurt very much to have your ears pierced?"

There was a moment of dead silence on the other end of the line. "Are you serious?" Cynthia finally demanded, sounding as if she were smothering a laugh.

"Very."

"Going to do it?" Cynthia prodded.

"I...I think so."

"Tomorrow?"

"If I put it off any longer, I may never bring myself to do it!" Leya confessed.

"Okay, boss, tomorrow it is. There's a department store across from the store that does it free if you buy the earrings from them. I'll go with you and hold your hand."

"I've...I've already got the earrings," Leya said slowly, having regrets already. The commitment she was contemplating seemed very final. But something told her Court was strong enough to handle it. She smiled to herself at the thought. She *trusted* him to know what he wanted, and he had told her he wanted her.

"Well, you can buy some more cheap ones from them, or I will, so we can get them to do the ear-piercing free," Cynthia said cheerfully.

"Thanks, Cynthia, for volunteering to go with me, I mean. But you haven't answered my question. Is it going to hurt?"

"Bring a bottle of wine down to the shop with you, Leya," Cynthia advised and hung up the phone.

The next day turned out to be one of those inexplicable workdays that is an absolute rush from the opening hour in the morning until closing. Leya and Cynthia, who came in at noon as scheduled, were swamped.

It wasn't until Cynthia finally was able to turn the Closed sign over in the window that Leya was able to talk to her about the earrings. Wordlessly, she handed the paper bag containing the unopened bottle of wine to her assistant.

"Do you mind telling me," Cynthia asked, taking the wine from Leya's grasp and carrying it to the back of the shop where she dug out two paper cups, "what brought on this momentous decision? I thought you had a thing about the ridiculousness of piercing one's ears!"

"Cynthia, I think I've gone crazy. This will probably be like getting a tattoo. I'll wake up in the morning and regret it!"

"No, you won't," Cynthia assured her, laughing as she opened the wine and poured it into the paper cups. "You're going to love being able to wear delicate little earrings. And it will be much more comfortable. No clips to pinch your ears. With your love of jewelry, I'm surprised you haven't done it sooner! Here, take a nice, big swallow."

Leya took the offered cup and did as she was bid. "Are we going to down the whole bottle before we troop over to the jewelry counter at the department store?" she asked interestedly, her eyes lighting with humor.

"Nope. Some for now, some for after. That's the way I did it. Let's see these earrings you've got that have made you take this big step."

Leya silently drew forth the green velvet box and handed it to her friend.

"Ah!" Cynthia breathed a moment later. "I understand. They're beautiful, Leya. A gift form Court?"

"Yes." Leya bit her lip and took another sip of wine.

"He knew what he was doing. They match your eyes perfectly."

Leya peered over to look at the emeralds. "Do you really think so?" She found it oddly touching that Court had thought of her eyes when he'd made the purchase.

"Definitely. It can't be a coincidence. These stones were

very carefully picked out," Cynthia declared with assurance, handing back the earrings. She searched Leya's face. "You're in love with him, aren't you?"

"Like I said, I think I've gone a little crazy."

"Same thing. Have another glass of wine and we'll get the bloody deed done!"

"Cynthia!"

Chapter 11

Friday morning, Keith remembered to invite Leya to his party.

"Can you come?" he demanded cheerfully of his sister. "Court will be there if he gets back into town on time."

"Is that supposed to be a lure?" she joked.

"Naturally. I figure you two will probably be panting to see each other after his absence, but I'm hoping you'll both come to the party."

"You don't think we're a little too old for your crowd?" Leya asked mockingly.

"Not since I moved into the staid business establishment. I figure the pair of you will fit in nicely."

"Poor little brother. Miss your disco floors?"

"Not since I discovered women go for that aura of power we businessmen have!"

Leya hung up the phone with a rude crash, her fingers going absently to her earlobes as they frequently did now.

There was no point in worrying about it at this juncture, she told herself later that evening as she dressed for Keith's party. The decision had been made; the deed done. It remained only to try and carry off the official signing of the peace treaty with a certain amount of style and panache. And if Court Tremayne had an ounce of common sense, she added grimly, he wouldn't tease her about it. She wouldn't be responsible for her actions if he dared to mock her!

She chose the emerald-green dress deliberately, liking the way it went with the earrings that blazed like small green stars in her ears. Cynthia had been right about one thing: Leya did like the more delicate nature of pierced earrings. It opened up all sorts of new design possibilities, she decided, glancing in the mirror yet again. She still couldn't get used to the sight of them, though, or what this particular pair of earrings represented.

She told herself at first that the last-minute decision to wear her hair down was a whim and then admitted the truth. The long, dark tresses cascading past her ears and over her shoulders provided a shield for the emerald earrings. With a small forward motion of her head, they could be hidden entirely, at least until another small motion, such as turning her head, caused the hair to fall back.

On the drive across town to her brother's apartment, it occurred to her that there was no absolute guarantee Court would be able to get back in time for the party, although he'd seemed convinced he would. It would serve her right, she told herself as her humor surfaced, if she'd gone to all this trouble and then had no grand scene to play!

That thought and the excitement radiating through her veins put a glow in the silver-green eyes that could only be compared to the tiny emeralds in her ears as she knocked on the door of her brother's elegant town-house apartment.

"The lady in green!" Keith grinned, opening the door an instant later and shepherding her inside. "You look quite ravishing tonight, sister dear. Can I guess why you're imitating an emerald?"

"A little too much green?" Leya groaned, glancing down the length of her long skirt.

"Not at all!" he assured her, following her into the living room, where a number of other people had already gathered. "The effect is terrific. Court will go crazy. What can I get you to drink? The usual?"

"That will be fine." She glanced around the room at the well-dressed, cheerful crowd. "You know, Keith, a year ago I wouldn't have been able to imagine you giving a party like this," she added in an admiring whisper.

"Upward mobility," he explained succinctly, splashing liquor over ice with casual flair. "You have to act like a success even if you haven't quite reached that point yet."

"You're really getting into this executive lifestyle, aren't you?" she teased, watching with wry interest as a lovely blonde detached herself from a group of people and made her way toward the bar. "Your date for the evening?" Leya added in a low tone.

"Haven't got one yet," Keith told her easily, sipping his whiskey. "But I suppose Janice here might do."

"I'll leave you to impress her with your aura of power." Tossing a smile at the advancing Janice, Leya made her way into the fringes of the crowd, searching out the people she knew and wondering how many here tonight had witnessed the dramatic exit she had made from her last party.

She was seized with a haste that would normally have surprised her. But tonight, as the nervous anticipation of Court's arrival began to mount, Leya hardly noticed the eager interest of several males in the crowd. She responded to it because the excitement in her needed some outlet and each new man on the scene was another object to absorb the energy that pulsed through her, lighting her eyes and curving her lips in a lazy, challenging invitation. More than once, she felt a stray hand unobtrusively come into contact with the sable hair as it swirled almost to her waist.

"Keith mentioned a sister," murmured a newcomer as Leya was handed a second drink by willing hands. "He forgot to mention the color of her eyes."

"An important omission?" she asked lightly, lifting dark lashes to give him the full benefit of the near-platinum green. The stranger was very good-looking, she decided clinically, and he had somehow managed to cut out the rest of her eager entourage. She glanced absently around and wondered how he'd done it. Somehow, she was isolated in a corner of the room, hemmed in by a potted plant on one side and the stranger on the other.

"Very important," the man assured her, dark eyes narrowing sardonically. "I have a weakness for green-eyed women, you see."

"Your weakness doesn't appear to have brought you to ruin," Leya grinned recklessly, tilting her head to study the waving black hair and handsomely cut features. Deliberately, she allowed her gaze to travel politely over the expensive, buttery-soft suede sport jacket and black shirt worn with a rakish air.

"Most of the time I'm able to control it before too much damage is done," he agreed, holding up his left hand to demonstrate a ringless finger. Then he glanced at her own bare left hand. "Apparently, you've managed to steer clear of the trap, too?"

"So far," she agreed, eyes laughing up at him. Where was Court? Perhaps he wouldn't make it tonight, after all. On the other hand, how was she going to behave when he did get here? The tension had strung her nerves to a fine pitch. The earrings tingled in her lobes.

"Something tells me you and I have a lot in common."

"But your eyes aren't green," she protested.

"Are you going to hold that against me?" he complained softly, bending his head down in an attentive fashion and bracing one hand against the wall behind her. He smiled. "I promise you I have other attributes."

"Have you?" she inquired dryly, arching one brow. "Let me guess. Do you play tennis?"

"Excellently," he chuckled, dark eyes warming.

"Golf?"

"Near par game every time!"

"Jog?"

"Every morning."

"And where's your favorite vacation spot?" she asked curiously, letting him mistake the teasing questions for genuine interest.

"Any place I can ski in the winter and sail in the summer. Do I pass?"

"I'm afraid you just flunked," she told him sadly. "I don't do any of those things." She looked up at him with laughing mournfulness.

"You prefer indoor sports?" His smile broadened seductively. "I have a talent for those, too."

"You're very accommodating."

"I do my best."

Leya parted her lips to make a flippant response and was suddenly aware of a change in the atmosphere of the room. The gathering excitement in her blossomed into full bloom, and she felt as if she were walking a glass-edged tightrope. Court was here. She knew it with every instinct in her body.

Affecting a casualness she was far from feeling, she allowed her gaze to sweep the large crowd until she focused on the door. Court stood there, talking to her brother. The tortoiseshell hair had been lightly ruffled by a chill evening breeze, and he was wearing the conservative gray suit he must have worn to his business meetings during the day. The coat had been discarded, probably left in the car, but the classic white shirt was still neatly buttoned and the dark tie in place.

Even as she glanced in his direction, the golden brown eyes swung abruptly and pinned her from across the room. Leya was very conscious of the attentive dark-haired man leaning over her, trapping her in the corner of the room, and of the grim narrowing of Court's eyes before he turned his attention back to Keith. Leya sighed. She would have a bit of explaining to do. Well, he couldn't expect her to attend a party and not mingle with a few guests, she thought righteously, beginning to edge out of the corner.

"Don't leave, green eyes. I haven't even gotten around to telling you my name," the man hovering over her complained softly, coaxingly. "And you haven't told me yours, either. Your brother forgot to mention that, too."

"My name is Leya," she told him idly, her eyes still on the door. "And I'm afraid I really must—"

"Hey, something wrong, Leya? Do you know the guy who just came in?"

"I know him. Look, if you'll excuse me—"

"My name," he said very distinctly, "is Alan. Alan West. Now about my expertise at indoor sports…"

Leya knew Court was starting toward her, pushing his way across the room. She couldn't see him now as the crowd came between them but she could feel the waves of his approach as surely as if they were made of water. They lapped against her skin in increasing frequency and power. She knew she had to get away from Alan West.

But even as she tried to dodge politely aside, Alan's hand fell protestingly on her shoulder. It did so just as Court emerged beside them.

"Good evening, Leya." His voice was a dark and unbelievably soft menace. "Say good-night. We're leaving." His eyes went to the hand on her shoulder, and Leya stared at him unhappily.

Alan, sensing the suddenly thick atmosphere, took one

look at the strained faces of the other two and removed his hand with a small exclamation of apology.

"Sorry," he murmured laconically to Court. "Didn't realize she was private property."

"She's having a little trouble understanding that herself, apparently," Court shot back coolly, grasping Leya's wrist and starting back toward the door.

"Take your hands off me!" Leya hissed waspishly as she was dragged forcefully through the crowd. "There's nothing for you to be upset about! I was merely chatting with Alan—"

"Flirting is the word," he growled stonily. "Did you bring a coat?"

"No."

"Good, then we don't need to delay any longer."

"My brother—"

"—Won't miss us."

"Court, I won't be dragged out of another party like this!"

"So sue me!"

"Damn it, Court—"

"What the hell did you think you were doing in that corner, anyway? Making comparisons? Or did you want to see what I'd do when I saw you? You once said something about being interested in genuine male jealousy, didn't you?"

"That's ridiculous!" she grated, a little frightened now.

"I agree. But since you're so interested, I'll be happy to show you what it's like to be standing under a ton of bricks when they come tumbling down!"

He turned at the door, his hands tunneling under the cascade of her hair to circle her neck. The tortoiseshell eyes were blazing. "I won't have it, Leya. Do you understand me? I won't let you drag anyone else between us. There's only you and me, and I'm not going to let you muddy the waters. Eventually, we're going to settle—"

His words cut off as he drew in his breath with sudden sharpness. Leya realized with a pang of panic that the movement of his hands had brushed back the fall of dark hair, revealing the emerald earrings. She stiffened, able to think only that the moment wasn't turning out as she had planned. She was helpless to deny the significance of the jewelry.

"Leya!"

Court's voice was a hoarse growl in his throat. His fingers moved urgently on the nape of her neck. "Leya, my sweet shrew, why didn't you show me right away? My God! You're determined to drive me insane first, aren't you?"

He didn't wait for an answer, dragging her close and covering her mouth in a rough possession that made her gasp. Then he held her a few inches away, his face intent, his expression urgent and demanding.

"Tell me, Leya. Tell me what it is you're going to ask of me. I gave you the right to ask anything, remember? Anything!"

Leya met his flaming gaze and gathered all her courage in the palm of her hand.

"I'm...I'm asking for marriage, Court," she breathed.

For a split second, he looked absolutely stunned. It must be her imagination, she thought wildly as the expression vanished in the next instant. He started to say something, and then Keith's voice was behind them, cheerfully interrupting.

"Hey, you two! This is a proper executive party! None of that around here!"

"This is a special occasion, Keith," Court whispered huskily as his eyes roamed with golden heat over Leya's revealing face. "Your sister just got herself engaged. To me."

Keith took the news much more in stride than Leya did.

"Well, congratulations, sister! Of course, I can't pretend to be astounded. I was pretty certain that was the way it would end. After all…"

"Later, Keith," Court murmured thickly, gathering a trembling Leya close against him. "We were just leaving. I'm sure you'll understand."

"So soon?" Keith grinned, smiling into his sister's bemused eyes. "But it's such fun seeing Leya struck dumb!"

"Treasure the memory," Court advised. "I'm sure it won't happen often. Now, if you'll excuse us?"

Leya realized abruptly she wasn't the only one who was trembling. She could feel the fine tremor in Court's hand as he guided her purposefully through the door. As she pulled her chaotic thoughts back into focus, she was at last aware that the moment had shaken him as much as it had her.

"If you must, you must," Keith was saying philosophically. "I'll see you both later." He smiled directly at Court. "Take care of her, Tremayne. She's the only sister I've got."

"You have my word on it," Court vowed with deep assurance, his eyes still on Leya's face. "I'll take excellent care of her."

A second later, they were alone on the steps. Wordlessly, Court hurried his silent captive down the short path and across the street to where his car was parked. He tucked her gently inside, then slid in beside her, turning to pull her close in the cold darkness.

"Let's go someplace very private and celebrate our engagement," he whispered as she buried her face against his chest. His hands stroked through the thick hair, pausing to touch the emeralds in her ears as if he couldn't quite believe they were there. "My God, Leya, you don't know what you've done to me tonight!"

"Did you…did you mean it, Court?" she said in a muffled voice, thrilling to the heat and strength of him as he held her close. "Are you really willing to marry me?"

"I said you could ask anything you wished of me, didn't I?"

She swallowed, not certain she should pursue that. "Are you still angry about Alan West?"

He sighed. "I can hardly blame the man for getting you off to himself. It's what I want to do every time I see you."

"You're being awfully noble about it!"

"Aren't I, though? Come home with me, Leya, and let me make love to you the way I've been aching to do since we first met!" he pleaded roughly, his lips in her hair and his hands moving tantalizingly along her back. "I want you so much, my little shrew!"

"Am I really a shrew, Court?" she asked, her body already responding to the need she could feel emanating from him.

"You can be anything you want to be," he told her magnanimously, "as long as you wear those emeralds in your ears!"

She could practically taste the lazy male triumph in him. Leya had told him everything he wanted to know by wearing the earrings. But all she knew about his side of things was that he wanted her. Wanted her badly enough to marry her.

Well, it would have to be enough, she told herself stoutly. She trusted him. Completely. He would not talk of marriage unless he was fully prepared to commit himself. Love would come in time, she vowed with the full depths of her willpower. She would *make* it happen!

"Where are we going?" she asked as he firmly disentangled himself and turned the key in the ignition.

"I told you. Someplace where we can celebrate our engagement!" His gaze glittered through the surrounding darkness, reaching out to touch her in an almost physical way. Leya shivered in reaction, aware of the weakness assailing her limbs.

"My house?" she managed after a few minutes as she recognized the route.

"It's that stairway," he grinned, much pleased with himself. "So romantic."

"Court!" She flushed, the laughter somehow seeming appropriate mixed with the passion. It seemed right.

But she found little else to say as he parked the car in

her drive, helped her out, and took the key from her hand. A moment later, she stepped through the door and turned to find him closing it behind them with a final-sounding clunk.

They stared at each other in silence, drinking in the need and desire that was fully mirrored in each other's eyes. The tension wafted around them, coiling tighter and tighter as the curious silence continued.

It was Leya who made the first tiny move to break it. Wide-eyed, she put her fingertips on the slubbed silk of his tie. An instant later, she was in his arms.

"Leya, my darling Leya! I've wanted you so badly!"

She speared her fingers through the brown and gold of his hair, luxuriating in the thickness of it as he crushed her close. His arms were under her hair, which swung loosely down her back, and she could sense the rising desire in his hard frame.

The essence of him filled her nostrils, tempted and warmed her on a primitive, very fundamental level. Once again, she touched the knot of his tie and slowly began undoing it.

"You used to talk in terms of golden chains," she reminded him throatily, her lips parting sensually as she worked gently on the tie.

"One of us will be on a chain by morning," he grated. "I'm no longer sure yet who will be chaining whom!"

"Does it matter?" she teased, pulling wantonly at the end of the tie and slipping it from around his neck.

"I'm past caring at the moment," he confided.

He bent, sweeping her into his arms, his eyes going to the swing of her hair as she was lifted high against his chest. And then he was striding toward the stairs, taking them steadily, purposefully.

As he climbed, Leya toyed with the buttons of his shirt, her eyes full of dreams and unspoken love. At the top of the stairs, Court turned toward her room and a moment later she was dumped lightly onto the bed.

"This is the way it should have been that night up in Oregon," he rasped, as he came down beside her, his solid weight sending waves of shimmering excitement throughout her body.

Her lashes drooped mysteriously, moving against her cheekbones with a pagan, inviting flutter that was as instinctive as it was unconscious.

"Tell me, Leya," he begged, his lips hovering over hers. She could feel the barely restrained desire in him and wondered at it. "It should be easy to give me the words now. Tell me there will be no more revenge!"

"I trust you, Court," she admitted, knowing what he wanted to hear and knowing, too, that she could tell him nothing less than the truth now. "It was myself I wasn't trusting. I didn't want to acknowledge I was so weak where you're concerned..."

"Damn it, Leya," he gritted. "If you're going to tell me that what you feel toward me is the same weakness you felt for Alex Harlow..."

"No!" she interrupted gently, her eyes shining. "That's not it at all, Court. Alex used me. I could never have forgiven that in a million years. But I believe now that your deception was only another Court Tremayne attempt to short-circuit the usual methods and get to the heart of the matter. I believe you're telling me the truth when you say you wanted me from the beginning."

"I did, I do! God, how I've wanted you!"

He was raining short, feathery kisses on her temple, her eyelids and the emeralds in her ears. "I must have you tonight. I can't wait any longer!"

"Yes, Court," she whispered softly, lovingly as her hands slid beneath his shirt and began to knead the hard flesh she found there.

She felt his fingers on her zipper and then the emerald-green dress was tugged off with a swift, impatient movement. The coolness of the room touched her skin briefly as Court levered himself up to skim off his shirt and slacks. Unself-consciously naked beside her, he began removing the rest of her few garments more slowly, lingering to touch his lips to each new area exposed.

She trembled as he slid his fingers under the elastic edge of her brightly colored briefs, but it wasn't from the coolness of the room, it was from the rising heat in her loins. He felt her reaction and leaned over to first kiss and then gently nip her shoulder. A moment later, he had slid the briefs down to her ankles and she was as nude as he.

"I'm going to make love to you tonight until you can no longer even remember my stupid deception in Oregon," he swore. "Until you can't think of anything else except our future!"

She shivered at the urgency in his words and in his body. She wanted to tell him it was unnecessary to atone for the past, but knew it would have to be done with her physical response, not words. Now, finally, was not the time for words.

His hardness impinged on her softness as he pressed himself against her hips. He was seeking to be enveloped by her in the way men have always sought with the women they needed.

"Oh, Court!"

Her head twisted on the quilt as she pulled him closer. Her toes clenched and unclenched against the soft material beneath her feet.

He gave an inarticulate groan as his hand sought the dampening, fiery heart of her desire, testing and probing. His touch made her gasp and one knee lifted in an agony of physical suspense.

"Leya, my wonderful Leya," he husked against her breast as first his lips and then his teeth circled each nipple.

Leya could say nothing more for a moment, reveling in the voluptuousness of the experience. Court's flame-igniting mouth traced delicate patterns on the hardened peaks of her breasts for a short time longer and then plunged to the soft alley between them. His fingers were arousing her to unbelievable heights, causing her hips to arch upward against his hand in delirious abandon.

"I want you, sweetheart," he gasped, his legs moving against hers, probing between her knees until she welcomed him.

"Ah!"

Her cry was soft, pleading, seductive. As if goaded by it and the small, quick breaths that betrayed her heightened desire, Court lifted himself, looming over her briefly before settling into the warm place he had made between her legs.

His body surged against hers, yet he held off from the final culmination of the embrace.

Instead, he used the intimate position to arouse her still further with threatening, teasing, unbearably exciting little movements that nearly drove her wild.

"Please, Court!" she begged, twisting to sink her nails into the hard muscles of his buttocks in an attempt to draw him closer and closer. His legs were tantalizingly rough against the smoothness of her inner thighs.

As if he was finding the softness of her as entrancing as she found his own hardness, Court reached down to stroke her from thigh to knee.

"Like silk," he blazed. "Hot silk."

Her nails in his hips dug deeper as he found the pulse in her throat with his lips but still he refrained from taking her completely. She delighted in the groan of response her small punishment brought forth from deep in his chest.

"Do you think you can control me in this because you know how much I want you?" he rasped.

She opened her eyes to find his half laughing, half challenging, wholly inflamed gaze eating her.

"Show me how much you want me!" she commanded softly, her lashes lowering in heavy, feminine invitation.

Without warning, his fingers closed around the curve

of her hip and she felt his nails lightly scoring the soft skin there.

"Oh!"

The cry was a small shriek of pain and pleasure as the exciting, erotic caress electrified her. With all her strength, she moved against him, feeling the crispness of his hair against her breasts. Her fingers raked the length of his ribs, pleading, cajoling, commanding.

"Leya! My maddening, passionate, irresistible Leya!"

He buried his mouth in the softness of her throat. Simultaneously, he gently seized her wrists, anchoring them on either side of her shoulders. Then, with the power and mastery that seemed an intrinsic part of him, he used his strength to hold her arching body still for a crucial instant.

"Court!"

His name was a broken sob of passion and need torn from her parted lips as he asserted himself against her and, at the same instant, surrendered to her.

There was a sharp sound of raw demand from him as he surged into a driving rhythm that carried her along in the way that a storm over the sea sweeps across the waves. All of Leya's senses were alive in that timeless moment.

As the storm they had created raged, Leya's hands scored the skin of Court's back in passionate intensity. It was an intensity she knew she would never feel with any other man, and it communicated itself to him. Her nails slid lower, digging into the strong thighs above her own and the tiny, sharp caresses she inflicted seemed to push him beyond all control. His mouth closed hotly on hers as if seeking to swallow the faint, choked moans that issued from far back in her throat.

Leya clung to him, having no other alternative but to let herself be absorbed by the intense claim he was making on her body. She felt him push to the depths of her femininity, taking everything as if he had a right to her. A right that didn't hinge on the trappings of engagements or wedding licenses but was somehow far more fundamental and savage.

She felt at once tamed and untamed, as if the man who was putting his brand on her sought not to restrain her but to chain her in such a way that her wildness would be released only by him.

Frantically, the love battle between them leaped forward to its ultimate conclusion, roiling both in its waves until neither could have escaped. But neither wanted to escape, and when the end came they reached for it with all the physical strength and mental will of two strong, healthy bodies and minds.

The deep, hoarse cries of mutual exultation would have left a listener wondering who had surrendered to whom. But in the depths of the huge brass bed, the participants in the small war were unconcerned.

Chapter 12

The remainder of the week passed in a confusion of plans, hastily contrived parties given by delighted friends and early conclusions to everything.

It was the early conclusions to the evenings that were making her a nervous wreck, Leya decided analytically on the morning of her marriage as she dressed in the wool suit she had bought for the ceremony. For a man like Court Tremayne, it just didn't seem natural. He was the kind who would have taken advantage of the availability of a fiancée. She would have bet money on it. So why had she spent every night of the past week alone in her bed?

His restraint was making her far more nervous than anything else could have done, she realized sadly. And underneath the bridal jitters lay her own sense of guilt.

It was she who had asked for marriage. She felt as if she'd tricked him into this final commitment. Leya remembered the brief shock she'd seen in his face the night she'd made her demand at Keith's party. Nervously, she bit her lip as she automatically went about dressing.

Would he convince himself at the last minute that he didn't have to honor such an extreme demand? she wondered. Visions of being left at the altar crashed through her brain for the hundredth time. If he'd really wanted marriage, why hadn't he taken advantage of her surrender? Why had he held his passion in check since that fateful night of the party?

She shouldn't have pushed him into marrying her, she thought abstractedly. She shouldn't have taken him up on his offer to let her make any request she wanted in exchange for her own commitment.

The waves of guilt and nerves ebbed and flowed around her as she hurried through the last of the morning ritual. What if he simply didn't show up at the church? Could she really blame him if he decided she didn't have the right to this much? Why had she pushed him? Whatever had possessed her? But she'd asked for the one thing she wanted. Or thought she wanted.

Leya shook her head wistfully. It was like being granted a magic wish and making it too hastily. Only in retrospect was it clear she'd asked for the wrong thing. She should have begged for his love. Not marriage. What was marriage without a guarantee of love?

Well, there was nothing left but to carry on now, Leya told herself bracingly as she surveyed the demure skirt and short jacket of her outfit in the mirror. The suit was of a decidedly neutral color, perfect for a wedding that was to be held in the minister's office with only a few witnesses, or so Leya had thought when she chose it. Now, as she looked at the abnormally pale color of the garment, she realized she had wasted her money on something she would never again wear. The lack of assertiveness in the color annoyed her. It didn't attract any of her senses, and the result was irritating. Still, one could hardly wear flaming red to one's own wedding!

The long length of dark braid had been twisted into a formal knot at the nape of her neck and the only note of color obvious in the mirror was that of the emerald earrings and her silver-green eyes. Leya hesitated over her jewelry box and then decided against adding anything else to her attire. She looked exactly as she felt: not quite herself. So be it.

The knocking on the door downstairs pulled her out of her reverie and, pausing to slide her stockinged feet into a cream-colored pair of heels, Leya headed for the stairs.

"Leya! You look beautiful!" Cynthia announced appreciatively, stepping inside and surveying her boss affectionately.

"Why do people always say that to brides?" Leya grumbled, not feeling beautiful at all.

"Because it's the truth. Brides always look beautiful!" Cynthia grinned, following Leya into the living room.

"You really think I look okay?" Leya's voice held a good portion of the skepticism she was feeling as she searched for her purse.

"Have I ever lied to you?" Cynthia demanded.

"Yes! The day you told me it wouldn't hurt to have my ears pierced!"

"I never came straight out and said it wouldn't hurt! You should have had a clue when I poured two glasses of wine down your throat before taking you over to the department store!" Cynthia retorted righteously.

In spite of her precarious mood, Leya laughed, "And by the time I found out it wasn't completely painless, it was too late to quit. One ear had already been done!"

"It was worth it. The earrings are fabulous." Cynthia located Leya's purse in the corner of the couch. "Ready?"

"As ready as I'll ever be, I suppose. God! I wish my stomach weren't so nervous!"

"Court's is probably just as bad," Cynthia assured her, ushering Leya out the door. "Where's your suitcase?"

"Good grief! I almost forgot it!" Leya flew up the stairs to collect the luggage Court had instructed her to bring to the church.

"Still no clue on where you're going for the honeymoon?" Cynthia asked when she'd traipsed back down the stairs.

"No," Leya said, smiling privately. "But I think I can guess. I expect it will be a beach somewhere." Assuming there *was* a honeymoon!

"I like him, Leya. I have from the first. He's the kind of man who will take care of his woman." Cynthia's voice softened and Leya glanced at her wryly.

"I always thought I took pretty good care of myself," Leya mumbled, secretly pleased at her friend's approval.

"It will be good for you to have a man around this big house," Cynthia said diplomatically as they went down the steps to her car.

"Fine words from a woman who's been keeping poor Mark dangling for months," Leya chided.

"You'll be dancing at my wedding one of these days, never fear!"

The closer they got to the church the more grateful Leya was that Cynthia had volunteered to drive her there. She really was out of whack emotionally today, she decided, taking a grip on her reeling thoughts. But, dear God! What would she do if Court didn't show?

And then, quite suddenly, there he was waiting beside her brother on the steps. Leya sucked in her breath and wondered at her own fears. Of course, Court wouldn't stand her up. He had given her his word, hadn't he? What had she expected? She could *trust* him! She took a grip on her emotions as Cynthia parked the car. She would make it up to Court, she vowed silently. She would teach him to love her as much as she loved him.

The queasy feeling in her stomach died. This was what she wanted. She yearned to marry this man regardless of the risks. She would never have run the same risk with Alex Harlow, her instincts said. But with Court, it would be worth it. She would see to it that he wouldn't regret being forced into this.

For the first time in a week, Leya managed a serene, confident smile. One of her normal smiles, she realized. She was feeling a little more normal, a little more sure of herself at last. It was only as she reflected on her personal turmoil since meeting Court that it became clear how far she had strayed from the routine of her rational thought processes.

"I almost didn't recognize you," Court teased in a whisper as he reached her and took her hand in his.

"You expected me to wear orange or red?" She grinned.

"One never knows with you." He looked as if he liked it that way.

The wedding passed in a solemn blur. Leya repeated her vows in a soft, firm tone and listened as Court did the same. The large hand wrapped around hers was steady and solid feeling but his kiss at the end of the short ceremony was curiously remote.

But there was no time to analyze his brief, restrained embrace. As soon as the minister finished, Keith and Cynthia were crowding around to congratulate the new couple.

"I have to hand it to you, Leya." Keith grinned, hugging her. "You picked a damn good way of ensuring that Court doesn't go to work for a rival firm two years from now. Regardless of what he does when his contract is up, he'll have to keep in mind the bonds of family loyalty!"

"Don't give your sister the credit for this wedding," Court complained good-humoredly. "I worked my fingers to the bone getting her to the altar!"

"Poor dear, you must be exhausted!" Leya mocked, aware of the heat in her face.

"I am. I intend to spend a good portion of the next few days in bed, recovering!"

"Court!" The heat in Leya's cheeks went up several degrees.

"You'd better get me out of here before I say something I shouldn't," he instructed pleasantly. Already he was leading her down the steps of the church as Cynthia, Keith and the minister trailed behind. "We'll be back first part of next week."

"Where are you going?" Cynthia demanded as Court handed his bride into the front seat of his car and checked to make sure the suitcase was in the trunk.

"For a nice leisurely drive up the coast, and then a nice leisurely couple of days at an inn I know in Oregon!" Court announced cheerfully. "Think you two can hold things together while we're gone?"

"For every day you spend on this honeymoon, I'm tacking on an extra day to the period of your contract," Keith warned.

"As far as I'm concerned," Cynthia declared, "you can stay away as long as you like. At this rate, I'm going to have the last of my school expenses paid well in advance!"

"What a pair of mercenaries!" Leya grinned as she turned to wave at her brother and her friend.

"Just old-fashioned businessfolk," Court told her as he pulled away from the curb.

"Court?"

"Umm?"

"Are we really going back to that inn in Oregon?"

"Yes."

She eyed his profile. "I have no objections. I mean, you know I love that coastline along there. But why that particular place?"

"Can't you guess?" he asked softly, flicking a short glance across the seat.

She hesitated. "We're going to start over? Go back to the beginning?"

"Not quite. I'm not that patient," he laughed.

The drive was comfortable and leisurely most of the way, although they ran into a lot of rain at several points en route. Court handled the bad weather with calm sureness, and by the time they had reached the isolated inn, it was almost sunset.

"If we hurry we can make it down to the beach to watch the sun disappear," he told her encouragingly as they checked into their room.

Ten minutes later, they had both changed into jeans and were wearing warm jackets for the small venture. Leya found herself inexplicably keyed up, as if now that the crisis of the wedding itself was past, some of her nervousness was returning. Firmly, she put the reaction aside, twining her fingers with Court's as he led her down the path to the rocky beach.

Surprisingly, they walked in silence for a time, allowing themselves to unwind. The winter sun sank quickly, though, and when it did the chill in the air increased rapidly.

Still they walked, and Leya let the elemental surroundings soothe her jangled but receptive senses. It was good to be back here with Court at her side.

And then, just as she fully relaxed and let herself absorb the pleasure of the moment, Court spoke, his voice a dark thread of sound in the evening shadows.

"What's wrong, Leya?" he asked carefully.

She lifted her head, startled at his perception. "Wrong?"

He gripped her hand in a small movement of impatience. "I know there's something bothering you. Don't deny it. I've told you before, we're very much alike. That means there's not much point in trying to hide things from each other. Tell me, please."

He stopped, turning to face her, his features an unexpectedly anguished mask. "What is it, Leya? Are you sorry you made the request that you did? Are you regretting our marriage already?"

She stood quietly under the weight of his hands on her shoulders and forced herself to tell him the truth. He was right. There could be only truth between them now.

"No," she whispered honestly. "I'm not regretting the marriage. But I think...I think I asked for the wrong thing..."

"The wrong thing!"

She nodded sadly. Tenderly, tremulously, her eyes full of love, she touched his cheek. "I should have asked for something much more important. Someday... someday, I will."

His fingers sank into her shoulders. "What's more important?" he bit out. "What do you wish you'd asked for?"

"Your love," she replied simply. "Someday, when you're ready, I will ask you for your love. Will you be able to give me that, Court?"

"My love!" The words were an explosion of sound between them. His eyes glittered in the darkness. "My love! Leya, you crazy little fool! I've loved you since that first weekend! You must have known that! Why else would I have given you the earrings?"

"Oh, Court," she breathed, her heart singing. "Why do you think I wore them? I love you, too. I think I have from the beginning." Her silver-green eyes gleamed in the fading light as she met his gaze. She made to move closer against him and was surprised when he held her away, his eyes searching her face anxiously.

"You love me?" he grated.

"Yes, Court."

"But you didn't think I loved you?" he persisted, as if unable to believe such stupidity.

"You never told me," she pointed out kindly, smiling. "All I knew for certain was that you wanted me."

"And on the basis of that, you were willing to risk marriage?"

"Or anything else you asked of me," she confessed.

He pulled her close then, warming her with his own body heat, his arms closed tightly around her. "Oh, Leya, Leya, I can't believe it. *I* was the one who was prepared to wait for your love. I was going to capitalize on the fact that you wanted me and then, finally, trusted me. I figured that sooner or later you'd see that what we have is something special, something precious. I thought that eventually you would respond to my love…" He hesitated, and then Leya heard the softly muttered oath.

"Damn!"

"Court!" she protested. "What's wrong?"

"I'm thinking of the time we wasted!"

She gave a little gurgle of laughter. "I hadn't noticed! It wasn't very long ago that we were standing exactly where we're standing now. I don't think you can honestly say that a great deal of time has been wasted!"

"Yes," he contradicted feelingly, "it has. We could have been married that first week!"

"Oh, Court," she whispered. "I'm sorry about all the misunderstandings. But for a time I couldn't think straight. I was so afraid..."

"Afraid that I saw you as some sort of conquest? It was never that way, Leya my love. Never! I am capable of getting my own way without going to such lengths as seducing the sister of the firm's owner!" He sounded mildly indignant.

"Yes, Court," she agreed meekly.

"I think I fell in love with you when I saw the way you laughed at me in that picture in Keith's office," he went on judiciously. "But I knew it for certain when I tracked you down to this inn and realized you were the only woman in the world I wanted to have with me when I went for a walk on the beach. I love you, darling Leya. Every inch of you from your sassy little tongue to your incredible response to me in bed. I'm going to love you for the rest of my life. We're so much alike, you and I."

"I suppose that was part of the problem."

"I kept telling you it was," he chuckled. "I knew you had to work your anger out of your system. If I'd been in your shoes, I'd have had to do the same. I thought I had it made the night you revenged yourself on Alex Harlow. If only your brother hadn't made his untimely entrance on the terrace!"

"I was angrier than ever at the thought of having been so weak as to nearly let you talk me into starting over. But I wanted to start again, Court. I wanted it with all my heart. If my brother hadn't shown up when he did, I wouldn't have been able to resist! But it was myself I was angry with, darling. I realized that finally. And it was myself I was hurting by not giving up the battle sooner."

"You're wrong there! I was the one who was hurt!" He groaned ruefully, squeezing her tightly against him. "I was so sure in the beginning that it was going to be easy to slide you neatly, simply into my bed after what we'd discovered here in Oregon. I knew you'd be angry when you found out about the deception, but I figured that if we'd made love by then, your anger couldn't last. I was a fool. I went about it all wrong!"

"Poor Court," she teased softly, lovingly. "You kept trying to short-cut things and I kept making it difficult!"

"I'm glad you appreciate what a little obstructionist you were!" he teased.

"Oh, I do. But it's probably been a good experience for you. Something tells me you've had everything far too much your own way in life!"

"No," he said with great certainty. "Until now I've never had the one thing a man really needs."

"What's that?"

"A woman who can't be bought. A woman who loves him in spite of his inability to handle her properly. A woman who trusts him enough to marry him, not even knowing for certain that he loves her."

"You didn't know for certain that I loved you," she noted gently. "Yet you were willing to marry me, anyway, and hope."

He sighed contentedly. "Like I said. We're a lot alike."

"I don't know about that," she protested laughingly. "You haven't behaved at all as I rather expected you to behave this past week. Somehow, I saw you as the type who would have moved right in with or without a ring."

His grin was a slash of white in the darkness. "The night I returned from San Jose and found you wearing those earrings, nothing could have kept me out of your bed. But after that I told myself that I had done enough short-cutting. It was time I gave you a proper courtship."

She heard the pride at his own self-denial in his voice and chuckled. "A whole week of it," she murmured with blatantly false admiration.

"Stop making fun of me! You'll never know what it cost to try and do things right for a change!"

"Yes, Court," she said sweetly.

"But that's all behind us now," he continued with vast complacency. "Now we can lapse into the quiet, humdrum routine of the average married couple."

"You sound as if that has great appeal."

"It does. It seems to me I've been running around without much rest since the first day I learned your name!"

"Such exertion! But it hasn't been exactly easy on me, either!"

"We'll both appreciate the peace and quiet from now on."

His hands moved along the back of her jacket, settling on the curve of her hips and forcing her into gentle contact with his hard thighs.

"Come with me, my dearly beloved wife, and let's get dinner and some peace and quiet."

He threw an arm tightly around her shoulders, curving her against his side, and they started back toward the lights of the inn.

"Court?"

"What, honey?"

"Really love me?"

"With all my heart. Do you really love me?"

"With all my heart," she echoed blissfully.

Dinner came and went in a haze of candlelight and music, sparkling silver and linen, but Leya couldn't remember later what she'd eaten. She remembered only the pleasure of being able to look across the table and let herself sink into the depths of a pair of gold-flecked eyes that watched her with a yearning hunger.

"The next step, following tradition," Court observed in a husky voice as he led her away from the table, "is to take you into that glass-walled room facing the ocean, find that little private alcove and let you seduce me. There's just one problem."

"What's that?" She smiled invitingly. "You don't think I can handle it?"

"I think that we might not make it back up the stairs this

time. You are filling my head and my senses like brandy this evening, sweet wife."

"It can't be much different from the effect you're having on me," she told him softly, aware of the fine tremor that went through him as he took her arm and headed toward the stairs.

At the door of their room, Leya suddenly smiled.

"What are you laughing at?" he asked indulgently, letting them inside the elegantly rustic bedroom.

"The fact that you got out of carrying me up that flight of stairs. Aren't you grateful? On the other hand, it would have kept you in practice…"

He shut the door and turned her into his arms, eyes all golden and warm.

"I would have carried you up a mountain if it had been necessary!"

"Greater love hath no man…"

"I'm glad you appreciate it. There was a time when I despaired of making you believe in my basically good intentions!"

"Did you ever really doubt me?" she teased.

"You had me quite terrified there for a while! Oh, Leya, I adore you!" His mouth covered hers in a kiss of curiously gentle passion. "I thought you were going to drive me crazy!" His hands undressed her lovingly.

"A woman likes to be sure," she murmured seductively, finding herself naked in his hands. Her words were a deliberate reminder of one of their first discussions.

"I was sure from the beginning. I don't know what took

you so long!" He smiled, lifting her into his arms and settling her gently between the sheets. And then he was sliding in beside her, warm, with a shocking power that immediately inundated her already awash senses.

"Oh, Court," she moaned, going into his arms with an eagerness that seemed to please him enormously. "Love me, please, love me!"

His fingers traced the line of her spine in a sensuous movement that made her arch like a cat. She shifted her legs unconsciously and then felt her ankle tucked beneath his foot as if he would hold her still. The small chaining sent a marvelously erotic shot of electricity out to her fingertips.

She felt him draw her close, so that the softness of her breasts was gently crushed against the rough maleness of his chest and the passion between them flowed back and forth, making first one and then the other the aggressor. Leya experienced the joy of being lovingly seduced by her husband and then the equally pleasurable thrill of seducing him. The constant trade-off carried an increasing emotional charge that intensified with each turn.

When Court's hands stroked the length of her inner thigh, Leya trembled, and he pulled her sprawling across his chest, her dark hair swirling against his skin. She held his face, showering tiny, desperate little kisses on his gold-and-brown hair, his eyelids and the tips of his ears.

"You're a temptress," he growled, his hands fingering her waist and finding the line of her ribs.

"It's your fault for tempting me first," she husked, her lips on his strong throat.

"Always arguing," he groaned hoarsely. "Even in bed!"

She felt the humor combined with the desire in him and knew that it would always be thus with them, a unique and loving blend that neither would ever want to lose.

"But a man has to exert himself on occasion," he continued on a note of seductive menace, pushing her flat on the bed and lowering himself gently, completely into her welcoming embrace. "And I want you so much, sweet Leya."

His desire could be no greater than her own, she thought dizzily, and was on the verge of telling him so, when his body claimed hers with a thorough mastery that made it impossible to speak. She told him with her response, giving all of herself and receiving everything of him in return.

The pattern of their lovemaking soared, making them one with the night storm that was rolling in off the ocean. The pounding of the rain against the window was in tune with the pounding of their blood, and the force of the gale set the primitive rhythm of their bodies.

And then, with a fierce cry that was muffled by the silky skin of her breast, Court reached down to clasp her hips, drawing her emphatically closer, losing himself in her softness as the end of their inner storm approached.

Leya's fingers clutched at the hard, muscled power of his back, and with a sobbing cry she surrendered to the impact of the tempest. She felt him being pulled into the vortex with her, and together they clung, riding out the winds.

Some time later, Court palmed the pink tip of Leya's gently curving breast and smiled down into her contented, gleaming eyes. He was propped on his elbow, his legs tangled with hers.

"Happy, Mrs. Tremayne?"

"Deliriously so, Mr. Tremayne."

"You're such an untamed little thing in bed," he laughed delightedly. "Do you realize that?"

"You don't mind the exercise?"

"Now what do you think?" He grinned.

"I think," Leya said laughingly, "that we're both much more energetic than we gave ourselves credit for!"

"You could be right. Personally," he drawled deeply, "I'm not too concerned about it now that I know the chain is in place!"

"What happened to all that humility down on the beach?" she demanded, running her fingers through his ruffled hair and smiling up at him with teasing green eyes. "You're starting to talk about golden chains again. Is the old Court resurfacing?"

"I know now that you love me and I love you. That does give me a certain amount of confidence," he said blandly.

"Egotist!"

"But look at the bright side," he urged helpfully. "You've got the same set of facts in your possession. And I always did think you were a reasonably bright girl."

"Meaning?"

"Meaning you were the one who once told me chains work both ways. Whoever holds the links is as much a captive as the one on the other end."

"I won't ask you which of us is on which end," Leya said

diplomatically. "Just promise me you won't let go of your end and I'll promise to hang on to mine!"

"It's a deal."

He bent his head and sealed the bargain with a kiss.

★ ★ ★ ★ ★

RECKLESS PASSION

For my husband, Frank, with all my love.

Chapter 1

"Exactly how far can I expect the seduction to go?" Yale Ransom inquired interestedly in his pleasant Southern drawl.

Dara Bancroft froze momentarily in the act of letting him assist her into the chic suede and leather coat. Some of the inexplicable warmth she had been experiencing all evening faded.

"Seduction?" she repeated carefully, her gently rounded chin lifting in a wary gesture. "I don't know what you're talking about. If that's the reason you think I've agreed to leave the party with you…"

"Don't take offense, honey," he soothed at once, his strong hands sliding the coat into place on her shoulders. The hands didn't look at all like an accountant's hands, Dara realized. Poor man. He tried so hard, but little things kept giving him away.

"I'm more than willing to be seduced," he went on easily, holding the door open and ushering her out into the chilly spring night. "After all, I'm in the market for a stockbroker, and your manager has made it clear Edison, Stanford and Zane would like my account."

"Mr. Ransom," Dara began firmly, hesitating on the top step as he took her arm. "I'm not sure how business is transacted down in Los Angeles, but here in Oregon we don't do things that way!"

"What a shame," he murmured, politely regretful. "And it can be such a pleasure, too."

Dara's expressive mouth curved into a knowing smile. "Careful, Yale. Your Southern-gentleman facade is slipping."

He grimaced wryly. "Already? And I try so hard."

"I know you do." Dara chuckled, yielding to the pressure of his hand and descending the steps toward a gray Alfa Romeo which waited on the street in front of the house. "But you don't have to pretend with me, Yale."

He shot her a slanting, hazel-eyed look as they walked toward the car, the dark horn rims of his glasses, not concealing the speculative expression in his gaze. "You know me so well? After only a couple of hours?"

"We stockbrokers are trained to analyze situations quickly," Dara responded with a satisfied smile.

"And in that short span of time you've decided I'm not the Southern-gentleman type, is that it?" he invited, settling her into the car.

"Oh, you've done a good job with the role and you've tried to create a proper, conservative accountant's image, but..."

"But?" he prompted, sliding onto the seat beside her and closing the door. It made that nice, solid sound that expensive car doors make.

"But I think you've been a lot of things in your life besides an accountant with a Southern accent!" she told him recklessly, unable to stifle the pleasant, heady rush which was swirling through her veins.

The sensation had taken her by storm almost two hours ago when she'd held out her hand for the conventional introduction her manager was making. Dara had smiled up into a pair of intelligent, interested hazel eyes and wondered what sort of expression she would see behind the lenses of his glasses when that deliberately neutral look was banished.

And then Yale Ransom had smiled back, a wide, faintly dangerous grin that must have been a reaction to her own challenging gray-green gaze. The flash from a gold-capped tooth added an astonishingly sharklike touch to Yale's raffish expression, and the strength of his grip on her hand told Dara a great deal more about the stranger.

He hadn't stayed a stranger for long. Almost instantly they had become paired off, with, Dara knew, the blessings of her manager, who was giving the party. But Dara didn't care if she was being used to attract Yale Ransom's account. She had other, more personal interests in the matter.

There was something about this man, she thought a little dazedly as Yale pulled away from the curb and drove down the quiet neighborhood streets of Eugene, Oregon. Something which pulled at her senses. Something had clicked between them.

On the surface, there was no logical explanation for her having singled him out of a roomful of people. He was exactly what he purported to be. Almost too much so, she decided, mentally casting about for what set him apart.

Perhaps that was the answer. Yale Ransom took great pains to conform to the image that was expected of him. The dark, amber honey of his hair was trimmed in a close, conservative style that went perfectly with the equally conservative horn-rimmed glasses. Folks here in the Willamette Valley of Oregon weren't inclined to be trendy, but even in this conservative atmosphere Yale Ransom's dark jacket, slacks and subdued tie could be considered sober attire.

The crisp white of his shirt collar contrasted with the deep tan of a ruggedly carved face that had crinkles at the eyes and a certain implacability around the mouth. He must have been around thirty-seven or thirty-eight, Dara thought fleetingly, eyeing his firm profile as they drove. The years showed.

Yes, everything about him said conservative, quiet, studied, trustworthy, professional, she thought in amusement. Even the faint Southern accent added a nice touch of the old-fashioned gentleman. She wondered if the drawl was a calculated addition to the overall image. Perhaps it was designed to give the impression of a man who still held such virtues as honor in high esteem.

Because if this man had been raised amid magnolia blossoms, genteel poverty or moneyed aristocracy, Dara would cheerfully eat her leather and suede coat.

The hardness about this man belied the image of a quiet gentleman. It was everywhere in him, from the harshly carved features of a face that had never been handsome to the six feet of smoothly muscled, hard male body. The conservative jacket and slacks did not hide the lean power underneath, at least not from Dara's eyes. And the lenses of his glasses couldn't conceal the perceptive, yet withdrawn expression of Yale's hard gaze.

Given her own analysis, Dara told herself she ought to be wary of the man. He wasn't her type, and at the age of thirty, she thought she ought to know exactly what sort of man wasn't her type! But when he'd smiled at her, that exciting, daring grin with the flash of buccaneering gold, his carefully contrived image had shattered.

After that, everything about him had intrigued her. The strong hands, the hazel eyes, the contrast between the look he was trying to project and what she felt was the real man—it all added up to a fascinating puzzle.

"Where are we going?" she asked presently, not overly concerned. They were driving past the two-hundred-and-fifty-acre campus of the University of Oregon located in the eastern part of town.

"Does it matter?" Yale asked politely, his attention on his driving.

"Yes, I think so," Dara told him, considering the issue with a delicate frown. "I'm not ready to go home with you now, Yale."

"I see," he murmured after a moment, slowing the car and guiding it to a halt at the curb. With an efficient, decisive movement he switched off the engine and turned to look at her in the pale light of an overhead streetlamp.

"Implying that you will be ready to go home with me

later?" he went on casually, hazel eyes flickering over her figure.

Dara's smile was slow and gently condescending. "I keep telling you, Yale, we don't do things that quickly here in Eugene. I left the party with you because you suggested we might go to a nightclub and have a drink and a few dances. Don't tell me you don't dance," she added, eyes glinting in the dim light. "Anyone who's worked on the image as much as you have must have learned to dance somewhere along the line!"

His answering smile spoke volumes. "I can manage. Where would you like to go? As you keep reminding me, I'm new here in town. I don't know all the places yet." He waited, deliberately putting the responsibility on her.

"There aren't that many of them," Dara said dryly. "Eugene is only a town of about a hundred thousand. But we get along. Let me see…" Idly she chewed a full lower lip and thought about it for a moment. Yale didn't move, his eyes centered on her face. There was a quiet patience about him that amused her. He was so sure he knew how the evening was going to end.

It wouldn't wind up as he assumed it would, of course, she told herself briskly. Dara didn't attempt to deny the strange attraction he held for her, but she knew herself well enough to know she could handle her own emotions.

Until she had unraveled the puzzle that was Yale Ransom, she would be reasonably cautious. What did he think of her? Dara wondered in the back of her mind. He had seemed willing enough to accept the pairing off which had occurred. Of course, he *was* new in town and probably hadn't met a lot of women yet, she assured herself.

She wondered vaguely how she looked to him after his previous two years spent in Los Angeles. Dara was an honest individual. She knew there was a softness about her which more than one male had assumed extended to her brain as well as her body.

She couldn't really blame a man for thinking that, Dara had decided several years earlier. The gently rounded outlines of her five-foot-four-inch body could most graciously be described as full-figured. She was not fat, she assured herself several times a week, but there was no denying the fullness of her high, curving breasts or the rounded outline of her hips.

Her eyes echoed the softness of her body. Wide, faintly slanting and gray-green in color, they were full of laughter and an abiding interest in life. A short nose which turned up slightly at the tip, a mouth designed for smiling and an unaggressive, rounded chin gave her an impish, amused look which somehow managed to conceal the lack of any real beauty.

The burnt russet of her hair was styled in a sleek, center-parted bell which curved over her ears and ended even with the line of her jaw. The entire combination could be termed reasonably attractive, if a little misleading in that it hid a finely honed willpower, but it would never be described as sophisticated, Dara knew. Or even sweetly beautiful. So what did Yale Ransom really think of her? Had he been joking earlier when he'd implied a willingness to be seduced in exchange for his securities account?

"If you can't make up your mind," Yale interrupted softly, "perhaps we ought to continue on to my house. We can enjoy a glass of brandy while you decide where you want to go dancing."

He moved slightly, shifting one large hand on the steering wheel. The small action drew Dara's attention and her eyes focused for a split second on the muscular wrist which extended, she felt certain, from a sinewy forearm. She met his eyes again and he smiled, unwisely revealing the gold tooth which gave him such a feral look. With a suddenness that was typical of her, Dara made up her mind.

"That's all right," she said kindly. "But I've managed to make a decision. Turn left up there at the corner. I'll direct you."

Yale hesitated, tilting his head consideringly. Then, with a shrug, he started the engine again and followed her instructions.

With a concealed grin, Dara guided him through town to an elegantly rustic restaurant and nightclub. The parking lot was full and the Alfa Romeo had to be left on the street.

"You're sure this is where you want to spend the evening?" Yale asked warily as he assisted Dara out of the car.

"It's the latest rage," she told him saucily, smoothing her coat as she stepped from the car. Dara lifted her collar against the night chill and it framed her mischievous smile as she looked up at her escort.

"We're, uh, not exactly dressed for it," Yale observed,

glancing down at his own conservative clothes and then at her. Under the leather and suede coat, Dara was wearing a softly cut, long-sleeved dress of emerald green. It shaped the fullness of her curves with a touch of sophistication which had pleased her when she'd surveyed herself in the mirror earlier.

"I think," she told him politely, "that if you take off your tie and unbutton your jacket, we'll get by. They get all types in here."

"All types but the one they're trying to imitate," Yale remarked, his fingers rising hesitantly to the knot of his tie. He glanced again at the jazzy sign with the neon-lit picture of a sequin-studded cowboy. The latest in country-western music drifted out into the parking lot.

"Well, you wouldn't want the real thing here, would you?" Dara challenged laughingly. "Genuine truckers and cowboys tend to be a bit rough around the edges, I'm told. The ones in designer jeans are easier to handle."

"You think so?" Yale asked, deciding at last not to undo the tie. Apparently he felt more comfortable in it, Dara thought in smiling amusement.

"Don't chicken out on me," Dara warned. "I'll take care of you."

He glanced at her over his shoulder as he closed the car door again. The hazel eyes flashed for an instant behind the lenses of his glasses. "Will you?" he demanded interestedly, taking her arm.

"Oh, yes," she assured him breezily. "I know this isn't

quite your usual style, but I think the experience will be good for you."

"Are you by any chance trying to tell me I'm a little too conservative for your taste?" Yale took her arm in a firm grip.

"I think, perhaps, you're a little too conservative for your own tastes," Dara hazarded.

"I would have thought that, as a stockbroker, you'd appreciate my conventional qualities," he told her dryly.

"Well, you see, I haven't been a stockbroker very long," Dara explained lightly.

"Really? What did you do before you became one?" He sounded genuinely interested, she thought, smiling.

"Remind me to tell you someday."

At the entrance to the disco, which had recently converted to high-gloss country-western, Dara and Yale came to a halt. The crowd of trendy would-be cowboys and their dates filled the room completely. A smoky haze wafted toward the wood-beamed ceiling and through it a bejeweled country-western band could be seen energetically twanging their electric guitars.

"See? I told you. It's a very popular place," Dara pointed out unnecessarily, scanning the room for a vacant table. From the height of five feet four inches she didn't stand a chance of discovering a spot.

"Over there." Above the noise Yale managed to get her attention.

"See something?"

He nodded and made his way through the crowd. He

had been right when he noted they probably weren't dressed for the occasion. The majority of the club's clientele was in designer jeans and pearl-buttoned shirts. Imitation Stetson hats were everywhere, as was imported beer.

"Marvelous going out with a strong male," Dara said in tones of mocking admiration as Yale forged a way to the table and commandeered it.

"We accountants have hidden talents," he told her, helping her off with the coat.

"How hidden?" she demanded immediately, gray-green eyes shining with warm laughter as he took the seat across from her. "That's what I'm trying to find out."

"Then you should have let me take you home instead of stopping off here," he retorted, looking up as a briefly clad cowgirl came to take their order. He requested two bottles of a distinctive English beer without bothering to check Dara's preference. She didn't mind. It was the proper thing to order in this atmosphere.

"Something tells me I shall learn more about you in this environment," Dara informed him blandly.

"You think I belong here?" Yale glanced around dubiously.

"Doesn't it remind you of L.A.?" she asked innocently.

"Nothing is like L.A.!" he declared flatly, a disgusted look crossing the hard features.

"You miss it?"

"Not in the least."

"I believe you said you lived here for two years," Dara noted. "Where were you before that?"

One amber brow climbed slightly as he folded his arms and leaned forward to rest them on the small table. "Am I going to be subjected to an inquisition?"

"I always like to interview my clients extensively before establishing a financial plan for them," Dara said smoothly, eyes glinting.

"As I said, you should have let me take you straight home." He smiled. "I could have given you a much clearer insight into my character."

"Who is supposed to be seducing whom?" Dara's laughing eyes hardened a fraction.

"You're right," Yale said, instantly apologetic. "I'm being much too aggressive, aren't I?"

"I'm afraid you're in for a disappointment," Dara said kindly, sitting back slightly as the English beer arrived. She watched him pay the cocktail waitress and then continued charmingly, "I don't seduce potential clients—physically, that is. I prefer the intellectual approach. Makes for a better long-term working relationship."

"The intellectual approach?" He looked skeptical as he poured the foaming beer into a tall glass. "You're going to wow me with your brilliant market strategy?"

"Something like that. After all, if I bring my taxes to you to prepare I'm going to want some assurance you can at least use a calculator."

"Meaning it wouldn't matter how good I am in bed?" he said wistfully, sipping his beer.

Dara gave him a haughty look, torn between laughter and the need to put him in his place. Already the polite, conservative image was slipping away. She had been right to force him gently out of his adopted element in an effort to discover what lay below the surface, but it suddenly occurred to her that what she uncovered might not be quite so manageable. At least in the guise of conservative accountant, Yale Ransom could be easily dealt with.

"Meaning you ought to have some interest in my ability as a stockbroker!"

"I'll find out soon enough, won't I?" he countered.

"You're going to give Edison, Stanford and Zane your account?" she pressed.

"Probably. This is a small town. It's not as if I had a great deal of choice," he said smoothly.

"True." She grinned wickedly.

"What remains to be seen is whether or not I get you for my personal broker."

"Surely you're not going to tell me that will depend on how agreeable I am tonight?" Dara said loftily, daring him to come right out and proposition her.

As she had expected, Yale backed down from a direct confrontation on the subject. Something flickered and was gone in the hazel eyes, and she nodded to herself, satisfied.

"I didn't think so," she said sweetly. "Now, are you going to dance with me?"

"I already feel rather out of place just sitting here," he complained ruefully, glancing over at the packed dance floor. "I'd feel an absolute idiot out there!"

"Give it a try, Yale. Please?"

"Where did you learn to pout so endearingly?" he inquired wryly.

"I'm not pouting, I'm being persuasive!" Dara snapped, slightly miffed at the comment.

"I beg your pardon," he said quickly, laughter in the hazel eyes. "I didn't mean to imply you were one of those annoying females who gets her way by threatening to sulk."

"Yes, you did, but I'm going to ignore it. I'm too anxious to get you out onto the dance floor."

"Why?" Yale tossed her an unexpectedly stark look which vanished almost immediately.

"Because I like to dance, of course. Why do you think I brought you here?" Dara smiled dazzlingly.

"You wanted to make me feel uncomfortable? Out of my element?" he guessed coolly.

"No!" But there was a trace of guilt behind the word, and Dara was afraid she might not have hidden it with complete success. She did want to jar him a little, watch him react to a situation where he could not hide behind his image. She felt an almost reckless urge to find out what lay behind that conservative, Southern-gentleman exterior.

"You're a little old to be playing games like this, aren't you?" Yale asked after a moment's thought.

"Games! I'm not playing games! You asked me to leave the party with you and then you asked me where I wanted to go dancing. I've been nothing but straightforward about the whole thing!"

He favored her with a narrow stare for a moment and then set down his beer abruptly. "All right. We'll dance."

"Now? But they've just changed to a slow number. I wanted."

"You wanted to dance. I'm offering this one. Take it or leave it."

Dara got to her feet without further argument. "It really is slipping, Yale. I feel in all fairness that I ought to warn you again," she whispered as he led her out onto the wooden floor and took her quite formally in his arms.

"My gentlemanly image?" he hazarded. "It's probably not surprising. You've been provoking me all evening. I wonder why. Did you think that getting my attention like this was the best way to go about getting my account?"

"Is it?" Dara leaned her head against his shoulder, forcing a closer intimacy than he had attempted.

"Beats me," Yale admitted, relaxing his grip and letting his body make contact with hers. "I guess we'll find out, won't we? What's wrong with my image, anyway?" He sounded interested.

"I don't know," Dara told him honestly, a slow smile quirking her mouth as she nestled her head against the expensive material of his jacket and closed her eyes. "Something about it isn't quite real."

"You don't believe I'm really an accountant?"

"Of course I believe you're an accountant! It's not that…"

"Are you sleepy?" he asked suddenly, ignoring her comment.

Gray-green eyes flickered open and she met his slightly frowning look.

"A little. I've had a long day. Stockbrokers get up early,

you know. I'm at the office by seven on weekday mornings. What's the matter? You don't like women falling asleep on your shoulder while you're dancing with them?"

"Not particularly."

"Then you should have danced a fast one with me. That would have perked me up considerably," Dara advised him.

"I'll remember that. In the meantime, try not to drift off completely, will you? I feel idiotic enough out here with all these fake cowboys. Carrying you off the floor isn't going to make me feel any more at home!"

"You sound annoyed," Dara told him, aware of the lean length of him as the dance grew a little more intimate. Strange how her soft curves seemed to fit the hardness of him. Was he responding to her? She couldn't be sure. There was an aloofness to Yale Ransom at the moment. As if he were deliberately trying to put some distance between them.

"Do I? Does that worry you?"

"Nope."

"Maybe it should," he suggested dryly.

"I'm not afraid of losing your account," Dara returned blithely.

"Edison, Stanford and Zane might not appreciate your losing it!"

"Am I in any danger of letting down the firm?" she taunted.

"You haven't got your hands on my money yet," he reminded her with a small smile.

"The evening's young," she teased.

"Perhaps, but you've already admitted you're in danger of falling asleep."

"So keep me awake. Tell me about yourself, Yale Ransom."

"Stop snuggling!" Yale muttered feelingly. "How old are you, anyway?"

"Too old to snuggle, I expect." Dara sighed. "I'm thirty. How old are you?"

"Thirty-seven," he answered shortly, as if his mind were on something else. "You're not married, are you? It would be just my luck to have an irate husband come barging in."

"Relax," she soothed. "I'm not married. Not anymore. Besides, I told you I'd take care of you in here, didn't I? Trust me."

"Not anymore," he repeated thoughtfully. "But you were once."

"Yes."

"What happened?"

"Do you really want to know?" she asked a little distantly.

"Yes," he said with sudden conviction. "I think I do."

"Six months into the marriage my husband realized he'd made a terrible mistake. Unfortunately for me, his ex-fiancée, who had broken off with him to marry another man, made the same discovery at about the same time." Dara shrugged philosophically. "It seemed my husband had been on the rebound when he set about sweeping me off my feet. When both he and his former lover realized they'd made a tragic error, there wasn't anything for them to do except apologize profusely to their respective spouses and ask for divorces."

There was a moment's silence above her head while Yale considered the brief story.

"You sound remarkably understanding," he finally said quietly.

"It all happened a long time ago," she said softly, opening her eyes to study the hard line of his jaw. "I don't think about it much anymore."

"But you haven't remarried, either."

"No. There are other things in life." She smiled. "What about you, Yale? Have you ever been married?"

"Yes."

She waited, and when no further information was forthcoming, Dara tried probing. "A long time ago?"

"Um-hmm."

"Before you became a Southern-gentleman accountant?"

"You are an inquisitive little thing, aren't you?" he charged with a stifled groan. His hold on her tightened, but Dara was inclined to think that it was more in irritation than anything else.

"I like to know my clients," she explained placidly, waiting with a hopeful expression for further details of his past.

"So you keep saying." Yale angled his head downward, the smoky light illuminating the honey-colored, neatly trimmed hair. "Are you sure you want to know so much about me?"

"Are you trying to warn me that I might not like what I discover?" She grinned.

"It's a possibility."

"Try me."

"It's tempting."

"I meant try telling me something about yourself!" Dara snapped tersely, mildly annoyed by his sexual interpretation of her words. Why did men always concentrate on the physical side of a budding relationship? Didn't they realize that there were more important matters between a man and a woman? Matters which should be dealt with before the physical side of things was explored?

"Oh."

She could almost feel him thinking it over and waited impatiently for his decision.

"Perhaps," Yale said slowly, "I ought to show you."

"Show me?" She tipped her head quizzically to one side as the dance drew to a close and they stopped moving.

"Mmm. How badly do you want to know me, Dara Bancroft?" he asked almost whimsically as he led her off the floor. His arm was wrapped rather casually around her waist, but Dara liked the feel of it.

"You make it all sound very mysterious," she countered impishly.

"It's not. It's just that no one's ever been so insistent about it. In fact," he told her with sudden decision, "I don't think anyone's ever even realized..."

"Realized what?" she pressed eagerly.

"Come on, my curious little tabby cat, and I'll show you." He grinned. The flashing gold tooth winked devilishly and Dara felt a small chill slip down her spine. What was she getting into by pushing Yale Ransom like this? One thing was certain. She couldn't stop now. She would spend the rest of her life wondering about him. She knew that much with crystal certainty.

It was unfortunate, though, she told herself wryly as he helped her back into her coat, that he thought of her as only a curious little tabby cat.

Without a word, Yale led her out of the glittering, rhinestone-cowboy nightclub.

Chapter 2

"Are you crazy?" Dara laughed, half appalled as she realized their destination some fifteen minutes later. "That's a roadhouse! A truck stop! The *real* kind."

"Afraid?" Yale asked succinctly, glancing at the parking lot full of trucks, large and small, and cruising on past to a point almost two blocks farther along the street.

"Talk about feeling out of place!" Dara exclaimed, ignoring his question. "What are you trying to prove?"

"I asked you if you were afraid."

She thought about that for a moment. "Well, no, not exactly. Not as long as you're with me, but…"

"I'll take that as a compliment." He grinned, parking the Alfa Romeo and climbing out.

"Why are we parking way down here? There was room in the lot." Dara watched, brow wrinkling in puzzled fashion as Yale slipped off his jacket and tossed it over the seat. His tie went next.

"Because I don't want to take a chance on coming back and finding the car door accidentally kicked in," he explained as if she weren't very bright.

"Accidentally?" she murmured, climbing out of her side

of the car and facing him across the roof. He was unbuttoning the top two buttons on his white shirt and rolling the sleeves.

"Accidents sometimes happen around places like this." Yale grinned.

She watched in growing fascination now as he removed his glasses and tucked them into a case in his shirt pocket. Then he raked a hand carelessly through his amber-shaded hair and the grin broadened. Gold gleamed in the moonlight.

"My God!" Dara breathed, her eyes full of laughter. "If I hadn't seen it with my own eyes I wouldn't have believed it!"

She turned as he walked around the hood of the car and came to stand beside her. Deliberately she ran an eye over him from head to foot.

"I can see that only one of us is going to feel out of place here," she finally groaned, shaking her head at the transformation. "You look like you just stepped off the rodeo circuit!"

"Don't worry about how you look," Yale told her consolingly. "I'll take care of you."

"You'd better! Remember that I didn't let anything terrible happen to you at *my* nightclub!" She slipped off her coat and left it behind.

"Trust me," he instructed, lacing her close to his side with a strangely possessive arm around her shoulders.

Dara shot him a quick glance from under her lashes at the familiarity of the grip but said nothing. In any event, her unspoken question was answered almost as soon as they stepped inside the loud, smoky tavern. Several male heads turned to run frankly sexual gazes over her rounded curves.

Dara felt like a prize palomino being led around an auction ring. This sort of inspection might be common in taverns and nightclubs the world over, but she was accustomed to it being performed in a more subtle manner. The crowd here was not subtle.

But the interested eye always came to a halt when they took in the sight of the sinewy arm anchoring her to Yale's side. After one last, assessing glance at her companion most of the eyes turned back to other subjects, such as the beer on the table or the sultry female lead singer with the band. With a wry grimace, Dara admitted that the possessiveness in Yale's hold was purely for her own protection.

"I suppose there's a point to all this?" she forced herself to say flippantly as Yale found a table and settled her into a chair.

"My bringing you here? You asked for it. Remember that," he went on with a touch of grimness. "Whatever happens tonight, you asked for it!"

Some of her laughter fading, Dara stared at him. "Are you angry with me?"

He stared back for another moment. "I can't decide whether I am or not."

Dara bit her lip, suddenly contrite. Her gray-green eyes widened in genuine apology. "Yale, I'm sorry if I've made you show me something you didn't want to show me about yourself. I never meant—"

"Didn't you?" he asked cryptically, signalling the blond waitress for two beers. American beers, Dara realized vaguely. That was the only sort the bar featured.

"Well, I admit I was curious." She sighed ruefully. "But I still don't understand everything. What's the big mystery? That you're at home in places like this? What did you do for a living before you became an accountant?"

He leaned back in his chair and studied her anxious expression. Dara would have given a great deal to know exactly what he was thinking.

"A lot of things," he finally said evenly, his eyes intent.

"You weren't raised on a charming, picture-book plantation with lots of history and money and the right Southern schools, were you?" Dara risked, her eyes smiling across the table at him. She willed him to respond, but he continued to watch her with that implacable gaze.

"Not quite," he said absently, fishing out cash for the impatient waitress. When she'd left with a fat tip, Yale finally seemed to come to a decision. "I was raised in the Blue Ridge Mountains. Know them?"

"North Carolina? Somewhere around Asheville?" At least he was talking, she thought hopefully.

He nodded.

"So?"

"So—" Yale drew a deep breath as if about to plunge into a cold pool "I've spent a lot of time and effort leaving those damn mountains and all they stood for behind me. I've put a couple of thousand miles between me and them, as well as a college education and a better accent. I've changed almost everything I could change, and over the past several years I've built a very successful image. Then you come along and in the space of a couple of hours tear through all my fine plumage demanding to know the real me."

"I see," Dara whispered, guilt rising now that she began to realize exactly what she'd done. "But I don't understand why you bothered. You could have told me to mind my own business. You didn't have to ask me to leave the party with you. You didn't—"

"I don't know why I did it, myself," Yale said quietly. "Would you like to dance?"

"Yale, I think we ought to talk about this first," Dara began earnestly. "I mean, everyone knows that part of the country has a lot of poverty, but I don't see why you should be so determined to forget you came from there. Everyone also knows the mountain people have a lot of pride and courage and—"

"Are you going to dance with me or not?" he interrupted as if she hadn't spoken.

Dara sighed. He wasn't in the mood for a philosophical discussion of his origins. That much was obvious.

"Yes, I'd like to dance," she said softly, getting to her feet.

The band slipped into a twanging waltz, the singer crying out a song of unfaithful men who spent their nights in taverns like this one and left their women alone at home.

"I thought the mountain music was more of the bluegrass type," Dara couldn't resist saying as Yale took her into his arms.

"Sorry. This was as close as I could get. I'm sure the band knows a few bluegrass tunes," Yale told her shortly.

There was silence between them as they moved round the floor to the country waltz. Dara tried to think of something to say, anything to break the strange mood she had created. At least Yale was holding her closer now, she told herself with determined cheer. He might be a little angry at her, but he wasn't trying to keep her at a physical distance the way he had earlier. Nestling her head against his shoulder, she took advantage of that small concession.

But she couldn't keep silent long. The urge to know the full truth about her escort was overpowering.

"What *did* you do before you became an accountant?" she finally dared to ask softly, speaking into the fabric of his shirt. She felt his arms stiffen around her.

"You don't seem to know when you've pushed your luck far enough," Yale observed almost mildly above her head.

"I'm sorry," she murmured humbly. "I can't help it. I want to know."

"Are you this curious about all your potential clients?" he drawled. Some of the aristocratic Southern accent was fading to be replaced by a slightly different inflection. From the mountains? she wondered.

"No," Dara admitted honestly.

"I suggest you don't ask any more questions tonight, honey," Yale advised very gently. "You've gone far enough."

Dara raised her head and opened her eyes at the faint warning in his words. Yet another question hovered on her lips, and she was on the verge of asking it when a gleam of purely masculine impatience lit the hazel eyes gazing down into hers. Before she could get the words out of her mouth, Yale took action to silence her very effectively.

Bending his head, he took her lips with a slow, forceful possession that startled Dara into momentary blankness. For an instant she struggled instinctively, not so much against the kiss itself, but against having her next question cut off so completely.

He never missed a beat of the waltz as he tightened his arms, stilling her automatic protest. Then he placed the hand he was holding around his neck so that her arms were circling him in an intimate dancing posture. His fingers moved with deliberate exploration down her sides, into the curve of her waist, and came to a rest on the flare of her hips.

Telling herself that he was beginning to get out of line, Dara made a move to break off the kiss, but he diverted the effort by using his hands to press her close against the lower half of his body. His mouth moved tantalizing on hers as he forced her into the hardness of his hips.

With growing shock, Dara finally realized she was being made love to in the middle of a dance floor. No one else seemed the least bit scandalized, she had to acknowledge. The other couples on the floor were equally involved with each other. But she wasn't used to this sort of public display, she told herself firmly, trying and failing once more to pull back.

Helplessly she found herself molded against Yale's lean length. She could sense the arousal growing in him, felt it in the deepening kiss which was threatening to swamp her senses. His tongue probed her bruised lips, seeking entrance to the warmth of her mouth.

Dara tried to remain firm in the face of the seductive invasion, telling herself this simply wasn't the place for that sort of thing, regardless of how inviting Yale made it seem. But his fingers began stroking the small of her back, finding the sensitive area at the base of her spine and massaging it sensuously.

"Oh, Yale," she groaned huskily against his mouth, and as she spoke the words he took advantage of the opportunity to force his way gently past her teeth.

The kiss exploded in heated sexual energy, destroying the last of her feeble defenses. Without another thought, Dara stopped trying to resist the impulse to simply let her full weight lean into the strength of him.

She felt her high, curving breasts crushed against the muscular chest, knew the power in Yale's thighs and felt his desire for her. It shocked her senses, sending answering thrills out to her fingertips, and she knew she was making small, helpless sounds deep in her throat.

When her arms tightened around his neck, Yale rasped her name into her mouth and she felt the tremor of barely hidden passion which went through him. He wanted her, she realized dazedly. He truly wanted her! All the hope and excitement which had blazed so unexpectedly into life earlier in the evening when she'd given him her hand in greeting was culminating in a sense of wonder. Who would have thought that she would have to wait until she was thirty to know this sensation...?

Or that she would find it in the middle of a honky-tonk dance floor? the humorous side of her nature tossed in for good measure as Yale's hands slid down to follow the curve of her buttocks beneath the soft material of her dress. She shivered at the caress.

The twanging waltz came to a close and sensuously entwined dancers began making their way slowly off the floor as the strains of a toe-tapping railroad song took over.

Yale's arm guided her through the smoke-filled, dimly lit room, past a table of raucous truck drivers who watched in open male appreciation as she walked by them. Self-consciously, Dara kept her eyes on the far wall, grateful for Yale's possessive arm on her waist.

"I think we've got a visitor," Yale said calmly as they neared their table. The sound effects of a nearby electronic pinball game covered his next words, and Dara glanced up curiously. Then she saw the husky stranger sitting at their table.

The large man, balding on to and wearing a belt which had to be buckled below his stomach to accommodate his bulk, stood up at once as they approached.

"Sorry, folks." He grinned good-naturedly. "Tables are kind of scarce, and I was taking a chance this one might have been recently vacated." His bright blue eyes dropped interestedly to Dara's neckline with the appraising look she was coming to expect. "I'll be moving on," he added, picking up his bottle of beer. "Reckon there's always a spot at the bar..."

"That's all right," Yale said easily, surprising Dara. "Why

don't you join us for a while? We don't mind sharing, do we, Dara?"

Dara shook her head and smiled politely, thinking that Yale's accent seemed to be changing more and more quickly. He was beginning to sound a little like the truck driver who had just taken their table.

"I appreciate that, friend." Their new acquaintance grinned, resuming his seat as Dara sat down. "I won't be staying long. Got a lot of miles ahead of me tonight."

"Where you headed?" Yale asked laconically, reaching for his beer.

"Sacramento."

"Home port?"

"You can say that again," the stranger breathed with an air of great expectation. "Got a wife and kid waitin' there. Name's Bonner, by the way. Hank Bonner."

Yale introduced himself and Dara, and when Hank's eyes strayed to her neckline, Dara felt obliged to try some sort of distraction.

"I, uh, expect your wife must miss you when you're gone on these long trips," she said gently. "I take it you drive a truck?"

"You take it right. And I surely hope to God she's been missing me!" Hank said in a heartfelt tone.

"How old is your child?" Dara persevered bravely, wishing he wouldn't look at her quite so interestedly.

"Two." Hank brightened suddenly. "Got a picture. Want to see it?"

"Oh, I'd love to." She smiled quickly.

She was aware of Yale's silent amusement as Hank Bonner began dragging photographs out of his wallet. He had several pictures, it seemed, of a smiling, dark-haired woman holding a young boy. He spread them out in front of Dara with obvious pleasure.

"Took this one out behind the house last month. That's the new camper I just bought, and this one's on the front lawn. Wife wanted that new patio furniture so bad I finally had to break down and get it for her," he said, shaking his head affectionately. "No peace at all until it arrived. Guess women are like that, huh, Ransom?" He grinned.

Yale's mouth lifted slightly at the corners. "I guess so. No peace at all until they get what they're after."

Dara ignored his sardonic glance, but she couldn't fully ignore his next words. "The interesting part is watching them find out if they really wanted it after they've gotten it."

"I'd be willing to bet that women know their own minds better than men ever will!" she stated firmly, shooting Yale a severe glance.

"That's a fact!" Hank Bonner agreed, chuckling. "Probably ain't a man alive who really understands a woman's mind!"

"No great loss, I reckon, as long as he understands the rest of her," Yale said smoothly, sipping his beer and watching the color climb in Dara's cheeks.

"The man who doesn't make an effort to understand both is only going to get half the satisfaction out of a relationship!" she heard herself say crisply.

"But it's likely to be the half that counts," Yale retorted coolly while Hank roared with laughter. Dara glared at him.

"I like this little lady of yours, Ransom. Don't suppose you'd let me have a dance with her, would you?" Hank asked hopefully.

Dara winced. It was obvious her feelings didn't matter. As far as Hank was concerned, she was private property and he had to request permission from the owner, not the property!

Yale shrugged. "Ask her yourself. I guess she can do what she wants."

"I'll keep her safe and sound," Hank vowed, getting to his feet and clearly expecting Dara to do the same.

Thoroughly annoyed but not yet at the point where she was willing to cause a scene in such unfamiliar territory, Dara allowed herself to be led off by Hank Bonner.

"Where'd Ransom meet a little lady like you?" Hank asked glibly as he took her into his arms for another country waltz. "You come here often?"

"This is my first time here," Dara said politely. "As you've probably already guessed," she added as Hank grinned broadly.

"No offense, ma'am, but you are a little different from the kind of woman I normally find here."

"Do I look so out of place?"

"Just different," he repeated soothingly. "So where did you meet Ransom if not here?"

"You mean he *does* look like he belongs here?" she asked immediately, curious once again. It would be helpful to have another opinion on the man, she thought.

Hank Bonner chuckled. "Sure. I'm just wonderin' where he had to go to find you, that's all."

"A party," Dara explained weakly.

"Must have been some party!"

Dara wisely let that one go and concentrated on following Hank's energetic waltzing. Eventually the dance came to an end and Dara turned with relief to head back to the table. Somehow, in spite of his less than gentlemanly behavior this evening, Yale represented safety in this strange place. She was turning that one over in her head when a very drunken cowboy loomed in her path.

"Is the lady beginnin' to circulate?" he drawled deliberately, dark eyes moving crudely over Dara. "It so happens I'm lookin' for a partner..." He stretched out a hand to snag her wrist and Dara instinctively withdrew, bumping against Hank's protruding stomach. His arm came around her protectively.

"Sorry, the lady's only on temporary loan to me. Got to return her to the rightful owner," Hank explained breezily. But Dara could feel the sudden tightening of his muscles.

Oh, Lord! she thought, horrified. She mustn't let this turn into a fight!

"Excuse me," she said very firmly. "I have to get back to my table."

"Come on, honey," the drunken cowboy said, his words slurring as he tried once again for a grip on her wrist. "I dance a hell of a lot better than this turkey, and as long as your man's lettin' you entertain others..."

"Let go of me, you idiot!" Dara grated, pulling her hand free with a totally exasperated movement.

"You heard her," Hank growled, and now Dara knew beyond a shadow of a doubt that her dancing partner was preparing for battle.

Beginning to panic, she scanned the teeming crowd for Yale.

"Stop it, both of you," she tried in desperation. "I'm not going to dance with anyone…!"

"Except me," the cowboy muttered.

"Yale!" Instinctively, Dara put herself between the two men who seemed on the verge of a fist fight. "Yale! Where the…oh! There you are!"

She saw him as he suddenly appeared behind the cowboy and tore herself free of Hank's protection to hurl herself into Yale's arms.

"It's about time you showed up!" she hissed as he curved his arm around her waist and held her against his side.

"Didn't take you long to start causing trouble, did it?" he observed placidly, his eyes on the drunk. "A slight misunderstanding here?"

"Ah, he's just bombed out of his skull," Hank explained disparagingly, sauntering forward. "Thought Dara was spreading the favors around. I was about to set him straight, but now you're here I reckon that's your right."

"No one is going to set anyone straight!" Dara yelped angrily. "I'm not going to dance with anyone! Is that clear?"

"As crystal," Yale confirmed, grinning down at her. "Ready to sit down?"

"Yes!"

"Then, if you'll excuse us," Yale told the cowboy imperturbably, "we'll be on our way. Unless, of course," he added silkily, "you have some objection?"

Dara froze, realizing with appalled comprehension that Yale was as fully prepared to fight as Hank had been. What was the matter with these men? Was that the only solution they had to "misunderstandings" of this nature?

"Yale, please," she whispered fiercely, tugging at his sleeve. He ignored her, his narrowed, waiting gaze on the cowboy.

"I thought she was being allowed off the leash," the drunken man muttered. "Not my fault..."

"As I said, a misunderstanding." Yale nodded pleasantly. But Dara could feel the tautness of his muscles and knew he was still coiled to strike. "I'm sure you can find another woman. This one's mine."

With a frustrated and angry glance at Dara, the man wheeled unsteadily and plunged off through the crowd.

"A sigh of relief?" Yale murmured, his fingers, which were resting just under her breast, correctly interpreting her long breath.

"You don't have to look so nervous, Dara," Hank told her soothingly. "Ransom ain't gonna let anything happen to you."

"I can't tell you how reassuring that is!" she snapped without thinking, her annoyance plain.

"Why are you so upset?" Hank demanded, genuinely

puzzled. "You don't want to dance with that creep, and we're here to make sure you don't have to!"

"Just another example of not being able to understand a woman's mind, Hank," Yale quipped, pushing Dara gently back toward the table. "Do what you think she wants and help her out of a situation, and the first thing she does is lose her temper!"

"The temptation to knock both your heads together is rapidly become irresistible," Dara informed them grandly, taking her seat. "You might be able to defend me against drunken fools, but who's going to defend you against me?"

"She's got a point," Yale conceded, grinning at Hank.

"That she does," Hank agreed admiringly. "A good point like that deserves another beer. I'm buying!"

Dara reflected much later that they might all still have managed to get out of the tavern without a fight if the frustrated drunk hadn't decided to take out his anger on the pinball machine.

At least, she assumed that was what initiated the disaster. There was a loud, shattering sound from the direction of the game machines shortly after the arrival of the beers Hank had ordered.

"What in the world…!" Dara swung around to stare in the direction everyone else was staring, but it was impossible to see exactly what was happening. The group of men standing around the machines seemed to turn into a brawling riot before her very eyes.

"It would appear this enchanting evening is about to come to a close." Yale groaned, getting lithely to his feet as chaos erupted. The band played on, oblivious to the shouts and yells and bodies spilling onto the dance floor.

"Yale!" she squeaked, once more seeking the sanctuary of his smoothly muscled strength. "What's going on?"

"Guess," he invited succinctly, turning toward the door and shoving her unceremoniously in front of him. "'Bye, Hank. Nice meeting you. Have a good trip down to Sac...."

"Reckon I will at that," Hank agreed cheerfully, grabbing his jacket and loping after them as he tossed a vaguely regretful glance back over his shoulder at the rapidly expanding fight.

The sounds of breaking glass and male war calls were all around Dara as Yale hustled her through the mob. She gasped as the path which had appeared momentarily clear toward the door was suddenly littered with brawling men.

"This way," Yale ordered, pulling her off course in an attempt to circle the melee.

"What the hell you think you're doin', pal?" Hank's voice demanded behind them.

Dara felt Yale hesitate and then turn to see what had happened to Hank. She swiveled with him, and both were in time to watch their table partner deflect a swinging beer bottle with his jacket-wrapped arm. An instant later he was planting a huge, square fist into the face of the man who had swung the bottle.

Before he could recover his balance, though, another man surged out of the mob, swinging a bottle. It was the drunken cowboy who had insisted on dancing with her, Dara realized dazedly.

She thought he was going to bring the bottle down on Hank's balding head, but before that could happen, Yale had left her side to intercept.

Hands across her mouth in the traditional pose of feminine shock, Dara gazed, stunned, as Yale stopped the drunk with an arcing fist. The drunken cowboy sank to the floor, blissfully unconscious.

"Hey, thanks, Ransom. That's one I owe ya." Hank beamed.

"Come on, both of you. Let's get out of here," Yale ordered, forcing his way once more toward the door.

From somewhere in the distance the wail of a police siren sounded.

"Some spoilsport must have called the cops," Hank muttered as the three of them made the door and staggered out into the parking lot. "Yup, here they come. Where you guys parked?"

"A couple of blocks away," Yale growled, grasping Dara's wrist and yanking her in the proper direction.

"You'll never make it, and they'll be lookin' for everyone they can get their hands on... Come on. My truck's out back!"

"Hank!" Dara exclaimed as she caught sight of a dark splotch on his hand. "What happened? You've been cut!"

"That bottle raked across my knuckles. Don't worry, I'll be all right."

"Driving's going to be tough," Yale gritted, pulling Dara along in his wake. "Want me to take over?"

"I'd appreciate it." Hank chuckled, nursing his injured

hand. "That's my baby there." He pointed to a huge gleaming tractor-trailer truck which stood like a monstrous prehistoric creature in the back parking lot.

"In you go, Dara," Yale said briskly, practically tossing her into the cab and climbing in beside her on the driver's side. He started the engine as Hank bounced up into the seat beside Dara.

"Yale, do you think we should be doing this? I mean, you're not supposed to leave the scene of a crime, or something like that. We're witnesses…"

"Nobody but a fool would stick around a situation like that," Yale told her kindly, shifting the massive gears and setting the huge truck and trailer in motion. "Trust me, honey. I know what I'm doing. This is my element, not yours."

Ruefully acknowledging the truth of that, Dara subsided as the huge truck lumbered off into the night. Bemusedly she watched as the Interstate sign flashed past. Yale was taking them onto the freeway.

Belatedly she remembered Hank's hand.

"Have you got a first-aid kit? I should put something on that hand," she said, turning in concern.

"Somewhere around here…" he said, rustling about behind her in the sleeping compartment. "Say, you seem to know what you're doing there, Ransom. Still doing it for a living?"

"Not anymore," Yale replied, catching Dara's quick glance out of the corner of his eye and grinning wickedly.

"Kind of feels good to get my hands back on the wheel, though."

"Yeah, must as I complain about it, I'd miss it if I had to stop tomorrow," Hank said, dragging out a first-aid kit.

Dara opened it quickly, pulling out necessary supplies and going to work on the cut hand.

"I don't think it's too bad," she finally said, taping the wound carefully. "Be sure to change the dressing. I've tried to clean it up as best I can, but you should probably still have a doctor look at it."

"I'll be home tomorrow. My wife can check on it," Hank said unconcernedly. "Thanks for the patching job, though. Between the two of you, you've been right useful tonight!"

"It's, uh, certainly been an adventure," Dara agreed carefully, slanting a greenish glance up at Yale's hard profile. He looked right at home. "How far are we going with Hank?" she asked softly.

"I don't know. Hadn't thought about it," Yale murmured. "Why don't you crawl in the back and catch some sleep? You were tired earlier this evening, so I expect you're exhausted by now."

"Yale," she whispered, "we can't just go off like this! What about your car? How will we get back to Eugene? Where are we headed, anyway?"

"Go to sleep, honey. I'll take care of everything," he instructed gently.

"Go on, Dara," Hank said soothingly. "Let your man have some fun. The sleeper's not as clean as it ought to be, but you'll be all right if you stay on top of the blankets."

"Fun?" Dara eyed her escort. "Are you enjoying this, Yale Ransom?" she asked accusingly.

"I don't know. Can't decide." He chuckled. "Stop looking at me like that and go to sleep. I'll wake you later."

Dara licked her lower lip in thoughtful contemplation. But she was outnumbered and she was exhausted. And she had brought the whole catastrophe down on her own head, she remembered in a surge of self-honesty. And it really had been rather exciting.

She smiled slowly to herself and climbed obediently into the sleeping compartment. Yale could handle everything.

Chapter 3

"Where are we?"

Dara's voice was a sleepy mumble as she stirred awake some time later. It was the lack of the muted roar of the heavy diesel engine which had roused her, and she realized the big rig had been stopped.

"A couple of hours south of Eugene." Yale's voice came calmly from the front seat. "Come on, honey, this is where we get off."

"A couple of hours south! Good grief! How are we going to get back tonight?" she demanded, scrambling out of the sleeper compartment. She was aware that the burnt russet of her hair was tousled and the emerald dress was badly wrinkled. The sleeping compartment had been strangely confining and she was glad to escape, even if she was still very sleepy.

"We'll worry about that in the morning," Yale told her, reaching out to help her back into the front seat. His mouth quirked in amusement as she blinked up at him sleepily. "You look like a tabby cat someone's just rudely awakened."

"Thanks," she muttered, knowing tabby cats tended to be plump and comfortable-looking, not sleek and racy. "How's the wound, Hank?" she added, eyes narrowing as she turned to peer at the other man's hand.

He held it up and grinned cheerfully. "Fine. The bleeding's stopped and I can manage things now."

"Oh. Well, I hope you have a good, safe trip on down to Sacramento," she said, returning his smile. "And...and I think you ought to consider finding another sort of job, Hank," she went on in an urgent rush. "This isn't a good life for a family man! Your wife shouldn't have to be raising that boy alone and—"

"Come on, Dara!" Yale's crisp drawl cut across the flow of words as he opened the door and grabbed her wrist. She was practically pulled down out of the cab and he had to steady her as she landed off balance beside him.

Hank's face appeared in the window above them as he slid behind the wheel. He was grinning.

"You take care of that little lady, now, Ransom. She looks to me like she's got about everything a man could want on a cold night! See ya!"

Yale wrapped an arm around Dara's waist and pulled her back out of the way as Hank brought the monster truck to life once more.

"Thanks, Hank," Yale called, lifting a hand in farewell.

"Anytime, pal, anytime!"

Diesel fumes filled the air as the truck and trailer growled past on its way back to the only element in which it was truly comfortable, an Interstate highway.

"It's cold out here!" Dara noted, wishing she hadn't left

her coat in the Alfa Romeo. She glanced around at the scattered buildings.

"There's a motel over to the right," Yale said conversationally, holding her close to his side and starting off in the direction of the flashing sign advertising rooms.

"A motel!" Dara frowned. "Aren't we going to head back to Eugene?"

"Not tonight. We'll find a way back home in the morning. It's too late tonight to scare up a ride and we're both tired."

"What time is it?"

"Almost two o'clock. Did you get any sleep?"

"Between Hank fiddling with the CB and you switching from one country station to another on the radio, no!" Dara lied feelingly. "And what's the idea of telling half the northbound traffic on the Interstate that you were traveling with your own personal stockbroker?"

"I didn't tell anyone that. That was Hank on his CB," Yale defended with a grin that exposed the gold.

"He got it from you!"

"Well, he wanted to know your status in my life so he could share the gossip with his road buddies. I had to think of something."

Dara was about to berate him further, but the truth was she had fallen asleep shortly after hearing Hank's cheerful announcement and she wasn't at all sure what had been said next.

"Do you think this place is clean?" she demanded skeptically, surveying the old motel with a critical eye.

"Hank assures me it's fine. Not elegant, but decent."

"We're going to look a little strange to the desk clerk." Dara sighed, lifting a hand to graciously cover a yawn. Even the chilly night air wasn't going to keep her awake much longer. "I mean, what with no luggage and no car..."

"I'll handle it."

"Uh-huh."

"Have some faith in your man, woman!" Yale gibed cheerfully as he opened the front door of the office.

"I'm your stockbroker, not your woman, remember?" she retorted sweetly.

"Actually, we haven't even agreed on that status yet, have we?" he noted. The door swung shut behind them, cutting off her next words.

A thin, elderly desk clerk detached himself from a small television set and came forward reluctantly.

"Can I help you?" he asked, not looking particularly anxious to do so.

"Two rooms, Yale," Dara remembered to hiss belatedly in his ear as he loosened his arm and started toward the desk. He ignored her, but the desk clerk didn't.

"Only got one. A double. Take it or leave it, and you pay in advance," the thin man growled with an owlish glance at Dara.

"We'll take it," Yale said quickly, fishing his wallet out of his pocket. Swiftly he counted out the money and collected the key. He had signed the register and hustled Dara out the door before she fully realized what had happened.

"I told you to get two rooms!" she gritted as the office door slammed shut behind them.

"You heard the man. He only had one!"

"Hah!"

"Don't take that tone with me," Yale instructed, sounding aggrieved. "Our being in this situation is all your fault!"

"My fault! Of all the nerve! It wasn't me who got involved in a fight in a sleazy bar, and it wasn't my idea to hitch a ride with a long-distance trucker and not get out of the truck for two solid hours! If we'd stayed at that nice country-western place I took you to earlier this evening, none of this would have happened!"

"Don't act the innocent victim," Yale muttered, sliding the motel key into the lock of number 53. "You had to keep pushing at me, trying to find out what was under my nice accountant image. You have only yourself to blame!"

"Oh, my God!" Dara breathed in grim resignation as the door swung open to reveal a stark but clean room. "There's only one bed. Where are you going to sleep?"

"On my side, naturally," Yale growled, closing the door behind them and switching on the light.

Since she had guessed the answer to the question before she'd even asked it, Dara squelched a retort. There wasn't much else she could do under the circumstances, and in spite of his almost blatant lovemaking on the dance floor earlier in the evening, Yale didn't look particularly amorous at the moment. And there was absolutely nothing romantic about the cheap, poorly furnished motel room.

"I'll use the bathroom first." She sighed gloomily.

Inside the spartan bath, Dara studied herself wryly in the mirror. She looked a little the worse for wear, she was forced to conclude, raking her fingers through her hair. Sleepy gray-green eyes gleamed back at her and she frowned as she realized there was a tiny hint of excitement in her own reflection.

Things hadn't developed quite the way she had imagined, but there was no denying she had found herself in an interesting situation. She grabbed a washcloth and began scrubbing her face while she considered that. Yale Ransom was turning out to have several fascinating layers. Surely after their shared experiences this evening he would feel a degree of friendship for her.

Perhaps enough friendship to give her his securities account. That would provide the excuse she needed to cement the relationship along business lines, and from there...

Dara broke off her hopeful thoughts and told herself not to get carried away. There was still a lot she didn't know about Yale. She wasn't even sure how he felt about her at the moment, although, judging from his reaction on the dance floor, she didn't leave him cold. Well, that was something, at least.

Hanging the threadbare white towel back on the rack, Dara unzipped the emerald-green dress and removed her lacy bra. Rolling the undergarment into a little bundle, she stuffed it into her purse and then rezipped the dress. It would be more comfortable trying to sleep without the bra, she told herself, wishing she could take off the dress, too. But that, of course, was impossible.

Yale was sitting on the side of the bed, his weight putting an alarming sag in the old mattress as he leaned over to untie his shoes. He had removed the white shirt and was wearing only his slacks.

"Your turn," Dara said cheerfully, determined to act with the casual comradeship the situation demanded. Damned if she would let him see her act like a nervous female! Not at her age!

He straightened, kicking off the dark leather shoes. The case containing the horn-rimmed glasses rested on the nightstand. His hazel eyes swept over her as she industriously began turning down her side of the bed.

"Thanks," he murmured, getting to his feet.

In spite of herself, Dara's gaze followed him as he disappeared into the bathroom. The broad shoulders and smoothly muscled back tapering into a narrow waist pulled at her awareness. She remembered how it had felt dancing with him earlier this evening and wondered at her own reaction. Never had she been so immediately attracted to a man.

Shaking her head, Dara slipped off her high-heeled shoes and panty hose and slid beneath the covers. Very carefully she arranged herself on the far side of the bed and lay on her back, gazing at the ceiling. Was there such a thing as love at first sight? she wondered. Probably not. But until tonight she wouldn't have expected to encounter attraction at first sight, either.

And attraction was a good place to start, she assured herself with a small smile, provided it was mutual.

"Don't tell me you're going to sleep in that dress!" Yale exclaimed, emerging from the bathroom and flicking off the overhead light as he walked toward the bed.

"As I didn't think to bring a nightgown, that's exactly what I'm going to do," Dara told him acidly and then winced as she heard the sound of a buckle and zipper being undone.

"Suit yourself," he remarked carelessly. She listened anxiously as he slung the dark slacks over a chair. A moment later the bed sagged once again and the large male body moving in beside her raised the temperature under the cold covers by several degrees.

"The least you could do is wear your slacks," she said in brisk annoyance, lying rigidly on her side of the bed as he shifted and stretched beside her.

"In order to keep warm, you mean?" Yale asked politely and reached for her with shocking swiftness. "That's what my own personal stockbroker is for," he informed her, dragging her into the curve of his body.

"Yale! Stop that! What in the world do you think you're doing?"

Dara flung out a hand in protest and encountered the pelt of curling hair on his chest. She pulled her fingers away as if they'd been burned. "Stop teasing me like this!"

"Teasing!" he growled, his arm moving around her waist to anchor her against him. "You're the tease in this little party. You've been badgering me all evening, and I've finally decided to give you what you want."

"I'm not in the mood for any more of your truck-stop

manners!" she snapped haughtily. "You've had your fun tonight. Behave yourself!"

The hand on her waist slid around to her stomach and moved upward to settle just under the full curve of her breast.

"So you don't like my truck-stop manners? That's unfortunate, isn't it? You didn't seem to like my more gentlemanly behavior, either. You're a hard woman to please, Dara Bancroft. But I'll try...."

Dara opened her lips to annihilate him verbally, but his mouth came down on hers before she could get the words out.

"Yale!" she managed in a muffled voice, and then the heated mastery of his kiss overwhelmed her senses. His mouth was like a narcotic, she realized dimly. A drugging, overridingly powerful thing that roused her emotions as nothing else had ever done. If she didn't stop him soon, she wouldn't be able to do so.

His fingers followed the under curve of her breast, seeking the nipple and finding it easily. She should have left on her bra, Dara thought wretchedly. Now his hand was shaping the softness of her as if the dress she wore was only a nightgown. The sensations he was causing began undermining her willpower, urging compliance.

"Hank was right," Yale said huskily against her throat as he dragged his mouth away from hers. "You have got what a man needs in bed."

"Don't talk to me like that, Yale. We both know you've

come a long way from the kind of world where men treat women like this!"

"I've got news for you, honey," he murmured, letting the tip of his tongue touch the rapidly beating pulse at the base of her throat. "Some things a man doesn't leave behind."

"No!" she gasped as he pulled her against his naked chest and reached for the zipper at her nape. "You're a gentleman, damn it! I'm holding you to that!"

His fingers hesitated, the zipper halfway open. "What makes you think I would have behaved any differently if I'd gotten you into bed tonight while I was still in my gentlemanly role?" His lips burned on her earlobe now, and she wedged her hands against the strong chest.

"We would never have wound up in bed like this if you hadn't taken over the evening!" Dara wailed.

"I really don't feel like arguing over whose fault this is," he soothed, lowering the zipper sensuously down to the base of her spine. "And don't try telling me you don't want me. I know what you were doing to me on that dance floor back at the bar and I know how you were responding."

"You don't understand!"

That brought a deep laugh from the back of his throat. "I understand, honey. Don't worry about that!" His fingers danced wickedly up her spine as she struggled futilely to lever herself away from his chest When they reached her naked shoulder, the bold fingertip slid under the fabric of the dress bodice and pushed it forward, exposing the rounded femininity beneath.

Dara gasped, knowing that by now both his eyes and her

own were adjusted to the darkness. He could see what his hands had revealed.

"Yale! Stop it! Please!" The cry was torn hoarsely from her throat as he lowered his dark amber head to taste the sweetness of her breasts. Her fingers curled unconsciously into the muscles of his shoulders and she heard him groan.

"You don't mean that," he rasped, his tongue circling a nipple, urging a physical response.

"Yes! Yes, I do, damn you! Please, Yale. This isn't the way I wanted things to be between us. It's too soon. We have to get to know each other. I want you to..." Her words trailed off. How could she tell him she wanted his love, not merely his desire? He would never understand how she could have fallen so completely for him in such a short period of time.

"You want me to what, sweetheart?" he whispered deeply, his teeth closing gently around the nipple his tongue had drawn forth. "Tell me. I'm willing to please...."

"I want you to stop making love to me!" She was lying through her teeth but she spoke the words with considerable forcefulness.

He stilled for an instant and Dara, too, froze, waiting for his reaction. When his head eventually lifted and his eyes met hers with a directness that sent a shiver through her limbs, Dara almost called back her own words. Almost but not quite. The future was what mattered between them. To preserve that she had to protect the present.

"Are you sure that's what you want, honey?" he murmured coaxingly, his hand softly cupping one breast.

"I'm…I'm sure," she vowed, unable to look away from the seductive expression in the hazel gaze. "Please, Yale."

"I bet you sell a lot of stock with that earnest little look, don't you?"

"Yale!"

He sighed. "You're old enough to know better than to play with fire, Dara."

"I never meant things to get so out of hand," she said contritely. "I only wanted to know more about you and somehow…"

"Couldn't resist opening Pandora's box, could you?" He grinned, leaning back against the pillows. She felt the sexual tension seep out of him and drew a deep breath of relief-relief tinged with regret, she was forced to admit privately.

"Was all this in the nature of teaching me a lesson?" she complained ruefully.

"No," Yale growled, rubbing the bridge of his nose with his thumb and forefinger. "I suppose I'd forgotten a few of the things that were still in the box, myself." His eyes closed and suddenly he looked tired.

"How long did you drive a truck, Yale?" Dara asked, knowing quite suddenly that she was safe.

The amber lashes flicked open immediately and hazel eyes gleamed in warning. "You really don't know when to stop, do you? Your curiosity must have gotten you into a lot of trouble over the years!"

"Not really. I've never been quite this curious about another person before!" she confessed.

He stared at her for a moment and then growled a soft command. "Go to sleep, Dara."

A little belatedly, perhaps, Dara acknowledged that it *was* time to stop. Without another word, she pulled away from the inviting proximity of his body, her hand brushing awkwardly against the material of his jockey shorts. Curling on her side with her back to him, Dara forced herself to stare at the wall until her eyes finally closed in sleep.

But her dreams were filled with fleeting promises of a happiness she craved, a happiness connected with a hazel-eyed man with honey-amber hair. In sleep her body remembered the feel of his hands, the strength of his chest and thighs and the laughter which sparked to life occasionally in the hazel gaze. There had never been a man like this one in her life, and he had even managed to invade her dreams.

It wasn't the morning sun which called Dara out of a warm sleep some time later. The shabby little motel room was still quite dark. It was a dream which was moving her into a drowsy, languid state of awareness. A dream which had followed her back into real life.

Half asleep, Dara's body reacted luxuriously to the warmth of a hand on her thigh. She knew that hand. She would know its touch anywhere, and her body accepted it instinctively.

Blissfully she turned toward the source of the gentle, insistent demand, her legs parting of their own volition. The half-conscious feminine invitation was accepted immediately. The hand on her leg began lazy designs which led to the soft inside of her thigh and simultaneously her mouth was warmly, tenderly invaded.

It was like drinking hot spiced wine, she thought dazedly, her arms moving to pull closer the source of this smooth, heated seduction. Her fingers closed first on the hard thrust of a shoulder and then they twined themselves into short, thick hair. Hair that she knew intuitively was the color of dark honey. The perfect shade.

"Oh..." The moan was from her own throat, thick with a growing urgency. It was as if her dream was merging with reality.

The masculine groan which echoed her soft cry was low and hoarse with undisguised male need. She responded to it, offering herself in an age-old desire to please.

There were no words. Somehow, far back in her foggy mind, Dara knew words would have destroyed the dream-like quality of the moment, and nothing on earth must be allowed to do that.

There was a curious floating sensation as the material which seemed to interfere with the searching movements of the demanding hands was slipped away. When it was gone, Dara felt the glowing sensation increase a hundred-fold. This was what she wanted; this was where she wished to be tonight and every night.

Eyes closed, she let the accumulating impressions pile up on her senses. Gently rough fingertips glided along the inside of her thigh until they closed on the heart of her throbbing desire. The electricity coursed through her veins, causing her nails to bite deeply into a taut male shoulder and score their way down to a lean waist.

Silently she called his name over and over, and then the word was a low, audible moan on her lips. It was the only word allowed in that moment out of time.

"Yale, oh, my darling, Yale!"

"Dara, sweet womanly Dara. I knew you were dangerous the instant I met you! And now it's too late. Much too late..."

The husky confession pleased her enormously and Dara curled closer, her hips arching into the touch of his possessive hand, trading her feminine secrets for the satisfaction Yale could provide.

"Yes, sweetheart," he growled, his lips moving down her throat, pausing to caress her breasts and then trailing down even farther to bury themselves in her curving midsection. "Give yourself to me tonight. I want all of you. All you have to give...."

She gasped as he dipped a wet kiss into her navel and then moved on, stringing kisses along the flare of a hip. His hand slipped down to grasp an ankle, tenderly forcing her legs even farther apart, and then she felt his teeth first feather and then nip the vulnerable inner length of her thigh.

Convulsively, her fingers locked in the dark honey of his hair and her body lifted into his urgent, demanding lips and hands.

"Oh, Yale. Please, please..."

"Tell me what you want," he rasped thickly, sliding his

hands under her buttocks and holding her body still while he rose to settle himself between her legs. "Tell me, Dara!"

The command was punctuated by tiny, velvet kisses along her stomach.

"Love me, Yale!" The cry was a feminine order of the first magnitude. "Please, please make love to me!"

He inched slowly upward, his hands sliding along her waist to palm her breasts as his mouth explored her silky skin in their wake. She was vividly aware of the heavy maleness of him, knew it would soon pour over her in a wave.

Hungrily she wrapped her arms around him, drawing him down into her waiting body. Her lips buried themselves in his throat as he loomed over her and she clutched at the tensely muscled back.

"I knew it had to end like this between us tonight," Yale gasped, shuddering as her hands clung to him, dragging him under into the rippling tide of her. "Sooner or later it had to end like this…."

"Yes, oh, yes," she panted, her breath coming in short, excited gasps that lifted her full breasts and crushed them softly against his chest.

Somehow it wasn't until she actually felt his unmistakable hardness against her that the last of the dream finally faded. Perhaps it was the stunning sensation of imminent masculine possession, or perhaps it was because she finally opened her eyes and took in the full significance of the cheap motel room. Whatever the cause, Dara was finally, fully aroused from her dreamlike state.

What was she doing? This wasn't the way she had meant

to conclude the evening! It was too soon, much too soon! They needed time....

"Yale, no! Wait, please, wait! I didn't want this to happen...!"

"It's too late now," he gritted against her mouth. "I'm going to make you mine. There's nothing in this universe that could stop me!"

He fastened his lips over hers, silencing her protest, and then everything seemed to explode around and in her at once. He held her with fierce urgency, forcing his tongue into her mouth even as his hardness took her completely.

Dara would have cried out with the ecstasy of it, but there was no chance. He dominated her awareness on every level, pulling her into the rhythmic surge of his body as if he would meld every inch of her with him.

Dara's fleeting moment of sanity vanished once more under the passionate onslaught. She couldn't think of the future when he held her like this, touched her like this, mastered her body with his own.

Deliriously she gave herself up to the thrilling wonder of the man to whom she had wanted to belong from the instant her eyes had met his. This was what she had been searching for all her life. This was the joy and exquisite excitement that had been missing from her short, ill-fated marriage.

Almost incredulously she felt her body responding in a way it had never responded before. Something tight and coiling was fighting to free itself deep in her loins.

Her hands slid down the violently arching male back, digging into the muscular flesh of Yale's buttocks and thighs.

"My God, woman! What are you doing to me!"

She reveled in the evidence of his unleashed need and sensuality, delighted in the now ungoverned response of his body to hers. His strength and power seemed to master her softness at the same time that they surrendered to it.

"I never knew..." she tried to say, "I never realized..." The words wouldn't come. How could she try to describe the indescribable?

Her teeth sank into his shoulder and her legs tightened violently around his rough thighs as the coiling passion in her lower body threatened to burst forth.

"Yale? Yale!" It was a plea. For what, she didn't know.

"Let yourself go, my darling," he whispered urgently. "I'll take care of you. Just let go...."

Unable and unwilling to resist the demand in him, Dara gasped, reacting unbelievably to an unexpectedly swift and erotic movement of his lean frame. It seemed to send her over the brink of a heretofore unseen cliff and she plunged into the chasm below, free-falling toward a velvet green earth, Yale's name on her lips.

As if he had only been waiting for the turbulent shudder which suddenly racked Dara as she lay beneath him, Yale cried out harshly. She felt the primitive convulsion take him completely in its power, giving him to her in an astonishing and fundamental way.

Willingly, joyously, Dara accepted the gift, clinging and clinging as together they plunged into the soft valley below.

He was with her in that moment, sharing the ultimate sensation which can be created between a man and a woman, and for Dara, that was all that counted. The future must be dealt with later.

Chapter 4

Languidly Dara attempted to move her foot, found it rapped beneath a heavy male leg and finally emerged completely from the sensual lethargy in which she had been drifting.

Her fingertips brushed a masculine chest and her soft gray-green eyes fluttered open to find a lazy pair of hazel ones watching her.

For an instant of silent communication, neither said anything, the recent memories mirrored in their eyes.

"I thought you were never going to wake up, sleepyhead," Yale finally murmured, his voice a deep dragon's purr in his chest. "It's been daylight for nearly an hour."

"You're in a hurry to go someplace?" Dara drawled, her mouth curving lovingly.

"Well, it did occur to me that there might be more interesting places to spend the weekend than this truck-stop motel!"

With a sexy, inviting grin, Yale rolled onto his back and reached out to haul her across his chest. It was as she came free of the sheet that Dara realized the green dress was no longer around.

The color rose in her cheeks as her breasts were crushed

softly against him. She saw his eyes follow the outline of her, a look of satiated pleasure in the hazel depths.

"You drove me wild last night," he rumbled, raking his fingers through the tangled wings of her deep russet hair. "You're a dangerous lady, Dara Bancroft. Very dangerous."

She smiled delightedly, toying with the curling hair beneath her hand as she met his gaze. She was in love! She could hardly believe it. How could it have happened like this after all these years?

"I plead innocent," she whispered laughingly. "You're the one who carried me off into the night. If we'd done things my way we would have danced a few dances at that nice nightclub I took you to and then gone home very properly to our own beds!"

"Never!" he vowed fervently. "I wanted you from the moment I met you. Whatever happened last night, we would never have awakened alone."

"Hah! I don't think you wanted me all that badly at first. As I recall, you were rather annoyed with me at times!" Deliberately she made a joke of it, wishing he could have used the word she wanted to use. He must feel something more than desire for her after what they had shared. How could a man make love like that and not be at least a little *in* love?

"Being annoyed with you didn't change my desire to take you to bed." He chuckled, framing her face with his hands. Dara felt the strength in the gentle grip and shivered with pleasure. "I don't think anything could change that!"

"No?" she dared lightly, eyes warm with her love and laughter and the freshness of what she had discovered.

"No," he agreed solemnly. "Rest assured, my sweet. The account is yours."

Dara blinked, certain she had heard wrong.

"What?" Firmly she kept her smile in place. He was making a joke.

"My stock account," Yale explained easily, laughing at her incomprehension. "It's yours. I'm entirely satisfied with the transaction. At the moment, in fact, I wouldn't care if you lost all my money in the commodities market! As long as you're willing to stand as collateral, naturally."

"Stop teasing me like that, Yale," she ordered carefully, some of the laughter fading from her eyes. "I'm not in the mood for that sort of joke. Not right now."

"What joke?" he demanded, shaking his head ruefully. "It's yours, honey, me and the account. I'm content with the deal and as far as I'm concerned it's all signed, sealed and delivered. I'll let you have the details you'll need to transfer it from my broker in L.A. on Monday. But right now we've got today and Sunday ahead of us to, uh, finalize the terms of our working relationship. What do you say we—"

"You're not joking, are you?" Dara pushed herself a few inches away from his chest, gray-green eyes widening as she stared down into his fiercely etched face as if she hadn't fully seen it until that moment.

"I never joke about money. Accountants rarely do!" he informed her loftily, eyes narrowing a fraction as he studied her tautening expression.

"Oh, my God!" she breathed as the full horror of the situation washed over her. He wasn't teasing her! He really believed she had slept with him in order to convince him to give her his account!

"What's the matter with you, little tabby cat?" he rasped soothingly, stroking a rough fingertip down her cheek and into the curve of her shoulder. "I had the impression you were quite satisfied with last night's deal, too! In fact, I'd be willing to bet from the startled look on your face at one point that you hadn't known just how much pleasure you could find in your own body!"

"How dare you look so smug and self-satisfied! Who the hell do you think you are?" The words were tight, tense, barely audible.

Slowly at first the anger kindled. Fed by her own humiliation, it leaped to life, shattering Dara's conception of herself as a mild, easygoing person with an even temper. After thirty years, she was finally discovering the full significance of the red in her hair.

"Dara!" The command was given as if she were a fractious child. "Calm down...!"

"Calm down!" she blazed, pulling free of his hand and fumbling her way off the bed to stand beside it, glowering down at the man she had fallen in love with during the course of one wild night.

"Calm down! Don't you dare tell me to calm down!'

Yanking a sheet off the bed and leaving Yale's sprawling form nude in the morning light, she wrapped herself in some semblance of dignity. The gray-green eyes were almost completely emerald now and the sun seeping in through

the crack in the curtains danced in the half-hidden fire of
her hair.

"You are a bastard, Yale Ransom!" she proclaimed as if
pronouncing a curse. "And I am a fool! I freely admit that!
God only knows where I got the idea we could…could
mean something important to each other. Believe it or not,
I'm usually a better judge of men than this! I haven't made
a mistake of this magnitude since I thought the man I was
marrying was in love with me!"

"Dara, stop it! You're behaving like a shrew. It doesn't
suit you, little tabby cat. Come back to bed and let me show
you…." Yale stretched out a hand, groping for her wrist.

"Don't you dare touch me, you arrogant, lying, *impostor!*" She moved back out of reach.

"Impostor!" For some reason he seized on that, mouth
hardening ominously as he slowly sat up.

"Yes! Impostor! Cheat! Opportunist! The language isn't
rich enough to supply all the words I need to describe you!"
she gritted furiously. "Oh, I knew you were something other
than what you were pretending to be last night. I knew
you'd been a lot of other things besides an accountant, but
I never guessed you were the kind of man who would use
a woman and then pay her off by handing over money or…
or your stock-market account!"

"Shut up and listen to me, you little wildcat," he grated,
getting slowly to his feet. The hazel gaze flickered as she
automatically backed out of reach.

"Don't get the idea I'm a bigger fool than I've already
shown myself to be!" Dara cried, her chin lifting defiantly.

"Listening to you was what got me into this mess! I don't intend to listen to you again! Ever! I try to learn from my mistakes, Yale Ransom. And you can rest assured you've just taught me one hell of a lesson! Even I can't quite believe how I could have made such an idiot of myself!"

"Good God! You're really intent on playing the woman scorned this morning, aren't you? But I haven't scorned you, honey. Just the opposite!"

"You've treated me like a…a commodity you could buy or sell," Dara hissed. "Last night you felt like buying it. Who knows? Tomorrow you might feel like selling it! What will you do then? Try to find another female broker who seems willing to pay the price? Let me give you a word of advice. Find someplace besides a dingy truck-stop motel to 'finalize' the deal. And the next morning, refrain from talking about the bargain itself until after breakfast. Much more civilized!"

"The choice of surroundings was yours!" Yale suddenly snapped, his fists planted on his hips. He stood in front of her, uncompromisingly naked and intimidatingly male. The deep amber hair was ruffled in a rakish, dangerous-looking style and the hazel eyes gleamed with determination. The Southern accent had lost most of its polish.

"There certainly isn't much to your gentlemanly veneer now, is there?" Dara taunted, her rage threatening to overwhelm her. "I even get the blame for choosing a cheap, one-night-stand sort of motel! Well, I suppose that's the proper setting, after all. A one-night stand is certainly all this affair is ever going to amount to!"

"The hell it is! I've got news for you, Dara Bancroft! You handed yourself over to me, lock, stock and barrel, last night. It's too late now to back out!"

"Don't be so anxious to conclude the bargain," she warned scathingly. "If I ever get my hands on your account I'd pump every last dime into surefire losers! I'd take great pleasure in ruining you! You're damned right I'm feeling like a woman scorned, and just remember hell hath no fury like one! Give me a chance and I'll pay you back a hundredfold for what you did to me last night!"

"Your warning is duly noted," he drawled, stalking forward with slow, deliberate strides.

"Don't come any closer," she ordered seethingly, holding the sheet in place as she backed away. "I mean it, Yale! I don't want you touching me. Not ever!"

"But I'm going to touch you," he promised with silky menace. "Often and in the most delightful places. You belong to me now, temper and all. Like I said, I'm satisfied with the transaction, and I'll make sure you are, too...."

Dara came up against the wall, her eyes blazing as she realized she was trapped. "You really can't get it through that thick head of yours that I didn't go to bed with you in order to get your account, can you? Well, try writing it on the blackboard a few hundred times. Because I didn't! I don't want your account! I never cared one way or the other about it!"

"Too bad, because you're stuck with it," he gritted, his fingers curling over her bare shoulders. He pulled her away from the wall, close to his naked strength. "And believe me,

I'll take every dollar you lose out of your soft hide." His mouth curled devilishly. "But I will also be very generous with my thanks for every dollar you make, too!"

"Take your hands off me!'

"I can't," he confessed almost ruefully. "I only have to look at you, and I want to touch you. Stop fighting me, honey. You know as well as I do that what we found together last night was very, very good. I'll admit we rushed into things, but—"

"*We* rushed into things!" she yelped, incensed at the blithe accusation. "*I* had nothing to do with it! You're the one who hitched a ride for us to the middle of nowhere! You're the one who got us one room in a sleazy motel when I told you to get two! You're the one who assumed that just because we were forced to share a bed, I would let you make love to me! You're the one who seduced me while I was asleep, long after I'd made it clear I had no intention of going that far! You took advantage of me! And you ignored me at the last moment when I finally realized what was happening and told you to stop!"

"Of course I ignored you," he murmured, bending his head to brush his mouth affectionately across her forehead and then the tip of her nose. "You'd really have been angry at me this morning if I hadn't!"

"You're despicable!" She brought up a hand, wedging it against his chest and trying to shove him away. It was like pushing the Rock of Gibraltar.

"What if I told you I was also sorry?" he whispered tantalizingly, his mouth seeking out the vulnerable place behind her ear. Lazily his hand toyed with the wing of hair in the way.

"Sorry! Sorry for what?" she challenged, wishing she could cry but far too angry to do any such thing. She stood rigidly in his embrace, stoically ignoring the inviting gentleness of his mouth and the sensuous heat of his body. She had learned her lesson last night. Never again would she let her emotions run away with her common sense. What a fool she had been!

"For getting you involved in that stupid tavern brawl last night, for the cheap motel room, for stranding you two hours away from home in strange surroundings, for taking you out of your world and showing you something of mine...."

"Beginning to realize you handled it all wrong, are you?" she flung back waspishly, closing her eyes fiercely against the tenderness in his mouth and hands. She would not let herself be seduced again!

"Yes," he admitted wryly. "I never meant to put you in a temper like this! I never meant to spend our first night together in a place like this and I never meant to wind up in a honky-tonk with you, either. But you just kept pushing..."

"So now it's my fault again, is it?"

He sighed. "Why don't we call it quits and start over again? I'll take you home and we can do things right this time around. I'll go back to my Southern-gentleman accountant role and show you that I've put truck stops and barroom brawls behind me. Trust me, Dara," he added on a low, husky note. "You won't regret it...."

"You're right. I won't regret it because I don't intend to let you try to repolish your image! I'll always have the memory of waking up in this place and hearing you tell me you were pleased with the transaction. Nothing will wipe that out of my mind, Yale! And I'm smart enough to know better than to cast pearls before swine twice!"

He whitened at that. She felt the sudden tension in him and knew a moment's genuine fear. Unconsciously, she touched her tongue to her lower lip, wondering if she really had gone too far this time. Eyes wide and reflecting an appeal of which she wasn't aware, Dara waited for his reaction.

"Your temper is as strong as your passion, isn't it?" he finally observed in an even tone which startled her. She knew he was exerting a considerable effort to avoid wrapping his hands around her throat. The knowledge gave her a perverse pleasure.

"You haven't seen the half of it yet," she vowed feelingly, tossing her head with scorn. "Give me an opportunity and I'll prove my temper is a lot more interesting than my passion!"

A slow smile twisted his mouth as he ran a reminiscent gaze over her face and bare shoulders. "Nothing could interest me as much as the feel of you coming alive under my hands!" he retorted gently, eyes softening. "You are all the woman a man could want, my sweet Dara. Go ahead and threaten me all you like, it won't make any difference. You're mine now."

Her eyes narrowed. "I don't belong to you or any other man. Take your hands off me, Yale. I want to go home."

He hesitated, as if considering the best method of handling her. "Maybe you'll be in a better mood after breakfast," he tried lightly, sliding his hands sensuously down her arms and catching hold of her wrists. "Shall I feed you, little tabby?" he asked whimsically, turning his head to kiss the delicate inside of her wrist. His eyes gleamed. "Will that put you in a more loving mood?"

"What do you care?" she challenged icily. "You're not interested in love. Only a business transaction!"

"I'll bet," he hazarded sadly, "that if I made an apology for that remark this morning you wouldn't accept it, would you?"

"No, I would not! Nothing you can say now will wipe out your earlier words! I know better than to trust you, Yale Ransom. I've learned my lesson!"

He drew a deep breath, and Dara knew he was still undecided about how to deal with her mood. "Well, we might as well try the food first. If that doesn't work, I'm sure I'll think of something else. Go and get dressed, honey. We'll talk this out eventually...."

She tugged free of his hands, walking regally across the room to retrieve her clothes and then sweeping into the bath without a backward glance. Damn the barbarian! She would not give in to tears. Not over a man like that!

She tried vainly to plot revenge in the shower, using the washcloth savagely in an effort to remove all traces of him. The rush of water over her face made the desire to cry even stronger. But she stifled it, keeping her anger whipped up instead.

By the time she had stepped out and toweled briskly, Dara felt she had herself under control. She had sternly opted for a cold, austere manner in the hope it would help her get through the next few hours with some dignity. It was all a woman had at a time like this. Revenge was wishful thinking.

"Well, it's safe to say there won't be many women dressed like that at breakfast!" Yale quipped humorously as she stepped out of the bathroom.

She chose to ignore him, turning to the mirror to run a comb through her hair. His eyes met hers there and he smiled, trying to coax her into a better mood.

"But you do look good in green," he tried, studying the dress. He was wearing his jockey shorts now, his tanned body looking lean and powerful as he held the dark slacks and white shirt lightly clasped in one hand.

"Go to hell," she told him briefly and had the satisfaction of seeing his eyes narrow.

Without another word he stalked into the bathroom.

Twenty minutes later he ushered her into the twenty-four-hour coffee shop next door to the motel, gallantly moving to put himself between her and the curious eyes which glanced up from early-morning coffee to blink at the sight of a woman in an emerald cocktail dress. Dara made no objection as Yale seated her in a far booth and slid in beside her.

He was wearing his glasses again this morning and his

sleeves were neatly buttoned at the cuff. The honey-colored hair was tidy and there was a general air of restraint about him. Dara's lips quirked downward in disgust. Nothing Yale Ransom did now would fool her. She knew the kind of man he really was.

"What would you like?" he asked politely as the waitress appeared to take their order.

"Cold cereal, please," Dara said crisply, giving her order directly to the brunette woman holding the pad and pencil. "And coffee."

"You need more than that," Yale interrupted with a frown, scanning the menu. "Bring her a number three. And the same for me."

The woman dutifully scratched Dara's order from the pad and wrote the new one. With a casual nod, she left.

"That was a waste of food and money," Dara informed him coldly. "I'm not hungry."

"You need a nice, hot breakfast," he began in a lecturing tone.

"Forget it," she gritted in resignation, lifting her eyes heavenward in silent appeal. "I'll eat it if it will stop you from talking to me as if I were a child!"

"You're not a child, you're a woman scorned, remember?" he muttered grimly. "Except that you're not exactly being scorned. But those are petty details to a female in your present frame of mind."

Dara refused to look at him, her eyes following the waitress as the woman returned to the table with coffee.

"At least she isn't staring at your outfit," Yale observed quietly when they were alone.

"She's probably been on duty since midnight. You see a little of everything sooner or later on that shift," Dara explained woodenly, sipping her coffee with care.

"How do you know?" Yale sounded mildly surprised.

"Because I've worked it." She shrugged, still refusing to glance in his direction.

"You've worked in a place like this?"

"Every summer while I was in college," she explained shortly, not particularly interested in pursuing the conversation.

"No kidding? What else have you done? I think you said something last night about only recently having become a stockbroker."

Dara favored him with a baleful gaze at that question. "Why do you want to know?"

He shrugged, lifting his coffee cup and eyeing her over the rim. "I suppose I'm kind of curious."

"Take a tip from me. Curiosity doesn't pay," she retorted flatly.

One amber brow went up. "We are singing a different tune this morning, aren't we?"

Dara gritted her teeth, about to dredge up a scathing reply when a deep, cheerfully rumbling male voice interrupted the conversation.

"Excuse me, folks, but the little lady in green wouldn't happen to be a stockbroker by any chance, would she?"

Dara glanced up, startled, to find a huge, friendly-looking

man in his mid-forties staring down at her with smiling gray eyes. He reminded her a lot of Hank Bonner in his choice of a size thirty-four belt for a waistline considerably larger. The man was dressed in a plaid flannel shirt and faded jeans. He had long-distance trucker written all over him.

"May I ask who wants to know?" Yale's question was polite, but there was a firmness to it that drew the man's respectful attention.

"Sam's the name. Sam Tyler," he said at once, extending a wide paw of a hand to shake Yale's. "And I'll bet your name's Ransom, right?"

"You seem to know a great deal more about us than we know about you," Yale pointed out with a deliberate smile.

"There couldn't be two ladies in green at this particular truck stop on this particular morning. Mind if I join you for a cup? Hank Bonner's the source of my information, by the way."

"I see," Yale said slowly, speculatively. "Sit down, by all means. Where did you run into Hank?"

"Having coffee a ways down the line. He knew I was headin' north and asked me to deliver a message if I found you two at this café. Also suggested you might be needing a ride into Eugene!"

"That was thoughtful of him," Dara said quickly, wondering why Yale seemed a little aloof. She had been wondering how they were going to get home.

"He also said to tell you the hand was doing fine," Sam added with a smile.

"I'm glad. What was the message?" Dara asked encouragingly. Yale seemed a little more relaxed now.

"Well, I guess I'd have to say that's a tad more serious...."
The big trucker's gaze sobered and he turned to face Yale.

"Trouble?" Yale's eyes were cool and more alert than the situation seemed to call for, Dara decided.

"A little, I reckon. Hank said he mentioned his, uh, special cargo to you?"

"He did," Yale said briefly, ignoring Dara's frown.

She glanced from one man to the other, perplexed. "What are you talking about? What 'special cargo'?"

A silent look passed between the two men. The sort of Do-we-tell-the-little-lady-about-this-or-not? glance that was enough to boil a woman's blood. And Dara was already on a high simmer.

Yale considered the relentless expression in the gray-green ice of her eyes and appeared to come to a reluctant decision.

"A short while before we met Hank last night he stumbled across something unexpected being shipped in his truck. Something which had been taped to the cab in an inconspicuous place by someone who apparently intended to retrieve it later. Probably after Hank had obligingly brought it down from Canada and across a couple of state lines...."

"What sort of 'something'? Drugs?"

"She's right quick, ain't she?" Sam Tyler offered admiringly to Yale as if complimenting him on a well-trained horse.

"A little too quick at times, I'm afraid," Yale growled, shooting Dara a withering glance. "At any rate, Hank removed the stuff and then put out a quiet warning to friends at a few stops. They didn't spill it on the CB because he had hopes of catching the guy when he came looking for his stuff."

"Why didn't Hank go straight to the police with it when he found it?" Dara demanded, brows drawing together across her nose.

Once again Yale and Sam traded glances, and Yale finally said quietly, "There were reasons. Besides, it was just a small, er, personal amount…."

"We all figure it's a one-man maneuver. It's been done before," Sam tossed in helpfully. "the logical place for the pickup is somewhere south of the California-Oregon border…."

"After it's been driven across the state line," Dara put in.

"Right. But it didn't happen that way. The guy came for his pickup at the first stop Hank hit after letting you two off. Even though they weren't really expecting him that soon, Hank and a friend damned near caught him." Sam hesitated. "They did get a description of him which, after what you might call due consideration—" he grinned "—they turned over to the police. The sonova—pardon me, ma'am—the joker's got both the cops and half the folks on the Interstate watching for him now. Sooner or later he'll turn up."

"The situation seems to be under control," Yale murmured, clearly waiting for a punch line. Sam delivered it.

"Hank's pretty sure the guy will be picked up soon. Which will be a great relief to all concerned, naturally…."

"Naturally." Yale grinned, and once again Dara had the feeling she wasn't being told everything.

"But it occurred to him that if this, uh, joker's monitoring the CB jabber it might explain why he came for his stuff before it crossed the border...." Sam let the sentence trail off suggestively.

"Damn CB gossip!" Yale muttered.

"Okay, guys," Dara began vengefully. "Let's not lose the 'quick' one in the crowd just as she's beginning to catch up! What's the real problem? Why is Hank sending messages back to us?"

Sam looked at Yale and lifted a huge shoulder. Yale nodded and turned to Dara.

"Shortly after he let us off last night, at the very next stop, in fact, someone came looking for the 'cargo'...."

"And...?" It was like pulling teeth, she decided grimly, but her pride wasn't going to get in the way of her overriding curiosity. Dara was determined to get all the answers.

"By then the shipment had been removed," Yale went on gently.

"Obviously! You said Hank removed it at once!"

"And you and I constitute the main alteration in Hank's normal routine on the Interstate through Oregon. Whoever taped that stuff on the truck wouldn't have had much trouble learning that Hank had given a lift to a couple of strangers. He might have come to check that the cargo was still in place after the hitchhikers got off. Finding it gone, a disinterested observer might be excused for wondering if the cargo had gotten off with us."

"Oh," Dara muttered weakly as the light dawned. "The guy might think we hijacked his drugs?"

"A perverted thinker who didn't know our sterling characters might have come to that conclusion, yes," Yale said patiently. "Eat your eggs, they're getting cold."

"I'm not hungry," Dara said absently, her mind churning with the unexpected news. "You meant that creep might come after us?"

"A lot of folks heard about you on the air last night," Sam put in kindly. "Frankly, we don't figure it's very likely the guy will bother chasing you down. In the first place, the cargo wasn't that, er, large. And in the second place, if he's still listening to the CB he knows he's being hunted. If he's got any sense he'll fade into the sunset."

"I'll keep an eye on her until we know for sure the guy's been found," Yale announced casually, digging into his sausage.

"I'll keep an eye on myself," Dara snapped, and then another thought struck her. "Do the police know we were with Hank last night, Sam?"

"Don't believe he saw any point in mentioning you two," Sam assured her smilingly.

"Good!" Dara heaved a sigh of relief. A lot of people knew she'd left that party in the company of Yale Ransom. A lot of other people knew she'd been out joyriding on the Interstate and had wound up at a cheap truck-stop motel. If somehow the first group found out what the second group knew via a newspaper story... She winced. it didn't bear thinking about. Eugene was a small town and she wasn't sure how much a stockbroker's reputation could stand. Or an accountant's, for that matter! People didn't like trusting their hard-earned money to wild and reckless types!

As if he'd been following her thoughts, Yale smiled cryptically.

"Worrying about your reputation, or mine?"

"You take care of yourself and I'll look after myself!" she told him morosely.

Something wicked glinted in the hazel eyes behind the lenses of Yale's glasses. "The police haven't been told about us, but an enterprising newsperson looking to beef up a tale of interstate smuggling might do a little more research than is absolutely necessary."

Dara stared at him, stricken.

"Eat your breakfast, honey," Yale growled, appearing almost contrite at having added to her fears.

"I think I'm going to be sick," she informed him grandly.

Chapter 5

"Are you going to sulk for the rest of the weekend?" Yale inquired with apparently detached interest as he opened the door of the Alfa Romeo two hours later and stuffed Dara inside.

"Why do you care? I'm not going to be spending the weekend with you anyway!"

He slammed the door shut with a narrow-eyed glance and walked around the hood. In the distance Sam Tyler's truck lumbered up the empty street in search of the Interstate entrance. In a short while Dara would be home. She was extraordinarily grateful for the knowledge.

"How long do you usually stay in this sort of mood?" Yale asked as he slid behind the wheel.

"Shut up and take me home."

"I can't. I don't know where you live."

Gritting her teeth, Dara gave him directions. As he pulled away from the curb she glanced back down the street at the now silent bar. As long as she lived in Eugene it was going to remain the landmark of her debacle, she decided sadly.

"I just wish Hank had gone to the cops before we ran

342 JAYNE ANN KRENTZ

into him." She sighed. "And if that wish could be granted, I'd go on to wish that we'd never run into Hank!"

"Don't blame him for what happened last night. That was strictly between you and me," Yale growled, guiding the car through the quiet morning.

"But why did he wait until the guy came looking for the stuff before going to the cops?" she persisted. That point bothered her.

"It wouldn't have been convenient for Hank to go to the police at the time he found the extra cargo," Yale said patiently.

"Why not?"

"Your curiosity is beginning to return, isn't it?" he noted in a cheerier tone.

"As you have already pointed out, I'm not in the best of moods this morning. Are you going to answer me or not?"

Yale sighed. "Hank wasn't anxious to drag the cops into this because he was carrying a hot load."

"What?" Dara swung around to stare at him in astonishment. "Hank was carrying stolen goods?"

"No, 'hot goods' means that he was just carrying an unauthorized load. Trucking regulations specify what kinds of goods drivers are allowed to transport. Hank was hoping he could take care of the guy himself and that would be the end of it. But when he and his pal missed snagging the man last night they decided it would be better to haul in the cops. So Hank probably got rid of his cargo—which, incidentally, was a shipment of T.V. sets—and then went to the police with his story."

"You and he certainly got chummy up there in the front seat while I was dozing in that sleeper!"

"We had...things in common, I suppose you'd say," Yale admitted.

"How much in common?" Dara glanced at him suspiciously. "Don't tell me you try to take the law into your own hands, too? Not a proper, upstanding accountant like you!" She didn't bother to keep the scathing tone out of her last words.

"No," he said, a strange smile coming easily to the hard mouth. A reminiscent sort of smile. "But I know what it's like to avoid the police. Remember, there are a lot of illegal stills up in those blue hills where I come from."

"Illegal stills?" Dara drew in her breath as realization dawned. "Yale! You didn't! You weren't a...a..." She broke off suddenly enthralled. "How did you work your way through college?" she demanded.

He flicked her a derisive glance and then brought his attention back to his driving. "I did what paid the most," he told her laconically.

"You ran moonshine? Illegal whiskey?" She was fascinated.

He nodded once, not looking at her.

"They still do that back there?" she pressed, intrigued.

"The business is bigger than ever. The Feds will never kill it. You folks on the Coast have your million-dollar drug busts, and back in the hill country we had our million-dollar illegal liquor busts."

"It seems different somehow, though. I mean, I've never

really thought of moonshine whiskey as being in the same category as imported drugs like heroin."

"You don't think white lightning's taken its share of victims?" he asked coolly. "It's a hell of a lot more dangerous than a lot of drugs!"

"Well, I suppose it's as dangerous as any alcohol..." she agreed slowly.

"Alcoholism isn't the only problem associated with it," Yale snapped. "Anyone buying it runs the same risk of getting contaminated stuff as someone scoring any other drug on the street. Some of it really will cause blindness. Not to mention the possibility of lead poisoning. There are a lot of 'shine addicts back in the states around the Appalachian Mountains."

"One thinks of it as a kind of folk tradition or something," Dara said, lifting a hand in a small, helpless gesture.

"Oh, it's a tradition, all right," Yale conceded bitterly. "Passed down from father to son. The kids grow up in families where being an adult male means being able to drink the stuff. They can't wait. And it goes on from one generation to the next."

"And the women?" she asked softly, curiously.

"They have to live with the men who are addicted. Most of the violence the stuff produces comes out in the home. You can use your imagination."

Dara sat silently for a moment, thinking of the memories she had stirred awake in Yale's mind by her rashness the previous evening.

"Did you know how bad the stuff was when you were running it?" she asked tentatively.

He just threw her a pitying glance. "Do I look like the naive type?"

"Er, no."

"It was the only game in town when I was growing up. About the only viable industry in the area. It sure as hell was where the money was at, and I knew from the start I was going to need two things to get out of those mountains: money and an education. I needed the first to buy the second."

"And you got it." It was a statement of fact.

"I got part of the education and then I got married to a high-school acquaintance who saw me as her ticket out of the mountains." His mouth twisted with astonishing bitterness. Dara felt a cold chill down her spine.

"Then what happened?" She knew she ought to stop asking questions, but something drove her on, demanding to know the whole story.

"Then I needed more money and a more legal way to get it." Yale shrugged. "I got a job driving trucks for a couple of years. It worked. We got out of the mountains."

"And…?"

He slanted a glance across the seat, taking in Dara's intent expression. "And she found someone who could take her farther than just out of the mountains."

"She left you?"

"Yes. Best for all concerned, as it turned out," he went on with a philosophical inflection. "She married someone who could give her a lot more than I could, and I had another chance to go back to school. Which I did."

"Emerging a proper, dignified accountant at last, hmm?" Dara smiled, relaxing finally now that she had the whole story.

"Satisfied?" he asked sardonically.

"Just think," she retorted, "if you'd given me all those answers last night we would never have wound up in that awful situation!"

"So it was all my fault again?"

"It's been your fault from the beginning!"

"The argument is academic at this point," he told her evenly, slowing as they approached the street on which her apartment was located. A jogger passed the Alfa Romeo, headed in the opposite direction along one of the many paths the town had established for cyclists and joggers.

"Meaning?" she challenged.

"Meaning you're mine. Regardless of how it all happened, the ultimate result is the same."

"Damn it! Don't talk like that!" she suddenly yelped as he parked the car in front of her apartment.

"Like what?" Yale asked innocently, turning in the seat to face her.

"As if...as if you own me or something because of what happened last night!" Her temporary satisfaction at having her questions about him answered evaporated in the presence of his continued threat.

"But I do," he explained gently, hazel eyes gleaming. He

moved, uncoiling with astonishing speed to forestall her effort to dive out of the car.

"Don't run away from me, honey," he soothed, his hand manacling her wrist with a grip that would only hurt if she struggled too hard. "I've told you I'm sorry about the way everything happened. It wasn't the hearts and flowers and romance you deserve, I admit that. Let me show you I can do better than a truck-stop motel...."

"You're out of your head if you think I'm going to let you hang around for...for more of what happened last night!" Dara gasped, appalled at the intensity in him. Dear God in heaven! Why did he have to look so *sincere?* But maybe he *was* sincere, she corrected herself grimly. Maybe he had decided he was in the market for an affair and she had practically invited him into one!

"Last night was good and you know it," he told her firmly, voice deepening with husky meaning. "Stop fighting it, Dara. It's happened and we're involved now. Nothing's going to change that."

"The hell it isn't! You may have decided you're content with the 'transaction,' but I've had a lot of second and third thoughts! I'm withdrawing from the bargain. Give your damn account to someone else!"

"I apologize for that remark..." he began, his fingers tightening on her wrist. "Let me explain!"

"Explain! Explain that you're accustomed to bargaining for...for love? I don't want to hear your explanations!"

"Love?" he questioned softly, mouth curving. "Was that what I was going to get out of the deal? Your love?"

"You'll never know, will you?" she charged violently, horribly afraid he might feel the trembling anger and pain in her. Desperately she tried to keep her voice cold and callous. "Because the deal is off!"

"How can it be when it was so perfectly consummated?" he murmured, pulling her forward until she fell lightly against his chest. "And you are quite perfect, you know," he went on whimsically, ignoring her struggles while he used his free hand to smooth the curve of her hair. His finger trailed from the burnt-russet wave to the edge of her angry mouth.

"Can't you at least try to resurrect some of those fine Southern manners you were showing off last night before you reverted to a...a trucker?" she managed breathlessly, aware of the heat and strength of him as he held her close. "I don't like being mauled on a Saturday morning in front of the entire neighborhood!"

"It wasn't my fine Southern manners you wanted last night," he reminded her, bending his head down until the hard mouth hovered an inch above her lips. "What you got was the real me, and don't try telling me you didn't like it. You were all softness and warmth and sweet, feminine demand in my arms last night. I'll never forget it, honey, even if the surroundings weren't what they should have been for the occasion...."

"No!" But the protest was issued as a small squeak of dismay which died beneath the onslaught of Yale's kiss.

Almost instantly, it seemed, his caress re-created the seductive aura of the dream-filled state in which he had made love to her last night. His mouth was firm and moved invitingly, coaxingly on hers. She heard his stifled groan of need as he urged her lips apart with his tongue, and when her mouth opened to him of its own volition her senses were throbbing.

It was hopeless, Dara thought dazedly. In his arms, she was too vulnerable and her love was far too exposed. Did he know the effect he had on her? How she longed to unbutton his shirt and lace her fingers through the amber hair of his chest? How her body pulsed with memories of the pleasure it had known last night and with the need to satisfy the man who had given rise to that strange pleasure? Did he know how very much in love she was?

When at last he lifted his head to smile crookedly down into her bemused eyes, Dara wanted to beg him to continue his lovemaking. She knew beyond a shadow of a doubt he was reading her state of mind in her wide, gray-green eyes. The crooked smile broadened.

"I'll take you out to dinner tonight," he promised caressingly, his hand stroking the length of her back to the base of her spine. "We'll do it properly this time, I swear..."

"That's...that's impossible," she finally got out with some semblance of haughtiness. She was not going to let this man treat her so shabbily again! Regardless of what her heart was willing to forgive, her mind still functioned and was in control! "I have a date this evening."

"Break it," he ordered gently.

"Why should I? His account might be even larger than yours!" That hadn't been particularly wise, but Dara was feeling driven. Nevertheless, as his hands tightened with sudden warning on her, she wished she'd found another insult.

"Dara, you ought to have learned something from last night," Yale growled thickly. "If nothing else, you should know by now that it's not wise to push me too far. Either break your date for this evening or take the consequences!"

"What consequences?"

"Honey, if you flaunt someone else in my face now that you're mine, I swear I'll take him apart," he gritted in such a flat, deadly voice she believed him.

"Another example of your good manners?" she scoffed, trying to hide her shock. "Is this the kind of behavior I can expect now that you've announced your intention to treat me as I deserve?"

The amber lashes flickered closed for an instant and Dara could feel Yale putting a rein on his temper. It was more than a little unnerving to be so close to the source of a potential explosion. When he opened his eyes again, the lenses of the horn-rimmed glasses couldn't hide the degree of control he was exercising.

"I'm doing my best to be patient with you, Dara," he said stiffly. "I know you've been through a lot in the past several hours. Much more than you bargained for...."

"You can say that again! I wasn't even planning on transacting business when I went to that party last night. Goes to show how life is just full of little surprises!"

"You know, I could cheerfully take a belt to you this morning!"

"Really? Is that how you treat your women?"

"You seem bent on finding out for yourself!" he rasped, shaking his head in quick exasperation. "And if you aren't waiting very meekly at the door for me this evening, I may treat you to a firsthand demonstration of my techniques! In you go, Dara. I'll pick you up at six. And don't wear your jeans. We're not going to any of your favorite nightclubs!"

Several hours later, after a lot of furious heartsearching and grim lectures to herself, Dara paced the floor of her apartment, for all the world like a restless cat. A tabby cat. She knew she was waiting for the sophisticated roar of the Alfa Romeo.

She couldn't deny it, she thought gloomily. She was in love. She had fallen in love last night, and nothing was going to change that fact that quickly. She was a woman who prided herself on a pragmatic approach to life. She would deal with the reality of the situation and not pretend she was merely temporarily infatuated. She knew what infatuation was. It was what she had felt for her ex-husband. And now she knew what love was.

There were cures for being in love, just as there were cures for infatuation, she told herself firmly. But the remedies for love were likely to have some severe side effects. And they didn't work quickly, as far as she knew. Time was one of them. Time and throwing oneself into work and perhaps finding another man… She would try them all. As soon as she could free herself from Yale Ransom!

Chewing absently on her lower lip, she came to a brief halt in front of a hall mirror and ran a quick, assessing eye over herself. There had been no date to cancel for this evening. Jeff Conroy, the research analyst from the office, was out of town on business and she hadn't felt like seeing any of her other assorted escorts. She almost hadn't gone to her manager's party last night, in fact. Too bad she hadn't followed her inclinations!

The curving bell of her deep red hair was brushed and polished-looking in the glow of the lamp. The floating material of the exotically printed yellow and green dress fell flatteringly over her rounded breasts and softly flaring hips. She had chosen her highest-heeled sandals in an effort to be on more equal footing with Yale, but she was very much afraid that wouldn't be a lot of help. He tended to dominate everyone in his vicinity.

On the whole, she had to be reasonably satisfied with the overall effect. She looked poised, cool and very much in command of herself. It was as much as she could hope for under the circumstances, she thought with a sigh as the sound of a car stopping out front caught her attention.

She opened the door to find Yale standing on the step, every inch the neat, conservatively dressed professional. For some reason she almost laughed, barely managing to stifle the flash of humor. But he must have seen it in her eyes, because the gold winked in his grin and the hazel eyes glittered wickedly behind the austere glasses.

"Why do you have to look past the surface?" he complained, stepping inside the cozy apartment and glancing around expectantly. "I really am an accountant, you know. Give me a chance!" He finished his quick perusal of the room and lifted her chin possessively with his hand. Dropping a light, proprietary kiss on her lips, he released her almost at once.

"I gave you a chance," she reminded him determinedly. "And you turned out to be something altogether different from an accountant!" She moved away from him. "I'll get my purse."

She disappeared into the bedroom and returned to find him studying her eclectic collection of books. He put down the small volume of eighteenth-century philosophy as she appeared in the doorway.

"Your interests appear to be wide-ranging," he murmured, coming forward. "Do you play that guitar?" He nodded toward the instrument on the wall.

"A little," she admitted carefully, eyeing him uneasily.

"And can you really cook stuff out of those fancy gourmet cookbooks?"

"Do I look like I've been starving to death most of my life?" she tossed back, reaching for a fluffy shawl.

He came up behind her, adjusting the shawl and then sliding his hands warmly down her sides, shaping her curves. "No," he whispered throatily. "You look like a woman who knows instinctively about womanly things like cooking and loving and—"

"And selling securities!" she interrupted, stepping hastily away from his touch.

"And selling securities," he agreed smiling. He flicked a glance over her interestedly. "Tonight's my night to ask the questions," he went on slowly.

"I thought you were going to take a lesson from me in the perils of curiosity," she muttered, turning briskly toward the door.

"I won't complain if my curiosity leads us to bed as yours did last night." He chuckled, following her out the door and into the dusk of the spring evening.

"It won't!" she swore. "Nothing will lead me into a repeat of last night! Unlike you, I've learned my lesson!"

"What did he say?" Yale asked almost conversationally as he helped her into the car and took his place behind the wheel.

"Who?" She frowned, momentarily at a loss.

"The guy you broke the date with tonight."

"That's none of your business," she declared regally, glancing pointedly out the window.

"Everything about you is my business now," he told her patiently. "But I'll let that question ride. After all, you didn't try to force a confrontation. I'll be satisfied with that."

"You're too generous!"

"I know, but that's probably because I'm feeling guilty."

"Over last night?" she scoffed. "I don't believe you."

"Try me. Give me a chance, honey. I'll make everything right this time around."

She slanted a suspicious glance across the seat, not certain how to react. This sudden earnestness to start over left her confused and wary.

"Tell me about yourself," he ordered in a rather business-like fashion some time later as they were seated in a charming downtown restaurant. One of the new Oregon-grown and-bottled wines was on the table, the atmosphere was elegantly subdued and the other patrons were well dressed and well mannered. Yale had brought her a long way from last night, Dara thought with fleeting humor.

"What do you want to know?" she asked, picking up the menu with a sense of anticipation. The food really was very good here, and Dara appreciated good food.

He shrugged. "Anything. Everything. Are you a native?"

"Native Oregonian? Definitely," she informed him, scanning the list of Continental specialties.

"Have you ever been outside the state?" he asked in amusement.

"Only when absolutely necessary," she told him with the blissful smugness of the classic Oregonian. "I was forced to go to California once for a time and I've made a couple of brief forays into Washington." She shuddered in recollection.

"I'm beginning to feel that way myself, and I've only been here a short while," Yale chuckled.

She glanced up and met his laughing eyes. "Most new immigrants want to be the last ones allowed over the border. They'd like to see the place closed off once they're safe here. You know, issue passports and visas to the rest of the folks who want to come for a visit!"

"You can't blame us," he said gently, watching her face with deep interest. "Oregon is so unspoiled and has so much to offer. We newcomers feel like we've found a paradise, and we know how easily paradises are ruined. What amazes me is that you natives are equally conscious of what you've got."

She nodded, perfectly aware of what he was talking about. "We've got everything that counts. The outdoors is everywhere, even in the cities. We're proud of our past and we've preserved it. We're very self-reliant, a heritage from that past, I suppose. A lot of us are descendants of people who came out west on wagon trains, you know. Our towns and cities are manageable in size. Portland's our only 'big' city, and that's only about four hundred thousand people. A lot of people make their living in the lumber industry, and that tends to breed an independent spirit."

"Everything about this state is independent," Yale murmured, trying his wine tentatively. It was his first exposure to Oregon wines. "Your environmentalist attitudes are famous throughout the rest of the nation, you know. You're all considered flaming radicals on the East Coast! Your state and local governments have spent a fortune taking care of your rivers and air and land."

"We know what we've got." She shrugged. "Land this beautiful doesn't last unless it's taken care of."

He nodded. "I'm aware of that."

"Why did you move from California?" Dara asked.

"L.A. turned out to be a little too far from the hills," Yale confided with surprising honesty.

Dara's lashes flicked against her high cheekbones as she considered that. "So you came looking for someplace a little more real, is that it?"

"Something like that," he agreed reflectively. "I don't ever want to go back to the mountains, but I found out I didn't want to give up everything I'd taken for granted as a child, either. I like smaller towns. I'll never be at home in a huge metropolis. And I like having the outdoors in my backyard."

"You can take the boy out of the country, but you can't take the country out of the boy?" Dara grinned in sudden sympathy.

"I guess that's it," he said slowly, returning her smile.

In that moment of communication Dara realized she had made a huge mistake. She had unwittingly allowed him to establish the truce he had been seeking.

"And that, my darling Dara," Yale continued, cementing the truce with sure instinct, "is something I hadn't even admitted to myself until you forced the realization on me. You're a witch, sweetheart."

"Do people back in the mountains still believe in witches?" she whispered, aware of the sensual tension she was experiencing.

"Definitely. Just because we talk a little slower than the rest of you doesn't mean we think any slower!"

He danced with her after dinner. Not in the restrained way he had danced at the flashy, ex-disco nightclub nor in the earthy, blatantly sexual way he had at the truckers' bar. This time Yale held her close, the embrace intimate but not embarrassing, and Dara foolishly allowed herself to revel in the swaying, enticing strength of his lean body.

She knew she was being seduced; knew it and for the life of her didn't know how to combat it. She loved this man in all his complexity, and saying no to him tonight was going to take more willpower than she might have in reserve. But it must be said. her whole future depended on it.

Chapter 6

As much as she had tried to prepare herself for the inevitable difficulty of ending the evening adroitly, and even with all her considerable experience at ending such evenings with other men, Dara had to acknowledge later that she badly mishandled the event. She found herself detonating the male time bomb in her hands with hardly any effort at all.

"I hope you're going to invite me to stay the night," Yale said deliberately, setting aside the guitar on which he'd picked out a couple of haunting mountain melodies for her and reaching for the glass of brandy Dara had poured.

So matter-of-fact! Dara drew a deep breath and said very carefully, "No, Yale. Not tonight." She sat quite still and watchful on her end of the couch and waited.

"Tonight, especially," he contradicted quietly, his eyes meeting hers with cool certainty.

In spite of herself, Dara shivered. "Why do you say that?" she whispered.

"Because I'm supposed to be keeping an eye on you, remember?" Yale allowed himself a smile at her look of astonishment.

Dara arched an eyebrow quellingly. "To tell you the

truth, I'd almost forgotten about that small-time smuggler. But it doesn't matter. We both know he's not likely to show up. He doesn't even know our names."

"He could have followed us this morning, waiting until tonight to come calling," Yale suggested helpfully.

"Don't be ridiculous! You're making excuses and you know it!"

"You're right." He sighed. "I really don't need any other excuse than the obvious, do I?"

"You're not staying here tonight, Yale. The evening has been lovely, I'll admit that much, but not lovely enough to cause me to make a fool out of myself again. This is as far as you're going to get with your seduction."

He considered that for a moment. "I'm going to stay," he announced flatly.

"Then you'll have to sleep outside in the Alfa Romeo, because you most certainly aren't staying here. Good night, Yale." With an air of determination, Dara rose to her feet.

He leaned back into the corner of the couch, one leg stretching out along the cushions with the foot dangling. The picture of the relaxed male, she thought in dismay. His dark tie had ben loosened and his jacket lay over the back of the couch. Some of the rakishness of last night was back. It set off all the alarms Yale had spent the evening silencing.

"Yale," she tried reasonably, "what happened last night was bad enough, but only a bunch of truckers whom we'll never see know about it. If you stay here tonight all my neighbors will know! As you yourself pointed out, this isn't

Los Angeles! If you're not concerned about my reputation, you ought to think about your own."

He sipped his brandy and contemplated the unicorn tapestry on the far wall. "An interesting notion." He turned his head to look at her speculatively. "It occurs to me that I *am* the injured party in all this. It was my reputation you set about tearing down last night…."

"Don't be an idiot! All I ever did was ask you a few questions! You're the one who—"

"Let's not get into that argument again. We're never going to agree on whose fault it was that we wound up at that motel last night." He groaned good-naturedly, wriggling his shoe a couple of times as he stared at the tip. "But I am staying, sweetheart. I'm a little concerned about that creep still being on the loose. I won't be comfortable thinking about you alone here."

"Yale…!" Dara opened her mouth in mounting frustration.

"I won't force myself on you, for God's sake," he told her irritably. "I'll sleep out here on the couch."

"That's not going to help the problem of my reputation!"

"Or mine. But I suppose we'll live it down," he said philosophically.

For some reason his nonchalance was the match to her kindling.

"Why you…you *bastard!* How dare you spend the evening behaving so perfectly when all along you were planning this! If you think I'm going to tolerate…oh!"

Her eyes blazed up at him as he leaped to his feet, all the lazy gentleness vanishing instantly.

"That's enough! You've called me a bastard twice today, and that's twice too often!" Yale had his hands on her shoulders before Dara could slip aside. The hazel eyes echoed her own simmering fury, and Dara was acutely aware of the fact that he had far more strength than she had to back his anger.

"I told myself I was going to be patient with you, give you a chance to cool off after this morning, but maybe the temper I saw then is routine for you! If that's the case, then I'm going to have to do something about it. Beginning now!" He gave her a small, decisive shake. "Apologize, Dara! There was a time when I would have taken a knife to any man who called me a name like that!"

"Why don't you try that approach?" she bit out recklessly. "You probably still carry one in your sock for old times' sake!"

"There are other tactics one can use on a woman," he warned silkily, forcing her closer.

"Don't you dare threaten me, Yale Ransom!"

"How are you going to stop me, Dara Bancroft?" he said with a hint of savagery. One hand sliding up to grip her nape and hold her steady as if she were a kitten, Yale snapped off his glasses and tossed them down onto the circular glass coffee table. Then his hand went to his loosened tie, pulling it free. It followed the glasses. His eyes never left her frozen face as his fingers went to the top button of his shirt.

"Stop it, Yale! I mean it, damn you!"

"I want an apology, Dara. A heartfelt one, I think."

"Why should I apologize?" she managed bravely. "It's the truth."

"I know. Which is probably why I want the apology," he retorted, his fingers on the second button of his shirt.

"You know?" she repeated in blank confusion.

"Umm. My father was killed in a fight before he got around to marrying my mother."

"Oh! Yale, Yale!" Dara lifted her palms to his face, her heart in her eyes. "You must know I never meant it literally! It's always been just another swearword to me. Please accept my apology."

His hand stilled and he regarded her solemnly for a moment while she waited contritely for him to tell her everything was all right again. Dara could have bitten her tongue out for having fought so unfairly. The gray and green eyes were full of her anxiety as she gazed up into his face, her hands still gently framing his hard jaw.

"How can I refuse?" he whispered a little hoarsely, his fingers gliding up her arm to capture one of her hands. "When you say it so nicely." He touched his lips to the sensitive area of her palm, first kissing it and then closing his teeth ever so tantalizingly on the flesh at the base of her thumb. The utter eroticism of the caress chilled her.

"Yale?" The question in her voice was clear and tremulous. He smiled gently down into her face. Without a word he drew her against him and kissed her.

"Do you always go from raging inferno to sweetly yielding female so quickly?" he breathed in amusement as his lips feathered across hers. "I find it fascinating, you know. So much fire and so much warmth."

"Yale, no!" Dara's voice was a plea as her eyes closed involuntarily against the force of her own passion. "I won't let you stay tonight. I can't!"

"We'll talk about it in the morning," he promised thickly. She knew he was letting the arousal he had held in check all evening begin to take command. She could feel it in the growing tautness of his thighs as he used his hand to force her close against him.

"Don't fight me, honey," he begged, shifting his leg so that it thrust between hers. Off balance and terribly aware of her vulnerability in the intimate position, Dara tried to resist.

"I won't let you do it!" she whispered, pushing at him even as her body longed for the embrace. "I won't conduct another…another business *transaction* with you, damn it!"

"No?" he mocked huskily, his hands moving down her sides, sliding across the high breasts with loving slowness before descending to the shape of her waist. He urged her closer so that his upper thigh pressed heavily against her. The thin fabric of her dress was little protection and Dara was fully conscious of the hard maleness of him.

The undeniable evidence of his physical response to her was a seduction in itself, she realized, alarmed. She felt the rush of longing she had known the night before and began to panic.

"No!" she gasped in answer to his mocking question.

"No, I will not allow another business deal between us, because you *couldn't afford the price* this time!"

The defiant words seemed to scorch the air around them. Dara froze as she felt the savage tension in him. His hands clenched into her soft flesh and his words came back angry and raw.

"What price, Dara? *Name it!* We'll find out whether or not I'll pay it!"

She was committed, forced to follow through on her wild threat. She felt backed into a corner and she came out fighting for her very survival.

"The price is marriage, Yale! I don't want you to get the idea I'm still selling myself for anything so paltry as a stock account! You'll have to marry me this time!"

A taunting wickedness flashed in the hazel eyes. "Is that your idea of revenge, little tabby?" he drawled.

"That's my idea of how to stop a Southern gentleman in his tracks!" she flung back, incensed at his barely masked humor. "Force yourself on me tonight and I will demand that you do the *honorable* thing!"

"I think," he informed her gravely, "that you're in the wrong part of the South. Where I come from we called that sort of thing a shotgun wedding. Have you got a shotgun?" he asked interestedly.

"Push me too far tonight and you'll find out!" A thoroughly ridiculous promise, Dara thought gloomily. How could you force a man to marry you? Unless, of course, his own code of honor required it....

"I do believe you're trying to threaten me, sweetheart,"

Yale murmured, gliding his hands down her back and capturing her hips in a kneading grip. His lips hovered in the vicinity of her ear and she trembled at the overpowering nearness of him.

"Those are my terms, Yale," she breathed, her face buried in the material of his shirt as she waited with agonized suspense for the results of her reckless play. Nothing should have been more guaranteed to stop his seduction routine than the knowledge that she would be expecting marriage! Dara was certain of her weapon. The only thing she wasn't certain of was whether or not she had really wanted to use it. Another night with Yale Ransom was a temptation beyond any she had ever experienced.

"I'm amazed you think so highly of my sense of honor," he observed coolly, dropping a featherlight kiss on her temple.

Dara gave a small start of surprise. "There's no doubt in my mind that you're a man who likes to stay on even terms with the world," she gritted. "You seem to have a pay-as-you-go philosophy about life. You proved that this morning!"

"When I told you you could have my account?" He groaned and then kissed her throat just below her ear. "You may be right."

"And you're not a fool…" she went on carefully, wishing her body didn't react so strongly to a man she had known such a short time.

"That's a more debatable point."

"Not foolish enough to commit yourself to marriage

with a woman you've only known a little over twenty-four hours!" she declared, bitter triumph lacing her words.

"I'll admit the price you're setting on yourself tonight is a bit steep," he hedged, his mouth traveling down to the curve of her shoulder.

"And I'm going to stick to it. I won't sell myself as cheaply as you seem to think I did last night!" she cried wretchedly.

"If that's the way you want it," he said slowly, and she thought she felt him tense. He was going to leave. She knew it. Knew it and wanted insanely to call back her words.

But it was too late. She had made her decision and she would force herself to abide by it. There was the future to think about tonight, not just a few tempting hours of ecstasy with a man who considered love a business transaction!

"As long as we understand each other," he whispered thickly, "we might as well get on with the transaction."

He moved, sweeping her into his arms with a smooth power that took away her breath.

"Yale! What are you doing?" she gasped as he started down the short hall to her bedroom. "Put me down!"

"Why? You set the terms. Don't tell me you're going to try to back out of them now."

"That's right!" she rasped furiously. "I set the terms. And I'm going to make you stick to them! I swear it!"

"Okay," he said simply, using a large foot to open the door to her darkened bedroom.

"What do you mean, 'okay'?" she yelped, the combination of passion and anger heating her veins until she felt liquid fire running through her body.

"I accept the terms," he explained evenly, dropping her lightly onto the old-fashioned country-patterned quilt that covered the four-poster bed.

She stared up at him, trying to make out his expression in the dimly lit room. She was curled in a shaft of light which fell onto the bed from the hall and she felt extraordinarily vulnerable. Everything was going wrong. She had been so sure her demand would send him fleeing into the night!

"You can't be serious!" she tried, her eyes fastened on him in utter fascination. "Do you know what you're saying?"

Even though he stood in the shadows, Dara couldn't miss the flash of gold in his slow, sardonic grin. "Don't worry about me," he advised, stripping off his shirt and letting it fall, unheeded, to the carpet. "You should be asking yourself that question. Between last night and tonight you're going to find yourself with both me and my account to handle. And we're both going to take a lot of time and attention."

Dara scrambled to her knees on the bed, not knowing whether to lash out at him or open her arms to receive him. Was he mad? She wasn't the sort of woman who drove men to rash extremes! She hadn't even been able to seduce her ex-husband away from thoughts of his former fiancée!

Dara put out a hand in uncertain appeal as Yale began efficient work on his belt buckle.

"Yale, listen to me. You're not talking about a…a short fling with a woman you happened to meet at a party! You're standing there, telling me you're going to marry me! In the morning you're going to have all sorts of regrets, call yourself a fool! Don't you understand?"

"After what we found between us last night, I don't see any reason why I should have regrets," he countered, stepping out of the rest of his clothes as if he were accustomed to undressing in her bedroom. Or as if he expected to become accustomed to it.

"Well, what about me?" she tried, unable to keep her longing gaze away from the tanned and powerful male body standing in front of her. "Think about what you're doing to me!"

"I don't have to think about that. You've already done your own thinking and set your own price. I'm willing to pay it. What could be simpler?"

He put one knee on the bed and reached for her. Panicked, Dara wriggled backward, getting shakily to her feet on the opposite side. She retreated swiftly, convinced he would pounce at her.

But he didn't move. Instead, Yale sat patiently on the edge of the bed and watched her with persuasive, gleaming eyes. His voice was unbelievably dark and silky on her nerves.

"Don't run from me, my darling Dara. Haven't I agreed to give you everything you've asked for? What more can a man do? I want you. Badly enough to pay your price. And you know you want me. Come here and let me show you...."

She felt her senses reeling at the seductive tendrils curling around her and she knew she was going to be caught up in the spell of him as she had been last night. How could a woman deny the man she loved? It was like denying her own breath. It went against all her natural instincts. *And he was going to marry her!*

"Come here, little tabby cat," he coaxed with electrifying tenderness. "Come and warm me with your passion and your need. I want to feel the curve of your hips and the swell of your breasts. I want to know that moment when you lose control and give yourself completely. I want to feel you take me inside and make me a part of you...."

"Oh, Yale," Dara whispered weakly, knowing her resistance was rapidly collapsing and helpless to stop it.

He held out his hand invitingly, and in spite of herself, Dara took a tentative step forward toward the bed. He was drawing her close with invisible bonds that had been forged last night and could never be unmade. She knew that in the deepest recesses of her mind. As long as Yale chose to chain her she was caught.

"I meant it, Yale," she tried valiantly as she stopped at the edge of the bed. His hand was still extended in silent demand. "I really meant it. If...if you go through with this I will expect nothing less than marriage!"

He moved then with unexpected swiftness, snagging her wrist and pulling her down beside him. He rolled heavily onto her, crushing her into the quilt and gazing down into her startled eyes with masculine triumph.

"I never supposed you didn't," he assured her with a low groan of desire.

And then he was covering her mouth with his own, plundering the warmth he found there as if the previous night had only whetted his appetite. She was held fettered beneath his heavy strength while he mastered her senses once more.

"Yale, why do I let you do this to me?" Dara said huskily, coming alive under his touch.

"When you know the answer to that, tell me," he ordered gruffly.

Confident now of her willing compliance, Yale shifted, moving onto his back and pulling her into an abandoned sprawl across his chest. He slid the dress from her shoulders, past her waist, leaving her to kick free of the confining folds.

"You fill my hands so perfectly," he marveled, deftly unsnapping the front clasp of her bra and letting her soft femininity spill into his waiting hands.

Dara moaned deeply with mounting anticipation as her nipples rose to the touch of his thumb and forefinger. Unconsciously she arched her lower body against the pulsating maleness of him.

"Show me how an Oregon woman treats the man she's going to marry," Yale growled roughly, his hands moving down to her waist and over the curve of her hips, urging her closer.

Dara closed her eyes and gave herself over to the need they shared. Throwing any remaining caution to the winds, she allowed her love full rein.

Her lips sought his willingly, enticing a response that was granted immediately. She felt him groan as her breasts brushed teasingly against his chest, and his undisguised response encouraged her as nothing else could have done.

Her excitement scaling ever upward, Dara probed against

the challenge of his tongue, defeating it utterly, and then she withdrew to explore the tips of his ears.

"You'll pay for that," he rasped in tantalizing menace as she carefully closed her teeth around one lobe. His fingertips sank sharply into her buttocks and scored a flickering pattern of excruciating, exhilarating stimulation which coursed down to her toes.

"Oh!" Dara's cry was one of feminine need and desire, and it seemed to act on him just as her hands and lips had acted.

But it also unleashed a totally unfamiliar aggression in her. A fantasy of power and seduction which Dara would never have dreamed she had. This man was hers. She had pushed him into a promise of marriage, a promise which she fully intended he should keep. He thought he was merely paying the price she had set, but there was more to it, much more. He was going to learn that he belonged to her, she decided exuberantly.

"My tabby cat is secretly a wildcat," Yale muttered in astonished wonder as Dara began a feverish exploration of his body. "My God, little one. You drive me crazy!'

She trailed kisses of damp passion down his throat, into the hollow of his shoulder and out to the sensitive inside of his elbow. His hands wrapped themselves in the heavy tangle of her hair as she kissed the warm skin of his stomach. His legs shifted heavily, restlessly, around her as she moved down to his thighs.

Once again she used her teeth, nipping with playful passion at the muscled tautness of him. She felt the rising desire that threatened to put an end to her bold loveplay and swiftly captured his wrists.

Dara was too caught up in the excitement and wonder of her newfound arrogance and aggression to realize she wasn't exactly mastering his strength with her own. The fact that he was submissive before her onslaught was enough. She would make him remember this night, she told herself as she moved upward again, straddling his hips and pinning his wrists beside his head.

"A wildcat," he grated hoarsely, no fighting the restraint of her hands as she leaned over to kiss him deeply, hungrily, persuasively. His body lifted, seeking hers, but she resisted, teasing him with a wantonness that amazed a small corner of her mind. This couldn't be her, that corner protested, quite shocked.

But it was, and Dara thrilled to the knowledge. She had known this man was crucial to her future happiness, but she had never dreamed he would open this door to her physical responses.

"Come and claim your man, woman!" Yale's soft command came tightly as she nibbled on his shoulder. She felt him arch upward again, urging her to complete the union.

But the wildness of her mood was not to be so easily coaxed back to the yielding Yale's body wanted. She would show this man he was at her mercy, make him acknowledge his desire for her. He would discover what it meant to be the one who submitted.

She lifted her head from his throat long enough to laugh a siren's laugh, gazing down into his gleaming hazel eyes.

"Do you want me, Yale?" she breathed.

"Want you, need you, desire you…" His head moved once on the pillow in silent disgust with the lack of sufficient words. Then he groaned with deep insistence. "Finish your seduction, tabby cat. Put me out of this misery. I can't stand your teasing much longer!"

"Misery?" She pouted, her fingertips toying with the masculine nipples. "I'm not sure I like that description. I wouldn't want to make you miserable, Yale…."

"Call it what you want," he breathed huskily, "but finish it before I go out of my head!"

"I would like to see that." Dara laughed throatily, bending to touch her lips lightly to his throat. "I would like to see you driven a little crazy by me…."

"You're enjoying your power?" he murmured, drawing in his breath sharply as she touched her tongue to the edge of his mouth and then his chin.

"Enormously."

"Have you ever played with fire before?" he demanded tightly.

"Not like this," she admitted.

"And now that you've chained a man in your spell, you're determined to extract all the pleasure from torturing him that you can, is that it?"

"I want to hear you beg," she agreed delightedly.

"I'm begging," he whispered.

"Not loudly enough." Still holding his wrists firmly to the bed, she scattered fleeting, alluring little kisses across his chest.

"You're a harsh mistress," he groaned.

"Not a mistress," she denied at once, angered slightly. "I'm going to be your wife!"

"In that case," he rapped suddenly, "you'd better start learning a little something about wifely obedience!"

He seemed to erupt beneath her, his hands coming free of her grip as if she had never attempted to bind him. Before she could do more than gasp her startled surprise, Dara found herself flat on her back, his broad shoulders looming over her.

Without warning she was thoroughly anchored to the bed, both her hands caught in one of his and drawn tautly over her head. His thigh moved over hers, pinning her writhing legs.

She felt the excitement flash through her in waves, as she reacted to the passionate capture with a thrilling awareness that was as strong as her previous sensation of power.

"Now, future wife," Yale gritted gently, his free hand beginning to move deliberately on her vulnerable midsection, "it's your turn to plead."

Dara smiled with dazzling witchcraft, her body already lifting against the touch of his hand. "Please, Yale. Please show me what being your wife will be like!"

"When you look at me like that, how can I refuse you anything?" he breathed, sliding his leg between hers with purposefulness and deliberate slowness.

He was going to keep her waiting, she realized dimly as she coiled and uncoiled beneath him. He wanted her to know the powerful need in every fiber of her being. She wanted to cry out her love for him, knew it was much too soon and cried out her desire instead.

"I want you, Yale. I want you so desperately!"

"I'm yours, sweetheart. I think I have been from the beginning!" He was poised above her in the darkness and then he was taking her with finesse and strength. She knew every inch of him along her skin, and her body vibrated in resonance with his.

He swept her along with him in the dizzying path of their mutual desire. Dara surrendered willingly to the demands he made of her, issuing her own demands in return. They were met with the same eagerness, and together they bounded toward the top of the cliff which overlooked the emerald valley.

Dara felt the shuddering release she had first known last night, still unprepared for the sensation even though she knew what to expect this time.

"Yale!"

Then he was leaping over the edge with her, a hoarse male shout caught in his throat as he slid a hand beneath her buttocks to hold her violently close. She felt him tremble, felt every muscle in his lean frame tauten. In that moment the taking and giving were so bound up together it was impossible to speak of mastery and surrender. Each gave and each took. Each mastered and each surrendered. It was a timeless cadence which required only love to make it complete. And that Dara gave with all her heart, even if it was in silence.

It was a long time later, deep in the heavy aftermath of

their passion, that Yale stirred and spoke softly, compellingly into the quiet darkness.

"You see, little tabby cat?" he said wistfully. "It doesn't really matter."

"What doesn't matter?" Dara murmured, luxuriating in the feel of him. She stretched like a cat beneath the soothing stroke of his hand.

"Where we come together like this," he explained. "A truck-stop motel or your bedroom or on a mountaintop overlooking the world. It's all the same. We're what counts, not the location."

She smiled against his damp skin and sighed blissfully. Secure in the knowledge that Yale couldn't have made love to her like this if he wasn't close to falling in love, she made her decision.

In the morning she would release him from his promise to marry her.

It was very simple, she told herself with catlike contentment. Yale would tell her he had no wish to be free of his promise and she would go to her wedding with the full knowledge that he wanted the marriage as much as she did.

How could it be otherwise after what they had shared?

Dara made her decision with the perfect certainty and confidence she had known when she finally realized she had discovered her niche in life as a stockbroker. Made it with all the absolute sureness with which she had first known she wanted to belong to Yale Ransom. Made it with a woman's sure instincts about herself and her man.

Yale would marry her because he wanted her, not because

he was bound to a promise. And she would teach him to love her after the wedding.

Perhaps it was inevitable that such complacency should not go unpunished. But the inevitability did not lessen the heart-wrenching shock Dara experienced when Yale calmly accepted his freedom and grabbed it with both hands, making no effort to step back into the net.

Chapter 7

"Okay."

That was his exact word the next morning when Dara, soft-eyed and full of love, told him she wouldn't hold him to the marriage promise. He was sliding out of bed, on his way to a shower in her eye-opening yellow and red bathroom.

"Okay!" she repeated to his disappearing back as the door closed. "Okay!" Dazed, she stared after him, unconsciously clutching the sheet over her full breasts. Only a short time ago he had awakened her with a kiss at the base of her spine, turned her over and made lazy, warm love to her.

And now he calmly shrugged and accepted his freedom as if he never had intended to marry her.

No! she told herself resolutely as she struggled free of the startled paralysis and got to her feet. Yale would have married her if she'd held him to his promise. She was sure of it. He was the sort of man who paid his debts!

But she'd blithely freed him of the obligation, and what male in his right mind wouldn't be willing enough to accept that freedom? What a fool she had been! For the second morning in a row!

In that moment it was hard to know which of them was the more inviting target for her anger: herself or Yale.

Grabbing a turquoise robe from the closet, Dara flung it on and stalked into the bathroom. It was already turning into a steam bath from the hot water Yale was using in such liberal quantities.

"What the hell do you mean 'okay'?" she demanded over the noise of the shower. She could see his shadowy movements behind the yellow curtain.

"Okay means okay," he called back laconically. "You set the price last night. If you don't want to collect full payment, that's your prerogative."

"The price! Is that all you ever think about? Yesterday you were willing to pay the price by handing over your account! This morning you were willing to...to marry me! Don't you mind the cost?" she bit out.

There was an instant's pause, and then Yale pulled back the shower curtain far enough to smile at her. There was a knee-weakening tenderness in the smile. There was also the devilish flash of gold.

"The fact that I'm willing to pay it should tell you how much I want you," he pointed out gently. "But if you're too generous to collect..." He let the sentence trail off significantly.

She glared at him, vividly aware of the way the water streamed across his head and shoulders, plastering the honey hair to his head and making the smooth, strong contours of his chest and arms glisten. She loved him, she acknowledged again, glumly, and he was playing games with her.

He had been from the beginning. She had no one to blame but herself.

And at last, two mornings too late, everything crystallized. She had fallen in love at first sight with a man who returned the physical attraction, but nothing deeper. It wasn't altogether his fault, either. She had allowed the situation to race out of control. She had succumbed so easily there had been no time for Yale to get to know her as a human being. On his demand during the past forty-eight hours she had handed over everything of herself with only token resistance. He was honest enough to be willing to pay her price, but he hadn't fallen in love.

With the cool, clear assessment of hindsight, Dara realized finally what she had done. At the age of thirty she should know enough about men to realize they didn't fall head over heels in love at first sight. A man's emotions were far more primitive. Men were quite capable of wanting a woman and wanting her badly after a short acquaintance, but falling in love was a much more complicated and lengthy business.

If there was to be any hope for her relationship with Yale Ransom, Dara told herself with chilling caution, she would have to go back to the beginning and start the relationship from scratch.

She drew a deep breath and smiled back at the man in her shower, a smile unlike any he'd had from her so far. A smile few people ever saw.

"It's not that I'm too generous," she began with icy sarcasm. He arched an eyebrow, waiting for the other shoe to drop. "But I am much too smart to let the emotions of a wild weekend lead me into making a major mistake. We've only known each other for two days, Yale. Marriage would be a horrendous mistake. I only said that last night to try to stop you from seducing me." She shrugged with deliberate self-mockery. "But you're good. Very good."

Something moved in the depths of the hazel eyes, but the wicked smile still played about his hard mouth. "Thank you for the compliment. I shall do my best to continue to live up to the expectations I've created."

She'd struck some sort of nerve, but Dara couldn't begin to figure out what was going on in his mind now. He had a certain watchfulness about him. As if he were paying out rope and waiting to see how much she would take before she obligingly hanged herself.

"I'm sure you will," she acknowledged politely. "With some other woman."

"I'm content with the one I've got," he drawled, ignoring the hot water which was being wasted by the gallon. He was deliberately challenging her, and Dara felt more than ready for the battle.

"How kind of you," she murmured. "My turn to accept the compliment, I suppose. But I'm afraid I have other plans for other weekends. This one has been…interesting, to say the least, but not something I intend to make a practice of repeating."

"No?" The single word was edged with humor and a masculine certainty that annoyed Dara.

"No," she replied very calmly. Then she glanced down the front of her fluffy robe, taking in her figure with an amused expression. "I'm aware of the fact that men some-times get the notion I'm a little…soft…"

"And cuddly?" he added helpfully, following her glance with an assessing one of her own.

"And cuddly," she agreed with a rueful sigh. "I haven't given you much reason to think otherwise, either. But I'm afraid the body nature gave me doesn't totally reflect the whole woman."

"What's hidden?" he asked lightly. "What haven't I al-ready seen?"

"Believe it or not, I can be extraordinarily stubborn." She chuckled.

"Are you trying to tell me in your own devious fash-ion that you're not going to sleep with me again?" he de-manded, looking fascinated.

"For a country boy, you're quite sharp at times." She smiled.

He ignored that. "What makes you think I can't make last night and the night before happen again and again?"

"Once I've made a decision and know what I'm doing, I'm quite unswerving." That was nothing less than the truth.

"You said something like this yesterday morning, as I recall."

"No," she responded coolly. "Yesterday morning I was madder than hell. It was inevitable I should get over that. I never stay angry long." She smiled reminiscently. "And you were very pleasant last night."

"You're not trying to retaliate for some imagined slight this morning?"

"Nope. I'm merely trying to tell you that the weekend is coming to an end."

"And if I said I wanted to go on seeing you?" he prodded, the smallest hint of impatience in his words.

"I'd tell you that you're welcome to call. Just don't expect to spend the night again."

"Why not?"

"Because, in spite of the impression I'm afraid you've gotten this weekend, I don't leap into casual affairs."

"The past forty-eight hours represent a temporary aberration, is that it?" he retorted broodingly.

"It happens to all of us on occasion." She sighed wryly. "But that doesn't mean one has to make a practice of it. If you want to continue seeing me, Yale, I'm willing. I enjoy your company. But I give you fair warning that I'm putting this weekend behind me, where it belongs, and returning to reality."

He watched her for a heartbeat and then he said very softly, "Come here, Dara."

She tilted her head, wary of his intentions. "Why?"

"I want to show you something."

"I can see all I need to see from here," she muttered, refusing to let her gaze slip farther than his chest. She wished he would close the curtain.

"Scared?"

"Of course not!"

"Then come a little closer, honey," he urged persuasively.

"Yale, I'd like you to hurry and get out of that shower so you can be on your way before my neighbors are all

awake," she instructed him resolutely, turning on her heel
and opening the bathroom door.

He closed in on her as her hand came down on the door-
knob. Dripping wet, he pulled her around and whipped the
fluffy robe off her shoulders.

"Yale! You're getting water all over the floor! What do
you think you're doing?" Her protest was a startled squeak
of alarm that didn't seem to faze him in the least.

"There are a few more things we need to discuss," he
told her, forcing her now nude body into the shower ahead
of him. "And something tells me we'll communicate better this way!"

"Stop it!" she snapped even as the hot water drenched
her. "I'm in no mood for any of your games!"

"Speaking of games," he began easily, wrapping one arm
around her breasts and holding her still while he industriously began to scrub her back, "just what sort do you think
you're playing this morning?"

She felt his strong hands working steadily down her tapering back, moving slickly on her wet skin, and she wanted
to give herself up to the sensuous moment. But that was
impossible. Too much was riding on her willpower, and
once the Bancroft will of iron had been invoked, nothing
could bend it.

"What games?" she charged tightly. "I've told you not
to assume from this weekend that I'm willing to engage in
a full-scale affair with you. That's all!"

"You've also told me you're no longer interested in col-
lecting the fee for last night's charming surrender. Funny,

I could have sworn at the time you had every intention of doing so!"

He soaped the contour of her waist and then, tantalizingly, began to make slippery forays over her hips. Helpless in the one-armed grip, Dara steeled herself against the onslaught.

"It was not a surrender, damn it," she grated, knowing her temper was beginning to fray under the pressure. "I don't know how things work back in the mountains, but out here on the Coast, women occasionally go to bed with men because they feel like it! It doesn't constitute a surrender in any sense of the word!"

"Then why the insistence on marriage?" he retorted, his fingers gliding more slowly now as he shaped the resilient flesh of her buttocks. "If you were only going to bed with me because I took your fancy for the moment, why demand marriage?"

"I told you, I was trying to stop you from seducing me!"

"You didn't have the willpower to simply say no?" he taunted.

"Not then," she admitted grimly. "But I do now. The weekend, Yale, is over!"

"I've got news for you, sweetheart," he growled, turning her in his arms and staring down into her upturned face without smiling. "It's just beginning. I want you now. You've pushed your way into my life. Seduced me would be a better term, I suppose. You know more about me than anyone else has known for years. You've given me just enough of your lovely, soft body to make me want a lot more, and you've let me see what I can do to you. One weekend isn't going to satisfy me. I was willing to pay for what I want with marriage, but if you don't want that, there isn't any way I can force you into it. I'll take what's left, which is an affair."

"Not on your life!" she flared, eyes burning an emerald color as she defied him.

His hands were around her waist, moving upward until his thumbs found the rosy tips of her breasts. "You don't mean that," he whispered deeply, circling the sensitive nipples deliberately. "You've already said I could continue seeing you...."

"You can," she flung back icily. "But if you want to date me, Yale, you must understand that this relationship is going back to square one. You would have to forget about the weekend and pretend we had just met."

"What man could forget a weekend like this?" he asked huskily, bending down beneath the hot spray to drop a knowing little kiss on her forehead.

"I know it's all my fault," Dara groaned, closing her eyes.

"Very generous of you to take the blame," he commended, his lips moving to her temples.

"I let things get out of control," she went on sadly. "I handled it completely wrong, I admit that."

"And now you're going to try and retreat to a position where you can handle it properly, is that it?" He chuckled, his hands cupping her breasts with increasing urgency.

"Yes!" she vowed.

"Such determination," he drawled with lazy interest. She

knew he was becoming aroused again. His stamina was a little frightening!

"When I finally get around to making a decision, Yale, nothing can change my mind."

"And you've decided you let me go too far, too fast?"

"Exactly."

"It's done, honey," he said silkily, propelling her closer until she could feel the sexual tautness in him. "You can't go back…."

"I'm thirty years old, Yale Ransom," she announced with cool fortitude. "I can do anything I damn please!"

Whirling so quickly she caught him by surprise, Dara stepped away from his slippery hold and out onto the rug. She grabbed the nearest towel and hurriedly pulled it around her dripping body. He tugged back the curtain once more and stood regarding her for all the world like an annoyed shark which had just lost its prey. Did sharks have hazel eyes that gleamed like the gold in their teeth?

"I don't understand you this morning," he complained, sounding aggrieved.

"Precisely my point," she flung back, starting for the door again. "The problem with wild weekends is that the activities tend to be too limited in scope. We've made a lot of love during the past two days, Yale, but you know almost nothing about me. The only reason I've learned something about you is because I kept pressing for information. We're still a long way from a genuine communication. I should have had the sense to realize that too much sex too early in a relationship severely hampers the task of getting to know each other! Frankly, I'm not interested in a relationship based solely on the physical side of things!"

With royal disdain, Dara slammed out of the bathroom. Her mind was made up. The future path lay as sharply marked before her as if it were lit with neon lights.

She was dressed in jeans and a snappy plaid shirt, cracking eggs into a skillet, when Yale emerged from the bathroom and came to lean in the kitchen doorway. She ignored his appraising glance even though it seemed to burn through the fabric of her shirt.

"So you're at least going to feed me before kicking me out, hmm?"

"Don't knock it. I'm a good cook." Dara surveyed the toast with a watchful eye. "The Sunday paper's over there on the table if you want to occupy yourself while I'm fixing breakfast."

"Very homey," he muttered dryly as he detached himself from the door frame and wandered over to the round glass table by the kitchen window. He stood beside the fern on the tall plant stand and scanned the headlines, hazel eyes narrowed behind the lenses of his glasses.

Eyeing him covertly, Dara knew his mind wasn't on the morning news. Encouraged, she poured a cup of coffee and carried it over to him. He looked up as he accepted the mug, the grooves around the edges of his mouth tight.

"Dara, about last night..."

"How do you like your eggs? Over easy or sunny-side up?"

"I don't much care at the moment," he rapped. "I'm trying to talk to you about us, damn it!"

"So talk. I'm listening."

She turned away, opened a kitchen drawer and began dragging out flatware. Yale flung himself into a chair and watched morosely as she set the table with smooth, efficient movements. She could sense him searching for the words he wanted.

"Honey, we can't calmly go back to the beginning and start over," he finally began in an eminently reasonable tone of voice that made her want to smile: the rational male was attempting to deal with the irrational female.

"Then we can call it quits right here," she said easily. "Or we can maintain a business relationship, I suppose— that is, if you still want to give Edison, Stanford and Zane your account. There, that's at least two other alternatives I can think of at the moment," she concluded brightly, dishing up the bacon and eggs and toast.

"I have no intention of following either suggestion!" he growled as she set the food in front of him.

"Then you can go back to the beginning and we can start from scratch. Take your pick." She sat down opposite him and shot Yale a dazzling smile as she picked up her fork.

He watched her through narrowed lids, the fingers of his right hand drumming with ill-concealed impatience on the cheerful striped tablecloth.

"What if I agree to do that and then prove you can't resist me?" he offered coolly.

His self-confidence hardened her resolve as nothing else

could have done. "You mean agree to start over and then deliberately seduce me? It wouldn't work. Not now. I've made up my mind, Yale. You haven't known me long enough to realize exactly what that means. We'll go as far as I want, and then I'll send you home. Just as I would any other date."

"Are you issuing a challenge?" he asked, finally picking up his fork, unable to ignore his food any longer.

"No, I'm telling you how it's going to be between us, Yale," she explained patiently. "I want a normal, properly developed relationship, or I want nothing at all. As interesting as this weekend has been, it was a mistake. It won't happen again."

"You're very sure of yourself this morning. Yesterday morning you were in a flaming rage," he noted calmly.

"Yes," she agreed, her mouth quirking wryly. "I was. But when I'm in a rage, which is rather rare, I'm not at my most dangerous. It's when I'm cool, organized and know where I'm going next that I'm a force to contend with."

"I'll remember that," he vowed, lifting his coffee cup.

"You certainly will," she promised sweetly. "More coffee?"

He held out his cup without a word. She could practically see him turning over her responses in his mind.

"You want the Southern gentleman back, is that it?" he asked finally. "You like the man you met at the party but not the one you found yourself with in a motel room out on the Interstate?"

"Stop trying to pretend you're two different men, Yale. Both aspects of you are part of the whole. There's no point trying to deny one or the other. Actually—" she smiled warmly "—they go together rather nicely."

He looked a little taken aback, as if he hadn't expected such an admission. But he was quick to seize on the apparent weakness. "If you're attracted to both sides of me," he pounced, "why are you so determined to keep me at bay?"

"Being attracted to a man is not a good enough reason for having an affair with him!"

"Why not?"

"Spoken with the essence of male logic." She groaned, shaking her head so that the russet ends, still damp from her unplanned shower, danced around her throat. "The female's reasoned response to which is *because it's not!*"

"Careful, Dara," he clipped, stabbing his egg vengefully. "I'm tempted to meet your response to my logic by turning you over my knee!"

"Now, that wouldn't be very reasonable, would it?" she murmured.

"I think you've been reading too much of that eighteenth-century philosophy I saw on your bookshelf. Just remember that back during the seventeen hundreds, during the so-called Age of Reason, it was still legal to beat one's wife! A very practical era."

"Ah! But I'm not your wife!" she murmured triumphantly, lowering her lashes to hide the mischief in her eyes.

"No," he agreed on a distant note. "You backed out of your deal the minute you woke up this morning. But I'm not at all willing to do the same. I want you, little tabby cat, and I can make you want me."

"The only way you can continue to see me is on my terms," she stated aloofly. "This weekend is simply not going to be allowed to set the tone of our relationship, and that's final."

"You *are* issuing a challenge," he accused, waving his fork at her briefly.

"The fact that you can say that only goes to show how little you know me."

"It won't work," he told her darkly.

"Our relationship?"

"Trying to put it on another footing," he elaborated. "It won't work."

"Then that will be the end of things."

"I accept," he gritted.

"Accept what?"

"The challenge. To put it in elemental terms, I will prove I can seduce you and make you eat every last one of your fine words. Before I'm finished you will be begging me to marry you!"

Dara forced down the excitement wafting through her senses. She was a long way from the finish line yet. With seeming casualness she raised her coffee cup in mocking salute.

"Is that the Southern gentleman or the moonshine runner talking?"

"That's *me,* Yale Ransom, talking, and I mean every word! Whatever else happened this weekend, the one abiding fact is that I made you mine. I'm going to make you admit it if it's the last thing I do on this earth!"

"Fine," she said easily. "Now, if you don't mind, would you hurry up and finish that coffee? I'd like to get you out of this apartment as quickly as possible. With any luck maybe the neighbors won't notice the Alfa Romeo...."

"Are you worried about being compromised?" he jeered.

"As you said last night, I'd probably survive it, but there's no sense deliberately inviting any more trouble, is there?"

"Speaking of which," he interrupted loftily, "what about the business with Hank Bonner's drug runner?" His smile was one of impending victory. "I still feel morally obligated to look after you as long as he's on the loose."

"Try looking at page A12 in this morning's paper," she invited kindly.

Shooting her a glaring frown, Yale flipped open the paper.

"It's in fine print close to the bottom of the page under the advertisement for tennis rackets."

His mouth moved into a harder line as he read the brief report. "So they got him last night, after all."

"He never stood a chance, what with all those truckers looking for him."

"And we're in the clear," he continued absently, finishing the few lines announcing the arrest of a man suspected of using interstate truckers to transport drugs.

"No mention of us at all." Dara grinned cheerfully. "Your reputation as a nice, staid, gentlemanly accountant is safe."

"And your habit of getting involved in barroom brawls and then going off into the night with a trucker or two is also safely hidden. It looks like we'll both be able to show our faces in downtown Eugene tomorrow."

"Something tells me you weren't as worried as you pretended to be about your reputation," she murmured, rising to clear away his plate in a pointed manner. She didn't offer him another cup of coffee.

"Were you?" he asked suddenly, looking up speculatively. "Would you have gone ahead and married me if we'd been made to look like a pair of reckless swingers?"

"It's an interesting problem, isn't it? We'll never know the answer, I'm afraid." She flicked a quick smile at him, mentally shouting, Yes! Yes! I probably would have been tempted by that excuse. My reputation wouldn't have mattered as much as having a legitimate excuse for marrying you. But I haven't even got that now. And I want you to marry me for far more important reasons, Yale Ransom. I want you to fall in love with me the way I've fallen in love with you!

"The answer might have been amusing," he drawled, sliding reluctantly to his feet, "but perhaps not as amusing as watching you trying to fend me off when you know you'll be aching to have me…."

Before he'd finished the last word, Yale had reached out and slid his arms around her waist as she stood at the sink. She went very still, bracing herself against the counter.

"Yale, it's time for you to go," she said steadily as he hugged her back against his strength.

"Don't worry, honey, I'm on my way," he whispered huskily into her hair. "I told you, I've accepted the challenge.

You can't go back to square one. We know too much about each other. We're lovers, Dara. We're going to stay lovers. You want me and I want you. Life is really very simple in some ways."

"A bit of Blue Ridge Mountain wisdom?" she murmured.

"A bit of Yale Ransom wisdom. And a young woman who didn't have enough sense to resist opening Pandora's box ought to pay attention. Because she's going to take all the consequences of her actions!"

His hands dropped away from her waist, leaving her feeling bereft. Dara spun around to watch as Yale strode out of the kitchen. She followed and stood in the doorway as he found his jacket and walked to the front door.

"Goodbye, lover," he called, letting himself out into the early-morning sunshine. "I'll be seeing you soon. You can count on it!"

She raced to the window and watched as he moved down the walk to the waiting car. As he settled into the front seat he turned and waved again. Even from here she could see the menace in his smile.

As the Alfa Romeo pulled away from the curb, Yale's hand was once again extended from the window. But this time he wasn't waving at her. He was acknowledging the gray-haired woman across the street who was peering eagerly through her kitchen blinds.

Dara muttered a decidedly violent oath and let her own curtains fall back into place. What was it they said about the devil living in those Southern mountains? She seemed to recall some old tales. Tales that sent chills of warning down her nerves.

Well, the devil was going to meet his match in her, she vowed silently.

A long time later as she whizzed along the bike path beside the Willamette River, letting the spring sunshine put the world back into proportion for her sadly chaotic senses, Dara tried to imagine Yale's mood. Automatically she shifted the gears of her ten-speed.

Was he frustrated the way a tiger is frustrated when its prey is rudely snatched from its jaws just after the feast has begun? Was he angry over her exposure of his past? He certainly hadn't been too pleased when she'd pushed him into revealing it.

Whatever his reasoning at the moment, she had the satisfaction of knowing he was going to play the dangerous game for which she was setting the rules.

Only now, in the clear light of day as she sped through one of Eugene's many parks, could she admit to herself how reckless she had really been.

Not because she had spent a "lost" weekend with a man she had barely met, but because she had risked letting him back out of the net after she'd secured him with a promise of marriage. Would she ever make him understand, or would he be more wary this time?

She was under no illusions about his determination to go on seeing her. She had deliberately challenged him, and his instincts had prompted him to accept. He'd even realized what she was doing and he'd still accepted, she reminded herself with a smile.

What he didn't realize was that she wasn't going to let him win. It was too important for both their sakes that she control the next crucial moves.

Dara knew she would be satisfied with nothing less than Yale Ransom's love. She was too proud, too determined, to settle for anything short of it. Once before she had done that, and she wasn't going to let it happen again.

She might have gotten the love affair off to a shaky start by allowing herself to be swept up into a reckless and dangerous forty-eight hours, but she would salvage the disaster or lose everything trying. Once Dara Bancroft knew what she wanted in life, she went after it.

Chapter 8

The hunt began the next day, and almost immediately Dara knew she had underestimated Yale's natural stalking skill. But who could have guessed that she would find herself the quarry of a split personality?

The first appeared shortly before her lunch hour on Monday. The conservative, gently spoken, fine-mannered Southern gentleman walked through the front door of Edison, Stanford & Zane, nodded to the secretary and strolled over to Dara's desk.

"Good morning, Dara." He smiled politely, only the hint of gold betraying the true nature of the expression. "I've got all the information here that you'll need to transfer the account from L.A."

Dara looked up a little warily, not quite trusting this genteel version of his accent. She was aware that more than one head in the office had turned in amused curiosity.

"Fine, Yale, won't you have a seat?" she murmured politely, indicating one of the client chairs in front of her desk. She reached for the sheaf of papers he extended. "I'll see to these today."

He settled his neatly suited leanness into the chair and

the hazel eyes were full of laughter which the lenses of his glasses failed to hide.

"I've got some time, so I thought I'd stop by and discuss my financial goals in the market. Always a good idea for client and broker to feel each other out, so to speak, don't you think?" he drawled politely.

"Of course," she agreed briskly, reaching for a pad and pen. She could play this every bit as cool as he could. It was, after all, her idea, damn it!

"I see your portfolio emphasizes growth stocks," she observed in her best professional tones, glancing at his statement from the other firm. "I gather you're not concerned with income producers?"

"I have no need of dividends. I'm looking for the long-term-growth stocks. Find me a few dozen bargains in the over-the-counter market and I'll be satisfied," he said easily.

"Bargains?" She half smiled. "What's your definition of a bargain?"

"Why, something that doubles or triples in the first year, naturally," Yale explained kindly.

"And you expect a few dozen such winners from me?" she inquired coolly.

"Your manager assures me you're good. Very good." He met her eyes, daring her to deny it.

"I am, but I'm not perfect." She smiled aloofly. "I happen to be following a couple of interesting electronics stocks at the moment, however. They're down from their highs for the year and selling at rather good P/E ratios. There's also a small cable television firm which hasn't been 'discovered' yet but which I think will really go places. Would you like to see some information?"

"I would be most interested in discussing all of them further. Over lunch? It is just after one o'clock, I believe. The markets should be closed back East...."

Dara slanted her new client a cautious glance. Yale was on his best behavior at the moment, but the humor in his eyes held more than simple amusement. The expression was compounded by something else, something she couldn't quite put her finger on but which the commonsense portion of her brain warned against.

"I'll have to be back in an hour," she began carefully. "I have a lot of work to do this afternoon...."

"I'll have you back by two. You have my word on it. I should be back in my own office shortly after that, myself." He got to his feet expectantly.

Dara hesitated and then took the plunge. This was what she wanted, wasn't it? Time for them to get to know each other on other levels besides the physical?

"I'll get my coat," she said calmly.

Whatever it was that was sending tiny warnings along her spine failed to materialize over lunch in a downtown restaurant. Yale was the complete and perfect escort, attentive, polite and charming. Slowly, as she worked her way through a large salad, Dara began to relax. If this was going to be his approach, she could handle it. It was exactly the sort of relationship she wanted at the moment.

"You never did tell me what you did for a living before

you became an account executive with Edison, Stanford and Zane," Yale said invitingly at one point.

"A great many things, I'm afraid. My résumé reads like the want-ads column. You name it and I probably tried it." Dara smiled at him, remembering her frequent job-hops. "I worked in an insurance office, a department store, a travel agency, a temporary secretarial help firm, city government, a restaurant, a hotel, an airline—"

"Okay," he interrupted, chuckling, "I get the picture. Is selling stocks merely another passing job interest?"

"Oh, no," she said in surprise. "Selling securities is what I wanted to do all along. I just didn't know it until I stumbled onto it," she explained.

"How do you know you won't lose interest and go on to something else?"

She lifted a shoulder, helpless to explain her instinctive knowledge of the rightness of some things in her life. "I know," she said, smiling. "I just know." The same way that I know I love you, she thought.

"You sound very certain," Yale said quietly, giving her an oblique look.

"I am. I've always been like that, going from one thing to another until something clicks. But when it does click, I know it instantly. I stick with it. For example, Eugene clicked after I moved here from Portland."

"Did your first marriage seem to click?" he asked softly, a little relentlessly.

Dara's eyes hardened for a second and then she relaxed.

"No. But I was a lot younger then and I hadn't learned to pay attention to all the important clicks or lack thereof."

"Were you passionately in love?"

"I was…infatuated, I suppose, is the word. He was very charming, very amusing and kind. I *liked* him. How can I explain it? I thought we had a lot in common and I thought we could make a go of it."

"But there was no 'click'?" Yale pressed deliberately.

"No. There was no click," she admitted.

"Has there ever been someone with whom everything feels right? Will you know it if it does happen?" he prodded, hazel eyes flickering with an enigmatic expression.

"Yes, to both questions," she said as lightly as possible. "but I'd rather not discuss it."

The amusement faded completely from his eyes as Yale studied her speculatively. "Where is he now? What happened to the relationship?"

"I told you, I'd rather not discuss it," Dara said with the serene sureness she was capable of projecting when she had made up her mind.

"Was he married? Does he live here in Eugene?"

"Yale, I'm not going to discuss it with you. Hadn't you better finish your steak? It's getting late."

"Dara…" he began determinedly, leaning forward with a surprisingly grim resolve. "Tell me about him."

"No. I'm ready to go, Yale. Are you going to take me back to the office, or shall I walk?"

"Did you run off into the night with him within a few hours of meeting him? The way you ran off with me?"

"Goodbye, Yale. I'll call you when I get the account transferred. In the meantime, I'll send you the information on those electronics firms I mentioned…." Dara was getting to her feet, smoothing the white skirt of her suit with a casual hand and reaching for her fawn-colored shoulder bag.

He stood up at once, and she could almost see the restraint he flung around himself like a cloak.

"I'll take you back," he muttered with determined politeness.

"Careful, Yale," she taunted gently. "The Southern gentleman is slipping a little."

"I'll behave," he promised, guiding her out of the restaurant with a hand on her waist. "Although I'll have to admit it was never this hard before I met you."

"Keep up the good work. I'm rather fond of you when you're good. You make a very charming escort."

His mouth twisted wryly as he held the car door for her. "In that case, will you have dinner with me tomorrow night?"

Dara smiled. "I'd be delighted." Privately, she wondered why the invitation hadn't been for this evening. But it was just as well. She had a variety of things to do, anyway.

He drove her back to the office in an almost meditative silence. The Alfa Romeo slid neatly into the curb in front of Edison, Stanford & Zane, and Dara's hand automatically went to the door handle.

"Thank you for lunch, Yale," she began with mocking formality and then stopped as his hand left the wheel to settle purposefully on her arm. She glanced down at his gripping fingers and then back up into his eyes with a questioning smile on her mouth.

"A little something to help you remember me by until tomorrow night," he said huskily and pulled her close for an unexpected kiss.

Before Dara could make up her mind how to respond, it was over. She fumbled briefly with the handle and jumped out of the car. "Goodbye, Yale!" She didn't turn her head as the car reentered traffic.

All things considered, it hadn't been a bad beginning, Dara decided several hours later as she stopped by the supermarket on her way home. Yale had been firmly in his Southern-gentleman role that afternoon. Perhaps he had determined to charm her back into bed. She smiled ruefully to herself at the thought. Perhaps she would allow him to do exactly that. After she'd decided he felt something more for her than simple desire.

She pushed the cart quickly down the aisle, scooping up milk and butter and other essentials from the dairy case. With a small frown she deliberated over dinner and decided on pasta. She would pick up some cheese and then…

Her train of thought halted abruptly as something familiar flickered at the corner of her vision. Curiously she turned her head to glance back down the aisle.

Yale stood at the far end dressed in black, close-fitting slacks and a black, long-sleeved shirt. He was watching her, his hands thrust into his back pockets, feet slightly apart and braced. The honey-amber hair was ruffled from the wind and he wasn't wearing his glasses.

"Yale!" Dara whispered in astonishment, smiling automatically and starting forward with the cart. What a coincidence, she mused.

He gave no sign of recognition, merely turned and disappeared around the corner of the aisle. When Dara reached the spot where he had been standing there was no sign of him.

Confused, Dara peered around and glanced out through the windows into the parking lot. Where had he gone? And why hadn't he waited to greet her? It *had* been Yale, hadn't it?

Of course it had, she reassured herself with a little shake of her head. Perhaps he hadn't seen her. With a shrug, Dara continued to the checkout stand.

Some time later she finished off her pasta with satisfaction. Dara had never allowed herself to fall into the trap of giving her dinner only minimal attention just because she happened to be eating alone. Her single place setting by the window was properly set with a glass of good wine and pretty china. Food was one of life's great pleasures and she refused to treat it as mundane.

She rose slowly to do the few dishes, her mind still churning with thoughts of Yale as it had been all afternoon. Idly she considered what she would wear the next evening and wondered if he would make a pass at her front door. The notion amused her in some ways, made her nervous in others.

But she could handle him, she told herself resolutely. Yale Ransom was going to learn that she wanted a real relationship or nothing at all. There would be no more wild, lost weekends!

She was still telling herself that when she finally slipped beneath the quilt of her bed and snuggled down to sleep. She had made up her mind, and once that had been done, she reminded herself firmly, nothing could change it.

The sound of a guitar woke her an hour later. For a moment Dara simply lay quietly, eyes still shut, and tried to remember if she'd left the stereo on earlier in the evening. She must have. The music was so close it couldn't be coming from a neighbor's apartment.

But why hadn't the stereo shut itself off automatically? her sleep-clogged brain demanded. Reluctantly her dark lashes fluttered open and she gazed at the pattern of moonlight on the far wall of her room. The guitar sounded so close, not at all as if it were seeping in from the living room....

The panic hit her like a crashing wave, driving her up into a sitting position against the pillows. In the darkness she saw the devil, dressed in black, sitting on the end of her bed and strumming the guitar.

"Yale!" She choked on a small scream. "My God! What are you doing here? You scared the life out of me!"

She clutched the sheet to her throat, her pulse pounding, and glared at him accusingly.

"I'm really much better with a fiddle," Yale confided softly, glancing up from the movements of his fingers on the strings.

"Yes, I can imagine!" she retorted on an infuriated shriek. "I believe your Southern mountain devil does play a fiddle!"

"Only when he's bargaining for souls." Yale grinned, the gold flashing wickedly.

In that moment it wouldn't have taken much at all to convince Dara that she was facing Lucifer himself.

"How did you get in? What in the world do you think you're doing?"

"Frightened?" He smiled, still picking out a mountain ballad as he lounged at ease on her quilt.

"You terrified me, and you know it! Now answer me, Yale!" she charged.

He was dressed as he had been that afternoon when she'd glimpsed him in the store. There was no sign of the horn-rimmed glasses. He was all dark, lazy menace.

"I'm here to serenade you to sleep," he murmured. "As for getting in, that was simple. I came through a window."

"Of all the nerve! Yale, what are you up to? This is… this is insane! And why didn't you speak to me in the store this afternoon?" she added belligerently as an afterthought.

He struck a few more chords on the guitar and then changed to another haunting melody, his amber head bent over the instrument.

"This afternoon? There was no need. I only wanted you to know I was there."

"But why?" Perplexed and a little angry, Dara sat very still, trying to figure out what he was doing.

"The quarry starts getting nervous when it realizes the hunter is right behind it. If there was one thing I learned to do back in those mountains, it was hunt."

"Hunt! Are you out of your mind? I'm not going to let

you hunt me down like some helpless animal!" she blazed, thoroughly incensed.

"I'll get to you somehow," he told her gently, looking at her through his lashes. "Either me or my alter ego."

"Will you stop talking as if you're two separate men?" she flashed, a shiver going through her whole body at the quiet certainty in him.

"Well," he told her casually, the soft rhythms of the guitar reaching insidiously into every corner of the room, "you're the only one who can bring them together."

"This is ridiculous," she stormed, pushing a curve of russet hair back behind one ear and glaring at her uninvited guest. "If you think I'm going to tolerate this sort of behavior—"

"The first thing you're going to have to do is keep your tactics straight," he cautioned helpfully. "The ranting and raving work on the Southern gentleman. After all, he would hate to distress a lady. But they aren't effective against the man sitting on the foot of your bed tonight."

"Really?" she shot back fiercely. "Then what do you suggest?"

"Sweet, soft submission, I think," Yale said reflectively as if seriously considering the issue.

"When hell freezes over!"

"Let's find out if your approach will work," he drawled, setting aside the guitar and sliding off the quilt.

The prickling sensation along her nerve endings exploded into full-scale alarm as Yale came toward her.

"Yale, no! I won't let you…!"

He sat down heavily beside her and reached out to pull her into his arms. She struggled, still trying to maintain her hold on the sheet, but he ignored her efforts, cradling her across his thighs.

"Go on fighting me, darling Dara, and we'll see where it gets you," he whispered, sweeping the sheet out of her grasp with a short, aggressive movement.

His hand came to rest just below the full curve of her breast and then began slipping down the satiny material of her nightgown.

"Stop that," she breathed tightly, trying to push against his chest with all her strength. "This isn't going to work, Yale Ransom. I'm not going to tamely let you seduce me!"

"Tame is a word I would never apply to you, sweetheart," he assured her as his fingers trailed lightly over her thigh. He anchored her arms against his sides and bent to kiss her angrily parted lips.

"No!"

But the word was lost in a muffled shout as his tongue forged into the warmth of her mouth. Effortlessly he held her still for the heavy, drugging kiss and the marauding quest of his hand.

Dara gathered her resistance, aware she couldn't fight him physically. He was simply too strong. But she would see to it that he gained no satisfaction from his bold lovemaking tonight. If there was one thing Dara Bancroft could do, it was to follow through on a project once she'd finally decided what had to be done.

Grimly she lay acquiescent beneath his touch, calling on

her total store of willpower to turn off the electric circuits his hands and mouth switched on. Never again was Yale Ransom going to think of her as an easy conquest!

"Relax, honey," he breathed encouragingly as he began a series of slow, lingering kisses down the length of her throat. "Remember how good it was when you gave yourself to me? You know you want that again...."

"It won't work, Yale," she hissed, turning her face into the black material of his shirt as his exploring hand slipped under the edge of her nightgown and found the silky skin of her inner thigh.

He said nothing but continued the patterns he was weaving on her skin, his fingers probing ever closer to the secret heart of her desire with knowing ease.

"I've learned a lot about you during the past couple of days," he told her insinuatingly. "I know how your body responds to my touch, how warm and soft and welcoming it becomes...."

"I've warned you before that the body I was given doesn't reflect the mind behind it!" she challenged, stiffening herself against his touch.

He kissed the nape of her neck and then sank his teeth gently into the skin of her shoulder. "I think it does," he countered when he felt her tremor of response. "Tell me the truth, Dara. Can't you hear the click of everything falling into place when you lie in my arms?"

"No, Yale, there are too many missing factors still...."

But she was lying and she knew it. The click had been

resounding and final the moment she'd looked up into his eyes that night at the party.

"What's missing, sweetheart?" he asked persuasively between kisses as he worked his way down the slope of her breast to the lacy edge of the nightgown. "Tell me and I'll provide it."

"You've already proved you'll say anything you have to say to get what you want," she swore bitterly. "You even agreed to marriage the last time!"

"But you didn't hold me to the agreement," he pointed out. "Why was that, I wonder? What made you change your mind about our bargain?"

"It was never meant as a bargain! I only wanted to find some way of stopping you!"

"I would have abided by it," he drawled, withdrawing his hand from her inner thigh momentarily to pull back the bodice of her nightgown.

"I'm flattered," she ground out furiously, aware of her breast being slowly, deliciously exposed.

"You should be. I don't marry every woman I sleep with!" he retorted on a thread of passionate humor.

"And I don't marry every man who claims he wants me in bed, either!"

"Waiting for love?" he taunted, lowering his head once again to her bared breast.

"Yes!"

His teeth closed around her nipple, sending a gasping wave of desire and helpless panic through her. She was fighting to recover from it when the second attack was launched.

The rough fingers probing her thigh swooped, claiming the intimate warmth of her.

Dara moaned and twisted in reaction. She was shivering from the physical exertion of trying to maintain her control and from the effects of his lovemaking.

"I'm going to steal your soul, darling Dara," Yale growled raspingly as he tightened his hold. "Your warm, inviting body will come with it!"

"Yale, please!"

"Begging already? What happened to the fierce resolve?"

"Damn you!"

"Don't say that, honey," he ordered hoarsely. "Accept the truth. You want me. I want you. Let yourself go and see where it leads…."

"I already know where it leads! To cheap motels and even cheaper love!"

"The surroundings don't matter! I've told you that!" he grated tersely and then punished her with his teeth.

She flinched at the small, sharp pain on her nipple and cried out softly. Instantly he relented, but his hand didn't cease its erotic pattern between her thighs. Dara felt the buildup of that strange, curling sensation in her stomach and wanted to shout her defiance of it and the man who caused it.

He felt her trembling against him and she knew his body responded to her weakness with the eagerness of the predator to the prey. Yes, she thought wildly, the *hunter*, wasn't that what he had called himself? She was being systematically hunted, forced to react to each new foray against her body.

But she had her own goal and she knew this wasn't the way to reach it.

"Stop fighting me, sweetheart," he urged. "Feel what your body is telling you. My God! It's almost screaming the message at me! How can I deny it? You're shivering with your need. You're moist and hot and shaking with it. How can you deny yourself?"

"I can, Yale," she whispered harshly. "When I've made up my mind, I can do anything. And the devil in you to-night can't change that!"

"The hunter in me tonight could take his quarry without too much effort, I think," he growled, letting his tongue taste the fine sheen of perspiration in the valley between her breasts.

"It would be rape, Yale. I swear to heaven, it would be rape! Because I'm not going to ask for it tonight!"

She felt the taut, muscular chest beneath her cheek, knew the still-leashed power in him and wondered if he would force himself on her, after all. Was there anything of the Southern gentleman in him now?

"I don't want you to merely ask for it," he rasped. "I want you to *beg* for it!"

"You won't get that from me, not tonight!"

He moved, settling her back onto the pillow and leaned over her. His hands were planted on either side of her, caging her. In the darkness he was a demon in black with amber-colored hair and she knew the overwhelming dominance in him, knew he was barely restraining himself from taking what he'd come to think of as his.

"Perhaps not tonight, Dara, but how long can you hold out? How long can you deny both of us?"

"As long as I have to!" she vowed, lying very still, instinct telling her not to provoke him physically or she would be lost.

"What are you waiting for?" he demanded brutally. "That so-called normal relationship you mentioned? Don't you know there is no such thing? Not between us. It's too late!"

"I don't believe that!" Her head moved on the pillow, sending the deep fire of her hair out in a fan which caught his eye for an instant.

"You're waiting for the magic click, aren't you?" he accused suddenly. "How long did it take before you felt it with that other man? The one you mentioned at lunch?"

Dara stared at him and then drew a deep breath. "With him it happened the moment we met."

There was a shattering stillness as the hazel fires raged in his eyes for an uncontrolled instant. "For everyone's sake, make sure he and I never meet, Dara. I'll take him apart. Literally."

She sucked in her breath at the violence in him. In that instant she could well imagine the dangerous, uncivilized man he had been in the past. She had a sharp vision of him taking a knife to anyone who dared call him names, she could see him risking the dark mountain roads with his illegal cargo and she could visualize him taking part in a tavern brawl. The Southern-gentleman veneer was thin, indeed.

"Don't worry," she flung back hastily. "I'm not anxious for any more violent scenes!"

"What happened to that relationship?" he asked between clenched teeth.

"I told you at lunch, I don't want to discuss it!"

"You told a *gentleman* at lunch that you didn't want to talk about it. He had to accept the answer, but I don't! Tell me, Dara. What went wrong with the magic click the last time?"

She felt the seething tension in him, knew he was determined to have an answer, and she was at a loss as to what to say. It had been a mistake to let him think there had been someone else, someone who was perfect for her....

"There were...are...complications."

"Complications! Are you implying it might not be over?" he asked incredulously.

"If we can get things worked out..." Dara hedged recklessly, wondering desperately if she was doing the right thing by goading him like this.

"Forget it!" he snarled. "Don't even *think* about him again, do you understand me? Whatever you had or didn't have, it's over and done with. It was finished the night you left that party with me! You aren't in love with him, you can't be in love with him. If you were in love with another man, there's no way on earth you could have given yourself to me the way you did this weekend!"

"How do you know?" she couldn't resist challenging.

"You hardly know me at all. You can't begin to guess what I might or might not be capable of doing!"

He glared at her for an instant as if he couldn't understand her argument. "No," he said with appalling emphasis. "I know you well enough to be sure of that much. *You aren't in love with anyone else!*"

"Whatever you say, Yale," she tossed back recklessly.

"Remember that!" he rapped. "The safety of your charming neck may depend on it!"

"Don't threaten me!"

"Why not? You belong to me. I can threaten you as much as I please!"

"One weekend out of my life doesn't give you any rights!"

"The hell it doesn't," he gritted. "Where I come from, a man takes the rights he wants."

"You may be from those lawless mountains, but you don't live there anymore! You're supposed to be maintaining another lifestyle now."

"You have only yourself to blame for shattering that lifestyle. You should have let well enough alone, been content with the Southern-gentleman accountant. He might have given you the time you seem to want. But you had to go and dig up the other half of me. Now you've got all of me on your trail and you don't stand a chance."

"You won't find me a casual bed partner!" she vowed.

"You *will* surrender! You can't give yourself the way you did this weekend and then change your mind about the relationship because it didn't develop the way you wanted!"

"You sound as if you're the one who got used this past weekend!"

"I did! You used me and then you tried to drop me. But it won't work, Dara. You're not going to walk all over my pride and get away with it!"

"You're doing this because of your pride?" She gasped, horrified.

"That's part of it," he retorted chillingly. "I'm also doing it because I still want you! With motives like that, a man doesn't give up easily."

"But those aren't the motives I want from a man!" she cried.

"I know. You have a preconceived notion of how things should be between yourself and a lover, but things don't always go the way we think they should. You're mine, Dara, and I'm going to make you admit that. You're not going to walk away and go flitting off to someone else who fits your mental image of the proper sort of lover!"

He surged to his feet and stood for a moment beside the bed, hazel eyes roving her slightly crushed and wholly abandoned looking figure.

"Tomorrow night you'd better keep in mind that I'm determined to have you! Sooner or later I'll get you where you belong in bed and pleading for more of what you discovered in that damn motel!"

Moving with the frightening grace of a leopard, the devil who had invaded Dara's bedroom disappeared.

Chapter 9

It was like dealing with two different men, Dara thought a little hysterically the next evening when she met her civilized accountant at the door.

Once again Yale was all good manners, sober suit and charm. The only clue to the devil in him lay in the gleam of hazel eyes through the lenses of his glasses and the flash of gold in his smile.

Dara was ready for him in more ways than one. She flung open the door and hurled the accusation at him before he'd even managed to step across the threshold.

"You followed me to work this morning!"

He arched one amber brow in polite inquiry. "I don't think that was me," he offered. His eyes swept her sleekly parted burnt-russet hair, the sun-bright, long yellow dress which flowed over her full curves and the sparkling challenge in the gray-green eyes.

"Of course it was you! I couldn't mistake that car, and you know it! It was the same you who came prowling into my bedroom uninvited last night!"

"Like I said, it wasn't me. Not quite. What honest,

Internal-Revenue-Service-fearing accountant would go around doing things like that?"

"You're going to stand there and deny you're...trailing me?" she snapped, dumbfounded. "Stop playing games, Yale."

"You really ought to take this up with him," Yale advised helpfully, lifting the shawl from the back of a nearby chair and placing it solicitously around her shoulders.

"I don't believe this," she gasped, whirling to stare at him in confusion and annoyance. "Stop pretending you're some sort of split personality!"

"Why not? Two hunters are much more effective than one. Come along, Dara, I've got reservations in half an hour."

"Yale," she protested weakly, uncertain how to handle the bizarre situation. A part of her found it vastly intriguing in spite of the danger she felt. "Yale," she went on determinedly, allowing him to guide her out to the car, "this is ridiculous!"

"I agree. You can call it off any time you wish," he informed her lightly as she slid into the leather interior.

"*I* can call it off! You're the one who's behaving in such a crazy fashion! They put people in straitjackets for this sort of thing!"

"Let's hope you don't let it go that far," he growled feelingly, starting the engine. "In the meantime, would you mind if we don't talk about *him?* This is my evening and I'd prefer to have your full attention."

She caught the hopeful, whimsical note in his gently accented words and stared at him in a combination of disgust and amusement.

"Don't tell me you're jealous of…of that hunter who was in my room last night!" she dared.

He flashed her a slanting, enigmatic glance. "Why not? He's had memories all day long of how you felt in his arms last night. As a proper Southern gentleman, I couldn't have barged into your bedroom without being invited. Is it any wonder?"

"Why should it bother you?" she demanded tartly. "You had the same memories!"

"This could get confusing, couldn't it?" He chuckled warmly, downshifting for a light.

"Does that mean you'll give up this crazy charade?" she said quickly.

"No, but let's talk about something besides me," he retorted easily. "Tonight you're on a date with a man whose manners you can rely on implicitly. Why not enjoy it? Have all those conversations you wanted to have that make you think we're developing a normal relationship."

"Are you making fun of me?" she muttered suspiciously.

"A gentleman never makes fun of a lady," he intoned piously.

It took a violent effort of will for Dara to stifle the laughter which threatened to bubble over inside her. As it was, the humor was clear in her eyes although she managed to keep her expression suitably haughty.

"And you, of course, are the perfect gentleman. Forgive me. I don't know how I could have made such an accusation. You'll have to understand, I've had a rather upsetting few days," she murmured with social apology.

"I'm sorry to hear that," he returned commiseratingly. "Life is full of the unexpected, though, isn't it?"

"Yes, but those with fortitude and endurance can cope."

"You have both?"

"Definitely!"

"Excellent. How did work go today? Did you put together the information on those securities you mentioned?" he asked politely.

"Yes. I have it at home, as a matter of fact. Remind me tonight and I'll give it to you." She eyed him coolly, assessing her decision to treat him exactly as he wished.

"What else are you following besides electronics? I want to keep the portfolio diversified," he began conversationally.

"Some of the new medical-research stocks may be good but very risky. The new emphasis on gene technology is bound to revolutionize the field, but a lot of starters are going to get left behind in the dust," she mused.

"I don't mind some high-risk stuff. I've got enough of the blue chips as it is," he told her easily, pulling into the parking lot of the restaurant he'd selected.

"Just how gutsy do you feel?" she asked challengingly.

"Whenever a stockbroker gets that particular gleam in her eyes I get nervous," he said, parking the Alfa Romeo with second-nature precision. "What are we going to short?"

"How did you guess?" She grinned.

"I've been burned on one short sale," he warned her, as-sisting her out of the car with male grace. "It would have to be a very, very sure thing...."

"There is no such animal as a 'sure thing'!"

He sighed. "Tell me about it."

"Well, there's this small computer company which got caught up in the run-up of technology stocks last year. But I happen to know they're on very shaky ground now. Their financial base is practically nonexistent. It can't be long before the market realizes just how precariously balanced the firm is," she said enthusiastically as they were shown to their seats.

"You enjoy your work, don't you?" Yale smiled, sitting down across from her and scanning her eager, excited face with amused interest.

"Love it. Knew I would the first day on the job! All the challenge and excitement and thrills..." She shrugged self-deprecatingly. "There's nothing quite like the day-to-day highs and lows of the securities business."

"So tell me more about this little computer company you're proposing to short," he murmured.

"The stock is almost bound to go down, and soon," she confided, leaning forward intently. "As a matter of fact, I'm going to short it in my own portfolio."

"You manage your own account?"

"Naturally. I don't intend making all those profits for other folks and not taking some of the benefits for myself!"

"So you're proposing we borrow some of this computer firm's stock, sell it while it's high and then buy it back when it tumbles. Our profit being the difference," he clarified, picking up the tasseled menu.

"A lot of people forget there's money to be made on a stock that's going down as well as on a stock that's going up," Dara reminded him.

"There's a hell of a lot more risk involved selling a stock short," he grumbled. "Ask me—I know!"

"How badly were you burned?" she asked sympathetically.

"I panicked when the stock was guaranteed to tumble started going up a point a day!"

She winced. "How many days before you bailed out and took the loss?"

"Ten," he told her wryly. "I lost about five thousand."

"Oh, dear. I suppose you're really not interested in trying another short sale, then?"

"A gentleman can nearly always be talked into anything by a woman he'd like to seduce." Yale grinned, glancing up from the menu with a deliberately sardonic expression in his eyes.

"I'll keep that in mind," she managed to fling back spiritedly.

The evening passed with surprising swiftness, the conversation moving quickly from one topic to another. Dara was astounded to realize hours later on the drive home that she had almost forgotten about the strange game Yale was playing. She was too involved in getting to know her Southern gentleman better and in getting him to know her.

She was floating on a contented haze created by what

she told herself was the success of the evening when they reached her front door. Smiling, she turned on the step.

"Would you like to come in for a brandy?"

"Yes." He smiled back. "I would."

She hesitated briefly as he took the key from her hand and inserted it in the lock.

"You will remember which role you're playing tonight, won't you?" she drawled in liquid tones.

"I'm still able to keep it straight," he assured her softly as she slipped past him to enter the apartment. "I'm hoping you'll let the two aspects of my personality reunite before any lasting damage is done to my psyche!"

Dara eased the shawl from her shoulders and knew a moment's inexplicable pleasure as his hand reached out to assist her, touching her nape lightly in the process.

"I refuse to take the blame for this double life you're intent on leading," she informed him coolly, walking toward the kitchen to get the brandy.

"You caused it."

He followed her, coming to lean negligently in the doorway as she went about the small domestic business. She could feel his eyes on her every move and determinedly refused to let it affect her.

"Do you suppose there was someone around when Pandora opened her box? Someone who forever after kept telling her that everything that happened was her fault?" She sighed.

"Probably," Yale said idly. "But, then, she deserved it."

"A woman can't help her natural curiosity." Dara handed

him the snifter and led the way back out into the cozy living room.

"Then she should learn to live with the consequences."

"What a pompous thing to say," she chided, sinking gracefully into a far corner of the sofa. The yellow skirts of her dress flared around her.

"Accountants sometimes seem a little pompous," he apologized, lowering himself casually across from her.

"*Men* sometimes seem a little pompous!" she corrected firmly.

"Whatever you say, ma'am," he drawled, his eyes laughing at her as he lifted his brandy glass.

"Now, there's a proper gentlemanly attitude. The lady is always right," Dara teased, inhaling the aromatic fumes trapped in the bell of the glass.

"Or else she's afraid," he added agreeably, sipping his drink.

"Afraid!"

Dara stared at him, the lighthearted teasing dying in her eyes.

"Umm," he confirmed as if he hadn't noticed her sudden irritation. "What else can I call it when, having opened the box, Pandora tries very hard to shut it again, even though she liked what she found inside?"

"Caution! Common sense! Intelligence!"

"All good qualities in a stockbroker, but when they appear in the woman behind the broker, one has to ask why."

"Yale, what exactly are you trying to say? Do you think

you can talk me into bed by calling me a coward?" Dara's eyebrows drew together in warning.

"No, I'm only trying to understand your actions. The only way they make any sense is if we accept the fact that there's a measure of cowardice involved here." He smiled at her in a lofty way that irked Dara.

"You might be feeling a little cowardly yourself if you found yourself the victim of a…a two-pronged hunt!" she gritted, swallowing a larger part of the brandy.

"No, that won't serve as an excuse," he told her softly, leaning back against the cushions and stretching out his legs contentedly while he considered the problem. "You can cope with both pursuers if you wish." He turned his head to look at her searchingly. "Tell me the truth, honey: Why are you trying to back off from the relationship we began this past weekend?"

"I've told you, Yale. I want a normal, properly developed one. I never meant to wind up in bed with you that first night, and you know it. It got everything off on the wrong foot," she said, speaking into her snifter.

"Maybe things between us didn't start out following the acceptable pattern, but that doesn't mean they're not right…" he started earnestly, breaking off when she flung up her head, brilliant eyes almost pure green.

"I let myself get rushed into a whirlwind relationship once before, and it was a disaster! I'm not going to let it happen again, and that's final! This time it will go along a reason-able, natural path, or it won't go at all!"

For a few assessing seconds he watched her, studying the grim resolution in her set face.

"Your marriage?" he hazarded coolly. "Or this other man?"

"What other man?" she clipped.

"The one you told me about last night," he said dryly.

"Oh, him." She bent over her brandy, swirling it carefully in the bottom of the glass. "I was…was referring to my marriage," she confessed at last, surprised at herself. She had never told anyone about the fears which had haunted her since that early mistake.

"Tell me about it," he whispered persuasively, putting out a hand to trail soothing fingers down the length of her yellow sleeve. "You said he was charming, kind, that you had a lot in common, but that you never felt the click…."

"It was all a long time ago, Yale. I told you, I hardly ever think about it anymore. I'm not bitter, just cautious."

"He rushed you off your feet? Pushed you into marriage and then, six months later, admitted he'd changed his mind?"

"That's it in a nutshell." She shrugged. "Not his fault or anyone else's except, possibly, mine for not slowing things down and letting the relationship develop more before committing myself."

"Your fault!" he muttered harshly. "How can you blame yourself? My God, woman! He used you! Can't you see that? How old were you at the time?"

"He didn't… At least, he never meant… I was twenty-two," she finished lamely.

"And how old was he?"

"Thirty-one."

"That settles it," Yale bit out succinctly. "You were used. He was old enough to have more integrity than to sweep a young woman off her feet and marry her just to punish his ex-fiancée! And you've spent the last eight years somehow thinking the disaster was all your fault, haven't you?"

She drew a deep breath. "I had six months, Yale, and I couldn't make it work. It started going downhill from day one. If I'd demanded that we get to know each other better before the marriage, not let him talk me into it until we'd developed our relationship into something besides a romance, it all could have been avoided. I would have learned about the ex-fiancée and, perhaps, understood what he was going through…."

"That's garbage," Yale informed her with complete assurance. "And if I ever meet the guy, I'll flatten him. Not for divorcing you—I'm grateful to him for that—but for leaving you saddled with this ridiculous guilt and fear!"

"You're starting to sound like your other half!" she managed flippantly, wondering how she'd ever let the conversation veer off into this particular channel. It was a channel which had been closed for a long, long time.

"Sorry, but even we accountants have our limits!"

"Yale," she began placatingly, not quite knowing what to say next.

"Sweetheart, I know what I'm talking about. I know what it means to be used. I know what it means to be married for an ulterior motive!"

"Did you love her very much?" Dara breathed, thinking of the young woman he had brought out of the hills with him.

"No," he said quietly, his eyes on the unicorn tapestry as if the truth were woven into it. "She was a pretty little thing and I was attracted to her. We'd known each other all our lives. I guess I felt some sort of responsibility to take her with me when I left the mountains. She wanted out as much as I did. I knew exactly how she was feeling and I couldn't leave her behind. We had everything in common, you'll have to grant us that," he said sardonically. "We knew everything there was to know about each other. And it wasn't enough to save the marriage."

There was a short silence.

"Is that why you mock my efforts to build a more solid relationship before we go back to bed?" she prodded in a surprisingly steady voice. "You don't have any faith in my approach?"

He shook his head slowly. "What I'm saying is that time and propinquity won't make much difference if two people simply aren't right for each other to begin with. As for the argument of getting to know each other well before the relationship moves to the bedroom, I don't have any problems with that—"

Dara interrupted with a quick, grateful smile. "Then you *do* understand something of what I'm trying to say!"

He eyed her consideringly. "I was about to say that in our case, we didn't violate your strictures the way you seem to think we did!"

"What are you talking about? We hardly knew each other a few hours before we found ourselves in that...that sleazy motel room!"

"Don't call it sleazy," he said with a lazy grin. "I have very pleasant thoughts of that motel room. What I meant was, even though we only spent a few hours together before we checked into that motel, we knew an awful lot about each other. You knew more about me by that time than you knew about your first husband when you married him!"

"Well, you didn't know much about me! The next morning you were convinced I'd gone to bed with you in order to secure your stock account!" she retorted icily. "And the next night you were willing to pay an even higher price! In both cases you acted as if you were involved in a business transaction!"

He set his snifter down on the glass table and reached to remove hers from her fingers. "Doesn't the fact that I was willing to pay any price you asked tell you something important?" he whispered, pulling her gently, coaxingly into his arms.

"It tells me you may not be a very good businessman!" she attempted bravely as his hands closed around her.

"Think what a fortune in commissions you'll make off me! I'll probably wind up buying any off-the-wall stock you pitch at me!"

He cut off any retort she might have made by sealing her mouth with his. The tip of his tongue probed persuasively at the gate of her fiercely clenched lips and his fingers began working their way suggestively down her spine to her waist.

"Oh, Yale," Dara murmured and heard his pleased masculine chuckle. An instant later he had gained the territory of her mouth. She gave in to the heated call of his body, nestling into the curve of his arm.

The intoxicating male scent of him was like a drug on her senses, senses that had already been seduced by an evening of tantalizing conversation and the undeniable excitement a woman feels in the presence of a man who wants her. She felt him free a hand to remove his glasses.

Telling herself that Yale in his Southern-gentleman role would be much easier to handle when the time came to say good night, Dara allowed herself to be drawn closer to the flame. Her cheek moved luxuriously against the roughness of his jacket as her head rested on his shoulder. Everything about this man elicited a response from her senses. Everything clicked.

"You have a way of feeding the fire in me even when you're sitting across the table trying to sell securities to me!" Yale's muttered accusation was heavy with undisguised desire.

His hands tightened in the thickness of her hair, holding her unmercifully still while he drank his fill of her lips.

"Touch me, Dara," he commanded huskily as her fingers crept up the front of his jacket and found the buttons of his shirt. "I love to feel your hands on me. You do want me, sweetheart. Admit that much, at least!"

"I want you, Yale," she whispered, eyes closing in utter pleasure as he lifted the hair aside and found her throat with his lips. "You must know that!"

"I know it," he growled against the skin of her shoulder. "I just want to make sure you do."

She felt a vague trickle of alarm stir at the back of her mind.

"Why?" she pleaded starkly.

"Because it will make it easier for you to tell that other man he has to go!"

She felt the abrupt tension in him as he pushed her slowly back against the cushions. Simultaneously he lowered the zipper of the yellow gown, and by the time she found herself beneath him, the bodice had been lowered to her waist.

Mutely she watched as he raised himself far enough away to shrug out of the jacket, flinging it aside, and then he was covering her again. His hands glided down her throat to her breasts and his legs settled with arrogant force between her thighs. The yellow skirt was hiked up almost to her hips and Dara felt ravished.

"You must tell him soon, Dara," he grated, dusting the valley between her breasts with tiny, stinging little kisses. "Tomorrow. Get rid of him!"

"Yale, let me explain," she begged, arching instinctively into his body.

"No, I don't want to talk about him anymore. Just tell him it's over. Tell him on the phone. I don't want you seeing him again," he rasped.

"You're starting to sound like your other self again," she told him tauntingly, filled suddenly with an inexplicable desire to goad and provoke. He made her go a little crazy when he did this to her, she realized. And the notion of his being jealous was satisfying, indeed. Even if it was terribly risky.

"The two of us are perfectly in accord when it comes to some things," Yale vowed, sliding slowly down her body. "We share a common goal, remember!"

"Oh!"

The exclamation was torn from her as his hands, moving forcefully down her ribs and waist, pushed the soft yellow fabric over her hips. His tongue went over her skin with a damp heat that made her writhe and her fingers clench fiercely in the amber of his hair.

"Oh, Yale!"

Her mounting excitement seemed to inflame him further and his lips teased at her waist and stomach. She moaned, her head tossing restlessly on the cushion, and tried to gain some semblance of control over her spinning senses. Desperately she made herself think of the previous night and how she had sworn she would not invite him to her bed again. Not until she was sure of him....

"You will tell him in the morning, won't you, Dara?"

"Tell who...what...?" It was becoming impossible to think, she realized. She had to get a grip on her emotions. It was too soon. She couldn't give in, not yet, not with so much at stake....

"That other man, damn it!" he said harshly, his teeth nipping with deliberate punishment at her vulnerable inner thigh. She flinched, and instantly his tongue came out to soothe the spot.

"There won't be any other man in your life except me!

You're building a relationship with me, no one else! Is that understood?"

"Yes," she breathed. "Yes, Yale, I understand. There won't be anyone else…." As long as you're around, there couldn't be anyone else, don't you know that? she added silently.

"Good," he said with such complete satisfaction that he gave himself away. Dara sucked in her breath in sudden, overpowering fury.

"Why, you…you bas—" She broke off of her own accord, knowing that even in the heat of her anger, she couldn't fling that particular word at him again. "You arrogant, overbearing, domineering, *trucker!* What makes you think you can make love to me until I'll do whatever you want?"

"Wait," he protested as her fingers tightened threateningly in his hair. She could feel the rueful laughter in him and tugged harder. "Wait, honey, that can't be me you're describing!"

"Don't give me that, you wolf in accountant's clothing! I'll teach you to try and seduce me!"

She began to struggle free of him, kicking at his leg with her sandaled foot and yanking unmercifully on the amber hair. How dare he play that game with her tonight? How dare he ruin her wonderful evening!

Yale must have realized she was beyond reasoning. He moved quickly, efficiently, grabbing her wrists and chaining them in one firm fist. He used the sheer force of his weight and strength to stifle her twisting, scrabbling efforts to be free.

He didn't hurt her, but he bore down on her, crushing her so completely into the cushions that she couldn't move. There he let her futilely struggle until she had exhausted herself.

"Damn you!" she seethed, infuriated at his patience while he waited for her to calm down. "You are the most annoying man I have ever met! And you were supposed to be a gentleman tonight!" she ended on a wail.

"I *am* behaving like a gentleman," he told her bluntly, hazel eyes hardening as he met her furious glare. "And you, my vicious little tabby, ought to be grateful at the moment! There are several very *ungentlemanly* things I'd like to do to you right now!"

"What's stopping you?" she demanded recklessly.

"The knowledge that I deserved the attack, I guess," he admitted with an abrupt, rueful little grin. "I was using a rather underhanded method to achieve my goal, wasn't I?"

"You certainly were!" she assured him fervently, her nearly green eyes narrowing. "And don't think this boyish, abashed little apology is going to make everything all right! It's time for my *gentleman* friend to leave!"

"Kicking me out again?" he asked sadly.

"With pleasure!'

He sighed, sitting up and releasing her carefully. Hastily she tugged her dress back up to her shoulders, aware of his mocking scrutiny.

"I meant it, you know," he said softly as she scrambled to a sitting position at the far end of the couch.

"Meant what?" she grumbled, trying to pull the zipper up far enough to hold the dress in place. She refused to look at him.

"Get rid of him, Dara."

She shivered suddenly at the cold intent in his words and her teeth unconsciously caught her lower lip in a small gesture of wariness as she turned her head to look at him.

"You and I have enough to do settling the matter of this relationship of ours. I won't have another man involved."

She stared at him for a long moment, aware of the strength of his will. She could feel the force of it flowing around her, binding her, defying her to ignore it. How jealous was he? Did his jealousy indicate love or was it merely an instinctive possessiveness toward a woman he happened to find himself wanting?

"It seems to me," she drawled with amazing daring, "that if I give up this 'other' man, the odds become rather poor."

"What's that supposed to mean?" he demanded roughly, picking up his glasses and putting them on with an impatient gesture.

"It becomes a case of two against one," she mocked, "Both of *you* against me...."

"That strikes me as just about even!"

"Yale!"

"Dara," he said with such quiet menace that she was positive both the devil and the gentleman were totally united for the moment. "This is not a negotiable point. Get rid of him!"

He snagged her wrist before she could answer, got to his feet and pulled her up beside him. "Give me your word that there won't be any other men involved, or I'll give you mine that I won't leave tonight until I have your promise!"

Locked to him by the savage grip on her wrist, Dara stared up at him, wide-eyed and knowing this was one way of playing the game that wouldn't work.

"There won't be another man in my life, Yale," she capitulated with a submissiveness that appalled her. But, then, she acknowledged to herself, it was nothing less than the truth.

Chapter 10

After he had extracted her promise to get rid of the nonexistent other man, Yale's hunting settled into a clear, dangerous pattern. Dara was helplessly intrigued by the novelty of being seduced by two men in the same body. She was also very much afraid at times that she would go crazy.

Her responses to the Southern gentleman and his alter ego were amusingly different and, she told herself ruefully, equally intense. With her accountant there were pleasant luncheons and evenings spent in conversation on a variety of subjects. They argued about the stock market, with Yale losing. He, in turn, talked of tax shelters and clever accounting strategies. They discussed mutual interests in books, films and politics.

"You know," he told her over a sinfully rich dessert of Burnt Cream which Dara had prepared one evening, "you have what used to be called a Renaissance mind. No matter what we talk about, you seem to have some information on the subject!"

"No." She smiled, scooping up a spoonful of the luscious dessert. "I'm a dabbler. People with Renaissance minds are

supposed to be accomplished in all their interests. I just dab-
ble around until I find the ones that…"

"Click?" he provided wryly, slanting her an enigmatic
glance.

"I'm afraid so," she admitted with an elegant little shrug.

The other advantage to the Southern gentleman, Dara
told herself time and again as she was bid good night, was
that he really did behave like a gentleman. There were no
more awkward scenes or threatened seductions when she
would deliberately draw the evening to a close. It wasn't that
Yale didn't kiss her with passion and a clear desire to carry
matters into the bedroom; he did. But he took his dismiss-
als with grace, and Dara knew that if the lovemaking ever
went further it would be entirely her own fault.

The times spent with her gentleman accountant were
civilized, casually sophisticated and delightful for Dara. She
loved this side of Yale. She could relax with this man. Relax
and enjoy herself while working on the construction of a
relationship that, she told herself, had a lasting basis.

The word *relax* was the antonym of what she felt when
the hunting devil from the hills appeared. Dara never had
any trouble telling the two men apart. Yale made no effort
to blunt the sensual menace which seemed to radiate from
him when he chose to pursue her in this guise.

He set her nerves on edge whenever he was in the vicinity. Glancing into her rearview mirror and finding the Alfa
Romeo following her to work or parked in the lot outside
a store in which she had been shopping was enough to send
chills down her spine.

He had the audacity to show up on her doorstep one night after she had gone to bed, leaning on the doorbell until she finally answered.

"To whom do I have the pleasure of speaking?" she demanded caustically when she'd finally dragged herself out of bed, flung on her fluffy robe and padded to the front door. The question was rhetorical. She'd known at once.

"Guess," Yale had suggested with his wicked smile.

She'd studied his negligent pose in the doorjamb with the wary, narrowed green gaze this version of Yale always elicited.

"I sent you home three hours ago," Dara had tried tartly, already aware of the excitement fluttering from her head to her toes.

"You sent *him* home," he'd corrected, sliding a foot over the threshold and gently forcing her back into the wall. "Me, I'm just getting started for the evening."

He had been dressed all in black again, the amber hair slightly ruffled, the glasses nowhere in evidence. Dara had instinctively clutched the robe more tightly around herself and sought for a way to deal with the dangerous situation.

"That's far enough, Yale. I want you to leave."

"Show me," he invited, clamping his strong hands around her shoulders and pulling her forcibly against the lean darkness of him. "Show me how badly you want me to leave!"

It had taken an extraordinary effort of willpower and Dara had found herself precariously close to surrender before she had managed the feat, but at last she had sent the devil away. His rage and frustration had been clearly evident, and the roar of the Alfa Romeo had been alarming as it disappeared into the distance.

Dara had leaned against the wall, regrouping her forces after the onslaught, and wondered how much longer she could survive the perilous game.

But the next day the gentleman was back, acting as if nothing at all had happened since he had wined and dined her so beguilingly the previous evening. Dara had given up berating him for the actions of his other half. Yale simply pretended a total lack of interest in the subject. She had drawn a long sigh of relief and relaxed once more.

The week slipped by rapidly, and by its end Dara was doing her best to see as much of the gentleman and as little of the devil as she could. Feeling a bit silly, she issued an invitation to the accountant. At least Yale was consistent in his personalities. Invitations made to the accountant were accepted by him. He didn't switch roles on her unexpectedly. It gave Dara a certain reassurance for which she was increasingly grateful.

"A picnic?" he repeated, sounding pleased. "That sounds interesting. What shall I bring?"

"Whatever will fit in a bike pouch." Dara chuckled. It was Friday night and she was once again bidding him farewell on her doorstep. "You do have a bike, don't you?"

"No, but I know where I can borrow one," he offered smilingly.

"Hmm. That won't do around here, you know. You'll have to get one of your own if you're going to become a genuine Eugene resident."

"Yes, ma'am," he agreed humbly.

She was carefully arranging the last of the sandwiches in her large bike bag late the next morning when he appeared. She turned at the hiss of tires on the sidewalk and found him dressed in jeans, mounted on a racy-looking red ten-speed. The collar of his brown pullover was open.

"You must have a very friendly neighbor! That's an expensive bike!" she said, admiring the lines.

He patted the low-slung handlebars. "My paperboy. He let me have it this morning after he finished his run. Nice kid."

She watched him swing lithely off the bike and push it over to where she puttered around her own yellow steed.

"You sure you wouldn't rather take the car?" he asked dubiously as she finished her preparations. His eyes scanned her tight-fitting jeans and open-necked green shirt.

The dark hunter would have reached out to pat the luxurious roundness of her derriere and the hazel eyes would have rested appreciatively on the full curve of her breast, but the gentleman was much more polite. Yale's smiling gaze warmed but he said nothing.

"Oh, no, this is a perfect day for a bike ride," she assured him, strapping the bag shut and mounting with practiced ease. "Ready?"

"Lead the way," he invited.

It was a delight to the senses to be whisking through the warm sunlight of an Oregon morning with the man she loved by her side, Dara thought blissfully. The bikes sailed over the road and the wind whistled past her ears.

"The river?" Yale asked, turning his head to glance at her laughing profile.

"I know a perfect spot." She grinned.

She led him through the wooded five-hundred-acre park, past the five-mile jogging trail and a long canal designed for canoeing, into a quiet landscape of green fields and tall trees.

"This is good country," Yale murmured quietly.

"The best," Dara agreed with the deep pleasure of the native Oregonian.

"I hadn't realized how important the Willamette River Valley was to the history of the settlement of the West," Yale mused reflectively.

Dara winced at his pronunciation of the river's name. "In addition to getting a bike, you'd better learn how to pronounce the name of the river." She chuckled. "It's Wil-LAMB-it. And you're right. This river was as much an influence on this region as the Mississippi and Ohio rivers were on their states. We used to have steamboats on it transporting the cargo between the different towns. People coming from back East thought they'd found heaven when they finally reached the Willamette Valley."

"I know how they felt," Yale said gently, flicking her an amused glance.

Warmed by the look in his eyes, Dara pretended to be busy searching for a suitable picnic spot.

"How does this look?" she suggested, indicating an isolated woodsy area.

"Fine," he agreed, gliding the bike to a halt. "But let's go a little farther from the path. I don't like spectators when I eat."

"Sorry I couldn't stuff a blanket into the pack," Dara apologized as they led the bikes off the trail and located a grassy spot on which to sit.

"That's what jeans are for," Yale said lightly, glancing around as if to assure himself of a reasonable measure of privacy. Then he bent over to fumble with his own bike bag.

"What did you bring?" Dara demanded interestedly as she withdrew the sandwiches, fruit and cookies from her own pack.

He produced a half-liter bottle of Burgundy, and she grinned approvingly.

"I even remembered a couple of paper cups," he told her virtuously, coming to sit down beside her on the grass.

"The perfect date," Dara said sweetly, opening sandwiches.

"I try."

"The other Yale could take a few lessons from you," she noted, not looking at him.

"I don't really feel like talking about him at the moment," Yale said smoothly, reaching eagerly for the nearest sandwich. "What have I got here?"

"Salmon and capers," she told him. "There's also one with a butter spread of dried herbs and wine and a chutney and cheese mixture."

"No tuna fish or ham and cheese?" he mocked, surveying the cleverly cut sandwiches with enthusiasm.

"I've decided it's time you expanded your food horizons,"

she retorted condescendingly. "Every time we go out you order steak-and-potatoes-type meals."

"I'm willing to learn. I always feel like I'm indulging my senses when I'm around you," he added meaningfully.

Dara flushed and took an industrious bite out of her sandwich while Yale calmly uncorked the wine.

"I've been doing some serious thinking about this streak of cowardice in you," he went on conversationally as he poured the Burgundy into the paper cups.

Dara nearly choked on her sandwich.

"Cowardice!" she managed, gasping for air.

"That's what it amounts to, I think." Yale nodded thoughtfully, slapping her helpfully between the shoulders. "Why else would you have backed off from where we had gone with this relationship of ours?"

"Yale, we've been through this," she began firmly.

"I realize that, but I'm starting to get worried," he explained patiently.

"Worried! What about, for heaven's sake!"

"You've implied you're waiting for the magic 'click.' What I'm wondering about is, how will you know it when it occurs? What are the signs? Are you just going to turn to me someday and say, 'Okay, Yale, it happened'?"

"Hardly!" She sniffed. How could she explain it had already happened?

"Then how am I going to know when you've come to your senses and realized you want this relationship as much as I do?" he pressed gently, his expression one of genuine, studious concern.

"Relationships should evolve over a period of time, Yale."

"Time can be telescoped under the right circumstances," he said quietly.

"Perhaps," she agreed carefully. "But it didn't happen like that in our case, did it? Our relationship didn't exactly take place in the right circumstances!"

"Are you going to hold that motel room against me forever?"

"Maybe," Dara declared. "It sure got us off to a bad start!"

"What about the next night, Dara? Why did you withdraw your demand that I marry you?"

"No woman wants to force a man into marriage!" she snapped, gulping a swallow of the wine.

"I was willing...."

"To pay a price. That's hardly calculated to convince a woman of undying love!"

"You never asked for my undying love," he pointed out softly.

Dara felt the red wash into her cheeks and glanced away from the intent hazel eyes.

"You made it very clear the next morning that your demand for marriage had merely been a means of trying to stop me from seducing you," he went on after a moment. "You withdrew it because it hadn't worked. And now you're using every other means at your disposal to keep from winding up in bed with me again. Why is that, honey?"

"Must you be deliberately obtuse?" she gritted. "I'm trying to let a normal relationship develop. How many times do I have to tell you? I want to be sure."

"There are no certainties in this life, Dara. You can't positively protect yourself against making the kind of mistake you made with your first husband. Sometimes you have to take a risk."

"I disagree," she said staunchly, glad it was the gentleman who was having this argument with her and not the devil. "I think one can take steps to ensure that things are right between two people!"

"Which brings me back to my initial question," he interrupted. "How will you know? How will *I* know you've finally made the big discovery?"

Dara was at a loss. There was no way to tell him she'd already made her discovery and was merely waiting for him to make his. He would either fall in love with her or he wouldn't.

"I expect one knows when one is in love," she evaded coolly.

"Ah," he breathed, "is that what you're waiting for? To fall in love?"

"I don't want a relationship based on...on sex, Yale. You must understand that. If that's all we have together, then—"

"Then you're going to break it off and go your own way, is that it?" he growled.

She shrugged helplessly. "I suppose that's the way it will have to be."

There was a tight pause. "How long did you know your first husband before you married him?" he finally asked.

"A...a few weeks," she confessed. "I told you, it was a whirlwind courtship. We were married less than four weeks after we met. He was eager to get on with it, I suppose, because his ex-fiancée had already married...."

"And how long would you have had to know him to realize it wasn't going to work? To realize you were allowing yourself to be used?" Yale probed.

Dara sighed. Resting her arms on her drawn-up knees, she gazed out over the wooded countryside. "I don't know. Perhaps a few months...."

"A few months!" he exclaimed, his irritation seeping through the gentlemanly exterior. "How many months? Six? Ten? How many?"

"In that case, I suppose three or four would have done it," she admitted, remembering how long it had taken before she realized another woman had a hold on her husband. An unbreakable hold.

"Four months," he repeated to himself. "Is that what you're proposing for us? A four-month period of getting to know each other thoroughly before we take up where we left off last weekend?"

"Is that too much to ask?" she flung back, suddenly annoyed. The burnt-russet sweep of her hair whipped about her neck as she snapped her head around to fix him with accusing gray-green eyes.

He met her gaze for an instant, and she swallowed unconsciously when she thought she saw a flash of the other Yale in his level stare. And then he looked away.

"Dara," he finally said quietly, absently shredding a blade of grass as he propped himself on one elbow and focused on the middle distance. "Are you sure you're not trying to punish both of us for what happened last weekend?"

"Of course I'm sure!"

"You said that first morning you would have your revenge," he reminded her.

"I was in a temper," she returned carelessly. "I didn't mean it." And it was true. Caution, fear, wariness, despair, all of those emotions had played a part in her subsequent actions, but not revenge. "I...I let myself wind up in bed with you again the next night, didn't I? If I had been bent on revenge that would hardly have happened!"

"I'm not so sure about that. You may not have been able to resist...."

"That's ridiculous. Pure male ego talking!"

"We have something special together, honey," he murmured. "It wasn't until the second morning we woke up in each other's arms that you erected the wall. Practically your first words were to withdraw your marriage demand, and then you kicked me out of the apartment."

"But I wasn't in a flaming rage," she reminded him virtuously. "That time I reacted in a rational, clearheaded fashion. No dire threats. That's when I'm at my most dangerous, Yale, when I'm thinking!"

"I see," he drawled, a trace of humor lacing his words. "And what you were thinking was that by the second time around you still hadn't felt this mysterious click, right? You still weren't sure of your feelings for me, so you decided to institute a trial period of getting to know each other."

"We need that time, Yale," she replied steadily.

"I don't think so," he returned almost casually. "I think you felt the magic in my arms and then tried to deny it in the morning. Maybe you're as much two different people right now as I am!"

"Nonsense!"

It was time to put an end to this threatening discussion, Dara decided firmly. She began picking up the sandwich wrappers and paper cups with a determined air.

"Time to get going," she told him lightly. "There's a long ride ahead of us before we get home!"

"Are you trying to exhaust me?" he demanded, the amusement in him telling her he was accepting the end of the picnic with good grace.

"That doesn't sound like a bad tactic. Maybe it would keep your alter ego from making late-night appearances in my bedroom!"

"Don't count on it. He's got a lot of stamina where you're concerned." He helped her with the trash, stowing part of it in his bike pouch until they could find a waste can.

It wasn't until they arrived at her apartment that he issued the invitation.

"Dara, will you have dinner with me tonight? At my place?" he asked politely as they braked to a halt in her drive.

She hopped off the bike and glanced at him warily. "Who's issuing the invitation?"

"A gentleman and an accountant," he intoned righteously. "The Yale you seem to trust."

"Oh, I trust both Yales." She grinned rashly. "It's just

that the other one is a little harder to handle! But I can always predict how he'll act, so, in a way, he's perfectly trustworthy!"

"But you wouldn't accept a dinner date with him?"

"Nope. But I will with the Southern gentleman. What time?"

"I'll pick you up at six."

"I can take my own car," she protested automatically.

"I wouldn't think of it. I'm issuing the invitation and I'll pick you up."

"A gentleman to the fingertips." She chuckled admiringly.

Chapter 11

Dara dressed with absent care for the evening, her mind on Yale. It was not the first time she had been to his modern, multiwindowed condominium near the river. She had teased him that first time, telling him it was exactly the proper setting for a bachelor accountant.

The visit had occurred earlier in the week and had been surprisingly short. Yale had taken her home for an after-dinner drink. She could still remember how he'd stood in the living room, a glass in each hand, and watched broodingly as she wandered around with undisguised curiosity. The liqueur had been rushed down her throat and she had then been politely rushed home. No explanations.

Yale's home had reflected the image he seemed intent on projecting. As she adjusted the zipper of the black, knee-length dress, Dara thought of the carefully modern leather furniture, the too-appropriate accessories and paintings and the expensive quality throughout.

It had all been very masculine and in very good taste. Nothing jabbed the eye or seemed obtrusive. Compared to her own rather eclectic decor, Yale's home was like a study out of a conservative home-and-garden magazine. He wanted it clear he had left the hills far behind. Dara smiled to herself. After they were married, she'd shake the place up a bit. It needed it!

Married! She scolded herself. She shouldn't be counting her chickens before they were hatched, damn it! A lot of time was still needed and a lot could still happen....

She broke off the chiding thought, the narrow, kicky pleats in her skirt floating around her knees as she went to answer the doorbell.

"Hello, Yale." She smiled, the impact of him hitting her senses with the usual force. Did a woman always react this way to the mere sight of the man she loved on her doorstep?

"Ready?" He grinned, the gold flashing briefly. "You look lovely."

Behind the polite barrier of his glasses the hazel eyes skimmed the scoop-necked dress approvingly and then lifted to the sleekness of her simply styled hair. It was all very subtly done, but the message was clear. He liked what he saw. Dara warmed under the quiet caress.

"Thank you," she said softly, thinking that he seemed incredibly attractive to her no matter what he wore. Tonight the dark slacks emphasized the lean power of his build and the properly buttoned white shirt was accented with a sober tie but no jacket. Amber hair still damp from a shower was neatly combed and the black shoes polished to a rich gloss. He looked every inch the quietly successful professional, and she still would have known there was a hidden side to him even if she'd never met him until now.

"Why the secret little smile?" he demanded easily, ushering her into the car before turning to lift a casual hand in greeting to Dara's inquisitive elderly neighbor. Mrs. Jenkins dropped her curtains at once.

"I wish you wouldn't do that," Dara muttered feelingly as Yale slid in beside her.

"It's the highlight of her day. I always wave."

"Oh, Lord!"

"Relax! At your age, what can they say?" he offered cheerfully.

"The same thing neighbors always say in such situations, regardless of the ages of the people involved. And I'm not exactly ancient!" she tacked on, ruffled.

"Of course you aren't, honey," he soothed. "You're exactly the right age."

"For what?" she retorted challengingly.

He ignored that, his hand going to the gearshift with practiced ease as they pulled away from the curb. "You didn't answer my question."

"The smile? I was just thinking how much more relaxing a date is with the gentleman than the...other Yale."

"Relaxed, are you? Good. I shall endeavor to be the perfect host," he responded, eyes warm with promise as he slanted her a speculative glance.

And he was. It was predictable, perhaps, that he'd prepared steaks, baked potatoes and a salad, given his culinary taste, but Dara loved every mouthful. His repertoire might be limited, but he did it to perfection.

"I enjoyed that ride today," he said reflectively some time later as he settled her into the deep, dark leather cushions of the couch and sat down beside her. "We must do it again, and soon. How about helping me pick out a bike next weekend? I can't keep sponging off the paperboy."

"It's a deal," she returned, resting her head against his shoulder as he put an arm around her and stretched out his legs with an air of replete satisfaction.

Two snifters of brandy sat on the low table in front of them, a selection of Mozart *Divertimenti* flowed from the expensive stereo and Yale had casually loosened his tie. He looked contented, possibly a bit sleepy and totally unmenacing. Quite the opposite of his alter ego, Dara thought with a hidden chuckle.

"Did you think about what we discussed at lunch, honey?" he asked after a moment, his eyes closed behind his glasses as he leaned his head against the sofa. The fingers of his hand were making absent, lazy movements on her bare arm.

"Yes," she admitted, curling her legs under her pleated skirt and giving herself up to the enjoyment of his warm, unthreatening embrace. "I thought about it."

"And?" he prompted almost neutrally.

"And what?" she murmured, eyes half shut as she burrowed into his shoulder.

"And how long do you think it will take before you're sure of us?"

"You can't put a time limit on things like this, Yale," she protested gently. "There are too many unknowns. Too many variables. Matters simply have to take their own course."

"I see," he said quietly after a moment. "You won't even give me a clue?"

How can I, she thought despairingly, when everything hinges on you?

"I'm not going to let myself be rushed into an affair, Yale," she finally said in a soft, firm little voice. "I'm going to be sure, and I want you to be sure."

"I am sure."

"No," she contradicted huskily. "You can't be. Not yet. You may be sure you want to sleep with me, but that's all."

He said nothing for a moment and then he leaned forward and deliberately set his glasses on the table beside the brandy snifters. He settled back into the couch, turning her slightly in his arms and lifting her chin with his free hand. The hazel eyes glittered down into her gray-green ones, and Dara had the first prickles of warning.

"You are a stubborn little thing," he mused, searching her face and lowering his head with lazy intent.

"Everyone's allowed one virtue," she teased, the warning twinges dying out as his mouth covered hers with warmth and masculine longing.

She sighed, twining her arms around his neck. This was the Yale she could handle. The one who would make passionate but gentlemanly love to her and then take her home when she insisted.

"You know this side of me very well now, don't you?" he whispered thickly, his fingers threading through the deep, lustrous red of her hair. Before Dara could answer he had fastened his lips on hers again, moving to deepen the kiss with his tongue.

She felt the gentle probing at her lips and parted them for him with a blissful little moan. After a week of his lovemaking, Dara knew exactly when to call a halt. But the time wasn't yet. For now she could indulge herself.

Her hands moved over his back, investigating the sleek musculature with hunger and the growing passion he elicited so easily. Someday, perhaps soon, he would once again be all hers. But for the moment she would take what she could, that which was safe....

"Dara!"

Her name was a hoarse groan deep in his chest as his fingers found the rising thrust of her breasts.

"I want you," he grated softly, finding her nipples and stroking them through the wispy softness of the dress and lacy bra. "You know that, don't you?"

"Yes, oh, yes, Yale," she breathed, arching into his hands and shivering with pleasure as he lowered the zipper.

It seemed to her that things were moving faster tonight than they usually did. All too soon she would be forced to gently break them off again. She wanted him to slow down so that the end needn't come too quickly. She didn't want to go home to a lonely bed. Not yet.

She closed her eyes as the bodice of the dress was lowered and then drew in her breath as the snap of the lacy bra was freed.

"I love the feel of you," Yale muttered achingly as he cupped her breasts and lowered his head to kiss the rising mounds in his hands. "Full and womanly and so very, very soft…."

"Yale," she began shakily as she was pushed gently backward beneath the weight of his slowly descending body. "Yale, it's getting late. I should be going home."

"Not yet, sweetheart. Not quite yet."

The vague sense of warning rippled to life along her nerve endings. There was a hardness in his words that was unfamiliar. A hardness which belonged to the other Yale.

He stretched out on top of her, his mouth beginning to rain hot, possessive little kisses across her breasts and the smooth skin beneath them, then up along her shoulders. She gasped as his teeth occasionally nipped at her sensitized flesh and her fingers dug into the muscles of his neck and back.

"Tell me you want me," he urged on a groan. "At least give me that much!"

"You know I want you."

"You've wanted me from the first, haven't you? Just as I wanted you!"

"Yale, I think we'd better call a halt," Dara moaned, supremely aware of the weight of his lower body as he thrust it against her in a surging, intimate movement.

"Dara, my darling Dara, I have a confession to make," he drawled, slowly, meaningfully.

"What…what are you talking about?" she whispered, opening her eyes wide to stare up at him.

His hands locked firmly around her shoulders as if to hold her still. But she was incapable of movement anyhow.

The weight of his body covered her softness with undeniable authority.

The hazel eyes glittered and the lines around his mouth tightened.

"I tricked you," he said intently. "You're not here with your Southern gentleman tonight. You're here with the other Yale. The one who makes you so wary. The one you found when you opened Pandora's box."

"Stop it, Yale! Don't tease me!" she hissed, her fingers clenching into his shoulders.

"I'm not teasing you. The time for that is past. And what's more, I'm not going to let you tease me any longer, either. I'm going to make love to you tonight, sweetheart, the way I did last weekend. I can't wait any longer. Not when you refuse to give me some sort of time limit!"

"Time limit! You want me to put a date on it? Tell you I'll sleep with you on a certain day? That's ridiculous! You know that!"

"This afternoon you were talking months. Honey, I can't wait that long for you! Don't you understand? This past week has been hell, and this afternoon when you started talking about endless weeks ahead I knew I had to do something."

"There's nothing you can do! I've made up my mind, Yale," she retorted gamely, a breathless feeling washing through her. He was serious!

"And I've made up mine," he flung back, a dangerous smile playing about the edges of his hard mouth. "Tonight both hunters are going to close in on you at the same time. I don't think you can resist them both at once!"

Appalled and feeling more helpless than she ever had in her life, Dara knew he was right. His heaviness beat on her senses, mastering her body in a way it seemed to crave.

Without further argument, Yale cut off her moan of protest, sealing her mouth with a kiss that first punished and then soothed. His legs sprawled across hers, anchoring them against the cushions, and Dara felt his hands moving on her body, stripping her clothing from her in long, sweeping gestures.

"Undress me," he ordered gratingly, his lips buried in the hollow of her shoulder. "Touch me with your sweet, loving hands. Touch me, Dara!"

"Please, Yale! This isn't what I want...!"

"It will be," he swore. "I'll make it what you want!"

His passion rolled across her like a wave. Soon she lay naked and trembling beneath him. When she refused to undress him, he ripped impatiently at the buttons of his shirt and flung it aside, coming back on top of her at once.

"I've wanted you so badly this week, Dara. I've ached for you. Every time you sent me away I wanted to ignore you. I wanted to tear off your clothes, pull you down on the floor and make love to you until you were no longer capable of speaking the words that would send me away!"

The feel of him was eating into her bones. Dara's senses swam as he talked to her of his need and desire. The passionate phrases were accompanied by an unrelenting assault on her body. His hands explored, caressed and enveloped until her breath came in quick panting gasps.

Through it all she realized dimly that he wasn't even aware of his strongest weapon. He couldn't know how her own sense of rightness was hammering at her, urging her to surrender to the power of the moment. How could a woman deny her man when his need of her was so obvious and so great?

It was impossible. She knew it was going to be impossible long before the first trembling, shuddering response seeped through her defenses.

He was aware of it immediately. When her hands began to slide lovingly over the skin of his back and down to the narrow waist he groaned in satisfaction.

"I knew it," he grated fiercely.

In exultation he strung kisses down her arms to the vulnerable, exquisitely sensitive areas of her elbows and wrists. His hands locked under her buttocks, reveling in the feel of her as he transferred his lips to her curving stomach.

Restlessly, Dara shifted her legs, hugging him between them with feminine strength that served to excite him all the more. Her nails danced on his neck and shoulders as she felt his tongue probing every square inch of her thigh and the soft warm heart of her.

"Oh, Yale, I do want you so…" The words were a ribbon of desire that wafted toward him on the wind of passion. He seized the end at once and tugged, drawing her closer and closer.

"Thank God," he cried softly. "Because I couldn't let you go. Not tonight. Not ever. I told you that you were mine!"

"Yes." It was the truth. It had been from the first moment. How could she fight it?

Abruptly he was moving, raising himself from the couch. Before she could ask him why, he reached down and lifted her high into his arms. She closed her eyes again, her hair falling across his shoulder as he carried her wordlessly into the bedroom.

She was gently deposited on the dark down quilt and a moment later, as he shed the last of his clothes and joined her on the bed, Dara knew beyond any doubt that both Yales were united tonight. He was right. She couldn't fight them both, and she no longer wanted to try.

Her arms opened to receive him and he moved against her soft, full curves, crooning like a man in a desert who has found an oasis. The tension between them mounted steadily to dizzying heights as Dara abandoned all attempt at defense. The need to satisfy this most important man in her life was too strong to deny any longer. She would worry about the morning when it came

"I've dreamed about this every night for the past week. The way you open yourself to me, gather me into you. The silk of your thighs, the responsiveness in you when I touch you like this…"

She moaned involuntarily as he claimed the intimate core of her with fingers that sent electricity flying along her veins.

He curled a tongue around one taut nipple and then bit gently, delighting in her reaction.

"Please, Yale. Please…" The muttered plea came from the heart of her as she pulled him close.

He obeyed the timeless feminine summons. In the darkness she saw him rise, knew he was going to complete the union and thrilled to the anticipation and need in herself.

And then, like a shattering mirror, everything seemed to fall apart.

"No!"

The cry was torn hoarsely from him as Yale suddenly threw himself to the side, his arm across his eyes in a gesture of abject denial.

"I won't, damn it! I won't do it this way!"

"Yale, what's wrong? What are you saying?"

Trembling, Dara turned her head to look at his rigid length, her eyes full of incomprehension and the still-flaming warmth of the passion he had aroused.

"Get dressed, Dara. For God's sake, get out of here and get dressed!" he rapped bleakly.

Slowly, confusion and fear driving her, Dara sat up beside him. He still refused to uncover his eyes and she could see the tautness in every muscle of his body.

"Yale, I don't understand…."

"Don't be a fool! I'm going to take you home. Exactly as you wanted me to do."

"Why?" The single word was stark and hollow-sounding.

"Because I don't feel like waking up beside you again and going through what I went through last weekend!"

"I...I see," she whispered, finally comprehending. Pain washed through her, replacing the love and longing in one fell swoop. She shut her eyes against incipient tears.

"No," he shot back harshly. "I don't think you do."

"Yes, I do," she breathed sadly. "You're afraid that I'll demand another price for the evening and that this time I won't let you escape payment. In the heat of passion you'll offer to pay it, but you suddenly realize that you may not get off the hook tomorrow morning as easily as you did last weekend."

"What the hell...!" he began angrily.

"Yale, what if I told you that this time there won't be any price?"

"I'd beat you. With a horsewhip, I think."

"Yale!"

He removed his arm from his eyes and even in the darkness she could see the fire burning in the hazel depths.

"I've had it with you backing out of our arrangements," he snapped, the fury in him unmistakable. "Do you understand? I've had it! You'll let me make love to you and then, in the morning, withdraw yourself from me again. I can't go through that."

"Will you listen to me?" she interrupted, a wild hope warming the cold which had settled on her when he'd broken off the lovemaking.

"No, you'll listen to me! We'll do this your way, Dara, because there doesn't seem to be any alternative, but so help me, when it's finally over I'm going to make you so thoroughly mine that you won't ever again think of that other man. The one with whom everything seemed to click for you!"

"Yale, there is no other man!"

"I know you got rid of him because I made you do it. I don't know why you couldn't overcome the 'complications' in that relationship. You certainly seem strong-willed enough where I'm concerned. But I'll have to be grateful for small favors, I suppose. But eventually you won't ever think of him. What we have between us will be right. You'll hear that magic click, Dara, if you'll listen. I'll make everything right, you'll see!"

"What an idiot you are, Yale Ransom," Dara whispered with deep love. "You were the other man. Everything clicked into place for me the night of the party. Why on earth do you think I left with you after only having known you a couple of hours? Why do you think I pushed so hard to discover the real you? And why do you think I let you make love to me in that sleazy motel room?"

"Dara!"

He sat up beside her, reaching out to grasp her arms and hold her still for his searching gaze. "Dara, are you telling me the truth?"

"I love you, Yale. I have from the first."

"Then why the hell have you put both of us through this?" he demanded violently, giving her a small shake. But she could feel the dawning wonder in him and smiled tremulously.

"Because I wanted you to fall in love with me. Is that so

hard to understand? The time I was trying to buy was for you, Yale, not me."

He swore softly, bluntly, and then he pulled her close.

"Dara, you're the idiot. I think I fell in love with you when you gave me your hand to shake so politely at that party and then had the nerve to laugh at me! I knew it for certain the next morning when you woke up in my arms...."

"No," she objected, her face pressed against the tantalizing hair of his chest. "The next morning you talked of fulfilling our arrangement. You were trading your stock account for a night in bed!"

"Sweetheart, it never occurred to me then that you might have fallen in love! The stock account seemed like a perfectly logical way to tie us together. There's nothing like a business arrangement to bring two people into constant contact. And then, the next night when you demanded marriage, I thought I had it made!"

"Only to wake up the next morning and have me tell you that you were free?"

He growled a response, his hands tightening around her. "How could you say that if you love me?"

"I was so crushed that morning when I handed you back your freedom and you took it." Dara sighed. "I thought that if you really cared you would insist on the marriage. Instead you just said okay and walked off into the shower. I could have killed you!"

"I felt the same way about you! I thought you had told me the truth when you claimed to have used the marriage demand only as a means of trying to stop me from making love. When you withdrew the demand, I figured it was because it hadn't worked. The next thing I knew, you were kicking me out of the house!"

"I fed you breakfast first!"

"Lucky me," he drawled, responding unwillingly to her small resurgence of humor. "I decided then and there that you were going to find out exactly what you'd done when you'd pushed past my carefully concocted image. As far as I was concerned, you had uncovered the truth and you were stuck with it!"

"I've always believed in being responsible for one's own actions," she teased warmly, trailing her fingers lovingly along the muscle of his arm.

"I almost flipped when you started talking about this mysterious other man," he grated. "The one with whom you claimed everything had 'clicked.'"

"I know." She smiled shakily, remembering his threatening lovemaking.

"Sweetheart, was it really me? The one you were so sure about?"

"I was sure about my feelings for you. I wasn't at all sure about yours for me! That was the complication I spoke of."

She felt the thankful sigh as he exhaled and held her more tightly than ever. "No other woman has ever been interested in knowing all of me," he said softly. "No one has ever guessed there was more than what showed on the surface. You took one look at me and started pressing for all the answers. I was stunned. By the time I had you in bed at that motel I knew I was going to have to make you mine. I couldn't let you go. You knew too much about me!"

"Well, I wasn't prepared for the split personality!"

"I was desperate and determined," he confided. "I had to find some way of throwing you off balance. You were so controlled, so cool about it all. I told myself I'd wear you down with a two-pronged attack."

"The old hunting knowledge from the hills?" She smiled, inhaling the musky scent of him.

"I was prepared to keep it up for quite a while, but today, when you started talking in terms of months, I decided I'd had it!"

"So tonight I was dating the devil in disguise?"

"Umm. Let's just say you had the whole me."

"An unnerving thought."

"You can handle it," he promised, pulling aside the dark sweep of her hair and pressing a hungry kiss to the back of her neck.

"This time you really will have to marry me, Yale," she vowed, sliding her hands down to his hips and sinking her nails ever so gently into him.

"Oh, no, you don't. I'm not taking any chances on your proposals. I will do the proposing this time. And you can bet your sweet life I won't renege like some folks do! Will you marry me, Dara? I warn you that if you say no, it won't make any difference. You're going to come and live with me regardless of your answer!"

"What can I say? You've closed all the avenues of escape! I'll marry you." She pulled her head back for a moment and smiled up at him dreamily. "I wouldn't want your reputation to suffer. Not after you've spent so many years building it!"

"I love you, Dara," he growled softly, the humor in him fading before the force of renewed passion.

"I love you, my gentleman devil. I always will."

He pushed her back into the thickness of the quilt, his hands running over her with a new possessiveness from ankle to thigh.

She felt the sudden urgency in him and knew it was echoed in herself. For both of them the need to consummate the private vows they had just taken was fierce and strong. The slow, leisurely lovemaking would come later, Dara knew. Now the urgency of committing themselves to each other was too great to allow for the languid, luxurious kind of love.

Within moments, Yale had restoked her level of excitement to what it had been before he had broken off so abruptly. She knew he felt the heat in her and the welcoming between her thighs.

With a groan of need and aching desire he covered her, surrendering to her femininity even as she surrendered to the bold, uncompromising maleness in him.

"Dara, my darling Dara," he husked, uniting with her in thrilling mastery.

She sang his name into his throat as he closed with her and pulled her into the surging rhythm of his body. Deliriously she gave herself up to the joy of the lovemaking, knowing even as she did so that he was demanding everything of her this time.

Together they sought the heights of the mountains above the verdant valley and together they sailed off into the currents of air that wafted them gently to the green fields below.

Dara was aware of the strength of Yale's hold and knew she was clinging just as tightly to him. This time neither would let go. Ever. This time everything really was right. It all clicked.

Much later, Dara roused sufficiently from the comforting power of Yale's arms to smile lovingly down into his relaxed features.

"And why are you sitting up there, looking like the cat that got the canary?" He grinned, ruffling her hair with deep love.

"I was just thinking," she murmured on a thread of laughter, "that when the chips were down tonight, the Southern gentleman resurfaced at the last moment."

He grinned back lazily, the gold in his teeth taunting her. "You think so?"

"Of course," she mocked. "Why else would you have stopped at such a crucial point earlier?"

"I've told you before, I'm a very good hunter," he drawled.

She blinked uncertainly. "Are you telling me you planned that?"

"Now that you've reunited both sides of my personality, you're going to have that problem a lot, I'm afraid," he told her with patently false sympathy.

"What problem?"

"Not knowing for sure which Yale you're dealing with."

"Hah! I know you, Yale Ransom," she declared with serene confidence. "You won't be able to fool me that easily!"

"Whatever you say, ma'am," he agreed politely.

Dara leaned down to kiss the Southern gentleman and surrendered in delight to the devil who reached out to pull her into his arms.

★ ★ ★ ★ ★